BRIAN DRINKWATER

FOOK

Twisted H2O Publishing

FOOK

For more information on this
and other titles, please visit:

AuthorBrianDrinkwater.com

Twisted H2O Publishing

ISBN: 0692234365
ISBN-13: 978-0692234365

A VERY SPECIAL THANK YOU TO…

…everyone in my life who's shown me nothing but support while I continue to follow my dreams.

…my devoted wife who has to suffer through my moments of distraction…even during important conversations, and for allowing me to bounce ideas off of her, even though it typically means spoiling the ending.

…everyone who's edited and proofread this book for me.

…Darren Hayes, who's 2007 song, "How To Build A Time Machine," triggered the first idea for this story.

AND…

…of course all of you who have purchased this book. Without you I'd simply be writing for my own sanity.

DEDICATION

This book is dedicated to my Grandfather. Though you may no longer be with us, you will never be forgotten.

I love you Papa.

"Within those veins, dark truths do dwell.
'Neath a kindred shadow, blood will tell."

William Grave, 1882

ONE

Only once before had a pair of eyes been so beautiful. It had been six years, three months and eleven days since he remembered first staring into a set of eyes as breathtaking and mesmerizing as the sleepy pair into which he currently stared. Now that original pair was probably tightly shut in the other bedroom, having given up on their husband's timely return.

As another flash of lightening illuminated the powder-blue nursery, followed by yet another newborn startling boom, Bill rechecked his math as his son began to once again express his fear of the unknown taking place beyond his bedroom windows.

"Six years...three months...and...no...twelve days," Bill quietly corrected his previous calculation, recalling the leap year that he'd previously overlooked.

As if intrigued by the still new sound of his father's voice, little Oliver Nesbit temporarily ceased his terrified rant to shoot his father a puzzled look.

"You think Daddy's strange?" Bill questioned his son with a grin.

The perplexed look on Oliver's face deepened.

"Daddy's a silly one isn't he? Well, you just wait.

You'll see how silly Daddy can be, because Daddy has no clue what he's doing. No, he doesn't."

Welcomed silence filled the room as the two just stared at one another, silently agreeing that neither one of them had any clue about what the future held, but at the same time seeming to believe that, no matter what, everything was going to be okay.

Another boom rattled the colorfully decorated room, replacing silence with the more familiar wails of the four day old in his arms.

"Yeah, I know. I've never been a big fan of this either," Bill continued to comfort his son. "I guess Florida's the wrong place for us both."

*****

"So where we going?"

Bill jumped at the sound of his wife's voice as he entered the dimly lit bedroom; the only source of illumination coming from the faint green glow of the indicator light on the baby monitor beside the bed.

"Huh?" he question, his temporary fear apparently inhibiting his ability to hear the question.

"Florida's not the place for you two. So, where are we moving?"

"I forgot about that thing," Bill smiled as he glanced at the monitor.

"What else did you hear?"

"Besides a musical recital of the alphabet?...followed by a brief, yet informative synopsis of American history, capped off by our national anthem in what I can only describe as the worst Eddie Vedder impersonation I've ever heard...I didn't hear anything."

"You heard all that?" Bill grinned sheepishly as he made his way across the room, removing his t-shirt.

"You think he'll stay down this time?"

"If I can get even an hour of sleep before the next

round, I can declare victory."

"I'll take the next one."

"No, it's my night. I'm gonna have to get used to this, so what good would it do to admit defeat on the very first night. Besides, I have no intention of showing such chivalry on your nights, so we don't need to be setting a precedent now."

"Fair enough," Jennifer welcomed her husband to bed with a kiss as he slowly slid under the covers beside her. "Maybe I can do something else to make your night a bit more enjoyable," she offered, her hand slowly tracing the faint outline of what used to be a solid six pack, now beginning to show signs of an eventual keg if diet and exercise continue to be omitted from their lives.

She hadn't married him for his looks but she couldn't complain. Though it embarrassed him to admit it, Bill had been a pageant child from the age of three when his mother had entered him in a local county fair pageant in Ohio. Having easily taken the title of Little Mister Hamilton County, Bill and his mother had been invited to take part in the state pageant a month later in which he'd once again come out on top and claimed the title of Little Mister Ohio. The only thing that had ended his domination of cuteness and stopped him from claiming the national title, was what his mother frequently recalled as "a breathtakingly impeccable, red headed, blue eyed bundle of sugar that must have been created by none other than God himself."

"Jonathan Mitchell Walker was his name," Mrs. Nesbit had often recalled whenever the conversation managed to wander down the path of her son's breathtaking good looks, which had been quite often. "It wasn't fair. That little thing was the most stunning creature I've ever laid eyes on," she'd continue, seeming to forget that her son was often in the room during such conversations.

Bill didn't mind though. He'd seen photos. He'd seen the miniature tuxedo that he'd worn when he'd claimed the state title, then once more when he'd suffered defeat at the hands of Little Mister Texas. He knew that his mother had been proud of him, even if he hadn't brought home the national trophy. Or, maybe she'd been proud of herself for creating such a breathtaking, human specimen. Either way, the thought of his mother and her silly, yet touching admiration for beauty always brought a smile to his face. She'd have been thrilled to see her new grandson. Though adopted and of no blood relation to her, Mrs. Nesbit would have surely thought young Oliver the most beautiful creature to ever grace God's earth.

Sensing his distraction as he showed no response to her hand stealthily slipping inside the waistband of his pajama pants, Jennifer paused in her seductive massage. "Are you okay?"

"What?" Bill reemerged from his memories to the realization of what was taking place just beneath the covers. "Yeah, yeah I'm fine."

"What were you thinking about?"

"Nothing...I mean...it was just my mother."

Quickly, Jennifer let go of her toy, withdrawing her hand from beneath the covers to a less erotic position on the pillow beside her head.

"No! Oh God no! That...that...well...that sounded horrible."

"No, this is good," Jennifer reversed her previous decision as she returned her hand to her husband's chest and once-again, began to caress her way south. "It's always good to learn new things about one another...even when it's disturbing. If thinking about your mother is what you need then who am I to judge," she continued, trying as hard as she could to hold back the grin, fighting to break free at the corners of her lips.

With each word Bill grew more at ease. Jennifer always did have a way of turning an awkward situation into a laughable moment.

As her fingertips again broke the loose seal posed by

her husband's plaid pajama pants, she purred, "You know, I never told you this, but just as I'm about to finish I often think of my father and the sensual way he used to—"

"—Okay..." Bill quickly interjected, putting an abrupt end to his wife's sick sense of humor as he yanked her hand from his pants, his uncomfortable reaction finally drawing the laughter that had previously been dying to erupt from her quivering lips.

Having accomplished her goal, Jennifer attempted to rebottle the humor as she slid even closer to her squeamish husband, who's hand was now firmly planted over his eyes, a broad, tight lipped smile doing little to contain the uncomfortable chuckles pouring out of him. A sensual kiss quickly brought back the moment of passion and Bill's hand slowly slid away, returning that original set of breathtaking eyes to his field of vision.

Another loud boom seemed to throw itself at the roof as concern replaced love and drew both of their attention to the monitor. The speaker remained silent, the audible absence reaffirmed by the lack of flashing lights along the top of the tiny white receiver.

Both remained silent for a moment, listening for the faint sounds of a shifting child and the telltale signs of an impending cry. The monitor echoed their silence.

"That was a close one," Jennifer whispered as she continued her lip's migration to her husband's neck.

"I know. You almost had to get up."

"Me? What happened to getting used to this and not wanting to set a precedence?"

"You and I both know that women are the more nurturing of the sexes. I think it would be best if you handled the nightly duties from now on. You know, so I can get more rest."

"Oh, you think so, huh? Well, I was trying to see to it that neither of us got any slee—"

"What was that?" Bill again hit pause on the adult fun.

"What?" Listening for a moment. "I don't hear

anything."

Bill continued to listen intently, sure that he'd heard something. Again the monitor confirmed silence in Oliver's room.

"Listen, I really want you right now, so you better quit delaying this and take care of business or I might just have to do it myself."

She knew how hollow that threat sounded. One of Bill's favorite things was to watch as she explored her femininity, usually bringing herself right to the brink of climax before he'd jump in and claim responsibility for the eruption of pleasure exploding within.

Bill showed little interest in the erotic threat, however; a look of concern and intense concentration dominated his serious face as he continued to listen to the faint patter of raindrops striking the skylight overhead. "Are you sure we're doing the right thing?" he suddenly broke his long silence with a recently common question that confirmed she was on her own.

"I've told you a hundred times, yes. Besides, it's a little late now," Jennifer responded, trying to be as comforting as she could, knowing how worried Bill had been about his new role as a father, but at the same time a bit annoyed at the thought of having the same conversation yet again.

She loved children, she always had. The youngest in a family of eight kids, Jennifer thrived on family and the sounds of chaos and family interaction. Every job she'd had since the age of fifteen had involved some form of child care; from babysitting for the Johnsons back home in Jacksonville; to working in a daycare all through high school; right up to college where she obtained her masters in education at Florida State. There was no doubt in her mind that she was ready to be a mother. Bill on the other hand hadn't been so sure.

It wasn't that he didn't like children, but growing up an only child in a house where his father was often out of town on business and his mother a bit on the over protective side, he'd never really had what most would consider a typical childhood. He'd had very few friends since his mother had always thought the neighborhood youth far too corrupting for her little angel. The only interaction he'd ever really gotten as a child had come from relatives and family friends at least thirty years his senior; so it was understandable that he'd never really seen himself as a father, a fact which he'd been very forthcoming about as soon as they'd both realized the seriousness of their relationship. But, he loved his wife and knowing how much being a mother meant to her, the two had decided to try for a family almost as soon as they'd been married. Unfortunately, the Lord had formulated a different plan for them and after nearly a year of unsuccessful attempts, they'd sought out the help of Doctor Huller who'd informed them that children, at least in the traditional sense, would never be an option. For some reason, which they still struggled to understand, Jennifer's ovaries were incapable of producing eggs and, therefore; would never be able to produce the genetic material needed to generate life.

Understandably, they'd been devastated by the news; Jennifer from of the loss of her only real dream in life and Bill from having to watch the woman he loved suffer such devastating news. For the next year, either out of denial or just a stubborn refusal to accept what they both knew deep down to be the truth, they'd continued to try and a year later, they'd remained childless. That year of refusing to accept reality, however; hadn't been a complete loss. It had allowed them to grow closer to one another. It had acted as a form of therapy and somehow had made the thought of not having children, though not ideal, somehow okay. It was at that point that they'd began to consider adoption and eighteen months and one unwanted teen pregnancy later, Oliver had entered their lives.

"You're going to be a wonderful father," Jennifer continued to reassure her worried husband.

"But how do you know? I hardly knew my dad. For all intents and purposes I didn't have a father at all. What makes you think that I can take care of a child? How do you know that I won't leave Oliver in the backseat of the car instead on dropping him off at daycare on my way to work? How do you know that I won't back over him with the lawn mower one day?"

"Really?" Jennifer responded, caught a bit off guard by his gruesome examples of bad parenting.

"What if I—"

"—Listen, you're going to be a wonderful father. You know how I know? Because you're a wonderful, loving husband who's taken care of me every second of our relationship and Oliver is blessed to have someone like you to call his dad."

He was still terrified, but somehow hearing those words of loving encouragement was exactly what he needed. At that moment, convinced by Jennifer's reassurance, Bill really did believe that everything was going to be alright.

"Now, forget about being a father for a moment and think more about being my husband," Jennifer renewed her attempts to bring pleasure to what had become a very heavy moment by gracefully sliding her right leg across Bill's lower torso and coming to rest face to face in a straddled position on top of her husband's excited partner.

Forgetting all worries, at least for the moment, Bill reached up, grabbing the back of Jennifer's head, and pulled her in for a passionate kiss. Like gasoline on an open flame, the touch of Bill's lips caused an explosion in her loins as Jennifer began undulating against her desired playmate, undeterred by the pair of lace panties and thick pajama pants currently obstructing maximum pleasure. It was a barrier that stood little chance of keeping them apart and like second nature, within seconds Jennifer managed to free her partner from his cotton prison and slip him past the lacy guard standing watch outside the palace walls.

"Boom!" another thunderous crash exploded from the night sky.

"What was that?" Bill once again allowed himself to be removed from the moment of ecstasy.

"It's just thunder," Jennifer continued her undulating dance as she attempted to keep her husband's attention focused on the task at hand.

"No, I know I heard something this time," he insisted, removing Jennifer from his lap and sliding off the bed to his feet.

"What did you hear?" Jennifer, frustrated, watched as he fixed his pants and quickly made his way to the doorway, disappearing into the hall.

He wasn't sure what he'd heard but he knew that it wasn't just thunder. Driven by adrenaline, Bill made his way along the dark hallway, the absence of light doing little to prevent him from making his way toward his son's bedroom. The nursery door was shut, just as he'd left it, Oliver's name proudly displayed on the plaque created by Jennifer's oldest sister and given to them during the baby shower two weeks earlier.

Bill placed his ear to the door, fearful that his worried imagination had created the sound and that he was about to burst into his son's room unnecessarily. The room seemed quiet and then there was a faint thud.

"Bill, there's a noise in Oliver's room!" Jennifer cried from the bedroom.

That was all he needed to reaffirm his suspicions. Quickly, Bill burst through the door, no longer worried about waking his sleeping son. The room was just as he'd left it. The fluffy white clouds, painted across the bright blue walls, seemed to dance around the room as always; their soothing presence topped only by the abundance of stuffed animals innocently resting upon the shelf lined wall beside the dresser and changing table. At the far end of the room stood Oliver's crib, the very same crib in which he'd spent his first years of life, nearly thirty-six years earlier. In it rested the colorful, Loony-Tunes bumper they'd picked out to prevent young Oliver from hurting himself on the wooden rails. Above it dangled the matching, animated mobile to provide sleep inducing comfort, and beside it stood a man, dressed in black, who was leaning over the low rail with a stuffed bunny in hand, suffocating the young child who had been innocently trying to sleep.

"Hey!" Bill yelled as he charged his son's assailant, struggling to pull the man away from the crib.

Seemingly undeterred by his discovery, the man continued to hold the soft pink bunny over the child's face, struggling to stand his ground as the angry father delivered blow after blow to his ribs and head. In the meantime, beneath the large stuffed animal, the young child's little legs seemed to slow in their struggle, the lack of oxygen finally taking its toll on the infant's failing lungs.

Panicked by the noises she'd heard, Jennifer appeared in her son's doorway to find the strange man standing over her son and her husband doing all he could to free him from the stranger's murderous grip. She screamed.

The distraction of the blood curdling scream seemed to momentarily startle the mysterious assailant, allowing Bill to finally pull him away from the crib and knock him to the floor with a swift right hook. With the intruder temporarily separated from his son, Bill turned back to the crib but Oliver was gone. Only the plain white onesie he'd been wearing remained in his place.

Quickly the assailant got to his feet and scrambled for freedom, knocking Jennifer to the floor as he scurried toward the front door before Bill could even process the impossible disappearance of his son.

More concerned with her son's well being than the man who'd attacked him, Jennifer got to her feet and ran to her husband's side, baffled by the empty crib.

"Where is he?" she cried.

"I don't know! He was just here!"

Just then, the unmistakable sounds of a terrified infant echoed from across the house. Both Bill and Jennifer turned simultaneously and ran from the room, following the new, yet familiar cries of their son.

The end of the hall opened up into the large livingroom. The front door stood wide open; the unwelcome visitor having apparently exited through it only moments earlier, and on the floor, in the center of the room, lay terrified little Oliver, naked but unharmed, screaming for the comfort of his horrified and bewildered parents.

"I'll call the police," Bill declared, frozen by confusion as Jennifer rushed to comfort their son.

TWO

Why do people feel the need to do this to themselves? What joy can come from a complete loss of self control and the possibility of making a decision that could utterly destroy the fabric of one's life?

These were just two of the many questions that seemed to always run through Jason Fook's head whenever he found himself in the presence of alcohol and it's enthusiastic consumers. Needless to say, he hadn't exactly been big with the popular crowd in high school. Stereotypes exist for a reason and he was living proof.

Nerd, Dweeb, Geek, Four-eyes…before *and* after he'd gotten contacts. He'd been the target of all those names. He'd worn his lunch a time or two and had been sprayed with water to make it look like he had wet himself. They'd even tried to hoist him up the flagpole one time. It had been before school and the flag hadn't yet been raised, so if they'd been successful, he at least wouldn't have had long to wait for the janitor to come by for his daily morning duty. Unfortunately, the janitor had been the one to place the hook around his belt loop. Luckily, Dockers hadn't accounted for a 128 pound belt so it had only taken one tug and an inch of air between his feet and the ground to set him free.

High school hadn't been the time of parties and fun that Hollywood always makes it out to be…at least not for him. He'd gone. He'd excelled in his studies. But when it came to any real, worthwhile interaction, he really couldn't think of one time that he'd stood out in any meaningful way. Looking back on those four years of his life, he'd often thought of high school as nothing more than a form of purgatory, a temporary layover on a road toward greater things, but now he was beginning to wonder if the layover had ever really ended. Sure he was a senior at M.I.T. and in a couple of months he would graduate at the top of his class, but what had he really accomplished. He was almost certain that, if he were to spend an entire day walking around campus, not one person would be able to guess his name, even with such a common name as Jason. And, if someone *did* manage to pull out the right name it would probably be one of those prick, fraternity guys who only knew who he was because of his last name's misfortunate similarity to the common four letter profanity.

"Yeah! Massive wiener!" a drunken patron yelled from the other side of the restaurant, drawing laughter and applause.

"I just don't get it," Jason quietly mumbled to himself. In actuality though, he was grateful for the sudden burst of vulgarity. Often his brain was his worst enemy. It was always looking for stimulation and more often than not, when left alone to wander, it did just that.

The departure of his date to the bathroom nearly fifteen minutes ago had left him in the situation of retrospective self evaluation. The short hallway leading to the bathrooms was in clear view on the other side of the restaurant, just beyond the bar and its sea of obnoxious lingerers. The door to the ladies room was only visible whenever it opened outward to welcome a new patron, or bid farewell to a freshly powdered female. Thirteen had entered in that time span but only twelve had exited. That bit of information was the only thing keeping him at the table, sitting across from a hardly touched, blackened chicken salad with no onions or tomatoes and a small cup of peppercorn ranch dressing on the side.

Though sad to admit, this wouldn't have been the first time that a girl had ditched him mid-date. Becky Tillmore had amazingly slipped away in line at "The Back Cracker", a popular roller coaster back home in Cannon, Massachusetts...or at least it had been until a few years later, when it had lived up to its name and crippled a woman by the name of Margery Millboro. Though just about everyone equated the accident to the key fact that Margery was a sixty-eight year old woman who'd just undergone extensive spine and neck surgery, somehow her lawyers had persuaded the jury to award her thirty-two million dollars. A few years later, "Cannon Amusement Park" closed and one more form of entertainment was yanked away from an already boring little town.

The loss of the rollercoaster wasn't that big of a deal to Jason though. He'd hated roller coasters at the time and after being tricked into getting on "The Back Cracker" alone, he still hadn't become a fan.

Two more women made their way into the bathroom as Jason continued to watch for the reemergence of his date, but the door swung shut once again with no sign of Miss Martin. "She was way out of my league anyway," Jason thought, beginning to accept the likely truth of the matter. Removing the napkin from his lap, he flagged down the waitress.

He wasn't surprised. He hadn't met Bethany on his own. They hadn't run into one another in any social setting. They didn't share any classes together. In fact, he wasn't even sure that she went to the same school or whether she was in college at all. The silence that had dominated their date right up to the point when she'd excused herself to the bathroom was so deafeningly quiet that he really didn't know a thing about her, other than how she ordered her salad.

Derek, his roommate, had set them up. "You need to get out there. Live a little. Dust off that lightening rod you keep tucked away in your pants," he'd said.

Though he hadn't been fond of Derek's implications, he was right. It had been nearly a year since he'd managed to somehow convince a woman into bed with him, if you could even call it convincing. She had been the less than attractive friend of the girl Derek had lured back to the dorm that night and based on the vulgar and, at times, repulsive things that came out of her mouth during the act, he'd gotten the impression that she probably would've given it up to just about anything with a pulse. The next morning he'd visited the school clinic and had every test known to man. Out of all the tests he'd taken up to that point in school, the results of those are still, to date, his favorite.

"Done so soon?" Lacey, as her name tag indicated, questioned, staring at the hardly touched food.

"Yeah, my date wasn't feeling well so I think we're going to go," he lied, not entirely sure why. It wasn't like he knew this girl and the likeliness of running into her again in a city of 617,594 people over the age of eighteen was—

"—She looks okay to me," Lacey stopped him before he could calculate the odds.

Jason turned to find Bethany standing on the sidewalk just outside the restaurant window, holding her phone in front of her as her fingers feverishly pecked away at the tiny screen. "Apparently the concept of glass and its transparent quality was beyond this girl's comprehension," he thought as he continued to watch her deeply, engrossing texting session. "Definitely does not attend M.I.T.".

"Would you like me to wrap this up for you?"

"What? No...it's fine. I'll just take the check."

"She's not worth it anyway. You seem like a nice guy.

I think you could do much better," Lacey offered her kind assessment with a smile before disappearing back into the busy restaurant.

That would've been a nice sentiment, Jason thought as he withdrew his wallet. Given that she was working for tips, he wasn't going to be fooled into reading much more into it.

*****

The March air was crisp, winter continuing its stubborn hold on the city, as Jason watched his texting date from the doorway of the restaurant.

Waiting for the waitress to return with his credit card and receipt, he'd contemplated what he was going to do about his deceitful date on the other side of the window. At first he'd decided to just wait her out and remain at the table until she'd gone, but as the girl continued to stand on the sidewalk, stubbornly refusing to put an official end to their date, he'd grown more and more frustrated. By the time Lacey had returned with his check he'd been fuming inside.

How could someone do that to another person? Sure he was on the shy side and a bit awkward. He wasn't the overtly fun type of guy that she was probably used to going out with but was it really that terrible to spend just one night with someone a little different? Hell, she was getting a free meal out of the deal. It wasn't like he was asking her to fuck him in return. He wasn't even expecting a hand-job or anything remotely like that. He'd just wanted to spend one evening with someone other than his roommate or his computer. Was that really too much to—?

"Excuse me," an elderly voice interrupted his internal rant.

Jason turned to see an older couple attempting to slip around him and through the doorway which he was blocking. "I'm sorry," he replied, stepping out of the way and fully outside as the door shut behind him. The anger that had been welling up inside began to subside and he contemplated once again just forgetting about the entire experience. What good would come from confronting the rude girl? He would probably end up saying something that would make him look even worse than she obviously already thought he was. There was no point.

Unfortunately, he now had to figure a way past the girl without being seen. Since he lived in the city there was really no need for a car. He'd walked to the restaurant from his dorm just a few blocks North, which would require him to stealthily slip past his ex-date if he didn't want to circle the entire block.

Shifting as close to the window, behind which he'd previously been seated, he began to slide along the building's exterior. Luckily, Bethany was still engrossed by her phone, making him feel more at ease about turning his slinking shuffle into more of a casual walk. As he passed the girl he attempted to catch a glimpse of the conversation but since he was trying to avoid detection, he was hesitant to get any closer and therefore wasn't able to obtain any more information about the secret conversation other than that it was taking place on an iPhone.

With Bethany now to his back he began to feel more at ease. She hadn't known him for more than an hour at most, so it was very unlikely that she could identify him from the back of his head or the clothes that he was wearing. His slow, cautious walk became more relaxed as the distance between them increased.

"Where have you been!?" Bethany shouted.

Jason froze, knowing that he'd been spotted. Instantly he began running the conversation that was about to take place through his head. "Where have *I* been?" he imagined his response as he remained frozen on the sidewalk, his back to the girl. "Where the hell have *you* been? I was sitting at the same table while you took the

longest pee in history or did you even have to go at all?
And, how the hell did you get outside without me seeing
you? You think you're so god damned special that—?"

"I had to climb out the bathroom window to avoid that
weirdo."

Confused, Jason turned as Bethany quickly lowered
herself into the passenger seat of a blue, Ford Mustang. It
was clear now that she'd been addressing the driver, an
attractive girl of similar height and build, with the same
long blonde hair and dimpled cheeks as his date.
"Probably her sister," he thought, turning to shield his face
as the car sped away.

"Weirdo," Jason repeated the familiar name aloud as he
turned and continued home.

THREE

"You said he was standing next to the crib when you entered the room?" Officer Eric Sanchez reconfirmed as he moved into the spot where Oliver's assailant had been standing forty minutes earlier.

"Yes. When I entered the room I saw a man standing beside my son, suffocating him with a stuffed animal," Bill again explained the attack for what seemed like the hundredth time to the middle aged officer.

"The bunny, right?" the officer motioned to the deadly pink plaything laying face down in the far corner of the crib.

"Yes," Bill, annoyed, reconfirmed.

"You mind if we take the bunny with us?"

"No, but what do you expect to get from that?"

"Probably nothing but just in the off chance that one of the man's hairs or some other evidence might have ended up entangled in the animal's fur. We're also going to want to dust the crib for fingerprints."

"Is that really going to work on wood?" Bill questioned, in no way an expert but familiar enough with crime scene investigations from television and books to know the basics.

"Probably not, but this plastic strip along the rail might lend a decent print," Sanchez tapped the rail with his pen.

"I need to grab a few things. I'll be right back. Just don't touch anything, okay?"

"Yeah, no problem," Bill agreed as the officer moved past him and disappeared into the hall, his presence replaced by Jennifer, still protectively clinging to Oliver in her arms.

From the moment that they'd discovered the young child on the living room floor Jennifer had refused to let anyone remove him from her grasp. Even as the paramedics had been conducting their exam of the child, she'd refused to let go. Her reaction was completely understandable given the terrifying events that had just occurred but Bill couldn't help thinking that his wife might now, never let go of Oliver again. Instantly, an image of his wife sitting at a school desk with seventeen year old Oliver on her lap, taking his S.A.T., popped into his head.

"They must think we're nuts," she whispered as she moved closer to her husband.

"Yeah, I got the same impression."

Oliver's eyes bounced back and forth over his bottle at his parent's exchange.

"Can you really blame them though?" Bill added. "I mean, if someone told me a story like that and I hadn't been there to witness it, I'd probably think the same thing."

"I know, but we're not making it up. We're good, upstanding, professional people. We're not the types to make something like this up for attention."

"They don't know that. They have no idea who we are. Besides...," lowering his voice even more, "...are we really sure about what we saw?"

"Yeah, I'm pretty damn sure." Jennifer paused, looking down at the pair of innocent eyes and ears intently focused on her. "I know what I saw. That psychopath was trying to kill Oliver." The tears, which had only tapered off ten minutes earlier, once again began to gather.

"I know. I'm not denying that. Hel...heck I was fighting the guy off. I mean..." Quiet again, "How did Oliver end up in the living room?"

"This will only take a few minutes," Officer Sanchez reannounced his presence as he reentered the room with a small box in hand. "Everything alright?" he questioned the couple, apparently sensing the intensity of the conversation, or perhaps having heard the tail end of it.

"Yeah, we...we just want this whole thing to be over," Bill responded.

"Do you have any idea who would want to do this to our son?" Jennifer added.

"I was actually going to ask you the same question," Officer Sanchez replied as he opened the small box to reveal a container of finger print dust and a small round brush.

On cue, Officer Sanchez's partner entered the room. The notepad that he'd used to take down Jennifer's account of the night's events was in hand and ready for any additional information he might be able to obtain.

"I don't know *anyone* that would want to hurt an infant," Bill rejected what he found to be an insulting question. He didn't associate himself with people capable of such an act. As far as he knew he was well liked by just about everyone he knew.

"I don't mean to imply that any of this was your fault. I'm just simply trying to come to an understanding of what exactly happened tonight. I, too, find it disgusting that someone would commit such a heinous act, but it doesn't change the fact that they did," Sanchez continued, as he began gently tapping the brush against the crib's railing. "Have you had any issues with a family member or someone close to you regarding your son?"

"No, of course not," Jennifer quickly answered.

"And you said that you adopted your son, right?"

"Yeah, the paperwork was just finalized at the hospital

a few days ago before we brought him home," Bill took his turn to answer.

"Any issues with the natural parents?"

"No, it was an unwanted teen pregnancy. The girl was only fifteen years old. Both of the girl's parents were involved in the process and everyone was more than happy with the arrangement. Tiffany—"

"—That was the girl's name," Jennifer interjected.

"Tiffany...," Bill continued, "...was very happy about the arrangement. I mean, she was understandably upset the other day after giving birth, but it's not like this was a spur of the moment decision. She chose us as the adopting family nearly six months ago and we made it very clear that she is more than welcome to be a part of our lives as much or as little as she wants. She's a great girl. Her whole family has been great."

"I don't think I'm going to get anything here," Officer Sanchez announced, giving up on dusting and returning the brush to the box.

"I didn't think you would," Bill, under his breath muttered.

Jennifer shot him a look and as he lifted his gaze from his wife's scolding glare he was met by another set of judgmental eyes looking up from the notepad in front of them.

Apparently Officer Sanchez had not heard the sarcastic comment, continuing the momentarily paused conversation. "What about the father?"

"Excuse me?" Bill asked, turning away from Sanchez's scrutinizing partner.

"The father. Your son's biological father. Any issues with him?"

"We don't know who the father is. Tiffany had apparently gotten drunk at some party and hooked up with a guy she didn't know. I think she said something about an Asian kid from another high school."

Not really noticing that Officer Sanchez's younger

partner was of Asian descent until he threw out the descriptive term about Oliver's biological father, Bill quickly turned back to the officer scribbling in the notepad as if to confirm that the use of the term Asian was still socially acceptable. The officer's eyes remained focused on his pen as he added the new information to the page before him, apparently undeterred by the term or just not willing to show his discomfort with the word.

"The father wasn't involved at all in the process," Jennifer took over answering the officer's questions. "As far as we know, Tiffany's family and the adoption agency were never able to determine who the kid was. As far as anyone knows, he isn't even aware that Oliver exists."

"Alright, fair enough. Well, I don't think that there's much else we can do here, so—"

"—You're not even going to go out and look for the guy?" Bill interjected.

"Mr. Nesbit," the entire department has been notified to keep an eye out for anyone in the area dressed in black jeans and a black hoodie but we really don't have much else to go by here, unless you've got some more information for us that we haven't yet heard."

Thinking for a moment, searching his brain for any additional details from the brief encounter.

"Listen, I'm going to make sure that a car comes through this neighborhood at least once an hour for the next few days. In the meantime, if you think of anything else, please give me a call."

Officer Sanchez removed a business card from his pocket and handed it to Bill.

"I suggest you get an alarm company out here first thing tomorrow morning and get this place secured. I know it can be expensive but the peace of mind is worth it. If we find anything else out, we'll be in touch."

And with that, Officer Sanchez and his partner exited the room.

"Do you think he'll come back?" Jennifer asked

worriedly, as if it was the first time the thought had occurred to her.

"Who, the officer?"

"No. The guy."

"I don't know. I'll get ADT out here in the morning and I know you don't like them, but I'm getting a gun."

FOUR

Out of Order

The Sharpie sign, taped to the elevator doors, was the perfect conclusion to a night Jason wanted nothing more than to forget.

The walk back to his dorm, though relatively short, seemed to take forever; thanks to the debacle that had been his date playing over and over in his overactive mind. By the time he had reached the ten story building he'd called home for the past four years, he'd wanted nothing more than to climb into bed and sleep away the remainder of the disappointing evening. Instead, staring at the broken elevator, he now realized that he had nine flights of stairs to continue his obsessive examination of his relationship failings, past and present.

He could forget about tonight. Sure, it hurt to find out that he was apparently too...whatever he was that made it so horrible to even complete a casual dinner. It would take some time to put it behind him but eventually he would. After all, it wasn't the worst thing that had been done to him by the fairer of the sexes. The memory of Jenna Bishop on the other hand; that was one that still lingered and probably would for the remainder of his days.

Jenna Bishop. The very thought of the name made Jason want to run and hide in shame. Even though no one in Boston, besides his longtime friend and now roommate Derek, knew about the incident, he couldn't help but think that, at times, people were still whispering the embarrassing little details to one another whenever they saw him. Looking back on the incident he couldn't believe how gullible he'd been, but it had been Senior year of high school and Jenna had been the aggressor, approaching him for a date, so for that reason alone he understood his puberty driven mistake.

The entire school had been in shock to find out that he and Jenna, a cheerleader, were going out. He'd overheard people ask her what she was thinking going out with someone like him, as if he carried the plague or something, but he didn't care. Jenna was beautiful and for some reason she wanted to be with him or at least that's what he'd been led to believe.

Only a week into the budding romance, they'd gone to a movie, they'd had dinner at her house with her parents and obnoxious little brother, who also seemed to question what in the hell their daughter and sister were doing with the frail, nerdy kid from school.

By the end of the weeklong relationship he'd felt on top of the world. Everything was going to change for him. He'd expected high school to be an unpleasant necessity in life. A sentence of abuse at the hands of kids more popular than he but now, having catapulted his way into the social elite with his romantic connection, everything was looking up, which was probably why he hadn't found it odd when Tyler Bidwell had invited him to a party that weekend.

The night had started great. His arrival had been marked by dozens of excited peers welcoming him to the party and offering him drinks, which he'd politely declined. He'd enjoyed the flirtatious advancements of numerous girls, which oddly Jenna hadn't taken offense to and by nine o' clock, he'd found himself in an upstairs bedroom with Jenna straddling his chest and his hands bound to the bedposts. The very thought of what was occurring should have been more than enough for him to finish right then and there given his lack of experience but amazingly he'd managed to contain his hormonal excitement.

Everything after that was a bit fuzzy. Likely, it was his brain's way of trying to protect him from the devastatingly embarrassing spectacle that had followed. All he could remember clearly was Jenna excusing herself for a moment and then, the next thing he knew, the room was full of people pointing and laughing at the half naked kid tied to the bed. There were jokes and names coming from all directions as he'd struggled to free himself from the silk scarves holding him prisoner. The flash of what seemed like dozens of cameras had been blinding, making it that much harder to undo the well tied knots. To make matters worse, there was a giant purple dildo laying on his chest. It had probably been a normal sized dildo, but no dildo is normal sized when you're tied to a bed with your pants around your ankles in a room full of your peers.

Thankfully, he'd managed to free himself, return his pants to his waist and with his head down, scurry to freedom. Needless to say, he hadn't even bothered talking to another girl until sophomore year of college when Derek had finally convinced him to go out on a date with Samantha Fishorn, a girl from his physics class. Samantha had been nice, but nothing had come of the brief romance so his solo existence had continued, occasionally interrupted by a date or two over the last three years.

IX

The crooked Roman numerals on the cold metal door were a welcomed interruption to his mind's once again, unwelcomed wandering. Pulling the door open, Jason exited the dim, concrete stairwell into the only slightly better lit, carpeted hallway that led to his increasingly desired dorm room, and within it, his bed.

It was nights like this that he wondered why he even bothered to go out in the first place. Nothing good had ever come from his attempts at social interaction. Just as he had done right after that incident with Jenna so many years ago, he needed to focus on what was truly important. He needed to dedicate all of his attention to the one thing that mattered most. He and Derek were on the verge of a major breakthrough. They were about to make science fiction a reality. That breakthrough was what mattered most and the night's failure was just the push he needed to bring this thing across the finish line. He just hoped that Derek was close on his end, as he'd been claiming to be for the last month and a half.

Slipping his key into the lock, a renewed energy had taken over and Jason couldn't wait to find out if his roommate was home. He couldn't wait to find out the status of the machine and the last component needed to test his theory. He turned the handle and pushed the door inward, the questions impatiently waiting on the tip of his tongue, fighting to be the first one uttered.

"So, did—?" Jason began to ask as he slipped into the room, closing the door behind him.

"—Where have you been?" an unfamiliar, female voice interrupted the winning question, causing all of the others to retreat back into Jason's throat.

Jason turned to see a topless blonde sitting in Derek's bed, her lower half likely equally as bare if not for the white sheets strategically positioned to show no more than an exposed upper thigh.

"Oh my god!" The girl's demeanor quickly changed from seductively playful to bashfully horrified at the sight of the unfamiliar company as she struggled to utilize more of the sheet's concealing surface.

Shocked and embarrassed as well, Jason quickly threw

his left hand up over his eyes.

"Jason, right?" the girl, recovering from her initial shock and now fully covered, nervously questioned the stranger.

"Uh huh," Jason responded, continuing to hold his hand over his face, not sure if he should enter further into the room or just turn and run from his own home. He shouldn't have been surprised. This was classic Derek. Just as *he* was *incapable* of interaction with the opposite sex, Derek couldn't keep them away. "Is Derek in the bathroom?" he questioned, knowing that he probably looked like an idiot standing in the short hall beside the bathroom door carrying on a conversation while self blindfolded.

"No, he said something about an electron multiplier and darted out of the room about twenty minutes ago. I thought it was some kind of toy or something he wanted to use."

Jason couldn't believe the unclothed girl's lack of embarrassment and sexual honesty. He could feel his face turning red. "Electron multiplier?"

"Yeah, I thought it might be a vibrator or something."

"Oh my god," he thought. "I'm going to go find him," Jason excused himself as he slowly backed up, reaching for the doorknob behind him with his eyes still covered.

The distracting presence of the naked girl on the other side of the room combined with the excitement that Derek might have finally solved the problem, which had halted their progress for the past couple of months, must have been enough to silence the opening of the bathroom door because it wasn't until he felt something warm and soft against his right hand that he realized that someone else was standing behind him.

"What game is thi—?" the second girl began to playfully question before realizing that she too had mistaken Jason for his roommate.

Jason dropped his hand from his eyes to reveal a

second, completely nude coed; this one a beautiful brunette who was standing between him and the door. They both just stared for a moment, apparently both in shock as he realized that, instead of finding the doorknob, his hand was resting against the girls upper thigh, in the crease between her hip and her more intimate of areas.

The girl screamed. Jason quickly withdrew his hand and doing everything he could to avoid further contact, slipped around the girl and out of the room.

*****

"Thanks to you, I'm probably going to prison," Jason announced as he entered the lab, ensuring that the door locked behind him.

"Huh?" Derek responded, the binocular like glasses remaining fixed on the small electronic device before him.

"Your company. I had a nice...brief...but nice little conversation with one of them. But I think I might have sexually assaulted the one in the bathroom."

"That's good," Derek mumbled, obviously completely engrossed in his work as a small puff of white smoke billowed up from the tiny soldering gun in his hand.

"Yeah, I thought so. Then, the strangest thing happened."

Derek remained silently focused on the small metal component before him.

"As I was banging the blonde one," Jason continued, now standing across the counter from his roommate, "and believe me, she was loving every minute of it, who would you imagine suddenly jumped out of the closet to join in?" Jason paused, looking for a reaction. "Your mother."

"How was my mother? I never heard a complaint from my dad," Derek replied, looking up with a grin.

"You son of bitch," Jason laughed. "You were listening the entire time, weren't you?"

"What?"

"Funny."

Derek, still smiling, went back to his work.

"Seriously though. You are aware that there are two naked girls in our room right now?"

"What happened to the third one?"

Based on the serious tone of the question and the very possibility of such a situation that involved Derek being true, Jason wasn't sure if his roommate was joking or not.

"I guess I lost track of time," Derek looked up at the clock on the wall then back down at the soldering gun as he lightly touched it to the metal, funnel like object again. "There."

"There, what?"

"It's done."

"You'll have to forgive me. I'm only a month away from graduating with a bachelors in astrophysics and molecular biology but that in no way has made me qualified to understand what that thing is," Jason motioned to the tiny silver funnel and wires.

"It's an electron multiplier," Derek answered, as if common knowledge, while holding up the small electronic device.

"The name's fairly self explanatory. What is—?"

"—This is the answer," Derek interjected, getting up from his chair, making his way toward a tall cabinet in the corner of the room.

"What was the question?"

"The question was, how do we amplify the amount of electricity to the machine's core without requiring a direct tie-in to a high tension power line or small nuclear reactor." Placing his thumb against the biometric scanner on the cabinet door, Derek waited for the click of the releasing lock.

"As I said before, I don't exactly know how much power we'll need," Jason reminded his friend.

Derek turned the handle on the safe-like cabinet.

"My calculations suggest that we'll need a significant

burst of power delivered directly to the machine's core all at once but I don't think it'll be anywhere on the level of a nuclear reactor."

"The nuclear reactor was an exaggeration," Derek felt the need to explain his apparently unfunny humor as he opened the cabinet.

"The most important thing is that the power is dispersed throughout the core at the exact same power level and at the exact same moment," Jason preached.

"I know," Derek agreed. Closing the cabinet door, the audible click of the automatically re-engaging lock filled the momentary silence followed by the thud of the steel briefcase on the counter beside the newly built component.

The design of the device had been entirely up to Derek. Jason had protested the metal briefcase design for fear that they'd be mistaken for terrorist lugging around a bomb or something; but Derek had insisted on the design, sighting its electrically conducive properties, as well as its ability to be easily transported without drawing too much attention. While he couldn't recall when he'd last seen a shiny metallic briefcase, it *was* better than his initially suggested, blender shaped design with a laptop fastened to one side. Unwanted attention would have surely arisen at the site of that monstrosity.

Watching as Derek again placed his thumb against another small biometric scanner beside the case's handle, Jason found himself eagerly anticipating the now familiar, though still exciting glimpse at the machine's innards. He hadn't been joking about his lack of electromechanical knowledge. That's why he'd sought the help of Derek in the first place. Other than their close friendship, Derek was a brilliant electrical engineer with a real knack for finding practical solutions for impractical ideas. He knew that his theory was possible. He knew that his calculations were correct. He just needed a little help proving it.

Lifting the upper half of the briefcase, Derek carefully

opened the top until the tiny hydraulic arms at each corner took over, propping it open at a one hundred ten degree angle. The iPad attached to the interior vertical surface sprang to life, welcoming them with the familiar Apple logo, followed by a desktop image of the DeLorean from "Back to The Future". The other half of the briefcase was filled with stacks of notepads and folders, or at least that's what curious onlookers would be led to believe if they happened to get a hold of it and somehow managed to get it open.

Derek again placed his thumb to the same biometric scanner beside the handle and with the enthusiasm of Doc Brown himself, uttered "Great Scott".

"Your obsession with those movies is troubling," Jason joked as the briefcase responded to the odd command, the notepad and folder facade splitting in the middle and raising like a paper drawbridge within the briefcase to expose the case's real contents.

The case was filled with neatly run bundles of wires bobbing and weaving their way around numerous circuit boards and, to Jason, unidentifiable computer and electrical components. At the center of the electrical maze was a four inch diameter, metal disk with the words "There is no future, without one's past" engraved in the center.

Jason's grandmother had repeated that phrase every night as she'd tucked him into bed, though he'd never really understood what it had meant. Every time he'd asked her what it meant she'd stealthily managed to change the subject. It wasn't until a little over three years ago, standing beside her deathbed in the house that he'd grown up in, that he'd learned the unbelievable truth behind its meaning.

"You just gonna stare or are you gonna open this thing?"

Realizing that he was blankly staring at the short phrase, Jason snapped out of it and placing his thumb against the same biometric scanner, reluctantly spoke "This is heavy Doc".

Derek smiled at his friend's annoyed tone. They'd both agreed, for security purposes, that it should take both of them to fully unlock the device but it had been Derek who had insisted on the voice coded passwords.

The small metal disk slowly slid aside to expose more wires and an even smaller circular cavity at its center. Derek grabbed the tiny metal funnel and with the touch of a surgeon, began working the tiny device down through the looping wires, positioning the narrow opening of the funnel through a tiny hole in the bottom of the spherical core.

After a few minutes of tinkering with the newly inserted component, Derek looked up at Jason with a smile and turning the case toward his roommate, uttered the words they thought might never be said.

"I think it's ready."

FIVE

"Do you have him?" the elderly woman on the other end of the line immediately asked, preventing Ty from answering the phone with the customary hello.

"No."

"What you mean, no?"

"Something happened."

"What you mean something happened? Is he alright?" the woman's inquisitive tone became that of worry.

If it had been anyone else asking the questions, Ty would have been more upset by the lack of interest in *his* own well being, but given that his grandmother had practically raised him from birth, he knew without words that she cared. Right now she was more concerned about her great grandchild and getting him back from the strange family with which he'd been placed.

"Remind me again why this is so important, grandma."

"Is he alright?" the woman persisted, apparently not interested in anything else until her question had been answered.

"Yeah, he's alright...I mean...I think he's alright."

"What you mean you think? What happened?"

"There was..." He wasn't quite sure how to explain

what he'd just witnessed. He'd been sitting outside the Nesbit's house for nearly two hours but just as the sky had continued to burn bright with the storm, so had the nursery windows. He'd almost been ready to drive away but the noise from the storm was the perfect cover. "As I was just about to get out of the car a..."

"Yes, a what?"

"Someone else showed up."

"Someone else? Someone who?"

"Some guy, a kid. I don't know. I've never seen him before."

"Ty, you been watching that family for weeks and you telling me that you never see him before?"

"I didn't get the impression that he was a close family friend, grandma."

"Don't you get snippy with me."

"Sorry."

"What he look like?"

"A white guy, in a black hoodie, kinda on the skinny side, you know, not very imposing."

"Well, did you scare him off then?"

"I couldn't. By the time I got out of the car he'd already slipped around the side of the house."

"Well, did you follow him?" Grandma continued, seemingly frustrated by the slow rate at which the story was being conveyed.

"Not at first."

"Why not?"

"Shock I guess. Does anyone else know about the baby?"

"Not less you said something."

"No, of course not."

"Then no."

"What was he doing there then?"

"What happened Ty?" she refocused her grandson's attention on the story at hand.

"I heard a window break so I ran to the side of the

house but..."

"What?"

"But by the time I got there the guy was already inside. Grandma, he was trying to kill him!"

"Who? Who was trying to kill who?"

"The baby. He was trying to kill the baby."

"What!" the woman's yell a mixture of anger and emotion. "Did you stop him?"

"I didn't have to. I mean I was going to but Mr. Nesbit burst into the room. I ducked out of sight of the window but I could hear screaming and a lot of commotion. I guess the guy got away because the next thing I knew he came bursting through the front door and ran down the street."

"The baby. Is the baby alright?"

"Yeah I think so. I mean..." He wasn't sure how to put what he'd seen into words.

"What?"

"Is there something you're not telling me, grandma?" I mean, I know he's your great grandson and my son but..."

"He our blood Ty. You and mine. There is no one else left in this family and this child very special; in ways you can never imagine."

"I think I've got an idea."

The other end of the line remained silent.

"He disappeared grandma. Not, he was taken away disappeared. I mean, he disappeared and then somehow ended up in the living room."

"The man must have grabbed him, left him in living room, then run off," the woman tried to explain away the peculiarity of what she'd just been told.

"I don't think so, grandma. During the commotion, I did take one quick look inside. I saw the stranger and Mr. Nesbit fighting beside the crib. I didn't look too long for fear of being spotted but the crib...the crib was empty. Shortly after that the man ran out of the house. A moment later I heard the baby's cries from another room."

"Is the child okay?" grandma's voice changed again, this time to a more calming tone.

"Yeah, I mean I think so. I knew the cops would be on their way so I got out of there as quick as I could.

"Good, and the stranger? Where he now?"

"He's in the car in front of me," Ty replied, slowly changing lanes but keeping his distance.

"He alone?"

"Yes."

"Follow him. Find out where he go and who he is. We need to know who else know about child and more importantly, if he know about us."

"Grandma, what's going on?"

"All in good time my son. Right now we need concentrate on getting that child."

"That might be harder now. The element of surprise is gone and the police are aware of the situation."

"The police don't know anything. All they know is what the Nesbits told them. They don't know anything about us. Not even the Nesbits know who you are. They don't know that you the father. That little slut doesn't even remember who knocked her up."

He didn't think Tiffany was a slut. He'd actually grown quite fond of her in the short time they'd spent together that night. Sure, technically the fact that she'd gotten knocked up at a party by some random, older guy that she didn't know, made her a slut but she'd seemed like a decent girl. He hadn't learned of the pregnancy until nearly four months later at which time he'd conveyed the news to his grandmother, who in turn had convinced him to keep quiet.

"The girl can't find out," she'd said. "She can't know who you are."

At the time he hadn't exactly been sure why his paternity should remain a secret. He'd figured it had been for financial reasons. If Tiffany knew who the father was, she would surely expect money for raising his child. It hadn't been until a little over a month ago that his grandmother's true reasons for secrecy had been made known.

Upon learning of the pending adoption, they'd considered coming forward and claiming the child. His family's shady past however, including his mother's current status as prisoner number 7865454 and his father's heroin overdose three years earlier, made it very unlikely that the state would award a child, even blood related, to the remaining members of such a dysfunctional household. That was when his grandmother had expressed her desire to take the child after its birth.

"We'll move back to family home and raise him," she'd said.

Even then he'd gotten the impression that there was something his grandmother wasn't sharing with him, but as usual, he did as he was told and kept quiet. He spent his time watching the Nesbit family prior to the adoption, tracking their habits, noting their routines, though he wasn't sure why, since a baby was sure to change all of it.

A month later his son had been born and all he needed was the right opportunity to swoop in and return him to his rightful family.

A horn blared as Ty watched the vehicle in front of him cross the double yellow line only to swerve out of the way of the startled, oncoming driver.

"What was that?" Grandma questioned.

"Nothing. Just traffic."

"Find out who he is."

"I will."

"I counting on you, Ty. Your son counting on you. Don't let us down."

"I know, grandma. I'll call you when I find out what's going on."

"Good boy."

And with those last two words of praise, the line went dead as the car ahead of him signaled and moved to the farthest right lane. Hanging back, he did the same, watching as the car then signaled again, turning onto West Columbus Drive toward Tampa International Airport.

"Where are you going?" he questioned aloud as he too signaled his turn.

SIX

"You think Christy and Amber are still in the room?" Derek wondered aloud as he watched the light bulb in his hand spring to life with each touch of the battery connected wire being held in his other hand.

"Huh?" Jason, engrossed in his calculations, only half acknowledged the first words uttered in nearly an hour.

"Nothing." Derek went back to playing with his light bulb. It was a simple toy but it had been his first introduction to electricity in elementary school. It was at that point that he'd become fascinated with the technology and knew what he wanted to do with the rest of his life. "Didn't someone say that the machine was ready? Oh that's right, I did, yet here we sit."

"I've explained this before" Jason sighed, spinning around in his chair to face his bored roommate. We can't just turn it on and hope for the best. If my calculations are off by even the slightest bit we could end up floating off into space. This concept isn't just time but also coordinate based. I have the ability to calculate some flexibility into the equation, compensating and adjusting our location within a few hundred feet and maybe about twelve hours or so, but that's about it. To accurately predict when and where we'll end up, we need to know the exact location and rotation of the Earth at—"

"—at the exact moment we intend to arrive," Derek finished the frequently received lecture. "I know. I get the concept but you've been working on that program for two years now. You've checked it over and over and over again. Sometimes you just need to let go and trust yourself."

Listening to Derek, Jason knew that his roommate was right. Derek was much more the type to just let go and let whatever was going to happen, just happen. They'd had the same classes all through high school and finished first and second in their class. They'd both been members of the math club and they'd both received full scholarships to attend M.I.T. but that was where their similarities ended. Derek's high school experience had been very different from his. While *he'd* suffered the socially stereotypical fate of a kid with his I.Q. in public school, Derek had excelled. He'd demonstrated an uncanny ability to blend in with just about any click. Though not the best player, he'd managed to work his way onto the varsity baseball team, giving him that all important connection that made him fit in just about anywhere, and while he was intellectually superior to his classmates, he was still somehow able to conceal that fact and let loose with them, participating in the most idiotic of drunken ideas. However, even with such socially opposite fates, they'd managed to remain best of friends since early childhood.

"Trust me Jason. You've got this."

Derek was right, he'd tested the program's accuracy thousands of times, not once finding a miscalculation. But he was a thinker, not a doer and as with most things in his life, he didn't like the idea of taking that first big step without knowing exactly what to expect.

"You understand the risk, right?" Jason questioned in a very serious tone.

"Jason, I don't even understand how what you're

proposing is possible, but we've been friends for nearly twenty years now, so if you say that you can make this thing work, then I believe in you."

After a pause, Jason uttered the word Derek had been hoping to hear.

"Okay."

Derek almost jumped out of his seat with excitement but, somehow managed to maintain his cool in light of Jason's apprehension.

Turning back to the screen, Jason powered down the computer and getting up from his chair, made his was to the very same cabinet from which Derek had withdrawn the machine. Placing his thumb against the scanner, the cabinet lock released with a click. The machine still sat open on the counter beside Derek, however they needed one additional item before the first test could be made. Swinging open the cabinet doors, Jason knelt down to reach the small refrigerator at the bottom of the cabinet. It too possessed a small biometric scanner, though this one didn't require any silly movie phrases like the machine, nor did it require both his and Derek's fingerprints to open. He'd installed the refrigerator himself as well as programmed the scanner himself. His thumbprint and his thumbprint alone could open the small black cube. Placing his thumb against the scanner, the refrigerator door opened with a soft click followed by a faint hiss as the airtight seal gave way, releasing wispy swirls of cool condensation.

Derek knew what was inside, though he'd only gotten a glimpse of the actual contents twice. The extent of his knowledge didn't go much beyond the machine that he'd assembled. He knew what the machine was supposed to do. He understood from an electrical standpoint what the concept was; deliver a massive, yet precise electrical jolt evenly across the entire core at precisely the exact same moment. It seemed simple enough at first. It wasn't until he'd started to assemble the components that he'd realized the difficulty inherent to such a task.

While electricity in the United States is the most stable in the world, there are still subtle fluctuations in the precise power delivered to any one location at any given time. To most people these fluctuations aren't a big deal. If they plug in their television or cell phone charger and everything turns on, they're perfectly happy, but when you're trying to calculate a precise voltage down to the nanosecond, the inconsistencies of the grid become clearly evident. This problem was the reason it had taken him well over a year to complete the build and the reason why it took an entire briefcase full of components to simply electrify a spherical space only four inches in diameter. Each component within the case was designed to not only amplify the electrical charge, but also clean it up, reorganizing the electron flow and storing the energy until the precise moment that the device is activated. At that moment, the stored charge would be released all at once into the fuel contained within the core; the very fuel that Jason was withdrawing from the tiny refrigerated safe.

"You gonna tell me what that is yet?" Derek posed the familiar yet unanswered question.

"This is the fuel cell that will power our little friend there," Jason replied, holding up the small, four inch sphere, the room's florescent lights illuminating the deep red liquid contained within the glass orb.

"Yeah, I know that much. I mean *what* is it?"

Carefully cradling the spherical cell in his left hand, Jason closed and locked the tiny refrigerator followed by the cabinet and made his way to Derek. "The sphere is a graphene enhanced crystalline vessel that—"

"—Smart ass. I know what the sphere is. Remember? I came up with the idea of utilizing graphene to enhance not only the structural stability of the vessel but its electrical properties as well. I meant what's inside, because it kind of looks like blood."

"Blood?" Jason laughed. "No, it's not blood. It's a

mixture of various chemical byproducts derived from the synthesis of albumins, globulins and fibrinogens, as well as a mixture of oxygen, carbon dioxide and nitrogen."

Derek just stared at Jason confused. While he hadn't been horrible at chemistry, he'd also never gotten a good handle on it. For all he knew, Jason could have been making up the names of those components and he wouldn't have known any better.

"This is what makes this whole thing possible," Jason reemphasized as he handed the small orb to Derek.

Holding the orb to the lights overhead, Derek stared at the crimson qualities of the dark liquid before slowly placing the sphere into the machine's core. He didn't know how this little red ball was going to make what Jason claimed, possible. If it was so simple why hadn't anyone else done it yet? Why was the concept still deemed science fiction and not reality? How had a twenty-two year old M.I.T. student perfected such an impossible concept when no one else could? Truthfully, these questions had been running through his mind ever since Jason had first proposed the possibility of such a device nearly three years ago. He wanted to believe that it was possible. The very idea of being the first to do what Jason was proposing was beyond words, but frankly, he didn't expect much more to happen than for them to plug the device in, press the button and then spend the next few minutes staring at one another as Jason tried to figure out what went wrong.

With the sphere inserted, Derek slid the tiny metal door back into place, concealing the red fuel behind Jason's familiar family quote.

"We can't do it here," Jason uttered.

"Why not?" Derek, confused, stepped to the side as Jason took over closing the device.

"Our first test has to be a small one. Twenty minutes at most...just to confirm that everything's working properly."

"And that can't happen here, why?"

"It's too dangerous here. We need somewhere more secluded. Somewhere no one's been for the last hour or so...including us. We can't risk being seen, but at the same time we can't risk occupying the same space at the same time."

"What are you talking about?"

"The 'Timecop' theory," Jason emphasized, as if that explanation would make everything clear.

He had no idea what Jason was talking about nor did he understand what a mediocre movie from nearly twenty years ago had to do with their experiment. "Are you talking about the movie from the nineties with Jean-Claude Van Damme?"

"The same person can't occupy the same space at the same time. I know it was only a movie but the theory is valid. The outcome could be catastrophic. Furthermore, we can't run the risk of overlapping the same space as each other or anyone else for that matter."

"Why?" the concept still eluding him.

"Picture yourself instantaneously becoming a conjoined twin with the person who's space you materialize in. Your bodies could fuse together, permanently joining you on a molecular level. If somehow you did manage to survive the instantaneous, biological reconfiguration, there would be no way to reverse the results without likely killing you and your new twin in the process."

"What if my new twin is hot?" Derek joked.

"I'm serious Derek. We have to be really careful."

The tone in Jason's voice making it clearly evident that he was in no mood for Derek's typical jokes, "Okay, so where do we do this test?"

"I have a place."

*****

"Are you luring me down here to kill me?" Derek joked as he and Jason carefully navigated their way down the steep flight of basement stairs.

More interested in the test than his friend's jokes, "Follow directly behind me," Jason instructed as he paused at the bottom of the stairs.

"Okay," Derek, confused, did as he was told, following his roommate step for step along the dimly lit hallway.

Their dorm building had been built in the 1800's, so he wasn't surprised to see the stone masonry foundation typical of the time. Obviously, over the past century, there had been some updates to the dark space. Electric lighting had been added at some point, providing some light to the narrow passageway. The plumbing running overhead looked fairly new, neatly running the length of the hall before ducking around a corner and disappearing into an unseen portion of the building.

"Remind me again why we're playing follow the leader."

"Do you want to end up a quivering pile of fused goo?" Jason, seemingly perturbed at Derek's lack of understanding, stopped and turned.

"Not really," Derek smirked.

"Then you need to follow me."

"You're worried about miscalculating the jump aren't you? You're afraid that you might misjudge the exact time and location of arrival and that somehow we might land in this very hallway at this very moment and that you and I will somehow meld together in some twisted, deformed mass of handsomely nerdy jello."

"Finally he understands," Jason thought to himself.

"As I understand it though, the arrival point isn't dictated by where we've been so really we could arrive anywhere within the margin of error. Ultimately we could end up trapped inside one of these stone walls or even buried alive in the ground adjacent to the building…if your calculations are off that is."

Jason thought for a moment…now he was questioning his own logic. Derek was right, but he knew his calculations were solid. He'd checked them eleven times before Derek had convinced him to finally leave the lab and get on with it. It was highly unlikely that they'd end up in the hall. If everything went according to plan they should arrive in the same location from which they'd left, at exactly 12:38pm. Checking his watch, it was 12:58pm. They had a twenty minute window. That should be plenty of time without any cause for concern.

"What are we doing?" Derek questioned, wondering why Jason had stopped.

"Just stay behind me anyway," Jason only half acknowledged Derek's solid logic. "By sticking together we minimize the risk," he added, continuing down the hall and through the same opening that the pipes had used to disappear.

Running his hand up and down the wall beside the doorway, Jason searched for the switch. This wasn't the first time he'd been down there. He'd spent many a night planning this test. He knew exactly the spot he intended to use. The back corner of the room in which they'd just entered was in actuality the front left corner of the building and the spot at which all of the building's power entered from the street. There was a switch on the wall just to the left of the doorway where his hand methodically searched.

"When that light comes on I'm not going to come face to face with some type of torture device, am I? You're not going to strap me to some table and have your way with me are you?" Derek continued to joke as he stared into the darkness before him.

Still focused on finding the switch, Jason continued to show no response to Derek's jokes. Suddenly, his finger detected a small patch of smooth plastic and a moment later, a soft click prompted a series of florescent lights to flicker to life.

While still not the most efficient lighting, the now visible room was much better lit than the hallway. In the back right corner stood a small tower of cardboard boxes.

The various company logos and handwritten labels suggested that the boxes contained supplies pertinent to the upkeep of a residential building, though their faded appearance suggested that their contents had been forgotten long ago and that the janitorial staff didn't frequent this portion of the building very often. Just inside the doorway was a series of empty wooden shelves which appeared to have been converted into a high rise condominium for spiders and other insects, but it was the back left corner that Jason had apparently been interested in as he quickly made his way to the caged off portion of the room.

Behind the chain-linked wall stood even more shelves, though these shelves, unlike their spider claimed counterparts, were lined with miscellaneous electrical supplies.

Arriving at the padlocked gate, Jason placed the briefcase on the floor beside him.

"I take it that's our power source," Derek guessed, motioning to the electrical box behind the indoor fence. "Too bad it's locked."

Without a word Jason began spinning the numbers on the padlock.

"I take it you've been down here before," Derek guessed again, now aware that maybe *he* hadn't been the catalyst in persuading Jason to finally test his long talked about theory. He'd obviously planned out this entire test and in true Jason fashion, had likely thought out every possible scenario. He'd just been reluctant, as usual, to take that first, risky step.

"Once or twice," Jason finally acknowledged as he aligned the last number and pulled the lock open.

Picking up the metal briefcase, Jason entered the cage. "Okay. We need to get this thing up and running as quickly as possible. We'll depart from this spot and it's also the location where we'll arrive, twenty minutes before now. The longer we stay in this spot the smaller our window for error becomes so you need to hurry.

"I understand," Derek acknowledged, more in an attempt to ease his obviously nervous roommate than himself. "Jello bad."

Jason quickly placed the silver briefcase on the third shelf from the floor and with a thumb scan and cheesy movie quote, the locks popped open.

Now aware of his role, Derek wasted no time as he popped open the electrical box. The machine needed a massive amount of power to run, which was apparently why, along with its remote nature, Jason had chosen this location for the test. Carefully he began dismantling the box's circuit breakers as he heard Jason speak the second password to access the case's hidden components.

"Here you go," Jason withdrew two electrical cords from the machine and handed them to Derek, who quickly began connecting them to the now exposed circuits.

The soft glow of the iPad added slightly more lighting to the dim space as the screen sprang to life, welcoming its owner. After waiting a moment for the tiny computer to boot, Jason quickly began navigating his way through the app that he'd developed to run his calculations. As an added level of security he'd disguised the program as a cheesy Pong style game. One, this boring game would likely draw little interest from anyone if they did manage to get into the case and two, only he knew the precise combination of shots that would correctly unlock the software hidden behind the simple program.

Sliding his finger across the screen, he launched the pixelated ball, bouncing the tiny square off the top of the screen before the computer sent the digital ball back his way. Sliding the linear paddle down, he redirected the ball to a precise spot along the far left corner of the screen before the opposing paddle again returned his shot. With one last motion, he ricocheted the ball one last time toward the first spot in which the ball had struck along the top portion of the screen. This combination of shots was the only one that his computerized opponent was programmed to miss. As the digital ball slipped passed the opposing paddle, the concealing game faded from the screen and was replaced by a blinking green curser much like that of an old-school Apple 2e computer.

There is no future, without one's past.

Jason typed the familiar phrase onto the screen and watched as instantly, the program which had previously appeared archaic in nature, flashed a series of modern, abstract shapes followed by a string of flashing numbers and letters before freezing on a screen that simply read:

Welcome.

Reaching over Jason, Derek withdrew two more electrical wires from the briefcase and began connecting them to the box.

With a few swift taps of the screen, a complicated formula began to take shape, followed by a message that read:

Coordinates accepted. Enjoy your trip.

"We're all set here. How's the power situation?" Jason turned to Derek who was still trying to connect the briefcase to the electrical box. It would have been easier if you'd told me what I'd be tying into ahead of time. I might have had the proper tools but I think I've got it," he announced as the iPad's screen brightened, followed by the appearance of a small lightning bolt in the program's upper right corner to indicate that the power connection had been made.

Checking his watch, Jason confirmed the time at the top of the screen.

"My watch is off by twenty seconds. Give me a

second."

Fiddling with the small buttons on the side of the cheap timepiece, Jason synchronized the time with that displayed on the iPad's screen.

Suddenly, a quiet rustling noise drew their attention to the tower of boxes along the opposite wall.

"What was that?" Derek questioned.

"I don' know."

They continued to stare at the motionless cardboard tower.

"Go check it out," Derek waved Jason toward the noise.

"Me? Why don't you go?" Jason retorted.

Before Derek had a chance to answer however, a large rat emerged from behind the boxes and began chewing on the cardboard, apparently unfazed by his guests.

Letting out a sigh, they both returned their attention to the task at hand.

"Okay, here," Jason spoke as he handed Derek two small silver orbs, connected by a pair of thin wires that ran from the briefcase and tied in at the machine's core.

Squeezing the small silver balls in each of his hands he watched as Jason withdrew two more silver orbs, also loosely squeezing them in each hand.

"You ready for this?" Jason questioned.

Derek just stared nervously. Before that moment he'd seriously doubted the likeliness of success but now, standing beside his determined and confident friend he began to question his previous doubt. Jason wasn't an idiot. He wasn't a fan of sci-fi. He didn't believe in the supernatural and he didn't attempt anything unless he was one-hundred percent certain that it would work. As impossible as the thought of time travel was, maybe Jason really had found a way to make it work.

"Take a step back," Jason instructed as he and Derek moved one large step away from the machine.

"Quivering jello, right?" Derek joked, this time a result

of nerves as opposed to humor.

"Here we go," Jason announced as he slowly depressed the small red button on the tiny orb in his right hand.

Closing his eyes, Derek waited for a swoosh of wind or a loud electrical snap as the machine activated, linking them to their recent past but no such noise came. No wind whipped through the dungeon like space and no electrical disturbance licked at the moist basement air. After a moment of confused panic, Derek slowly opened his right eye to check on their situation. Fear limiting his ability to fully see through the tightly squinted slit between his eye lids, he could only, faintly, make out a blurred image of his equally confused roommate holding what he assumed was the orb up to his face as he repeatedly pressed the button.

"Did it work?" Derek nervously questioned.

"I don't know. I...," Jason's answer trailed off as he continued to examine the small metal ball in his hand.

Feeling more at ease, Derek relinquished some of the strain on his eyes, though continued to keep them shut. "Oh well. It was a good first try. Maybe it just needs a few more adjustments," he attempted to comfort his roommate, now confident that he'd been correct. Time travel was a sci-fi fantasy just as he'd thought. There was no way that two M.I.T. students with a few sophisticated electrical components, an iPad and some electricity could manage to accomplish what millions had dreamt of for centuries. Slowly he began to open his eyes. "I mean, we'll just go back to the drawing board and...Jason...why are you naked?" he questioned, wondering not only why his roommate had decided to strip down but also, how he'd managed to do so in such a short time and with such stealth.

Seemingly surprised, Jason glanced down at his body, confirming the validity of Derek's question. Honestly, he didn't have a good answer but looking up he did have a question of his own. "Where are *your* clothes?"

Derek too, glanced down at his nude body. "What the fuck?"

Just then a pair of voices echoed from the hall, causing them to both forget their nudity as they returned their attention to the machine. Without thought, Jason quickly returned his tethered orbs to the briefcase before snatching Derek's out of his hands and doing the same. Derek quickly began disconnecting the wires from the electrical box, attempting to be both quick, yet silent, as he returned the electrical components to just as he'd found them.

"Come on," Jason whispered urgently as the voices and now sounds of footsteps drew nearer.

Reconnecting the last circuit breaker, Derek quietly closed the thin metal door to the electrical box as Jason closed the briefcase.

"Crap," Jason proclaimed in a whispered tone.

"What?"

"The lock."

Derek turned to the chain-linked door. Previously left wide open, it was now closed. The same lock that they'd earlier removed was again hanging securely in place on the outside just above the handle.

"Open it."

Jason quickly passed the briefcase to Derek before shoving his fingers through the gate in a desperate attempt to realign the numbers that would grant them their freedom.

"Come on. Come on," Derek pushed as the voices in the hall grew closer.

"I'm trying. It's harder from this angle," Jason complained as he knelt to the floor in an attempt to get a better view of the numbers along the bottom of the lock. "It's too dark. I can't see the numbers."

Jason was right. He hadn't noticed it before but the lights in the room were off. The glow of the device must have been enough initially that he hadn't even noticed, but now with the briefcase closed, the blackness of the room was obvious. "Here," Derek spoke as he held his thumb against the lock on the case. The faint blue light on the scanner lit up momentarily as he held the new light source close to the bottom of the lock beside Jason's head.

Jason continued to fumble with the numbers, getting the first two in place.

"You're worried about miscalculating the jump aren't you?" Derek's familiar words echoed from the hall, no more than twenty feet from where they were currently trapped.

"I'm asking you about your calculations," Derek informed Jason.

"I know. The light."

Derek looked down. The light on the case had timed out. "Oh." He placed his thumb against the lock and again the blue light lit the cage.

Dialing in the last two numbers, the lock released with a faint click. Quietly, but in a hurry, Jason displayed amazing dexterity as he managed to remove the lock from the handle without dropping it, while at the same time opening the door and letting them free. Both scampered from their temporary prison toward the boxes on the other side of the dark room.

"The lock," Derek pointed to Jason's hand as they reached their hiding spot.

Looking down, Jason realized that he'd forgotten to reattach the low budget security system.

The footsteps resumed in the hall as the familiar, yet unexpected company continued its advance.

"Never mind. Forget the lock," Derek instructed.

"I can't. I'll know something's wrong," Jason disagreed as he quickly made his way back to the cage, slipped the lock back through the handle and made his way back behind the cardboard wall just as his counterpart's hand slipped around the doorway and flipped the switch, illuminating the room.

Derek and Jason, while attempting to remain as hidden as possible, watched in awe as the ten minute younger versions of themselves made their way toward the locked cage.

"I take it that's our power source," the other Derek offered up the familiar guess.

"Deja Vu," Derek mumbled.

Jason turned with a shushing stare.

He couldn't help himself though, as he leaned closer to his naked roommate. "Is this really happening?" he whispered.

Jason's disapproving stare deepened.

"Okay. We need to get this thing up and running as quickly as possible," the other Jason instructed as they made their way into the cage.

Knowing the rest, Derek turned his attention away from the familiar action taking place on the other side of the room, suddenly more interested in their current surroundings. The boxes that were concealing their presence from themselves had obviously been down there for quite some time. The dank space had caused a fair amount of mold to form along the bottom of the boxes that were in contact with the floor; the yellow-green life creeping upward toward the higher stacked containers. The sides of the boxes were lined with various people's names and short descriptions like, *bathroom* and *books*; likely the current contents of the moldy brown squares. Other names and descriptions had been crossed out on various boxes, indicating that this had not been their first storage task, though their condition would suggest that it would likely be their last.

The remainder of the dimly lit corner was fairly empty. The floor, though covered in a thick layer of dust, was remarkably clean given the condition of the boxes, suggesting that, at least occasionally, someone must take a moment to visit the secluded space with at least a broom and maybe a dustpan in an attempt to tidy up the place.

Scanning further he didn't see any oil containers or paint cans, as he would expect to find in such a space. There were no tools or spare pieces of wood for miscellaneous repairs by the building attendant and there was no old food or random crumbs of any kind.

Now, of course he didn't expect to find food stored in such an unsanitary place, but its presence might have helped to explain the rather large rodent currently scurrying toward Jason's left foot.

"Jason," Derek whispered as he tapped his friend's shoulder.

Jason showed no signs of acknowledgement, still focused intently on the two men in the cage.

"Jason," Derek whispered again, a bit louder this time as he peeked around the boxes to see if he'd heard himself.

His counterpart continued to work on the electrical box as the other Jason set up the machine.

Glancing back toward the quickly scurrying rat, Derek watched as the small animal disappeared beneath his crouching friend, but before he could offer another warning, Jason quickly jumped, almost springing to his feet as the unexpected rodent brushed against his dangling, nether region.

A warning obviously no longer of any use, he quickly slapped his hand over Jason's mouth to muffle the yelp that he was sure would follow as Jason locked eyes with the rat who'd paused in his journey to offer up his own 'what the hell' look.

"What was that?" the other Derek questioned.

Jason, Derek and the rat froze, all seeming to exchange the same, 'we're busted' glance.

"I don't know," the others continued.

"Go check it out."

"Me? Why don't you go?"

With Derek's hand still over his mouth, Jason could only offer up an 'I told you so' stare.

The rat, apparently bored with its newly discovered

company, continued on its way, making its way around the boxes and into plain view of the cage.

Realizing that they were safe again, since neither of them had investigated the strange noise after seeing the rat, Derek removed his hand from Jason's face.

Allowing a moment to pass before moving again, Derek and Jason again slowly peeked around the boxes, watching as the others made final preparations and now stood holding the tiny wired orbs in their hands.

Derek knew what the other him was thinking. He wanted to stand up and tell him to go for it; to not doubt his genius roommate and push the button, but he knew he wouldn't and moments later the button was pressed and the men in the cage vanished, their clothes dropping to the floor where they'd previously stood.

"I guess that explains where our clothes went," Derek laughed as he pictured the look of shock on both of their faces when they'd discovered their nudity. Given all that had just happened in the last ten minutes however, he'd almost forgotten that he was naked. Jason on the other hand was defensively cupping himself, likely in an attempt to preserve what little dignity he had left, as well as protect himself from anymore curious scavengers.

"The conductivity was poor," Jason mumbled.

"Excuse me?"

"How could I've been so stupid?" he continued. The machine works because of the electrical charge. The same charge that passes through the core then passes through us, linking us to the machine at the exact moment of transition."

"We were good conductors but our clothes weren't," Derek finished Jason's thought.

"Exactly and since they weren't good conductors, while they *were* attached to us, they weren't technically connected to the machine and therefore were left behind."

"Speaking of behind," Derek motioned behind Jason who jumped, expecting to see another rat quickly approaching for another inspection.

Other than their first, furry visitor, now chewing at the corner of one of the boxes, they were alone.

"Come on. Let's get out of here," Jason motioned, unamused as he spared one hand from its protective duty to pick up the briefcase.

The two made their way back into the cage.

"Give me the wires. I'll hook 'em back up," Derek held out his hand.

"We don't need to do that," Jason responded, unsure why the reasoning, that was so obvious to him, seemed to elude his equally intelligent friend. "We've already caught up with time. If we go back to where we started we'll be going back to the exact moment that we watched ourselves disappear."

He could tell that Derek was processing the information.

"Jello, right?"

"It's too risky and completely unnecessary since we're already here," Jason reaffirmed his logic.

"Can I at least get dressed then?" Derek motioned to the pile of clothing on the floor.

"Please do."

SEVEN

The lamp post lined entrance to the Turtle Creek apartments joined the car's gauges in illuminating the interior of the Chevy Impala as Ty crept to a stop. Anticipating that the large, wrought iron barrier would momentarily slide out of the way, he waited but received no welcome from the automated gate.

"Fucking thing," he sighed, annoyed at the still malfunctioning scanner.

For a month now it had been on the fritz, scanning the resident barcode on his window only half the time. Setting the car in reverse, he checked behind him and slowly backed up, again passing the scanner, then put the car in drive and rolled forward for a second time.

It still didn't budge.

"Really?"

He was going to have to buzz the apartment to get inside. Though he knew his Grandmother was eager for an update, it was nearly one in the morning and at the ripe old age of 83, she was most likely passed out on the couch, having succumbed to the sandman while awaiting the phone call he'd never made.

Putting the car in reverse again, intending to use the

visitor's turn out where the call box stood, Ty began to back up. He considered randomly dialing another apartment, but what would he say when the groggy voice on the other end answered? He couldn't claim to be FedEx making a middle of the night delivery. On the other hand, Everyone knew that the gate wasn't working. Maybe he could just tell them the truth and they'd buzz him through the damn thing. No. The odds of finding a friendly night owl were slim. "Fuck off," would be the likely response. Grandma Ushi was his only option. Either that or spend the night parked on the side of the road.

As he rolled passed the scanner and prepared to pull into the visitor's lane, a soft, electronic click drew his attention back to the gate, followed by the sound of the motor engaging as the metal guard began to slowly step aside.

"Thank you," he sighed in relief as he placed the car in drive and slipped through the gate.

Ahead on the left stood the main office where the mailboxes, fitness center and pool were. He turned left at the side road just before it, following the road around the complex. His grandmother's apartment was toward the back of the property, just opposite the athletic fields of a middle school, which stood on the opposite side of an eight foot tall, wooden fence separating the two properties. Parking was always an issue, no matter what time of day you came home, but in the middle of the night, with everyone in the complex home, it was damn near impossible. To make things even worse, the back of the property had a tendency to flood in heavy rain, limiting the available spaces even more.

Slowly rolling along the dimly lit parking lot, Ty searched for an open space. As difficult as parking was and as run down as the complex seemed when compared to other apartments in the area, it was still better than where he'd lived just two years earlier. Though only five or so miles away from his current home, he and his mother had resided just off of Florida Avenue. He didn't recall parking being an issue and the gate at that apartment had always worked, but that was about the only upside to those apartments. The wiring had either been installed incorrectly or the degenerates living in the complex had harvested so much copper wire from the building that they'd managed to disable half of the outlets and even though management was required by law to maintain the property to the city's strict building codes, neither the city nor the police seemed to care. The abundance of drug dealers and prostitutes prowling the street just beyond the property's walls was probably of bigger concern to them, though nothing ever seemed to get done about that either…except in his mother's case.

A couple of years back, in a typical display of poor judgment, she'd brought one of her clients back to the apartment. Unfortunately, the john had been an undercover cop and even though it had been her first arrest for prostitution, she was no stranger to the court. The fact that she'd brought the officer back to her home while her son slept on the pull out sofa in the living room had rubbed the judge the wrong way, and in the end, earned her a six year sentence in the Bradenton Correctional Facility for Women. Since he was only sixteen at the time, the state had two options; place him in state run care or allow a family member to take over as legal guardian. Grandma Ushi, having already been in essence a parental figure in his life, had thankfully been awarded custody.

Water splashed against the wheel wells as the car reached the flooded corner of the property. As expected, there was plenty of parking in this portion of the lot. Lacking a pair of waders, he continued on, passing his grandmother's apartment on the right.

Amazingly, there appeared to be a space just up ahead, that is until he got closer and realized that it was being occupied by a tiny Ford Fiesta, hidden between a pickup truck and a van. Maybe he could push the car out of the way, he thought as he passed the half open space. It couldn't weigh that much. If he had a friend with him they could probably just pick the tiny car up and carry it to the lake at the other end of the parking lot. Lucky for him though, and the Fiesta, the parking gods were smiling down on them that night and just another twenty feet ahead on the left was an open spot between a Ford Escort and an out of place, brand new BMW convertible…likely an overnight visitor. More interested in getting some much needed sleep than pondering a neighbor's out of place company, Ty swung the Impala into the open space, placed it in park and swung open the driver's side door.

"Ty," a faint voice struggled to compete with nature's dominating sonnet of frogs and insects.

Stepping from the car, Grandma Ushi came into view, standing on the sidewalk just beyond the front door of the first floor apartment. She must have been watching for him through the front window, miraculously fighting off sleep for the past two hours while waiting for the update that had never come. It was also possible that she'd been sitting on the plastic patio chair beside the door where she could be seen most mornings sipping tea and waving to random neighbors as they came and went on their daily routines.

"Why didn't you call?" she continued as he crossed the parking lot.

"It's late grandma, I thought you'd be asleep."

"You know I can't sleep at time like this."

"I'm sorry. I just thought—"

"—Sooo," Ushi interrupted, not interested in his excuses.

"It's fine," he responded as he slipped between the parked vehicles and joined his grandmother on the sidewalk.

"Fine? What you mean, it's fine?"

"I mean there's no problem."

"So you know who he is?"

"Well..."

"We can't take any chances here, Ty," the old woman went into her familiar, lecturing tone.

"I know Grandma. I took care of it."

"So he dead."

Surprised and not sure how to respond to that, "No, I lost him at the airport. I couldn't get past security, but the only flights leaving that terminal were to Denver, Chicago, Atlanta and Boston. He's far away from here."

"Ty, we cannot have strangers getting in way. Too much at risk. This your child...our blood and now somebody might know."

"He doesn't know who I am."

"How you know?"

"He can't know. You said it yourself. No one knows anything about us. I'll get my son and we'll get out of here before he can come back. He won't be a problem."

"You don't know that. He knows something or he wouldn't been there."

"It doesn't matter. I know what he looks like now so I can be on guard while watching the Nesbit's for my opportunity.

"We might not be able to wait for right opportunity. This getting too dangerous. We need to act soon."

"I'll bring him home, Grandma. Please, don't worry. It's late. Now let's get you inside and in bed."

"That boy is the last of our blood. Our name must live on and it's up to you to make happen."

"I know Grandma," Ty agreed as he urged his grandmother back toward the open door of the apartment.

"That boy is very important," the elderly woman once again eluded to his son's mysterious importance.

He'd asked her why on numerous occasions, but every time had been greeted with the same vague explanation about the blood line and every other generation or something like that. All he knew was that his grandmother was a wise woman and that, since she'd taken him in, his life had improved tenfold. He owed her everything and would do anything for her, even if he didn't fully understand why.

"You a good boy, Ty," she paused in the doorway. "I love you very much."

"I love you too, Grandma," he kissed the old woman on the cheek before shuffling her into the apartment and closing the door.

EIGHT

"Katie!? What's burning!?" Phil Bishop yelled to his daughter as he made his way to the bottom of the stairs, trying to refold the morning paper.

No answer.

Rounding the banister he began down the hall. A faint cloud of smoke clung to the ceiling overhead. He was certain that any minute the nearby smoke detector would also awaken with the new day.

"Katie," he called again as he reached the end of the hall and stepped into the kitchen to the sight of flames leaping from a frying pan on the stove and his sixteen year old daughter attempting to put them out by swatting at the air almost five feet away. "Jesus!"

Dropping the disheveled paper on the island countertop, he yanked the dish towel from the oven door and tossed it over the flames as he slid the pan from the lit burner and killed the supply of gas just as the smoke detector let out its first cries for help. Pulling the towel from the extinguished pan, he rushed back into the hall, waving it overhead until the emergency device ceased its ear piercing rant.

"It must be genetic," he mumbled as he lowered the

66

towel from overhead, remembering countless occasions being awakened to the same situation by his wife's kitchen follies. It had been three years since her passing and since then his daughter had made it her mission to fill in for her departed mother, right down to her tragic inability to cook.

"Sorry Daddy," Katie timidly lowered her head as her father reentered the room.

"That's ok sweetie. I appreciate the sentiment. So, what *were* we having, bacon?" he questioned as he made his way back to the stove, turning on the hood vent. The blackened remains of the pan vaguely resembled bacon but he couldn't be sure.

"Eggs," Katie replied.

Looking at the pan again he couldn't figure out how his daughter had messed up eggs so badly. The charred remains weren't white or yellow but pure black and compressed into three relatively neat rows that he would have sworn were strips of bacon if it weren't for the uncooked entrails of egg whites puddled on the stove top beside the burner.

"The bacon's in the oven," his daughter quietly added.

He knew what to expect as he opened the oven, but for some reason he kept his face directly in front of the door as he pulled it open and a thick cloud of smoke billowed from the inferno within.

"Son of a...!" Phil yelped as the smoke struck his eyes, instantly drawing tears. Quickly he pulled his face away from the continuing plume, waiting for the burning sensation to subside. He was aware, however; that with every second the door remained open, the smoke detector was preparing for its next rant.

Quickly he closed the oven and spun the knob to off, only briefly catching a glimpse at the cause of the fire within it. Apparently, his daughter had chosen to line the baking sheet with wax paper instead of aluminum foil and to make matters worse, she'd chosen the cookie sheet without raised edges to trap the abundance of grease. A river of flammable fluid poured from the edge of the pan to the hot surface below as the paper glowed a bright orange, ninety percent of its surface already consumed by white hot flames.

"We'll just let that burn itself out," he coyly remarked as he wiped at his still burning eyes.

"I'm sorry Daddy," Katie apologized as she hurried to the sink, grabbing a paper towel from the dispenser and running it under the faucet before handing it to her father.

Still caught off guard by the near inferno that was his home, he didn't notice the warmth of the wet cloth until he applied it to his face. His daughter wasn't the brightest of girls. At age five she'd attempted to plant a nickel in the garden out back, claiming that a money tree would soon grow and help the family pay for her mother's expensive treatments. Of course at the time he and his wife had found the claim adorable and thought nothing of it. They had even bought a small tree and planted it overnight in the exact spot where the nickel had been buried. The next morning they'd been awoken by young Katie jumping up and down on their bed, shouting at the top of her lungs, "It growed! It growed!". She'd led them down to the garden, barely giving them time to put on their shoes before dragging them outside to show them her tiny tree with dollar bills taped to its branches. Now the tree was ten feet tall and on occasion he would still tape a few dollars to the lower branches for her to find, though at times he wondered if she understood the joke or really did believe that money grew on trees.

Her questionable intelligence aside, he loved his daughter more than anything. She was the spitting image of her mother with the same long, blonde hair and hazel eyes; everything right down to the tiny dimple on the right side of her mouth whenever she smiled. And even though she'd managed to end up six months pregnant at the young age of sixteen, he couldn't be mad. In his opinion she was perfect and the tiny grandchild in her womb was a blessing.

"I'm so sorry Daddy," she wet another paper towel before rushing to her father's side.

Anticipating the scalding cloth, he blocked her advancing hand with his. "That's okay, sweetie. It happens," he attempted to comfort her while watching the glow of the oven window and imagining what the inside of the appliance would look like once the flames subsided. He also couldn't help but wonder if they'd ever have a meal again that didn't taste and smell of bacon or ash.

"I could make something else."

"No, that's quite alright," he quickly interjected, discarding the now cooler first paper towel on the island beside the newspaper.

"How am I ever going to raise a baby? I can't even cook a simple breakfast," Katie slid closer to her father, placing her head against his shoulder.

"Listen," he took ahold of her chin, lifting her eyes toward his. "You're going to be an excellent mother. You know how I know? Because, just as you seem to have inherited your mother's infamous inability to cook, you've also been blessed with her amazing ability to nurture."

A glassy quality took over his daughter's eyes.

"You're going to be an amazing mother because your mother was an amazing mother and wife and I'm positive that you couldn't be anything less."

"Thank you Daddy," his daughter replied, obviously trying to fight back her emotions as her voice quivered and she buried her face deeper within his shoulder.

"Now, how about a fool proof breakfast? A real American classic."

Katie raised her eyes from her father's shirt, the evidence of her emotions displayed by the dark spots on his police uniform.

"You get the Cheerios and I'll get the milk."

NINE

"This is the best system you have, right?" Bill continued questioning the alarm technician as he wandered from window to window, installing the sensors that would alert the Nesbits to any future intrusions into their home.

He'd been amazed by the company's response. After the police had left, Jennifer had demanded that he call about the security system immediately. He'd insisted that it would probably take at least a couple of days to get someone to come out and look at the house, let alone install it, but she'd continued throughout the night until he'd finally caved and called the alarm company around 3:00 am; if for no other reason than to satisfy her persistent nagging. To his amazement, an actual person had answered and after a five minute conversation, he had an appointment for 8:00 am that morning. With he, his wife and newborn son sharing the same bed, they'd been able to get a patchy three hours of much needed sleep.

"This is your entry sensor," the technician began the now familiar mantra as he pointed to the pair of sensors that he'd just attached to the window. "And this is your shatter sensor," he motioned to the thin wire running from the previously indicated sensor to the large pane of glass. "Nothing can get through this window without tripping at least one of these sensors which in turn will trigger the alarm system, which in turn notifies us. There's one of these sensors on every window and door, not to mention three security cameras which will begin recording at the moment an alarm is triggered. If someone even thinks about entering this house uninvited, we'll know about it."

"What about the skylights though?" Jennifer questioned as she entered the room, clinging to little Oliver, still reluctant to let him out of her grasp.

"The skylights too ma'am," the young man answered, attempting to be as respectful as possible, but unable to fully conceal his frustration with his customer's persistent interference and questioning.

As if understanding what his mother was asking, Oliver lifted his gaze skyward to the skylight overhead.

"We had a break-in last night. I just want to make sure that my family is safe," Bill attempted to explain he and his wife's constant questioning.

"Yes sir. I understand. I'll make sure that you and your family are as safe as possible," the young kid assured them with what appeared to be the first moment of understanding and sympathy he'd shown since beginning his inspection of the property.

"Thank you..." glancing at the name stitched on the technician's shirt, "...Ty."

"My pleasure sir."

*****

It had been unexpected and frightening, yet a pleasant surprise when he'd arrived at work earlier that morning and had been handed his list of appointments for the day. Typically he didn't read the list of customer's names that he'd be visiting that day; only the type of services being requested. He didn't typically care who the service was for, only what type of day he was in for.

Installations varied depending on the size and age of

the house. Newer houses were typically built on concrete foundation with cinder block walls, stucco finishes and high vaulted ceilings. Such houses could be tricky when installing an entirely new system. On the other hand, many of these houses came wired with an existing system when built, so installation simply meant swapping out a couple of keypads, window and door sensors and maybe a motion sensor or two. Nothing too tricky.

Older homes usually possessed the same style foundation but were built in a style more typically seen further north, away from the annual threat of hurricanes. Those houses typically had hollow, insulation filled walls and plenty of space in the low, flat ceilings to run and conceal wires from the system's central hub to the numerous security points in the house. Unfortunately, those houses had been built before fear had taken such a fierce hold on society; back when a knock at your door was likely your neighbor welcoming you to the neighborhood with a dinner casserole or freshly baked brownies, rather than a 9mm and dufflebag in which to shove all your shit. This in turn also meant that the entire house had to be wired from scratch; a job that could easily take an entire day, not to mention countless hours squeezed into the sweltering heat of a tiny attic crawl space.

Three upgrades and one install in a house built only six years ago, the list read as Ty had made his way across the parking lot toward the row of matching company vans. But it hadn't been the list of services that had stopped him in his tracks mid parking lot. The name beside his first appointment might as well have been printed in 3D the way it leapt off the page at him.

Nesbit, Bill.

Suddenly he'd recalled his boss mentioning the first appointment being very important. That the man who'd called the twenty four hour appointment line in the middle of the night had been very adamant about getting the very first appointment that morning. Even after the scheduler had informed him that they didn't have an available opening until early next week the man had persistently argued that it was urgent and that he was willing to pay for the top of the line system as long as they got out first thing that morning. Eventually the scheduler had given in, bumping what would have been his first scheduled service that morning to later in the day and placing Mr. Nesbit's name at the top of his list.

He couldn't remember how long he'd stood motionless in the center of the parking lot staring at the impossible name on the page before him. It hadn't been until Bob Holvis had laid on the horn of his van that he'd been startled back to reality and continued the rest of the short journey to his company issued vehicle.

Now he was standing in the living room of the very house he'd been parked in front of only ten hours earlier.

"Thank you, Ty," Mr. Nesbit smiled as he took a step back, apparently finally at ease with the young stranger's ability to perform the job for which he'd been hired.

"My pleasure sir," he politely responded, though unable to look Mr. Nesbit in the eyes. All of his attention was focused on the young life nested in the arms and against the bosom of the attractive woman he feared his son would someday call mom.

He'd contemplated reaching for a screwdriver from his utility belt and plunging it into Mr. Nesbit's left temple. His cunt wife wouldn't know what hit her, until another screwdriver had been drawn and firmly buried in her likely barren womb. She'd slowly slump to the floor, the look of shock and pain causing her eyes to widen as he slowly loosened her grip and removed the undeserved life from her grasp.

But then what, he'd considered. The company knew who he was. They knew that he was there and he was driving their van. If he went back to pick up his car before his shift was over, he'd surely be questioned, especially if he was seen removing a newborn child from the passenger seat. Just the same, he couldn't try to run either. The cops would find him in no time.

No, his only option was to wait. He would lay claim to his son soon enough. For now, he had to leave it up to the Nesbits to take care of him. Besides, he wanted to know more about last night's unexpected visitor.

"So, tell me about this break in."

TEN

"What are you doing!?" Derek gasped as he opened the door and stepped into the dorm room to the sight of half his wardrobe in a pile on the bathroom floor. The other half was hanging from an impromptu clothes line made of telephone and computer cables tied to the shower rod and haphazardly strung across the bathroom to the light fixture above the sink before crossing the room once again, ending in a knot on the other end of the shower rod.

"I figured it out," Jason laughed excitedly as he picked up another Calvin Klein dress shirt and dunked it into the watery, pale green concoction that currently filled their bathtub.

Derek was sure that the white shirt would reemerge from the foaming green sea with a similarly unappealing hue, however when it did reappear, it was as white as when it had gone into the tub.

"Figured what out?" Derek chose to ignore his roommate's utter disregard for boundaries in exchange for an explanation.

"Huh?" Jason distractedly responded as he draped the shirt over the indoor clothesline before grabbing a pair of jeans and sentencing them to the same watery fate.

"What? What did you figure out?"

"Oh, the clothes issue," he continued in the same excited tone.

Derek just stared, expecting an explanation as he again watched his assaulted garment reemerge from the opaque liquid and get tossed across the same sagging wire.

"The electrical current wasn't sufficiently transmitted through our clothing so they didn't go with us."

"Yes, I know. I was there. Remember?" Derek reminded him, still unsure what this had to do with his wardrobe's unscheduled bath.

"The machine focuses electricity through the core, bending space and time around it, allowing for it and anything attached to it, with sufficiently conductive properties that is, to travel through time.

He didn't need an explanation about how the machine worked. He knew exactly how it worked. He'd built every component that had gone into that briefcase. He knew exactly what every chip, wire and tube in the thing did. The only components that he didn't fully understand were the red liquid and the software used to run the amazing device.

"Don't you get it?" Jason questioned as he saw the still confused look on his roommate's face. "Our clothes couldn't conduct a great enough charge to bind them to the machine."

"So we're going to do it wet next time?" Derek struggled to understand how his clothes taking an unneeded bath had anything to do with Jason's explanation.

"No," Jason laughed as he tossed another of his roommate's shirts into the water. "This liquid contains ultra high ion levels that I developed by using the school's IDE plants, otherwise known as Electrodionization plants."

"Yeah, yeah, I know what Electrodionzation plants are," Derek interjected, feeling the need to remind his friend that he wasn't a complete idiot when it came to chemistry, especially electrochemistry. "You're talking about pure water."

"Exactly."

"But you know that pure water simply means water with a higher concentration of ions, hence a greater ability to conduct an electrical current than standard, impure tap water. It doesn't change basic properties, namely the inevitable fact that it will eventually evaporate. How do you plan on bonding the ions to the fabric?"

"With this."

While continuing to hold his latest victim underwater with his right hand, Jason reached for what looked like a large bottle of bleach sitting on the floor beside him. The typical Clorox label had been replaced by a hand written label displaying the unfamiliar and unpronounceable name, "Perchlorododecahedrane".

"As the water evaporates, the green stuff you see will chemically bond the additional ions to the individual fibers of our clothes, ensuring that they possess the conductivity levels needed to bond with the machine, hence allowing them to travel with us and ensuring that we arrive fully clothed at our destination.

"Okay, but did you need to chemically alter my entire wardrobe. I mean, I don't think I'll be wearing pajama pants during our travels," Derek motioned to the pair of cotton, flannel pants dripping over the toilet.

Jason stared up at the flannel pants, realizing that maybe he'd gone a bit overboard in his excitement.

Sensing Jason's waning enthusiasm, triggered by his questioning, Derek rolled up his sleeves and grabbed a pair of his underwear from the pile.

"Move over. I'll need these."

ELEVEN

"So, explain to me why we're driving all the way out into the middle of nowhere this time. The basement seemed to work fine last night," Jason inquired from the passenger seat.

"If seeing your scrawny ass, squatting behind a pile of moldy boxes suddenly jumps to the top of my to do list, I'll let you know."

"All I'm saying is that it's safe. That building has been there for well over a hundred years. Other than a few electrical and piping upgrades, the basement has hardly changed in all that time. It's the safest option I could find."

"Safe yes, but it doesn't contain the amount of power we need for a real test. That fuse box can't handle the amount of power we need for a trip of any significance."

"Based on my calculations, it was capable of providing the device with enough power for a jump of nearly six months."

"Our first trip was supposed to take us twenty minutes into the past but instead we only traveled a little more than five. Your calculations were wrong."

Jason didn't argue. He'd spent the previous night wide

awake, contemplating not only the clothing issue but his error in timing as well. Derek was right. There had been a serious miscalculation between the time he'd expected them to arrive and the brief step back that they'd actually taken.

"Don't be too hard on yourself," Derek assured his visibly bothered friend. "The miscalculation didn't come from your program, at least not your part of it. The power estimates I gave you were embarrassingly inaccurate. I blame myself."

"Then so do I," Jason agreed with a smile.

"Thanks."

"No problem."

"There isn't enough power in any typical electrical panel for us to make any significant jump. We need a larger source if we're going to test this thing's real potential," Derek motioned to the briefcase in the backseat.

Jason had insisted on strapping the device in like it was their own little, scientific love child.

"Derek, the further back we go the greater the risk of miscalculating the arrival point, not to mention the countless unknown risks such as other people or objects occupying the space. We could instantaneously become—"

"—Become fused to the other person or object like Siamese twins," Derek finished the familiar warning.

"All I'm saying, is that we need to run more small scale tests before we risk too large a jump."

Letting some of his frustration with his straight laced roommate finally seep out, "you need to loosen up a little, you know, let those balls of yours drop and take a risk every now and then".

Jason didn't know how to respond. He knew Derek was right. He *did* live his life by the rules. He never made a move without contemplating every potential consequence or calculating every possible outcome, but he didn't like surprises. He didn't like the uncertainty of the unknown, so a change in this behavior was unlikely.

"Sorry," Derek, recognizing Jason's contemplative pause, quickly recanted. "All I mean is that you need to live life. You can't always be concerned with what might happen. Sometimes you need to just take a chance and see what comes of it."

"The last time I took a chance, what came of it was a night, followed by the remainder of high school, filled with ridicule as well as what I'm sure are dozens of photos of me and a dildo."

Derek remained silent. He and Jason had never actually talked about the Jenna Bishop incident. He knew about the events of that night. There probably wasn't a kid in their high school who didn't, past or present but the topic hadn't actually come up between them before; likely due to Jason's understandable embarrassment and *his* disinterest in causing any unnecessary pain.

"There's no need to worry. I've found the perfect location," Derek chose to change the subject instead of continuing down the current, uncomfortable path. "It was actually a place I looked into right after you'd come to me with what I, at the time, thought was a crazy idea."

Jason shot Derek a surprised look. Derek had voiced his opinions regarding the likeliness of success before, but never had he called the project crazy.

Aware of his roommate's stare, but keeping his eyes on the road ahead as they traveled further into the densely wooded area, "I had actually run all of the calculations in anticipation of maybe one day using the site to make a leap of unbelievable distances, you know, like the Middle Ages or Victorian times or something like that. I'd love to go back and pick DaVinci's brain a while, you know? Unfortunately there would be no power source capable of allowing a safe return home, so I guess that would be a one way trip," he paused to contemplate how he could have previously overlooked that bit of information.

"Anyway, based on last night's little experiment and my latest calculations, courtesy of a wasted hour in Professor Billcock's class this morning, I've determined that there's no power source in the world large enough to make possible a jump of that magnitude; not even a nuclear power plant could provide us with enough juice."

"This news was a bit deflating," Jason thought. He too had dreamt of one day using the device to travel back to a time when dinosaurs had roamed the earth. His bedroom walls had been lined with posters of the magnificent beasts; hung in chronological order of each species' existence from the Triassic Period all the way to the moment of their extinction at the end of the Cretaceous Period. He'd spent countless nights staring at the prehistoric animals lining his walls, wondering if scientific investigation had recreated the magnificent creatures accurately or if humanity's need for exaggeration and grandeur had somehow skewed the reality of these grand giants. He wanted nothing more than to go back and see for himself but if what Derek was saying was accurate, and he was sure that it was, he would never get the chance to witness those long dreamt about creatures, thriving in their natural environment.

"By my calculations, I estimate that the largest jump we could possibly make would be approximately twenty-five years, give or take a month or two," Derek continued, unaware of his passenger's roaming thoughts.

Jason, still lost in thought, showed no reaction to the significantly shortened timeline.

"Did you hear what I said. The machine is only capable of a twenty-five year window."

Reemerging from childhood memories to the reality of his suddenly shattered dreams, "Twenty five years?" Contemplating the shortened window, "We also have to take into account the factor of space and time," he fully reengaged himself in the conversation. "Just because the device is capable of going back that far doesn't mean that a landing spot is possible. If we max out the machine's capabilities without taking all three planes of space into consideration, we could end up arriving in the middle of deep space and ultimately to our deaths.

"Always the optimist," Derek joked at Jason's consistent need to point out the worst of possible scenarios. "Don't worry, I ran your space time calculation as well and I've determined that the furthest back we can go, based on available power sources and the earth's orbital location, is May 22nd, 1991."

"A few days after my birthday," Jason added.

"That's right."

"How did you run my program from class this morning?" Jason questioned curiously. You didn't take the device with you? Did you?"

"No. Of course not," Derek laughed, surprised that Jason would even suggest such a thing.

"So how did you come up with 1991?"

"I...I sort of uploaded your program to my phone," Derek admitted as he held his iPhone up, the simple looking program filling the screen.

"I didn't realize we'd made it available on iTunes," Jason joked.

"Yeah, I was just as surprised as you when I saw it advertised beside the 'Porntube' app."

"Well nothing beats good product placement."

Smiling at his roommate's uncharacteristic quick wit, Derek's excitement at the pending trip grew.

"So, you still haven't told me where we're going yet," Jason reminded him.

"I told you. The year of our birth, 1991," Derek answered as he slowed the car, turning off of the paved road, onto a narrow dirt road that wandered even further into the dense woods.

"You're not going to kill me are you," Jason, taking a page from Derek's book of humor, commented on the remote nature of their destination.

"Kill you?" Derek laughed. "No, I'm not going to kill you, but that might if you're not careful," he motioned to their destination as the remote transformer yard came into view just ahead.

"You're going to tap into that?" Jason questioned, concern evident in his tone.

"Tap into? No, I'm going to harness the shit out of it," Derek replied with a grin, knowing that his plan would likely knock out the power to nearly every home and business within a fifteen mile radius.

Jason looked at his friend's wide grin with concern as Derek slowed the car, coming to a complete stop only ten feet from the large fenced facility.

"And how exactly do you propose we get in? I'm sure there's security."

"There is. Every inch of this facility is covered by at least one camera at all times," Derek confirmed his roommate's assumption. "Not to mention that the gate is not only magnetically locked but also equipped with security sensors that trigger the cameras to begin recording from the time that it's opened until ten minutes after one of the hundred or so motion sensors on the property ceases to sense any signs of movement.

"So let me guess. You hacked into Mass. Electric and planted a virus that will allow you to temporarily disable their security systems and hence allow us to access the facility undetected."

"No," Derek laughed. "When have you ever known me to be the hacker type? I wouldn't know the first thing about hacking into a utility company's digital infrastructure, let alone how to write a program that could temporarily disable an entire security network."

"Then how are we going to get in there without being seen?" Jason wondered aloud.

"With this." Derek removed a single key from his pocket, holding the simple device of entry up for Jason to see.

"A key?" Jason questioned, surprised by the simplicity of the proposed solution.

"Not just any key. A key that I had copied during my internship with Mass. Electric last summer."

Jason was impressed. He'd never doubted Derek's intelligence, but at times he *had* questioned his commitment. Derek had always come across as the 'whatever's going to happen will be' type and not one to plan things out in the long term, but seeing that key firmly grasped between his index finger and thumb, he now realized that he'd seriously underestimated his roommate's commitment to the project. Derek had obviously been planning this moment for quite some time now, which somehow made him feel more at ease about the dangerous leap they were about the take. At the same time though, a key seemed too simple a solution for what sounded like such a sophisticated security system.

"You're telling me that the state's largest electric company probably spent a small fortune to install a state of the art security system on this site and all that it takes is one key to get inside?" Jason questioned.

"That and the passcode that I got by making my boss, and I quote, 'cum so hard that, not only her husband, but her vibrator as well would forever pale in comparison'."

"There's the Derek I know."

"Thanks," Derek's grin widened at the perceived compliment. "Now come on," he opened his door and excitedly jumped from the vehicle.

Jason watched as Derek almost skipped his way to the security gate, unable to conceal his excitement. "Here we go I guess," he spoke as he opened his door and followed more cautiously.

*****

"You throw like a girl."

"I am a girl," Autumn Lively responded to her

brother's taunt as her first pitch bounced in front of the pizza box, currently standing in as home plate.

"You couldn't hit it anyway!" Callie yelled from the other side of the large back yard.

"I think you should back up a bit more!" thirteen year old Jonathan yelled back at the mouthy outfielder as he took up position beside the pizza box one more time.

Grabbing another ball from the bucket beside her, Autumn stepped to the side of the stick that they'd placed in the grass as an impromptu mound, kicked her leg in the air and delivered the next pitch. This time the ball sailed from her grasp, passing over the cardboard plate and just under the bat of her overconfident brother.

Callie began laughing from the outfield. "See! I told you!"

"Shut up Callie!"

"Hey, don't yell at my friend just because you suck!" Autumn scolded her embarrassed brother.

Jonathan didn't say a thing. Instead, he retook his position alongside the plate, slamming the end of the bat into the box as he'd seen his major league idols do countless times. Autumn grabbed another ball from the bucket beside her, staring her brother down before winding up and releasing the ball with another girlish delivery. The ball sailed toward him. Intent on showing up the year older girl in the outfield, he focused all of his concentration on the spinning projectile hurdling toward him. Rearing back, in preparation for an all or nothing swing, he took one quick glance at the pretty redhead in the outfield. As much as he wanted to show her up; to prove just how good he was, even more so, he wanted to impress her.

Callie had been friends with his sister for nearly five years now, ever since she'd moved in next door. He'd always liked her. She'd always been nice to him and they'd always enjoyed each other's company, but in the last year or so something had started to change. What had been a secondhand friendship had begun to take on a more exciting quality. Callie had always been Autumn's friend, but lately he'd realized a greater excitement beginning to take over whenever she and his sister got together to play, which is why he'd blown off going to the beach with Billy and his parents that morning and, to his sister's surprise, had suggested baseball instead.

He wanted nothing more than to hit the ball coming toward him. He intended to hit the ball so hard that the leather cover simply peeled away, leaving only the ball's core sailing toward the other end of the yard, over Callie's head and into the adjoining woods. She would have no choice but to be impressed. Rearing back, he prepared to swing.

As the ball approached the plate, he lunged forward, putting all he had into the swing as the bat and the ball crossed the plate at the exact same moment but one inch apart. Just as the previous pitch had done, the ball struck the hockey net backstop with a soft swoosh as the momentum of the swinging bat compromised his balance and dropped him to his knees. Female laughter erupted from the outfield, replacing Jonathan's previous confidence with adolescent embarrassment.

"My turn," Callie yelled between laughs as she sprinted toward the plate.

Embarrassed by his failure, Jonathan didn't say a word, simply dropping the bat in exchange for his glove. He couldn't explain how he felt. Hell, he couldn't explain how he'd been feeling for the past year. Instead, he chose to avoid eye contact with the source of his confusion and jogged out to the mound to take the place of his sister who was currently trotting to the outfield.

"Right here," Callie poked as she slammed the bat into the plate, just as her unknown admirer had done moments earlier.

Refocusing his attention away from his confusing, early teen emotions and back on the task at hand, Jonathan stepped back, preparing to deliver a perfect strike. Displaying perfect form, just as his father had taught him, he kicked his leg high into the air, lunging forward and released the ball with all the strength he could muster.

The ball erupted out of his hand as Callie prepared to swing. Shifting her weight to her back leg, she pushed forward, toward the approaching ball. The sound of the metal bat striking the spinning leather was almost inaudible as the baseball instantly changed course. Within a millisecond, the leather orb was sailing over his head and moments later, his sister's as it broke the wooded barrier and continued its airborne journey deep within the distant woods.

He was devastated. The very thing that he'd intended to do, to impress his unaware love, had just been done to him and now she was rounding the loosely laid out bases in an almost ballet like dance as her closest friend scurried off into the woods to retrieve what would momentarily become an embarrassing home run.

*****

He didn't have to admit it. Jason was sure that his worried look was all the evidence Derek needed to understand just how nervous he was about this improperly planned and dangerous test. Or, at least it would have been if his friend hadn't spent the last ten minutes consumed by the dangerous task of connecting the device to the two-hundred-twenty kilovolt transformer that Jason continued to admire from afar.

"And you're sure that the device can handle this much power?"

"Again, yes," Derek reassured his nervous friend for what was probably the fifth time since they'd set foot inside the gate. "The charge only passes through the case for a brief nanosecond before we're gone. It's *this* place that I'm more concerned with," Derek displayed a half worried grin as he took a quick look around at the multimillion dollar equipment surrounding them.

"Why, what's going to happen after we're gone?"

"Likely, nothing," Derek reassured as he connected the last of the spider web of wires to the large equipment and then to the case. "If anything, the sudden surge will probably just trip the breakers, knocking out power to half of the town, or...,"

"Or?" Jason's concern grew at the trailing thought.

"Or, the sudden redirection of power could cause this transformer as well as the other three behind it to erupt in a massive ball of fire and sparks capable of being seen from space," Derek shrugged dismissively.

"Great. Let's just hope we're no longer standing here when that happens.

"Right, now come on," Derek held out the pair of wire tethered orbs that would connect his friend to the machine.

"What's that then?" Jason motioned to the red backpack, propped against the fence behind him.

"Oh shit, wouldn't that have sucked," Derek laughed as he placed both of his orbs on the ground and jogged over to the bag.

"What?" For the first time in his life he felt completely confused and in the dark about what was going on.

"Spare parts," Derek explained as he picked up the bag and trotting back toward the device, grabbed Jason's arm to encourage him.

"Spare parts? Encouraging," Jason hesitantly moved toward the briefcase.

"Don't worry about it," Derek reassured. "Everything will be fine. I just wanna be prepared for anything."

"You, prepared?" Jason almost began laughing at the comical statement.

"Hey, I can plan ahead when necessary," Derek assured as he bent down and picked up his orbs. "You remember those two girls in our dorm room?"

"You mean the one I assaulted and her friend," Jason recalled the embarrassing encounter, his face turning red.

"Yes, them."

"What about them?" Jason searched for a point.

"Well, before bringing them home, I made sure that I was well protected.

"But weren't you just telling me in the lab the other night how you needed another box of condoms and wanted me to run to the convenience store to pick them up for you."

"A task which you have yet to complete."

"Sorry. I'll get right on that."

"Anyway, yes you are correct. I was out of condoms but I knew that I was out of condoms so I made sure to engage our fine young female friends in a very specific and provocative line of questioning before inviting them home. A line of questioning which ultimately provided me with the knowledge that not only were both on birth control, but also that the lovely blonde occasionally left her back door unlocked."

"What does having no condoms have to do with her poor security habits?"

The grin, which had continued to grow as he'd recounted his previous night's escapades, suddenly faded at his sadly inexperienced friend's tame existence.

"Never mind," Derek sighed. "You ready?"

"What?" Jason's confusion continued. "Oh wait."

"There you go," Derek's smile returned.

"How are we going to get back?"

Derek's grin again faded. "What?"

"Here. How do we get home? How do we know if there's a suitable power source on the other side that can safely return us back to this time?"

Realizing that the joke had been completely lost on his friend, Derek switched back to a tone of reassurance. "What does that plaque over there say?" he motioned to a small silver sign mounted on the exterior wall of the gate house.

"1990," Jason stuttered as he adjusted his glasses in an attempt to read the distant numbers.

"Right, a whole year before our programmed arrival point. So there's nothing to be concerned about. This place will exist to provide us a safe journey home."

"But if the calculations are off, we could arrive in the wrong year."

"If the calculations are off we could be dead," Derek let out an uncomfortable chuckle.

"Excuse me!" a young, female voice suddenly interrupted.

Both Derek and Jason turned to find a young girl holding a baseball and standing on the other side of the fence at the edge of the clearing.

"Time to go," Derek announced as he pushed the tiny button on his orb.

"Wait! What about the transfor—" Jason was cut off mid-sentence as a loud snap followed by a deafening pop erupted from the equipment around them.

Autumn stumbled backward at the eruption of noise and a sudden burst of wind that swept through the large clearing, tripping over a root and falling backward onto her butt. The home run ball that she'd just retrieved, before stumbling upon the two strange men standing at the center of the large facility, rolled from her grip and stopped against a nearby tree.

Though the fall had temporarily jarred her head back, she quickly returned her focus to the two strangers, just in time to see them, the wires and the odd box at their feet, vanish into thin air. The popping, sizzling noises slowly faded as the air calmed, but the same couldn't be said for her nerves. Stumbling to her feet, forgetting about the ball and reluctant to remove her eyes from the spot on which the two men had just been standing, she began making her way back to her two friends who were now standing at the other edge of the woods, intrigued by the odd noises taking place just beyond their property.

"Go back!" Autumn yelled as she waved her friends toward the safety of their homes, her nervous stagger quickly becoming an all out sprint.

"Where's the ball?" Jonathan asked confused.

"Forget the ball! They disappeared!" she replied as she ran passed them.

"The ball's lost?" Callie asked.

"You didn't hit it that hard," Jonathan attempted to regain some of his dignity.

"I hit it harder then you did," Callie poked fun.

"Come on!" Autumn yelled again.

Forgetting the ball, Jonathan also bolted for the house, quickly being overtaken by the pretty redhead.

TWELVE

"Explain to me again why we're participating in this antiterrorism thing," Officer Michael Lucern questioned from the passenger seat as he peered out his window at the tree lined, rolling hills along Interstate 90.

"Because the Chief asked us to," Phil Bishop fed his partner the simplest explanation he had. He didn't want to make the long trek from the quiet, rural streets of Cannon to the monstrosity that was Boston. Early on in his marriage and his career, he and his wife had spent three years living and working in the city. Out of those three years came more experience then he could have ever asked for and was glad to receive, but it also made him realize that, while he loved police work, he didn't love that type. He didn't want to be dealing with drug addicts, gang members and prostitutes day in and day out and while he understood the inherent risks involved with his chosen profession, the thought that he might leave his then pregnant wife and future daughter without a husband and father never did sit well with him. It was a feeling very vocally shared by his wife. So, six months into their pregnancy, they'd made the decision to up and leave the big city, leaving their small apartment in exchange for a large country house deep in the secluded woods of Western Massachusetts. With the highest of recommendation from his chief back in Boston, he easily found a position in the Cannon Police Department where he'd remained ever since.

"Really? Do you do everything the Chief asks you to?" Michael joked.

"Yes."

"So if the Chief asked you to jump off a—?"

"—Given that the highest bridge in Cannon is a whopping ten feet tall...yes," Phil instinctually guessed where his partner was heading with his typical, childish humor. While a great police officer and his best friend, Michael Lucern was the most immature thirty-eight year old he'd ever met.

"Building. I was going to say building," Michael finished his previous sentence with a smug tone and equally smug smile.

"Well, I'm sure that you're thinking of the tallest building in Cannon, which we both know is the church at the center of town...if you're counting the steeple that is...and since I am a God fearing Christian who attends church every Sunday and believes that my Lord and Savior would do everything in his power to protect me, my answer would still be yes."

"Do you have an answer for everything?"

"Yes," Phil ended the exchange with a smile.

"Seriously though," Michael changed the subject back to the road trip. "What second rate terrorist would think that a small town in rural Mass. would make a good target?"

"I don't know? That same woman attacks the chili cook off with her atomic butt burner concoction every year."

"Hey, my mother's chili is delicious and you know it. I've seen you put down more than one bowl at a time."

"It wasn't me that always complained about it. It was

93

Trish who wouldn't let me sleep in the same room with her afterwards."

Michael still wasn't sure how to handle the subject of his partner's deceased wife. Their families having been so close, he'd witnessed firsthand the pain that Trisha's cancer had caused them. He'd always been amazed at how well Phil had handled the situation, never letting on just how torn up inside he likely was. Phil and Trish had fought that battle together for nearly nine years before finally losing and not once had he seen his partner break down.

"Well," Phil broke the growing, awkward silence. "Speaking of burning concoctions, you should have seen my kitchen this morning."

"Katie trying to cook again?" Michael laughed, more than a little familiar with his godchild's culinary gifts.

"The eggs looked like bacon," Phil shook his head, still trying to grasp how that was even possible.

"Well it could have been worse, they could have looked like meatloaf. At least they were in the same category this time. If you ask me, it sounds like she's getting better."

"Funny."

"She means well," Michael reassured.

"I know she does. It just worries me sometimes. Trish was the better parent. I'm afraid that without her around I might have stunted Katie's ability to fully blossom into the woman that I know she should be. I mean, she's only sixteen and she's going to be a mother. Trish and I didn't even think about having a child until we were in our mid twenties and well established in our lives and careers. What is she going to do?"

"She's going to thrive," Michael reassured his partner in the first real moment of vulnerability he'd seen since the loss of Trish. "She's a strong girl with a strong father and even though the situation might not seem ideal right now, God always has a plan. Eventually that plan will become clear and you'll discover that this whole situation is actually a blessing in disguise."

"How do you do that?"

"What?"

"That. How do you go from obnoxious, post-pubescent, middle aged teenager one moment to mature, reassuring adult friend the next?"

"It's a gift I guess," Michael smiled. "Don't worry, it'll pass. Before you know it I'll be stealing your car, telling you how much I hate you and raiding your liquor cabinet again in no time."

"As long as you don't end up pregnant," Phil grinned as he signaled to pass a vehicle.

"I can't promise anything."

THIRTEEN

"...Transformers!" the shouted completion of Jason's sentence greeted their familiarly different surroundings. However, as worked up as he'd been just prior to making the jump, nothing could distract him from the strange, tingling sensation running up and down his spine. "Do you feel that?"

"I think we made it," Derek whispered, quickly scanning their surroundings as he patted himself down, looking for any odd or unfamiliar limbs. His one fear, other than miscalculating the landing point and ending up floating out in space was that, by some stroke of very bad luck, they would appear in the exact spot as some unlucky maintenance worker from the electric company.

"Do you feel that?" Jason asked again, in an even more excited tone.

"Feel what?" Derek responded confused but at the same time relieved to have all of his limbs and no extras.

"That! The tingling sensation!" Jason emphasized his enthusiasm over what seemed an almost orgasmic experience for him. Closing his eyes, the sensation grew, spreading from his spine until every part of his body, right down to the hairs on his head shared the same odd sensation.

"Are you alright?" Derek questioned, concerned and a bit confused since he felt nothing whatsoever.

Jason gasped, holding his breath momentarily before releasing it with a long sigh as the sensation faded.

"I hope you brought a clean pair of pants," Derek joked as he watch a wave a relaxation overtake Jason's body.

As the tingling sensation dissipated, Jason opened his eyes to find Derek staring at him, both concerned and confused. "You didn't feel that?" Jason questioned the strange look.

"Did I feel that? No. Have I felt that? Just...not with another guy by my side."

"It was unbelievable," Jason closed his eyes again, trying to get it back.

"I didn't feel anything but it could have been because I was too excited about not being...you know...dead."

Realizing that the sensation wasn't coming back, Jason once again opened his eyes while at the same time remembering the little girl that they'd seen just before activating the device.

"Shit, the girl!" Jason announced as he turned toward the fence.

She wasn't there. Quickly he scanned the perimeter of the transformer yard; still no little girl. "What do you think happened to her? Is she ok?" he questioned, remembering the popping noises and loud, electrical snap that had erupted from the surrounding equipment just before they'd jumped.

"Just the equipment reacting to the sudden power surge. I'm sure she's fine. If the equipment had exploded we would have likely heard or seen it just as we made the jump. The moment we left, the surge was over and the equipment, if still functioning, probably returned to normal as if we'd never even been there."

The explanation made sense. The electrical noises that

had come from the equipment had been loud but they definitely hadn't been explosions. Looking through the fence, to the tree line where the little girl had stood, Jason realized that he could no longer see the houses from which she'd probably come. It was likely that the neighborhood, that would eventually reside only a hundred or so yards away, hadn't been built yet.

"They really let this place go didn't they?"

Jason turned to see Derek disconnecting the device from the surrounding equipment.

"I mean look at this stuff," Derek admired the transformer to which the machine had just been connected. "The paint looks so fresh and the wires don't show any signs of deterioration."

Jason couldn't say that he'd paid much attention to the site's condition prior to that moment but everything did appear to be newer than he remembered. Even the steel plaque on the gatehouse wall seemed to gleam beneath the morning sun. They had obviously traveled back a significant amount of time and since they'd ended up with their feet planted firmly on the ground, he could only assume that they'd hit their desired target.

Kneeling beside the briefcase, Jason tapped at the iPad, scrolling through the thousands of lines of data that had been transmitted between the tablet and the device.

"System core stable," Jason read the three word sentence displayed on the screen with a sigh as he patted his right, front pocket. Just as Derek had brought with him a bag of spare parts, he'd brought with him an extra core.

"So now what?" Derek announced as Jason continued to stare at the sentence on the screen.

Swiping at the screen, Jason closed the program as he lowered the lid and engaged the latches on the case. "What do you mean now what?" he asked confused as he got to his feet with the case. Derek was standing beside him, his backpack of electrical toys slung over his shoulder as if he were ready for class.

"I got us here, so now what do we do?"

"Don't ask me, this was your trip."

"I'm just joking, come on," Derek motioned as he started toward the gate.

"Where are we going?"

"We came all this way. Don't you wanna take a look around?"

"Just a quick look and then we need to get back," Jason agreed as he followed.

"To hell with that. We didn't risk our lives to just poke around the woods for a few minutes."

As the gate slowly retracted, Derek slipped out of the yard. Carrying the case, Jason quickly followed.

"I hope you brought your hiking shoes," Derek continued as he began walking down the dirt road that they'd previously traversed by way of the car still parked outside the gate in the future.

"Why?" Jason glanced down at his brown loafers and khaki pants.

"Because it's a long walk back to the city," Derek's voice faded as the distance between them grew.

Jason jogged to catch up to him. "We can't walk all the way back to the city. Heck, it took us almost twenty minutes to drive here and this thing isn't exactly light," he motioned to the metal briefcase as he caught up to his speed walking partner.

Stopping in his tracks, Derek thought. "You know, you're right."

"Yes, I know I'm right. Now, let's just take a look around and then—"

"—I guess we'll have to hitchhike," Derek announced, in an excited tone, the plan he'd obviously decided on already.

"Hitchhike?" Jason responded, hesitant to follow. "It would be safer to test the machine again," he shouted as he again played catch up.

"Nonsense. It's the nineties, you know, the time of peace and love."

"That was the sixties," Jason argued as he caught up. "The nineties had AIDS, Dessert Storm and George Bush...the first one."

"Yeah, but we have Obama, so how much worse could it have really been?"

*****

"This is a stick-up!"

Dustin Hendrix turned to see his five year old daughter standing beside him with what appeared to be a crude gun cut from the side of an empty cardboard box. From the print on the side of the paper weapon, it appeared to have been a shipment of Jameson Whisky.

"Don't shoot," he played along, throwing his hands in the air.

"Bang! Bang!" the little girl yelled as the improvised gun jumped in her hands with each shot.

He realized that he wasn't going to win any father of the year awards by encouraging his five year old daughter to hold up a liquor store, let alone kill the clerk. He figured he'd probably been knocked out of the running the moment he'd chosen to bring her to work in the first place, so, grasping his chest, he stumbled backwards and dropped to one knee.

"You got me," he gasped.

"Daddy, they aren't real bullets," Abby laughed as she lowered the gun.

Still pretending to be shot, Dustin partially removed his hands from his chest to peek at his wounds. "Oh no. Abby, look," he groaned.

"Daddy," Abby's laugh turned to concern as she approached her father.

Grabbing his daughter as soon as she was in arm's reach, Dustin pulled her close, tickling her sides as screams of joy poured from the little girl.

"Daddy, stop!" Abby struggled, pleading through her laughter to be set free until her father did just that.

After a moment of shared laughs, they both regained their composure and locked eyes.

"I love you Daddy."

That statement never got old. From the moment he'd witnessed her birth, his little girl had become the most important thing in his life. A relationship with her mother may not be possible but he knew that he would love and cherish his daughter forever. "I love you too sweetie," he reached for his daughter again, this time taking her in his arms for a hug.

The bell above the door, suddenly sprang to life.

"Daddy has to work now, so go back in the back room and watch the rest of your movie," he released his embrace as he watch his daughter comply and retreat back into the storeroom where he'd set up an Elmo tape on the television and VCR used to give new employees a brief training video.

"Cute little girl," Derek greeted the clerk as he returned to his feet, taking his place behind the register.

Dustin eyed the two men before him. Unfortunately, the store he worked in was in a somewhat rural and remote area with some...less than upstanding clientele. The man commenting on his daughter was dressed in a t-shirt that read *Fall Out Boy* (whatever the hell that was) and a pair of khaki shorts and for some reason he reeked of trouble. His Asian friend, however, put Dustin's mind at ease with his neatly pressed Polo shirt, Dockers slacks and nerdy glasses.

"What can I do for you boys?" he addressed the two men in a stern, elder tone, even though they both appeared not much younger than he.

"Do you have a phone that we can use to call a taxi?" the 'Fall Out Boy' asked with a smile.

"Pay-phone's outside," Dustin bluntly replied.

"I saw that, but we don't have any change. Can you break a twenty?"

"Register only opens for paying customers," Dustin continued his stern demeanor.

"But we don't need alcohol. We're just looking for a ride."

"I can't open this register without a sale."

"Like I just said though, we aren't interested in buying anything. I just need a dime for the phone," Derek's voice took on a tone of annoyed frustration at the clerk's unpleasant personality.

"No booze, no phone," the clerk matched Derek's tone.

"Listen," Jason jumped in, realizing Derek's growing frustration and wishing to avoid a shouting match that could likely turn into being questioned by the local authorities. "We've been walking for quite a while now and we just need to call a cab to come pick us up. I'm sure that you can help us out," he spoke in as friendly a tone as he could manage.

"No booze, no phone," the clerk repeated.

"I'm sure there's a button on that keyboard that will open this thing," Derek, fed up with the man's unjustified attitude, leaned across the counter to get a better look at the register.

"Get the hell back!" the clerk raised his voice as he reached beneath the counter.

Seeing the man's hand disappear beneath the counter for what he could only assume to be a gun, Jason pulled Derek away from the register.

"Get off me," Derek protested. "This guys a lying prick," he argued as Jason pulled him into a nearby aisle.

"Daddy?" Abby appeared in the storeroom's doorway.

"Go watch your show sweetie," Dustin instructed his daughter while keeping his hand firmly around the .38 below the counter.

Abby did as her father instructed just as the bell greeted

another group of customers.

"I told you girls before, unless you miraculously aged three years in the last few months, you ain't buying shit," Dustin greeted the familiar group of teen girls.

"Let's go," the attractive brunette turned to the other girls as they headed back out the door. "That asshole's working again."

The bell rang again as the girls exited.

"You're just friends with everyone aren't you?" Derek re-greeted the unpleasant man behind the counter.

"I told you guys, no booze, no pho—"

Placing a bottle of Vodka on the counter, Derek stopped the clerk mid-sentence.

Dustin just eyed the two men before him.

"If you can manage to pry your fingers from that shotgun or revolver or whatever you have below the counter...," Derek smugly addressed the man, "...we can finalize this transaction and forget that we ever met."

Releasing the revolver, "Twenty-one, fifty," Dustin replied after a pause.

"Oh, look," Derek taunted as he pulled a twenty from his wallet. "And here's a couple of his friends," he continued obnoxiously as two dollar bills followed.

Reluctantly the clerk's hand reappeared from beneath the counter, retrieving the money from the counter and with the push of a few buttons he added the cash to the open drawer and tossed two quarters onto the counter, ignoring Derek's outstretched palm.

"You keep it," Derek glanced down at the spinning coins. "Maybe you could buy some manners."

With the transaction complete, Jason quickly swiped the coins and grabbing Derek's arm, ushered him toward the door as the bell thanked them for their business.

"Can you believe that asshole?" Derek complained as they stepped back into the warm, May sun that had kept watch over them as they'd unsuccessfully searched for a compassionate motorist.

"So now what?" Jason questioned, making his way along the sidewalk toward the pay phone. "This thing says it takes a dime. Do quarters work? I've never used one."

No response.

"Derek?" Turning, Jason realized that Derek hadn't heard a word he'd said. He hadn't even been following him. Instead, he was standing at the driver's side window of a tan Volvo station wagon, laughing and chatting it up with an apparent new friend. "Typical."

Making his way toward the car, Jason noticed that the passengers inside the unattractive, square vehicle were the three girls and one of them was now holding the bottle of Vodka that Derek had just purchased from the uncouth clerk.

"Jason, come on," Derek waved him over. "Melissa and her friends here have agreed to give us a ride into town.

"Already on a first name basis with the hot one...typical," Jason thought to himself. Another ten minutes and he'd probably know which ones were on the pill and which ones left their backdoors unlocked, whatever that mean— Finally getting the reference, he paused, shaking his head at his deviant friend and his own cluelessness.

"Come on, hurry up!" Derek shouted again as he lowered himself into the passenger seat, somehow convincing its current occupant to move to the back.

Watching the sandy haired girl open the rear passenger side door and climb into the back with her friend, Jason suddenly began to sweat as he realized the uncomfortable situation that he was about to encounter. It wasn't that he had any fear of the girls. None of them seemed like crazed serial killers. He did, however, fear the conversation or uncomfortable lack of one that would likely take place in that car. He knew exactly how the next fifteen minutes of his life would go and with every awkward second he imagined, a new bead of sweat began to form.

"You okay?" 'Sandy' asked as Jason squeezed in beside her, fumbling with the door before successfully pulling it shut.

"Good," was all he could manage, realizing that he'd forgotten the "I'm".

"Jason, this is Melissa," Derek motioned to the driver.

"Hi," Melissa smiled as she offered a small wave before returning to the task at hand by putting the car in reverse.

"And that's Michelle and...I'm sorry," Derek continued the introductions, pausing on the sandy haired one beside Jason.

"Sandy," the pretty girl introduced herself with a bashful smile and southern drawl.

"Really?" Jason thought, trying not to laugh at the coincidence.

"I love your accent," Derek continued to lay on the charm. "Let me guess, South Carolina?"

"Georgia," the girl corrected.

"I was going to say Georgia. Hey, Jason, aren't you from Georgia?"

"No. You know where—"

"—Oh, that's right. Florida, only a mile from the Georgia state line. I always screw that one up," Derek continued.

Jason just stared in awe of the master at work.

"Oh really?" Sandy's shyness melted away as she turned to Jason. "My family lives only a few miles *north* of the border. That's so funny. What town?"

Jason froze, both mesmerized and terrified by the set of baby blues peering up at him.

"Gator...ah...Disney...I mean," Jason stumbled.

"Gatora-disna-hachie," Derek interjected. "It's a very small town in what used to be Indian territory. Most people don't even know it's there."

"Oh, yeah, I think I've heard of it," Sandy responded, wrinkling her nose as either a sign of confusion or in response to the smoke bellowing up beside her as Jason went down in flames.

"So, where to?" Melissa questioned as she paused at a stop sign.

"You girls ever been to M.I.T.?" Derek asked.

"What's Mit?" Michelle spoke for the first time since being introduced.

Glancing over at the cute redhead, Jason now knew who would be Derek's primary target. It was no secret that he preferred blondes, but he was also lazy, so stupid was usually an easier option. On occasion the two went hand in hand, but not as frequently as the stereotype would have one believe.

"You have an amazing smile," Derek focused his attention on Michelle, even though she wasn't currently smiling.

"See?" Jason spoke softly, confirming his prediction to himself.

"See what?" Sandy asked, still confused.

This time he didn't respond, afraid that if he spoke he'd just utter another stupid Florida landmark.

"We're college students, in Boston," Derek continued to address the girls as a whole. "M.I.T. is where we go."

"Don't you have to be pretty smart to get into there," Melissa asked as she drove.

"Well, yeah I guess so. I mean, don't get me wrong, I'm no genius but my friend here is."

"Well at least that wasn't a complete lie this time," Jason thought. He had tested well into the genius range in high school, but that wasn't typically something that played well with the ladies, at least not the ones their age.

"Really?" Sandy's interest peeked, her stare intensifying and inducing more perspiration from her back seat neighbor. "I think I took one of those I.Q. thingies last year in my sophomore year. At least that's what everyone said it was. They didn't come right out and tell us. I just remember it being really hard."

"Oh, yeah? What college do you go to?" Derek

continued to carry the conversation, well aware that his terrified friend couldn't.

"Oh we don't go to college. We're still in high school; Silver Lake. You know it?"

"Yeah, I think a couple of guys in our dorm went to school there," Derek continued the lies.

Jason could see the excitement in Derek's eyes at the news that they were surrounded by high school chicks. This news only made Jason more uncomfortable. Not only would he have to explain to the police who he was and why his license said that he had just been born, but he was probably also going to have to help Derek fight off three angry fathers and possible statutory rape charges as well, if this conversation ended where he figured it would.

"Don and Paul. I think they went to Silver Lake," Derek continued. "Isn't that right, Jason?"

He didn't answer, his mind incapacitated by thoughts of the under aged teens around him and the risks that went along with Derek hooking up with even one, let alone all three of them. They weren't supposed to be there. They weren't supposed to exist in this time and every interaction that they had with a person from this time was a previously nonexistent ripple in the space time continuum. God forbid Derek slip one by the goalie with someone from the past. He'd be a father before he was even born. That *had* to be somehow devastating to the future. They had to be careful. Moreover, he had to keep Derek under control.

"Earth to Jason," Derek waved his hand in front of Jason's face.

"Herpes," Jason muttered, his thoughts of how to stop Derek slipping past his lips.

"Ew," Michelle responded from the other side of the car.

"What?" Derek looked at Jason in shock.

Already committed, Jason continued his unvetted plan. "We forgot your medicine back at your girlfriend's house.

Derek was horrified. Each of the girl's faces went

blank as they all turned their attention to the nearest window, avoiding eye contact with their new passengers. Derek just stared at Jason with a look of confused anger before facing forward in his seat, convinced that the conversation was over.

FOURTEEN

"Is it bath time? Yes it is. It's bath time!" Jennifer leaned over little Oliver as she unbuttoned his onesie.

Oliver just stared up at his mother. She was sure that he had no clue what was coming, since this was to be his first bath since leaving the hospital. His excited smile hadn't come from seeing the little blue chair in the kitchen nor had it come from the few drops of water that his mother had splashed on his legs. His focus was on the long strands of his mother's hair, that swayed back and forth above him.

Reaching for the source of his fascination, Oliver's fingertips brushed through the end of his mother's long hair, sending his legs into a frenzy of excitement.

"Whoa there, Pelé!" Jennifer laughed as she battled to keep Oliver under control as she slid the onesie over his head and released the tabs of his diaper.

For a newborn, Oliver was a complete contradiction to everything she'd read prior to the adoption. According to the books, at this age, he shouldn't be able to do much more than cry and poop, but already Oliver seemed to have developed amazing dexterity and control in not only his limbs but his neck as well, making him an unexpected handful at times. While this development had struck her and Bill as odd, it hadn't raised any real concerns. The doctors had declared him perfectly healthy and that was all that mattered.

Oliver let out a squeak as both legs began kicking in unison the moment the cool air breached his diaper.

"Seriously Oliver, you're going to kick yourself right off this table," Jennifer took on a more serious, yet still light hearted tone as she removed the thankfully, gift free diaper and lifted the excited infant into her arms.

Being picked up only excited Oliver even more as he was now closer to his new, favorite toy. Getting a handful, he pulled on the long blonde strands of excitement.

"Ow, hey," Jennifer laughed as she freed herself from her son's surprisingly strong grip and much to his displeasure, swung her hair over her other shoulder. "It's not time to pull mommy's hair because what time is it?" she went back into her high pitch baby talk. "It's bath time! Yay!"

Oliver just stared at his mother, perplexed by the sudden changes in her voice as they entered the kitchen and approached the sink.

Testing the water, which had been hot when they'd left the room but had since cooled to the perfect temperature, Jennifer shifted Oliver in her arms and began lowering him into the sink. As his butt made contact with the mysterious liquid, Oliver's look of playful excitement switched to that of complete and utter shock. If the look of surprise wasn't enough to indicate his displeasure with this new experience, the tears that followed were. With no interest in the wet chair, Oliver let out a howling cry.

"Oliver, sweetie," the baby talk ceased, replaced by a tone of comfort. "It's just bath time. Everyone takes baths. There's nothing to be afraid of."

Oliver didn't care as his cries continued.

Worried that the water may have been too hot after all, Jennifer lowered her hand into the shallow tub. The temperature seemed right; just slightly warmer than room temperature. To be sure though, she reached for the cold faucet, giving it a slight twist and allowing a few seconds of cold water to mix with the warm.

Oliver paused at the sound of the running water, but losing interest quickly, he turned his attention back to the fact that he was naked, wet and scared and continued his rant.

"It's okay," Jennifer continued as she proceeded to wash her son, convinced that the water was fine and that Oliver's negative reaction was nothing more than confused fear over the unfamiliar situation. "Next time will be better," she told herself as she poured water over his chest, rinsing away the soap that she'd just applied. "There's nothing to be afraid of," she continued to comfort her son, though probably more in an effort to make herself feel better since she would've felt horrible just standing there in silence while her son cried for her help. "Shh, nothing bad is going to happen."

Instantly, she wished that she'd chosen a different set of comforting words as a loud crash and sounds of shattered glass boomed from the front guest room, followed by the ear piercing siren of the new alarm system and a monotone female voice repeating the phrase, "Intruder alert. Guest room. Intruder alert. Guest room".

Jennifer screamed, hoisting Oliver out of the water and into her protective arms. Either satisfied that he was no longer lying in that horribly, wet place, or simply startled silent by his mother's scream, Oliver ceased all noise as he and his mother hurried out of the kitchen, down the hall and into the master bedroom at the back of the house, but not before grabbing the phone from the receiver hanging just inside the arched kitchen entry.

Closing the door behind them, Jennifer stood at the foot of her bed, not sure where to go from there. Catching a glimpse of the partially open, closet door to her right, she and Oliver slipped inside, crouching beneath the neatly hung clothes in hopes of concealing themselves within the dark shadows. Holding the phone receiver in front of her face, she pushed a random button as the keypad sprang to life. Quickly she dialed 911 but as she held the phone to her ear, there was nothing on the other end. No dispatcher, no dial tone...nothing. Hitting the end button, she dialed again and again got the same lack of response.

"Shit!" she exclaimed as Oliver just stared up at his terrified mother, confused by what was happening, but obviously not as scared as he had been only moments ago in the sink, since he didn't make a sound. "Okay, the phone is out which is why the alarm company hasn't called to confirm the alarm like the man said they would," Jennifer attempted to calm her nerves by talking herself through the situation. "If they can't get a hold of me they'll probably call Bill who will, of course, tell them to send the police. And if they can't get a hold of him, they'll send the police anyway."

Jennifer pulled Oliver close to her chest. What was she going to do? Was she really going to just hide in this closet while that son of a bitch from the other night came back to finish the job. A flash of the previous night's horror overtook her thoughts as she looked down at the innocent life held firmly in her arms. It was her job to protect Oliver, no matter what that meant. Bill had fought off the attacker the other night. There was no reason to think that she couldn't do the same, or at least slow him down and possibly divert his attention away from her son just long enough for the police to arrive and take out the bastard.

Spotting the shallow, half empty laundry basket on the other side of the closet, Jennifer slowly crept toward it and lowered Oliver inside, covering him with a couple of shirts, careful not to cover his face or tangle anything around his neck.

"You stay right here and be quiet," she instructed her

son as if he understood and might issue an, "I understand mother," in return. "I love you." Leaning over, she kissed Oliver on the forehead and stood to face the closed, closet door. To her right was Bill's golf bag from which she withdrew an iron and slowly exited the closet.

Standing just inside the closed, bedroom door, Jennifer scanned the bedroom windows, overjoyed to see that she'd forgotten to open the blinds that morning, which prevented anyone from looking in and possibly spotting Oliver's hiding spot. Reaching for the doorknob, she listened but heard nothing but the sounds of the alarm and the repetitive female voice. Cautiously, she stepped to the side of the door and raising the club, ready to strike anyone who might be hiding on the other side, she slowly pulled open the door to the empty hallway.

The pounding in her chest felt like a drummer who'd lost his rhythm as overwhelming fear caused her heart to skip a beat or two. Poking her head out of the bedroom, she scanned the hall. It was empty. Cautiously she crept out, quietly closing the bedroom door behind her and keeping as close to the wall as possible as she made her way past the linen closet and past Oliver's bedroom, pausing as she approached the large opening that lead to the living room. The guest bedroom stood just off the living room to the left.

"Do you think they're inside?" a faint, unfamiliar voice competed with the alarm from within the guest room.

"I don't see anybody in there," a second voice responded.

"This is crazy," Jennifer whispered as she took a moment to think about how ridiculous she probably looked, pressed against the wall clutching the club, but Oliver's life depended on her. Placing her hand on the brass handle, she pressed down but stopped as a police siren cried out from down the street.

"Thank God," she sighed as she released the handle and retreated back to the bedroom for Oliver. As she opened the closet door, light from the bedroom poured in, illuminating the small hamper and the tiny life within it. Oliver was just laying on his back as she'd left him, the word *Angel* printed across his chest in big, pink letters as she noticed the pair of Victoria's Secret shorts that she'd used to keep her son warm as well as hidden. Lifting Oliver out of the basket, keeping him wrapped in the fitting garment, she returned to the hall just in time for the doorbell to ring. Still cautious about who it might be, but confident that the intruder was likely long gone, given the police presence outside, Jennifer made her way to the front door, peeking out of the narrow, curtained window beside the door and spotting her savior dressed in blue.

Unlocking the door, Jennifer yanked it open, greeting the officer with a "Thank God you're here!"

"Ma'am, are you alright?"

"Yeah, I'm fine but somebody tried to break into the house! I think they broke the window in the guest room! It's over there!" she began rambling.

"Ma'am," the officer attempted to interject.

"I was so scared! Last night someone attacked my son!"

"Ma'am."

"My husband fought him off but I think he came back!"

"Ma'am!" the officer finally stopped the hysterical woman with a raised voice.

Jennifer just stared, shocked and a bit perturbed by the officer's rudeness as she waited for him to speak.

The officer just glanced in the direction of the keypad, mounted on the wall beside her.

"Oh," Jennifer finally realized that she'd been competing with the alarm and the electronic voice, still announcing the location of the breech. Fumbling with the new keypad, she finally managed to enter the correct four digit code and with the press of the disarm button, the siren and the female voice fell silent. "As I was saying—," she instantly went back into her rant before being cut off once again by the rude man before her.

"—You don't have an intruder, ma'am," the officer explained.

"Bullshit!" she wanted to respond but kept her mouth shut.

"It was just a tree," the officer continued.

"What?"

"A tree, ma'am. Those men were taking down a tree next door and lost control of it. It looks like it crushed your fence and some of the branches went through your window. There was no intruder."

"I'm so sorry!" a man shouted from the sidewalk.

Jennifer looked around the officer to see two men standing beside the police cruiser. One man was shaking his head, seemingly unable to make eye contact with her while the apologetic man strangled his hat in his hands.

"But what about the phone? It's dead," Jennifer asked confused.

"Are the connections on that side of the house," the officer asked.

"They are," she thought as she shook her head in the affirmative.

"The tree probably took out the box or severed a wire. Just give the phone company a call and they'll come out and fix it. You never answered if everyone was alright."

"Yeah, yeah. We're fine."

"Is anyone else in the house?"

"No. My husband's at work. No one was in that room so everyone's okay; just a little shaken up," Jennifer nervously laughed at the situation.

"Understandable," the officer responded, he too showing signs of relaxation, now that he was sure that no one was injured and that this was simply an accident easily fixed with the exchange of information and a few phone calls to the insurance companies. "I'm going to need you to come outside for a minute so I can get your information and take a brief statement.

"Can I put some clothes on my son first?" Jennifer glanced down at Oliver wrapped in her shorts.

"Of course ma'am. Come out when you're ready."

"Thank you officer."

Leaving the door open she retreated back toward Oliver's room as the officer made his way to the two men waiting beside his car.

"This is not your typical bath time," Jennifer looked down at Oliver who stared back, offering his mother what appeared to be a slight grin.

FIFTEEN

"Katie. Hey girl," Latisha waved as she shoved her way through the crowded hall to her best friend's locker. "Where were you this morning? I didn't see you on the bus."

"Yeah, my dad thinks he should drive me from this point on," Katie answered, looking down at the lately, unable to be concealed lump beneath her blouse.

"You know he's just trying to look out for you, right? He loves you."

"I know. He really has been great, with this whole baby thing and all," Katie smiled as she placed her hand on her stomach. She'd been terrified from the moment she'd seen the blue plus symbol. Ever since her mother had died, she'd felt lost, not sure how she would be able to move on with her life. Her mother had been everything to her. Though a small town, her father had always taken great pride in his work, which meant long hours and many nights and weekends away from the family. But she hadn't faulted him for that. They had a great life. They lived in a great little town and in a big, comfortable house with everything they could ever want, and she understood that it was all because of her father's hard work and dedication.

In his absence though, her mother had, at times and in essence at least, acted as a single parent which had only made the bond between her and her mother that much stronger.

She'd been devastated the night that her parents had sat her down to tell her about the cancer. She hadn't really understood what the whole thing had meant at the time, except that it was bad and that her mother would likely not live to see her reach adulthood. She wouldn't be there for her graduation. She wouldn't get to witness her vows in St. John's cathedral at the center of town and she wouldn't get to be there for the birth of her first grandchild.

She'd cried herself to sleep that night, as well as all those in the three weeks that followed. During all those tears though, she'd also been thinking. There had to be something she could do to help her mother get better. There had to be something she could do that the doctors couldn't. She'd been seven at the time and the thought that she could perform some miraculous cure that the medical world hadn't yet imagined had been childish. Her mother had survived years past the doctor's best expectations, a feat that her mother had attributed to, "the best medicine money can't buy," she'd often said, "love." Right up to the moment that life had escaped her body, she'd spoken of their love being responsible for keeping her alive. She'd also instructed them to take care of each another and that, no matter what, she'd always be watching over them.

"I'll be there for your graduation," her mother had struggled to form each word in the five minutes they'd shared together while the rest of the family waited down the hall. "I'm going to be right there beside you at the alter. You're going to be so beautiful in that white gown. I can already see you," she'd closed her eyes to picture the moment as a wave of discomfort caused her to wince ever so slightly. "And your daughter...," she'd continued. "...my granddaughter. She's the most precious thing I've ever seen," she'd spoke as if she could see her tiny face on the back of her closed eyelids.

She'd seemed so convinced that she'd have a little girl. She'd even fought through the pain of a few more words to describe the angelic child from her vision.

"She's going to have long blonde hair, blue eyes and the cutest dimples anyone has ever seen," she'd described with a broad smile.

Even as another wave of pain overtook her frail body, she'd held that smile. Her mother had died ten minutes later with her husband by her side.

Katie had known it was coming; that didn't make it any easier though and with her mother gone she'd sort of gone on a wild streak. She knew what her mother had told her, about the family taking care of each another. She remembered every word but for a while she hadn't known how to go on, so she'd filled the void left by her mother's death, with drunken parties at houses of previously unknown friends and drug induced encounters. No matter how many times she found herself lying there, some unknown boy writhing around on top of her, all she could think of was the image of that little girl that her mother had described to her. Each time she'd just closed her eyes, as her body shook with each thrust of reality, and imagined that little girl's face. She was beautiful; just as her mother had described and she wanted nothing more than to give her mother what she'd found so much joy in imagining in her final moments.

Looking back on it, the decision was probably stupid, though something inside of her wasn't completely convinced. The little girl currently growing inside of her was nothing short of a miracle and, though a potential detriment to her future, she wouldn't trade her situation for anything in the world.

"Katie. Kaa-tieee. Hey, Earth to Katie!" Latisha shouted, startling her friend out of her trance.

"Sorry," Katie smiled as she grabbed her math book

and closed her locker.

"Your mother again?"

"Yeah, but I'm alright."

"I'm sure you are, but if you need to talk..."

"I know. Really, we're alright," she held her stomach again.

Latisha smiled at her natal embrace.

"Katie," another voice suddenly cried from the flowing sea of students.

"Oh, here comes Mark again," Latisha spoke with a devilish grin. "The poor boy just won't give up. Maybe you should give him a chance this time."

Ignoring the advancing boy, Katie looked to her friend for assistance in diverting the impending situation.

"Would you look at the time," Latisha announced loudly as Mark broke through the crowd, arriving by her side. "I'm going to be late for class. You can tell me all about it in science. Hey Mark," she greeted the new arrival before disappearing into the crowd.

"Latisha, wait," Katie unsuccessfully called for her friend's return. "Bitch."

"Hey, Katie," Mark nervously greeted her.

"Hey Mark," Katie hesitantly responded. It wasn't that she didn't like Mark. He was a great guy. He was one of the brightest kids in the school and despite his high GPA and horrendously bad taste in clothing, he actually wasn't all that bad on the eyes either.

"So, I know I asked you this before...," he began.

Katie knew where this was going. He'd already asked her to the junior prom twice last week, both times to which her response had been "no". It wasn't that she didn't like him. They shared many of the same classes together and in the last year they'd actually grown to be fairly good friends. She just didn't feel right about going with him to such an important event. He deserved better than to waste such an important coming of age experience with some messed up, pregnant chick. He was going to go on to do amazing things with his life and he didn't need to run the risk of falling for someone who would only hold him back.

"...but I've been thinking," Mark continued. "I know you said no and I respect that, but I don't really think you have a say in the matter."

"Excuse me," Katie, caught off guard, responded.

"That's right. You don't have a choice in the matter because I know for a fact that your daughter would love to go to prom with me."

"Okay, this is getting a bit creepy," she thought but chose to play along to see where he was going with this new approach. "Is that right?"

"Yes. It is."

"And you know this how?"

"She told me," Mark spoke confidently, as if he really believed what he was saying.

"She told you huh. How exactly do you know that it's a she?" Katie asked, sure that she hadn't told anyone about the sex of her unborn child yet.

"You told me a few weeks ago in psychology, remember? Well, you didn't actually tell me, but one of the times we were talking you'd mentioned a pink dress that you'd seen at the store and how you wondered if they made the same dress for children. I could only assume you were talking about..." he motioned toward her stomach.

She did remember the conversation. For months she'd managed to conceal the fact of her pregnancy from the rest of her peers but since word had spread about her condition in the last month or so, most of the school just looked at her as that poor pregnant girl...but not Mark. He didn't seem to be fazed by her condition. He was her friend before the pregnancy and after finding out about the life growing within her, other than Latisha, he was the only one who'd continued to treat her the same as always.

"So, like I said, you don't have a choice in the matter,"

Mark reaffirmed.

"And what exactly did you and…," glancing down at her stomach, "…talk about?"

"Oh, you know, the usual, the weather, music…the growing of appendages."

Katie stood silent at the odd remark.

"Nevertheless, the most important thing is that she would like nothing more than for all of us to go to the prom together and I couldn't agree more."

Overhearing the odd conversation, the girl two lockers down turned to offer a perplexed look before closing her locker and making her way to class.

"I've got something," he suddenly announced as he removed his backpack from his shoulder and dropped to a knee to open it.

Given the oddity of the situation, Katie wouldn't have been surprised to see him withdraw a ring from the overstuffed bag and profess his love to her right there in the hall, but instead he withdrew a neatly wrapped box with a large pink ribbon, which had been crumpled and deformed by the hardbound contents of the bag.

With the box in hand, Mark returned to his feet, holding it before him for Katie to take. "I got this for you."

Not sure what to expect, she nervously took the box from his hand.

"Go ahead. Open it."

Reluctantly, she pulled at the ribbon, watching it unravel and release its grip on the flat, rectangular box.

Mark stared at the box with a smile.

Lifting the lid, she couldn't even begin to guess what might be inside. Beneath the lid was a layer of snow white tissue paper, neatly folded over the box's true contents. As she lifted the corner of the tissue paper, a silky pink fabric slowly appeared. Intrigued, she lifted the tissue paper further, revealing a lacy trim along the edge of the pink material.

Mark's smile grew as his present was slowly revealed.

Lifting the paper aside, Katie just stared in amazement at the tiny pink dress within the box. It was exactly as she'd described, however it was only a fraction of the size...just big enough for a newborn baby.

"I hope it's the right one," Mark broke the silence, pulling Katie's gaze away from the gift. "I remembered you mentioning lace but I couldn't remember if it was pink or white."

"It's perfect," Katie spoke as she returned her attention to the gift before her. It was almost exactly as she'd described it. At the time she remembered wondering to herself why she'd been telling him about the dress. He was a guy and probably didn't care about some stupid dress but, staring at the tiny article of clothing, it was clear that he'd memorized every detail, right down to the tiny bows on the end of each shoulder length sleeve.

"I know she can't wear it yet, but I was wondering if her mother would mind wearing it to the prom."

Looking up, Katie saw Mark holding another, similarly wrapped but larger box. Since her mother's death and her unplanned pregnancy, her future had been questionable and she'd done everything in her power to push away those who she feared might sink right down beside her. "Maybe it was time to stop pushing," she thought. Maybe this was all part of her mother's grand scheme from up there in heaven. Staring into Mark's hopeful eyes, the only answer she could give was, "yes".

SIXTEEN

"Herpes? Really?" Derek finally broke the long silence that had loomed over them since their unforgettable ride into town.

An elderly man sitting in the booth behind Jason lifted his head from his bowl of soup to look around his wife and shoot Derek a disgusted look.

Ignoring the old man's disapproving stare, "I mean, you could've said that I forgot my inhaler or something not so...cock blocking."

This time the old woman turned, joining her husband in the silent scolding.

"And what girlfriend? I mean, what were you trying to do?"

"I couldn't allow you to sleep with any of those girls and the way that it was heading, I almost expected the car to suddenly pull to the side of the road so you could toss me out while you took turns banging each one of them in the back seat."

"That's ridiculous...there's no need to take turns."

Apparently no longer hungry, the old man signaled his server for the check.

"Besides, just in case you weren't aware, I was selling

you like crazy to the cute southern chick who definitely seemed interested," Derek continued to defend his behavior.

"Was she?" Jason thought. His lack of skill when it came to the opposite sex wasn't a shock, but was it really so bad that he couldn't even tell when a girl was genuinely interested in him? "That's not the point," he snapped out of his introspective detour. "The point is you, me, neither of us can risk disrupting the past just so we can get our rocks off."

"Get our rocks off?" Derek chuckled at the expression.

"Yes. Us being here already poses a potential threat to the future. Everything we do, every interaction we have with the people of this time could potentially have time altering affects. Something as simple as a passing conversation on the street could lead to a mosquito killing a future Nobel prize winner or worse."

"You lost me," Derek stared at Jason confused.

"The person you talk to might be distracted from killing the mosquito that otherwise would have been dead and unable to bite someone who…never mind," Jason gave up, realizing that his explanation made perfect sense in his head but wasn't coming out in a logical, coherent manner.

"So what you're saying is that we should make sure to wear insect repellant while we're here?"

"No," Jason sighed. "What I'm trying to say is—"

"—I know. I'm just screwing with you. I understand. I don't know how I figured it out since that was the worst example I've ever heard, but nonetheless. And this is the U.S.. Who gets killed by mosquitoes?"

Annoyed, Jason picked up his menu.

"Nothing was going to happen you know," Derek pulled Jason's attention away from the laminated list. "I'm not an idiot. I may act like it at times but remember who built that thing," he motioned to the case on the seat beside Jason. "I'm well aware of the risks inherent to us being here. I wouldn't have taken the conversation in the car any further than just that, a conversation."

"Well, good. I'm glad to hear that you were at least thinking with the right head this time," Jason spoke as he returned to the menu once again.

"It doesn't hurt to have some fun and flirt every now and then though," Derek continued. "Just because you can't do something doesn't mean you can't test the waters to see if it might have been possible."

"And what would be the point in that?" Jason glanced up from his menu again.

"I don't know...fun. Jason, not everything in life has to have some predetermined outcome. Sometimes the most memorable things in life are those that happen spontaneously; you know, when you're just kicking back and having fun. A conversation with a girl doesn't have to lead to a relationship and marriage and children and houses with white picket fences. Sometimes it can just be an enjoyable conversation with a person you find to be both interesting and attractive, regardless of whether or not you're looking to batter dip the corn dog."

Jason watched as a couple with two young children, in the booth behind Derek, lifted their gaze skyward at the off color remark.

"Mommy, I want a corn dog," the youngest of the two boys suddenly announced from the other booth, causing both parents to look Jason's way.

Awkwardly, Jason mouthed, "sorry," as the parents returned their attention to performing damage control.

"All I'm trying to say is that you need to let go," Derek continued his lecture. "Stop being so uptight with your constant need to control each and every aspect of life. I think you'll find all social interactions much more fulfilling, not just the ones with the taco vendors."

"Jesus!," the mother in the other booth responded. Again Jason mouthed an apology, though no one looked his way to receive it. The mother, though offended, kept her back to Derek and instead appeared to be complaining to her husband for him to do something about the situation. Based on the timid, beaten down expression on his face, Jason assumed they were safe.

"I need to be more spontaneous?" Jason returned his attention Derek's way.

"God yes."

"I need to just let go and do something wild."

"Well I don't think I said wild but, yes, I guess."

"Okay. I can do that."

"Good, now let's eat," Derek sighed, glad to shift his attention away from Jason's shortcomings and onto the menu before him.

"Excuse me!" Jason suddenly called out. "Excuse me, miss!"

Derek looked up to see Jason waving at someone behind him. Moments later an attractive young girl wearing black dress pants, an eye matching, hazel colored top and holding a long white cloth of sorts, stopped at their table. She just stared at Jason confused as he appeared suddenly nervous to place his order.

"Can I help you?" the girl finally spoke with a bit of an attitude.

Closing his eyes, Jason whispered, "spontaneous," before reopening them and asking. "So, who's a guy gotta fuck to get some God damned service around here!?"

The café fell silent, other than the sound of utensils dropping to their plates. Derek too, sat stunned at what he'd just heard.

"Excuse me?!" the girl replied.

As if shocked himself by what he'd just heard come out of his own mouth, Jason began melting into the brown, vinyl bench. Derek, along with the rest of the restaurant's patrons, turned their attention to the girl.

"One, I don't work here," the girl addressed Jason with a more appropriate, hushed tone, her voice dripping with venom. "Two, if I did, I wouldn't...how did you so eloquently put it...oh yes...fuck your scrawny ass if my life depended on it."

Derek just stared at the girl as she leaned closer to Jason with each biting word, forcing Jason even further into his seat.

"Get some fucking manors, prick," she ended the verbal assault as she took a step back and made a b-line for the exit.

Jason remained two inches tall in his seat as the smile on Derek's face grew.

"That was awesome," Derek announced. "I think I'm in love." Excited by the encounter, he leapt from his seat, to follow the rapidly departing girl.

Jason remained motionless in his seat as the rest of the customers began clapping.

"Will there be anything else? sir," their *real* waitress approached the table, addressing Jason in a condescending tone that suggested he leave as well.

Fumbling for his wallet, Jason pulled out a five to pay for the sodas and quickly scampered for the door.

*****

"Hey, wait! Ma'am!" Derek shouted as he crashed through the café doors and spotted the annoyed girl hurrying down the sidewalk.

"Ma'am?" the girl stopped in her tracks. "First you insult me, and now you're calling me old!," she turned, surprised to see Derek without his obnoxious friend.

"Whoa, whoa," Derek slowed his approach, afraid that the hot headed girl might actually take a swing at him or pull a can of pepper spray from her purse.

"I'm sorry. I thought you were..." She finished her sentence with a hand gesture back toward the restaurant.

"I know. I'm not," Derek spoke as he finally caught up to the now motionless girl. "I'm his friend."

"Yeah, I saw you at the table. You should get better

friends."

"He's a work in progress," he joked, but got no response other than a stare that suggested that her next statement might be on the lines of, "so, what do you want?". "I mean, he's actually a really nice guy...probably too nice at times, which is why he said that."

"He's too nice, so he verbally assaulted a complete stranger...makes sense to me. Listen, I've gotta go," the girl announced as she started to turn and leave.

"No, what I mean is..."

Delaying her departure, she waited for an explanation.

"I guess...I sort of told him to say it."

"Then I guess you're just as big a pig as your friend is. Good bye." She turn and continued down the sidewalk.

Following, "I didn't exactly tell him to say anything, especially to you. I was simply suggesting that he might have better luck with women if he were more...spontaneous and not so uptight all the time."

The girl stopped. "I don't think he understood."

"No, clearly not," Derek shook his head in agreement.

She continued walking.

Derek continued to follow. "He really is a nice guy though. Like I said, he's just not good with women...or should I say, he's terrible with women."

The girl stopped again. "Why do I feel this conversation's leading to you asking me something?"

Caught off guard by the girl's perceptive and upfront approach, "I...I mean...listen, I can tell that you're in a hurry."

"You think?"

"Feisty, this one is," Derek thought. "May I ask why?"

"Because my water broke and I'm on my way to the hospital."

Sarcastic as well, but just to make sure he hadn't overlooked something he quickly glanced at the girl's stomach...baby free.

"Why would I tell you where I'm going? So you can

follow me and kill me?"

"Well, I've already been following you," Derek spoke with a grin. The look he received apparently didn't see the humor in the comment as the girl once again began walking. "Wait! I'm sorry. It was a bad joke."

The girl stopped again.

"Trust me, I'm not a serial killer."

"Sounds like something a serial killer would say."

Derek wanted to smile at the girl's wit but, figuring that he'd pushed his luck enough already, he maintained a straight face. "Just humor me. What's the big hurry?"

Reluctantly, "Well, if you must know, I have class in...," she checked her watch, "...twenty-five minutes, and I have to run to the store on campus now to pick up a new coat, since I can't go home to get my other one without fearing that you'll show up at my door in the middle of the night." She held up the white coat that she'd been holding in the restaurant. A large pink stain covered a large portion of the crumpled article of clothing.

"Are you pre-med?" Derek guessed.

"Pharmacology major actually. I have a lab and Mr. Malone requires that each and every student be dressed the part," she sarcastically ranted before realizing what she was doing. "Sorry, but I really do have to go. Either way, home or store, will take me at least twenty minutes, leaving me only five to make the fifteen minute walk to class. So, either way I'm screwed."

"What if I could ensure that you got your coat and got to class on time?"

"What, are you going to teleport me or something?" she joked.

"No, of course not," Derek laughed at how close she actually was.

"Then how are you going to do that?"

"I can have a new coat to this very spot in less than five minutes," Derek confidently proclaimed.

"Oh really," she laughed.

"Don't laugh. I'm dead serious. If I'm not placing the coat in your hand within five minutes from the time I leave I'll—"

"—You'll streak through Lilly's dinner," the girl interjected.

"Lilly's Dinner?" Derek paused as he turned to look back at the restaurant from which they'd just come. Until that moment, he hadn't noticed that the Irish pub he'd come to know as 'The Belligerent Leprechaun' had previously been a colorful, peace and love establishment in the nineties. "Okay."

"Really?" the girl questioned Derek's quick acceptance of her terms. "No backing out. A deal's a deal."

"A deal's a deal," Derek agreed. "I mean, we haven't even gone out on a date and you're already trying to get my clothes off, but really, how could you resist," he joked as he looked himself up and down.

"I knew that this was all just a creative way of asking me out. And, you really shouldn't be too full of yourself," she flirted.

"Ouch, but no. It's not about me. It's my friend."

"You want me to go out with the asshole?" her newly flirtatious demeanor returned to that of contempt.

"Remember, not an asshole. Nerdy, awkward, uptight, boring—"

"—I thought you were his friend."

"Listen, like I said, he really isn't a bad guy and it would really mean a lot if you just went out on one, *full* date with him."

"Full?"

"I mean don't ditch him by climbing out a bathroom window or by having one of your friends make up some lame excuse so you can cut the date short."

"Has that happened?"

"More than once," Derek confirmed with a nod. "He just needs a good experience with a beautiful woman to get him on the right track."

Smiling at the compliment, "I'm not sleeping with him though."

"Oh God no. I wouldn't want you to. That might kill him," Derek joked. "Just one PG date."

"Alright. That seems fair enough, especially since I don't think you can pull it off with only three and a half minutes left," she looked at her watch again.

"Three and a half minutes? I said five from the time I left."

"I'm just joking."

"No, no. I can do it," he assured as he turned to head back toward the restaurant. "Just wait right there!"

She motioned to the spot where she stood.

"Right there!" he reconfirmed before stopping at the realization that, "I don't know your name!"

"What!"

"Your name!"

"Sarah!"

"Nice to meet you, Sarah! I'm Derek! Right there!"

She smiled as he turned and disappeared into the crowd of people on the sidewalk.

*****

"Where were you!?" Jason shouted as he spotted Derek walking quickly towards him.

"Come on. We need to get out of site," Derek insisted as he grabbed hold of Jason's arm.

"Out of site? Of who? What did you do?"

"I didn't do anything. She thinks I'm hurrying off to get her another coat," Derek quickly explained as he dragged Jason along.

"Get who a coat? It's eighty degrees out here. Who needs a coat?"

"Not that kind of coat. A lab coat. You know, like the ones doctors...or pharmacists wear."

Pulling back on Derek's persistent guidance, Jason

stopped them in their tracks. "From the beginning. Who are we talking about?"

"Sarah," Derek answered before realizing that Jason had no idea who he was referring to. "The girl from the restaurant."

"The girl I insulted?" Jason asked shocked.

"Yes. Her name is Sarah and she's very nice."

"I don't doubt that, seeing that I was the asshole back there, but what were you doing talking to her? I came out of the café and when I didn't see you, I picked a direction that I thought you might have gone. Apparently I picked wrong. What were you talking to her about?"

"You, actually," Derek answered with a grin as he glanced back in Sarah's direction. From what he could see through the moving sea of bodies, she was still waiting and still watching to see where he was going. "We need to keep moving," he insisted as he grabbed hold of Jason's arm again.

Jason didn't fight.

"We need to get out of view. I told her that I would get her a new coat for her lab class."

"That's nice. Why?" Jason asked nervously as Derek pulled him around the corner of the building, stopping just out of Sarah's line of sight. "You can't sleep with her, Derek."

"Yes, yes. I understand," Derek assured him. "I'm doing this for you."

"You don't need to apologize on my behalf."

"I'm not doing it as an apology. I'm doing it to get you a date," Derek explained.

"With her? I don't want to go out with her."

"Why?"

"Well, for starters, my first and only words to her were to imply that I wanted to sleep with her for a cheeseburger and some fries.

"Oh, it's fine. She's over that," Derek dismissed Jason's concerns.

"Oh, okay. Well that's good to hear," Jason sarcastically breathed a sigh of relief. "Are you nuts? How could she be over it? You're good, but your not that good."

Derek just stood there with a confident grin.

"Are you?"

"Listen Jason, I talked you up to her and told her that you weren't a complete ass."

"Oh, well, I guess it's better that I'm just a bit of an ass."

"Actually, it is," Derek replied. "But anyway, I made a bet with her that I could get her a brand new lab coat and deliver it in less than five minutes. And if I did, she agreed to go on a date with you."

"I can't go on a date with her. What if we somehow screw up the future?"

"It's just one date," Derek assured his nervous friend.

"What if she falls for me. I can't have a relationship with someone from the past and we definitely can't tell her about the machine."

"Jason, it's one date, not marriage," Derek placed his hands on Jason's shoulders to calm him.

"Okay, then how do you plan on accomplishing this task? You must be just about out of time by now."

"That's the beauty of it. I have all the time in the world," he patted the case held firmly at Jason's side.

"That is pretty brilliant," Jason agreed.

"All I have to do is get a coat and, some time in the future, come back to this very moment to make the delivery and you've got yourself a date."

"I don't really want a bet to be the only way that I can get a date," Jason responded, defeated.

"Hey, take what you can get man; besides, she's hot, right?"

"She was pretty," Jason agreed. "So what does she get?"

"Huh?"

"The bet. What does she get if you fail?" Jason asked.

"Oh, nothing big. I told her that I'd run naked through The Belligerent...Lilly's Café."

"Lilly's Café?" Jason questioned as he turned to look back at the restaurant, forgetting that they'd ducked into an alley around the corner.

"I know. I don't know how I didn't notice either," Derek acknowledged his friend's shared confusion.

"Didn't you already do that though?" Jason questioned as he turned back to Derek.

"Once...maybe twice before."

"And didn't the owner call the cops?"

"No, the cops came when that girl smashed a beer bottle over her boyfriend's head for trying to trade her for weed."

Jason nodded as he recalled the memorable night.

"The owner insisted on helping me get dressed in the back room, if you know what I mean," Derek's grin grew.

"Yeah, yeah. I remember. That's why I can't order anything with potatoes anymore," Jason scowled at the memory.

"The Irish really *love* their potatoes."

"Okay, so you can't lose the bet but I still don't think I want to go on that date," Jason protested.

"Listen," Derek's grin faded as he once again took hold of Jason's shoulders. "You need this. Trust me."

"Well...—"

"—Good," Derek took Jason's hesitation as a yes. "Now we need to find a replacement coat." Grabbing Jason's arm again, he pulled him through the alley toward the opposite street.

SEVENTEEN

"Grandma, I'm home!" Ty announced as he closed the front door and turned to find the tiny living room littered with boxes; the apartment's contents haphazardly filled to the brim and in some cases, spilling out onto the coffee table and floor. "Grandma?"

"Back here, Ty."

Rounding the corner, more boxes came into view, partially blocking the hall to the bedrooms. Stepping over the low cardboard wall and pushing the open closet door as far as its scattered contents would allow, Ty made his way toward his Grandmother's bedroom.

"Grandma, what are you doing?" he questioned as he entered the bedroom to the sight of his grandmother shoving clothes into a large, black garbage bag.

"We're going home," she responded as she dumped an arm full of clothes into the bag before heading back to the dresser for another load.

"But what about my son?"

"You're going grab him tonight," she nonchalantly proclaimed, shoving another arm full of clothes into the bag.

"Tonight? I don't think we're ready yet. I mean, after

the other night—"

"—Exactly," Ushi stopped her frantic packing. "There someone else out there with unknown interest in our boy; someone who obviously wish harm. I been thinking about this all day, Ty. We can't rely on Nesbit's to look out for him. We have to act now before that monster comes back." And with that forceful declaration, she continued packing.

"I told you. He's gone."

"He be back. May not be today or tomorrow, but give it enough time and he return. We need to act now before he get chance."

"Yes, but the police—"

"—I don't care about police," she interrupted.

"Great, but they need to be considered. They'll probably be making frequent passes through the Nesbit's neighborhood, not to mention a likely quicker response to 911."

"You will get in quick and you will get out quick," she paused again, this time placing her hands on her grandson's shoulders as she looked up at him. "It was blessing from Lord that you were called to install alarm system. It was sign that this meant to be. No calls to police because you can get in and out before anybody even know you there."

"She was right," he thought. When he'd installed the alarm system he'd programmed a backdoor pass code that would silently disarm the entire system while still giving the Nesbits the impression that their new, top of the line system was still up and fully functional.

"You can do this, Ty," Grandma Ushi reaffirmed as she squeezed his shoulders. "By end of night our family will be complete. Now pack. We must hurry." And with that, she went back to hurriedly shuffling about the room.

He still didn't understand the sudden urgency but he also didn't understand why anyone would be after his son, which admittedly made him uneasy. So, trusting his grandmother's always flawless judgment, he did as he was told and added to the black, plastic suitcase.

*****

"I don't know what you're expecting to see on there," Jennifer sighed as she stood holding Oliver while Bill rewound the security footage. "I mean the tree came through the guest bedroom window and there's no camera in there."

Oliver stared at his mother as she spoke, then turned to his father as if he too was waiting for a response.

"I know. I just wanna make sure this thing works," Bill pleaded for patience as the four squiggly images dance across each quadrant of the television.

"Oh, it works. Trust me. If you'd been here you would have known," her tone changed from impatience to frustration.

Picking up on the change in his wife's inflection, Bill turned his attention from the screen to face his wife and son. Oliver was nestled in his mother's arms with an almost equally annoyed expression as if to second his mother's frustration. "I'm sorry that I wasn't here," Bill got to his feet, loosely wrapping his arms around his wife and son. "I know you told me to go to work and that you didn't want us living our lives in fear but I shouldn't have listened. I should have stayed home to look out for the both of you."

"No," Jennifer sighed as she leaned into her husband's shoulder. "I told you to go. I shouldn't be mad."

Oliver, smooshed between them, didn't know what to think or who to concentrate on as his eyes darted from side to side.

"I still should have been here."

"I guess it wasn't that bad," Jennifer commented in a much lighter tone. "The police did respond quickly and the two workers were very apologetic about the situation and had the window covered up in less than fifteen minutes."

"And they said that they'd have someone out here tomorrow to fix the window?" Bill confirmed.

"First thing in the morning, they said."

"See, then everything's fine," he loosened his hug to look her in the eyes. "But I guess more importantly, are you alright?"

"Aside from psychopaths and trees breaking into our house, yeah, I guess I'm just peachy."

Smiling, Bill returned to his seat, still facing his wife and Oliver who could once again easily watch his father from a comfortable distance. "So what did you do?"

"What?"

"When the alarm went off," he clarified. "You said you were giving Oliver a bath at the time but what did you do when the alarm went off?"

"I really don't remember," she lied, embarrassed to say that her natural reaction was to hide in a closet. The only thing worse would have been if she and Oliver had shimmied under the bed. "We went into the bedroom but the police showed up so quickly, we couldn't have been there long."

Oliver looked up at his mother as if to say, "just tell him that you hid me in the dirty clothes."

Suddenly a loud siren filled the room, though not as loud as it had been earlier that day. Bill turned to see the cluster of videos now playing on the screen. The audio of the triggered alarm echoed from the speakers before being quieted to an almost inaudible muffle as he turned down the volume.

Startled by the sudden and frighteningly familiar sound, Oliver let out a soft whimper.

"It's alright," Jennifer comforted her son, preventing the whimper from becoming a full blown cry.

"Just went into the bedroom, huh?" Bill smiled as the video showed his wife frantically darting from the kitchen and into the master bedroom where she and Oliver disappeared into the closet.

"I was scared, Bill," she defended her reaction. "You'd have done the same if you'd been home alone." She didn't really believe that. Since she'd known Bill, she couldn't recall ever seeing him scared. Hell, he'd dove right in to protect Oliver the night before, without thinking twice. If he had been home he would've probably just gone and investigated the noise, seen the tree and turned off the alarm.

"I wouldn't have hidden in the closet," Bill laughed at his suggested cowardliness. "I would have hid under the bed."

Jennifer chuckled at the joke as she kept an eye on the continuing footage. "Okay, I think it works. I don't think Oliver needs to relive the entire thing, she glanced down at her son who was staring, fascinated by the array of images.

"Okay," Bill agreed as he returned his attention to the television, prepared to turn it off but not before the closet door on camera four reopened to display his wife firmly grasping one of his golf clubs. "Is that my nine iron?" he asked with a grin.

"Actually, I think it was the six."

"Wait a minute," he hit rewind, taking the footage back a few seconds to the moment his wife reemerged from the impromptu safe room.

"I was scared so I grabbed the club," Jennifer continued to defend her actions. "Someone had to protect our son."

"Is that Oliver?" Bill leaned in toward the screen.

"I left him in the closet for safety," Jennifer explained.

"It looks like you treated him like a pair of dirty underwear," Bill chuckled as he caught a glimpse of his son partially buried in the clothes hamper.

Oliver turned to his mother as if expecting an apology.

"They weren't dirty," Jennifer protested her husband's claim. "And they weren't underwear," she then offered

Oliver his own explanation. "There were only some shirts and a pair of shorts in there. I had to keep him hidden," she continued to defend herself.

"I'm only joking with you," Bill laughed as he reached for her hand and pulled the two of them closer. "I'm proud of you. You did everything you could to protect our son." He lightly brushed Oliver's thick, dark hair with his finger tips. "Everyone knows that Victoria's Secret shorts are like an invisible cloak for babies," Bill smiled.

"Ass," Jennifer playfully swatted at her husband as Oliver smiled.

EIGHTEEN

"We're going back tomorrow, right?" Derek asked as he unlocked the door to the lab, flipping on the lights as he and Jason entered with the briefcase and backpack full of wires.

"Well...I think we should really analyze the data from this trip before we go running off on another so soon. We don't know what kind of stress might have been put on the core...or *any* of the components for that matter," Jason voiced his opinion as he returned the case to the securely locked cabinet. "Such a dramatic test so soon was dangerous enough. We might not be so lucky next time."

"Lucky my ass," Derek laughed, their successful return having boosted not only his mood but his ego as well. "We're a couple of fucking geniuses. I'm still not sure how the whole thing works, but it does. The god damned thing works and we're going to be fucking rich as hell!" he exclaimed.

"We're not going to be rich as hell because we're not going to tell anyone about it, remember?" Jason reminded his momentarily delusional friend as he locked the cabinet and made his way over to the computer to review the data on the device's iPad. "Why are you so excited now? You seemed very nonchalant about the whole thing when we successfully arrived back in 1991?"

"That's because I fully expected us to die trying to get home," Derek, in the same nonchalant tone, replied.

Jason turned from the computer shocked. "That's comforting."

"Yes, but we didn't," Derek's excitement returned as he quickly made his way to the counter beside Jason, pulling his attention away from the data being transferred from the iPad. "Do you understand what we've just done?"

"Of course I understand," Jason thought. He was the one who'd come to Derek with the idea in the first place.

"We've just traveled over two decades back and forth through time. Now, yes it's not an extraordinarily large amount of time in the grand scheme of things, but our little five minute jaunt the other night was impressive enough which means this is amazing. I know we can't tell anyone right now, but you have to at least admit that this is the coolest fucking thing you've ever seen, let alone had a part in creating."

"It was awesome," Jason responded, his tone nowhere near the level of Derek's excitement.

"It was awesome," Derek mocked. "Come on. Admit it."

"I agree."

"No, like you mean it."

Just wanting the distraction to end, Jason turned his focus away from the computer, giving Derek his full attention.

"Come on," Derek urged. "Oh, wait!" Running to the opposite counter, on which he'd sat the backpack, he unzipped the front pocket and withdrew the Northeastern medical coat that they'd picked up before returning home. "Just pretend I'm your waitress," he continued to pick on Jason for his outburst earlier that day as he slung the coat over his right forearm. "Now...go!"

Jason just sighed. He knew that this childish behavior

wouldn't end until Derek got what he wanted. "That was the coolest fucking thing I've ever seen or done," he ad-libbed what he thought might satisfy his obnoxious roommate. "We are the smartest fucking human beings to walk this orbiting ball of stupidity and one day we will be considered gods amongst sheep."

Derek just stared at him confused. "Not exactly what I was looking for, and unexpectedly a bit mean, but I guess it'll do."

"Oh shut up," Jason smiled as he returned to the computer.

"At least admit one thing," Derek continued.

"If I do, will you leave me alone?"

"Probably not."

"He may be obnoxious but at least he's honest," Jason thought as the transfer finished and he began processing the new data. "What?"

"The real reason you're hesitant to go back."

"I told you. It might not be safe," Jason replied, his attention split between the new data and the meaningless conversation in which he was being held prisoner.

"No, that's not it," Derek rebutted.

"Oh, okay. You tell me why then."

"Sarah."

"I told you that a relationship with someone from the past is extremely dangerous and not worth the risk involved."

"Then why did we spend almost an hour trying to convince the clerk, at the student store, that we'd lost our student IDs and weren't just pretending to be students in order to buy the coat."

"I didn't do anything," Jason protested as he again focused his attention away from the conversation. "The coat thing was all you."

"Yeah, but I got the coat for you. Poor Sarah is still standing on that corner, expecting us to bring it to her."

"First off, I never agreed to go on the date, and second,

we both know that she eventually went home, or to class or somewhere. Then, later she probably graduated, got married, started a family and right now is working as a pharmacist somewhere."

"Michigan."

"What?"

"She lives in Michigan, has no kids and has a relationship status of single," Derek replied.

Confused, Jason turned to find Derek on his phone. "How the hell did you find her Facebook page that quickly. I swear, you're like some sort of social media ninja." He returned to the computer.

"See, there's no need for you to worry. You wouldn't be preventing her from having the children she apparently wasn't going to have anyway, and the husband, that you'd be depriving of a meaningful relationship, doesn't exist, so there's nothing to worry about," Derek explained.

"How do you know she didn't get divorced?"

"Maybe she did," Derek agreed. "You could be saving her from making the biggest mistake of her life."

"Unbelievable," Jason muttered.

"Huh?"

"I said, you're unbelievable. You always find a way to turn a situation around and make is sound so...positive," Jason sighed.

"Well, that's because I'm a positive guy, which is why I'm confident that it won't hurt for you to just go on one date with her."

Jason just turned and stared at Derek.

"Come on man!" Derek's upbeat tone turned to desperate plea. "She's fucking beautiful. You'd be an idiot to pass this up."

"She *was* stunning," Jason thought, but beautiful or not, it was too dangerous. "You're a smart guy, Derek...maybe not right now...but you have your moments."

"Thanks?" Derek replied confused.

"You know that I can't do it. You know the danger

and we just can't risk something like that."

"Unbelievable, I go through all of that to get you a date with what is probably the hottest woman you've ever met...and still is by the way..." he flashed Sarah's profile picture on his phone, "...and you tell me you can't go on one simple date with her?"

Jason just stared at Derek as he completed his rant, avoiding eye contact as he returned his attention to the picture on the phone.

Looking up Derek saw that Jason was watching him. he glanced back down at his phone and then back up at Jason. "Alright, fine. I get it," he finally gave in to Jason's logic. "You're right. I understand the risk, but...just look at what you're giving up," he flashed the phone again, this time holding it up longer for Jason to see.

"Derek was right," Jason thought. Even in her early forties she was still stunning with her long blonde hair blowing in the wind in what appeared to be a photo shot on a beach somewhere.

"You've gotta promise me one thing though," Derek insisted as he returned the phone to his pocket.

"What's that?"

"You, me and shots of whiskey at The Belligerent Leprechaun tomorrow night."

"I—"

"—No! You have no say in the matter," Derek interjected before Jason could decline. "I'm going to get you laid my friend because whatever backup you have in your piping down there...," he motioned to Jason's crotch, "...is causing you to make some piss poor decisions."

Jason knew better than to argue. Derek had made the declaration, so it was decided. He knew exactly how the night would go though. They'd go to the bar and meet two relatively attractive women. But, instead of getting his chance at one of them, Derek would get drunk and, if he didn't bang them both in the bathroom, he'd bring them back to the dorm, leaving Jason with a choice, run off to the lab for a night of number crunching or lie awake listening to the sounds of the ménage á trois taking place only ten feet from his bed. He did have a lot of data to sift through, so maybe that plan wasn't so bad after all.

"Fine," Jason agreed, looking forward to the likely productive evening.

"Good. It's settled then," Derek declared. "Now, I'm going to bed. They don't tell you in movies but time travel really takes a lot out of you. You coming?"

"No, I'm going to get started on this. I'll be up in a bit."

"Well, don't be too late honey. Time travel apparently makes you horny as well," Derek joked as he used his hand, tongue and cheek to mime a blow-job before laughing and disappearing through the door.

Not surprised by Derek's vulgar humor, especially when floating on cloud-nine, Jason just smiled and returned to the thousands of lines of data on the screen.

NINETEEN

"I'm home!," Phil announced as he walked through the front door to his daughter standing at the foot of the stairs, arms crossed with the look of a parent who just caught their teenage son sneaking back into the house in the middle of the night.

"Where have you been?"

"You knew that I had to go into Boston for that convention today. It took longer than expected. I'm sorry I didn't call," Phil apologized for his tardiness. "What's that smell?" he suddenly noticed the surprisingly pleasant aroma of non-burnt food, lingering in the air.

"I cooked you dinner," Katie grinned.

Instantly he dreaded the culinary crime scene that awaited him in the kitchen. He wasn't sure that the stove could take another one of his daughter's meals. Kissing her on the cheek, he made his way down the hall, Katie following close behind. Rounding the corner, he was glad to see the kitchen still intact and remarkably clean. Then he spotted the bucket of KFC on the dining room table and three empty plates in front of the surrounding chairs. Laughing he turned. "Cooked, huh?"

"You were late, I had to reheat the sides a couple of

times. That counts."

"Thank you sweetheart. That was very thoughtful. I'm sorry I'm late."

"That's okay," she smiled, giving her father a hug.

Looking over his daughter's head with his arms around her, "What's with the third plate?"

"Miss Moore was over for a bit."

Phil broke the embrace. "Katie," he playfully scolded.

"What?" she smiled. "Miss Moore is hot, Dad. Besides, she really likes you."

"I thought we talked about this. You can't keep trying to set me up with every single woman in town."

"Miss Moore lives just outside of Cannon, Dad; in Dalton."

"You know what I mean," Phil smiled.

"You deserve to be happy too Dad."

"I am happy. I have two of the most important people right here," he placed one hand on his daughter's shoulder and the other on her stomach.

"Beyond this I mean," Katie looked past the sweet remark to remain on point. "I mean, you deserve to find love again. You can't keep running away from the chance to be happy again. Mom wouldn't have wanted it that way and you know it."

"I know sweetheart and you're right. I should get back out there. Trust me. I want to love again but you have to understand that it has to happen on my own terms and when I'm ready. Right now my focus is on you and that precious little girl in there. Right now, that's all the love I need. I promise you, when I'm ready, you'll be the first to know and then you can fix me up with whomever you see fit. Deal?"

"Deal," Katie smiled.

"So how was your day?" he changed the subject as he began building a plate of food from the containers on the table.

"Mark asked me to the junior prom today," she replied.

Caught off guard, Phil froze, the chicken leg in his hand hovering only inches from the plate on which he'd intended to place it.

"Mark?" he bought himself some time to recover as he continued filling his plate.

He knew who Mark was. He was the youngest of the three Fossy kids. As far as he could recall he was a decent kid, kept to himself and didn't really cause any problems. The same couldn't be said for his older brother's however.

"You know Mark, Daddy."

"Yeah, I remember Mark. So, did you say yes?" he asked, all the while "please say no, please say no" was looping through his mind.

They'd had enough problems with boys lately, namely Jordan McCandlis, the fifteen year old father of the little angel currently inhabiting his daughter's womb. When his mother found out that he'd gotten Katie pregnant, she'd shipped him off to live with his father somewhere in California. They hadn't heard from him since, but frequent encounters with Miss McCandlis in town never seemed to get any less uncomfortable.

"I said yes, Daddy."

"Damn," he thought as he turned with a smile and a plate full of food for the microwave. "That's great dear."

"I know what you're thinking Daddy and you have nothing to worry about."

"What could I have to worry about?" he commented, glancing at his daughter's stomach and instantly wishing that he hadn't.

"I'm sorry about Jordan and this," her nervous happiness grew hostile.

"No, sweetie," he put the plate down, moving closer to his daughter. "I didn't mea…"

"I know," she lowered her head. "I didn't mean to get upset."

Placing a finger under her chin, Phil lifted his daughter's gaze to meet his. "I love you very much, and while this isn't exactly the situation that I wanted for you, I'm still very proud of you and wouldn't want things to be any different. Now, tell me about Mark."

Looking into her father's eyes she could tell that he was being genuine. Early on in the pregnancy they'd had their blowouts. They'd said everything that needed to be said and had even gone into family counseling to help work through the less than ideal situation. Quickly they'd come to the conclusion that yelling and fighting wasn't good for anyone, so they'd agreed that, whenever a situation turned negative or angry words were about to be exchanged, they would both just take a breath, acknowledge each other's sides and move on. It had proved an effective method for dealing with things.

"Sooo?" he awaited a response.

"He was so sweet, Daddy. I knew what he was going to ask. He'd already asked me last week but I'd said no."

"Last week?" Phil thought. This was news to him.

"I just couldn't say no this time. Remember that dress we saw in the store a while back?"

"The pink one?"

"Uh, ha. I told him about it and he remembered and bought it for me.

"He's a crafty one," he thought. Maybe he would have to take a closer look at the third Fossy kid after all.

"And not just that, he also found a tiny one for little Isabella. Oh, that's right. I didn't tell you yet. I'm thinking Isabella for a name."

New boy, new dresses, baby names; there was way too much information being thrown his way.

"Anyway, he's really nice and there's nothing for you to worry about so don't go being big, mean mister cop if you see him around town. He already knows you're a cop and I told him you were really a big softy and not to worry."

"Well, that's emasculating," he thought.

"Do you want to see the dress?"

"Do I have a choice?"

"Daddy," she scolded.

"Of course I do, where is it?"

"It's upstairs, I'll be right back," she exclaimed as she hopped in place, then ran for the stairs.

Phil returned to the microwave, but instead of inserting his plate, he stared at the machine, wondering if he could fit his head inside and still manage to turn it on.

TWENTY

Disarmed

Ty stared at the single word on the transmitter in his hand. If everything was functioning as planned, the Nesbit's new alarm system displayed 'active' on every control panel, even though he had just deactivated it from almost a block away.

"Now remember Ty," Grandma Ushi continued to offer advice from the back seat of the car. "In and out. Don't let them know you there."

"Yes, Grandma," he responded, somewhat annoyed. He knew what he was doing. He'd been watching the Nesbit's for weeks now. He knew their patterns. He knew their habits. This being his grandmother's first time however, she apparently felt that it was her duty to point out every potential situation, unaware that a solution for nearly every scenario had already been carefully considered.

"Which one theirs?" Ushi questioned as she leaned forward between the seats.

"It's around the corner," Ty replied.

"Why we so far away?"

"Because, after last night's events, the police have increased their presence in this neighborhood."

"Well, I have not seen a cop yet," Ushi huffed as she sat back in her seat.

As much as he loved and respected his grandmother, at the moment, he just wanted to tell her to shut up. He knew what he was doing. He would have preferred to have left her at home but she'd insisted on coming along. Just in case something did go wrong, she wanted to be on the road and out of town as quickly as possible, which is why she'd insisted that he load the trunk with all of their belongings as well as install the carseat in the backseat beside her.

"This is best plan," she'd proclaimed and honestly, he couldn't argue with her logic. "What you waiting for?" she grew impatient in the backseat. "Go get him."

"I am, Grandma. I just disarmed the alarm," Ty fought his frustration.

"Remember, in and out."

"Yes, Grandma." With that last bit of unnecessary advice, he pulled at the door handle and quickly hopped out of the car, quietly closing the door and ending his grandmother's incessant nagging.

With an abundance of vehicles parked along the residential street as usual, he didn't see any reason why *his* would stand out to a passing police cruiser, and with heavily tinted windows, no one would be able to see the elderly woman quietly waiting inside. He, on the other hand, was now out in the open, and not wanting to risk being seen, quickly made his way down the street, the view of his car and watchful Grandmother disappearing as he turned the corner onto the Nesbit's street.

*****

A flash of lightening, followed by distant thunder startled Jason awake.

11:45 pm

He'd returned to the dorm around eleven to find Derek already asleep, which had initially come as a surprise given his roommate's love of the night and utter distain for the time wasting activity, but given the excitement of the day, his choice was understandable, and by eleven thirty, he too had drifted from reality.

Another flash of lightening lit the room, followed by an even quicker, louder clap of thunder. Glancing toward Derek's bed, Jason attempted to make out the shadowy figure asleep in the bed across from him. Since the day they'd moved into the dorm together, there hadn't been one night that Derek hadn't rattled the walls with his obnoxiously loud snoring. The first few months had been torture for Jason. He'd tried everything from a pillow over his head to noise canceling headphones but, after nearly strangling himself with the cord one night, he'd opted to just deal with the noise, which is what made his roommate's current state seem so odd. Though Derek was dead asleep, the room was completely silent.

While the peace and quiet was a welcomed change, it was also a source of concern. Derek hadn't felt the strange sensation when making the initial jump that morning nor upon their return...or at least that's what he'd said. Meanwhile, Jason had felt it both times, even more so the second time. Wondering if Derek really had felt the odd sensation, Jason quickly sat up in bed, placing his hand to his heart as he recalled the quickened heartbeat which had accompanied the full body tingling. What if Derek had experienced the same sensations and cardiovascular response? While *he'd* recovered relatively quickly, the sensations fading only minutes after arrival, what if Derek had been experiencing something different? The quickened heart rate could account for his amped up energy in the lab earlier and for his almost euphoric demeanor. It could also be the reason why their room was now completely silent.

"Derek," Jason whispered in a concerned tone.

There was no response.

"Derek, are you alright?"

Again nothing.

Tossing back the covers, Jason got to his feet. "Derek, are you dead?"

He instantly wondered why he'd chosen those exact words. If he *was* dead, he certainly wasn't going to audibly confirm it.

Along with having to adjust to sleeping in a room with a running lawn mower, Jason had also grown accustomed to sleeping in complete darkness. Derek had insisted that he couldn't sleep if even one ray of light, whether natural or manmade, struck his eyelids. As far as he could remember, he'd always slept with some sort of night light, but as with the snoring, he'd managed to adjust, and now the darkness was as much a comfort to him as it was to his nearby roommate. What he couldn't get used to was navigating the cluttered floor, which made midnight bathroom visits an often frustrating and sometimes toe busting experience. Now the cloak of darkness was limiting his view of his hopefully sleeping friend.

"Derek, wake up," he spoke louder. He had to know that he was alright, even if that meant stumbling over to Derek's bed and shaking him awake.

Another bolt of lightning lit the room and this time, Derek's empty bed.

Surprised, Jason fumbled for the lamp, filling the room with a soft artificial glow. The shadowy figure that he thought he'd seen was nothing more than a body double made of covers and a couple of pillows.

"Derek?" Jason called out as he made his way toward the bathroom.

Again no answer, as confirmed by the empty adjoining room.

"Where did you go?" he wondered aloud as his eyes fell upon the desk at the foot of Derek's bed. "Unbelievable," he sighed as he quickly hurried to his dresser, pulling out a t-shirt and pair of jeans.

When he'd arrived home less than an hour ago, the backpack, which had contained all of Derek's wiring had been lying on the desk, but more importantly, the medical coat that they'd gone out of their way to obtain, had been resting beside it. Now both were gone.

Quickly, Jason threw on his clothes and fumbled with his shoes, nearly falling as he neglected to untie his right shoe before attempting to shove his foot inside.

"How could he?" he mumbled. "He knows the risks. We agreed to wait until I was done analyzing the data. How could he just run off without me and—?"

A sudden chime from Derek's nightstand ended the one sided conversation as Jason glanced in its direction to see Derek's personal iPad lit up beside his bed. Curious, he wondered toward it. On the screen was a text, but by the time he got close enough to read it, the tablet went dark. Curiosity getting the better of him, Jason picked up the computer, sliding his finger along the bottom until it fell into the familiar, circular depression. He pressed it, but at the same time, lost his grip on the device and watched in horror as the expensive toy slipped from his hands, bounced off the corner of the nightstand and struck the floor at the exact moment another boom of thunder shook the room.

"Oh, crap!" Jason exclaimed as he dove for the device, expecting to see a shattered screen as he flipped it over beside a dirty sock and half eaten banana.

Thankfully, the screen was intact, but his relief was short lived. Getting to his feet, his eyes remained fixed on the fuzzy image filling the screen. Somehow, between the fall and being picked up, the photo app had been activated, displaying one of the hundreds of photos currently housed in the tablet's flash memory. No other photo could have caused his heart to sink deeper into his stomach however. It was grainy and had obviously been taken in a low light situation with partially obstructed visibility but it wasn't the poor quality of the image that sickened him. Lying on a bed, pantsless and with a massive, purple dildo on his chest, was none other than the sixteen year old version of himself.

"What?" Jason questioned the photo confused, trying to process what he was seeing.

This was the first time that he'd seen a photo from that horrible night…which he'd always found surprising. He knew there were others out there. There had to be. He recalled seeing cameras before managing to free himself and run from the room, but remarkably, no images had ever surfaced…until now and on his best friend's computer nonetheless.

Before he could analyze what he'd found any further, the iPad chimed again as another text message appeared at the top of the screen. As if the image before him wasn't enough to get his stomach churning, the new words to accompany it were.

Bethany: I analyzed that red fluid you gave me.

Quickly, Jason swiped at the message, displaying the conversation taking place between Derek and none other than the female counterpart to last night's failed experiment in blind dating.

Derek: What is it?
Bethany: Blood.
Derek: What?
Bethany: That's it. Blood. Simple Type O negative blood. Where did you say you got it from again?

His heart completing its decent, Jason bolted from the room.

*****

Splintered remains of what used to be a fence laid all around Ty's feet. Happy to have made his way from the car to the Nesbit's front yard unseen, he now stood in the open, staring at the demolished fence that had once divided the Nesbit's side yard from their neighbor's. As far as he could remember, the fence had been fine earlier that morning, but now only the back half of the fence still stood. Looking around, the freshly cut stump and random small branches, scattered about the neighbor's yard, told him everything he needed to know about the events that had unfolded after he'd left.

Suddenly realizing the vulnerability of his position, he quickly stepped through the debris field, attempting to avoid any potential nails in the fallen boards and ducked into the shadows of the side yard where the damage became even more evident. Not only had the fence fallen victim to the since cleared tree; the house had also suffered a significant blow.

"The guest room," he thought, trying to recall the floor plan from that morning's installation as he stared at the damaged window, which had since been covered with a bright blue tarp and an abundance of duct tape. "Not the most secure fix," he thought while at the same time appreciating the Nesbit's carelessness. While the alarm system was deactivated, this window still provided an easier point of entry and exit. His son was only one room over and with the Nesbit's bedroom all the way at the back of the house, he figured he'd have no problem peeling back the tarp, slipping inside, and sneaking away with his son without anyone even knowing he was there.

Confident in his new plan, Ty removed a pocket knife from his back pocket and began carefully cutting at the crease were tape met tarp. Avoiding the ripping sound of the sticky fabric, the temporary cover slowly succumbed to the blade as the corner gave way from the smooth stucco finish and inch by inch the blue barrier fell to the side as an opening, large enough to quietly slip through, was made. Folding the knife, he returned it to his pocket and cautiously stepped over the low sill and into the room.

Darker than the shadowy yard, the dim street lights that had aided him outside, barely penetrated the unlit room. Ty attempted to remember what the room looked like as he pulled his second foot through the window, bringing it to rest on the invisible floor beneath him. From what he could remember the room was furnished sparingly.

"Bed over there," he thought, turning his head to the opposite side of the dark void, picturing the neatly made, double guest bed. "There's an easel over here," he reached his hand out, checking the distance to the recalled wooden tripod. "And over there is the—"

Standing chest high, penetrated the dark from the direction of the recalled dresser, was a tiny red light, floating in the darkness.

"Did I install a camera in here?" Ty recalled the system's layout. "No. There's a camera in the main entry, living room, nursery and master bedroom."

Whatever that light was, he hadn't put it there. Terrified that maybe the Nesbits hadn't been so careless about their security after all, Ty stared in the direction of the door, expecting Mr. Nesbit to come bursting into the room, fist swinging like he had the night before but the door remained closed. The lights remained off and the house remained quiet.

Remembering that the room had been clean and fairly spacious, he quietly made his way toward the beacon. The outline of a small white object, sitting on the remembered dresser, came into view as he grew closer. Beside it stood the door to the living room and beside that, the light switch. Light no longer necessary however, he ignored the switch and reached for the door knob, slowly turning the surprisingly noisy handle and carefully pulled the door toward him. The light from the dimly lit hall, poured in through the crack, bringing out the dresser's deep cherry tones and illuminating the ghastly attempt at art currently resting upon the easel. More interested in the surprise piece of surveillance equipment though, Ty paused in his departure to take one last look at the tiny device and smiled as he read the brand name along its base.

Tyco

"A baby monitor," he smiled. "Hardly a sophisticated peace of surveillance equipment," he thought.

Glad that the device hadn't been a camera but still cautious of its powerful microphone, he released his grip on the noisy doorknob and carefully slipped through the opening that he'd already made.

Not sure if it was the fear of being caught or the excitement that only twenty feet of floor space and one door was separating him from his son, Ty suddenly realized that his heart was pounding; so hard in fact that the thought of his heart being so loud as to register on the monitor crossed his mind. Disregarding the brief, illogical thought however, he carefully crept toward his sleeping son's door.

Taking the door knob in his hand, he considered the very likely possibility of another monitor in the child's room. Thankfully quieter than the previous knob however, Oliver's door silently pivoted on its hinges, welcoming him into the room.

Similar to the hall, two night lights illuminated the happily decorated room. Admiring the cheerful decor as he made his way toward the crib, Ty made note of each detail with every intention of replicating it in their new home. Slowly creeping to the edge of the crib, he again became aware of his pounding heart, though only for a moment as it all but stopped at the sight of the empty crib.

"What the fuck?" he whispered, forgetting about the

possible second monitor.

Scanning the room, another monitor stood atop the changing table, thankfully with its power light off.

"He must be in their room," he thought as he contemplated what to do next. Logic told him to get the hell out of there; that this wasn't going to work right now and that he'd be better off coming back once the Nesbits began to feel more comfortable again. Logic was typically a powerful persuader, but logic had never met Grandma Ushi, and he knew what she would say if he returned to the car without her great grandson.

"Failure! You are failure and disgrace!" she would scold him. "My great grandson count on you to rescue him from impostors and you let him down. Shame! Shame!"

Practically hearing the disappointment in his grandmother's phantom voice, Ty quickly made his way out of his son's room, back into the hall and before he even realized it, to the Nesbit's closed bedroom door.

"This wasn't part of the plan," he thought. He didn't know what he was going to do. All he knew was that he couldn't...no...he wouldn't leave without his son. He hoped to find him asleep in a little bassinet, away from his stand-in parents' bed and close to the door so that he could just poke his head in, snatch him up and disappear into the night but as he slowly opened the door, his hopes faded as Mr. and Mrs. Nesbit came into view, asleep on the queen size bed with little Olive peacefully passed out between them. At a loss for what to do, he proceeded into the room anyway, pushed by his grandmother's persistent nagging until he found himself standing beside the bed, staring down at the woman who had the audacity to call herself mom.

Only a few feet away, Ty wanted nothing more than to just grab his son and run, but there was no way to reach him without disturbing the sleeping parents, so he continued to watch the trio, contemplating just how he was going to pull off this abduction. He didn't have much time however as Oliver began to shift, his motion shortly followed by a couple of short "Cacks" and eventually the start of a cry.

"I'll get a bottle," Mr. Nesbit announced as he got to his feet and as Mrs. Nesbit rolled over to comfort the hungry child, her eyes still closed and mind still partially focused on sleep.

Receiving the embrace of his temporary mother, Oliver quieted but remained awake as Mr. Nesbit stumbled past the closet and out, into the hall.

Thankfully, the closet door had been open, so quickly ducking inside had been silent and easy. "This is it," Ty thought as he watched the father's departure through the now only partially open, door. Reaching into his back pocket, he began to withdraw the pocket knife but quickly reconsidered as he thought about what that meant. He'd come there willing to do whatever it took to claim his son, even if it meant murder, but the knife was to risky. What if Mrs. Nesbit got out a scream before he was through, or even more concerning, what if she struggled and in that struggle the knife slipped and ended up coming to rest inside Oliver's tiny body? No, the knife wasn't going to work. He let the small blade drop back into his pocket. Looking around he spotted a silky, purple robe on a hanger beside him. Quietly he wrapped the end of its belt around his left hand as he drew it from the loops and exited the closet. Careful not to make a sound, he slowly retook his position over the sleeping woman as his son, catching a glimpse of his true father, turned his head and offered an excited smile.

Sensing the child's movement, Mrs. Nesbit opened her eyes to see the boy smiling at something behind her. "What are you so happy about," she offered Oliver a groggy form of baby talk as she turned and came face to face with Ty.

Shock delaying her scream, Ty took the opportunity to

deliver a devastating blow to the woman's face, stopping the scream and leaving the mother teetering on the verge of unconsciousness.

"It's okay," Ty comforted his son as he slipped the robe's silk belt around the woman's neck. "You're almost home."

Oliver's smile grew and he let out an excited squeak as his father tightened the purple fabric.

Mrs. Nesbit's body tensed as the blood flow to her brain was suddenly cut off and the veins in her neck began to bulge with the added pressure.

Seeing this, Ty pulled harder, bracing his foot against the frame of the bed as the thin fabric began to cut into the woman's skin. Given her nearly unconscious state, she wasn't putting up any fight and it wouldn't have surprised him in the least to see the skin around her neck suddenly tear under the immense pressure, adding a loss of blood to the cause of death. He pulled tighter.

"Who...!"

Ty turned to see Mr. Nesbit charging at him, lowering his shoulder and launching him backward into the fragile drywall beside the bed. The two men, jarred by the sudden impact, both fell to the ground, though Mr. Nesbit, less affected by the blow, quickly got to his feet and continued his assault with three swift blows to Ty's head.

The room spun with each additional blow as Ty struggled to maintain his grasp on reality. Acting on pure survival instinct as Mr. Nesbit continued to deliver blow after blow, somehow the pocket knife ended up in his hand. Pushing the release, the blade slid out of the handle as he buried the knife into Mr. Nesbit's thigh.

The father let out a painful cry as he stumbled backward, tripping over a pair of shoes and falling headfirst through the fragile closet door.

Trying to make the world stop spinning, Ty stumbled to his feet, grabbing his face as he realized that his left eye was already swollen shut.

Lying halfway inside the closet, Mr. Nesbit lifted his leg toward his hands and with another cry, yanked the blade out of his leg. Fighting back the pain, he reopened his eyes just in time to see his seven iron barreling toward him, instantly turning his world dark.

Standing over him, Ty continued to deliver blow after blow with the club, leaving Mr. Nesbit's head unrecognizable and relocating its previous contents to the surrounding walls and neatly hung clothes.

Exhausted, Ty dropped the club, ready to claim his rightful spot beside his son, however before he could fully turn around, the lamp that *had* been beside the bed, struck his right temple with a crushing blow. Falling to the floor beside his victim, Ty only momentarily caught a glimpse of Mrs. Nesbit before his knife came to rest deep within his only remaining good eye.

With the delivery of the knife to the assailant's eye, Jennifer watched as the man's body twitched momentarily before going limp. Struggling to get to her feet, tears began to flow as she stared at Bill's lifeless body and the urge to vomit battled with the wails of sorrow erupting from her lungs as she struggled to remain upright, leaning against the closet door jamb while she stared in horror at her dead husband.

"Oliver," she suddenly remembered and pulling her eyes away from the tragedy that lay before her, returned to the bed.

Oliver just stared at his mother as she made her way back to him. The smile that he'd had just prior to the attack was now a cold, almost inquisitive stare as his eyes suddenly shifted toward the door.

Jennifer turned just in time to see the white burst of the muzzle as a bullet struck her forehead, repainting the wall behind her.

Standing in the doorway, Ushi lowered the revolver as Mrs. Nesbit dropped to the floor beside the bed. Carefully tucking the gun back into her purse and refocusing her attention on her great grandson, she made her way to the bed.

"Who that?" Ushi asked in a playful tone.

The smile returned to Oliver's face.

"That my little angel?"

Oliver kicked his feet.

"That my precious little angel?" she continued in full blown baby talk. "I think it is."

Kicking one of the fallen woman's legs out of the way, Ushi stood beside the bed and reaching down, hoisted Oliver into her arms.

Oliver just stared up at her, his smile still beaming.

"That my great grandson. That little Oliver. But I no think you look much like an Oliver. Do you?"

Oliver giggled.

"What horrible name. I going to give you new name."

His smile faded as he appeared to listen.

"From now on your name...Jason...Jason Fook."

The smile returned.

*****

"Jason! Jesus! You scared the shit out of me," Derek jumped as he caught a glimpse of his roommate, standing silently in the lab's doorway.

Jason didn't say a word as he continued his silent stare.

Putting his phone down on the counter next to him, "How long have you been standing there?"

Still no response.

Tracing Jason's blank stare to the medical coat beside his phone, "Oh...I..."

"Going somewhere?" Jason broke his silence.

"No...I mean. Shit," Derek, at a rare loss for words, realized that there was no use lying. "I was going to—"

"—to see her?" Jason completed his nervous roommate's sentence.

"Yeah," Derek admitted. "I'm sorry man. I know we

discussed not going back so soon but you did say that you weren't interested so I figured—"

"—It's fine," Jason issued an emotionless approval as he slowly advanced toward the counter at which Derek sat.

"Really?" Derek responded, confused but relieved.

"Sure. I mean, what kind of friend would I be if I got in the way of true love?" Jason continued his slow advance.

"I didn't say anything about true love. I just wanted to go back and give her the coat and..." Derek hesitated as he noticed that Jason's hands were hidden behind his back. "I know that nothing can come of it but I just figured it wouldn't hurt to..."

Jason stopped at the opposite side of the counter.

"What do you have?" Derek motioned to Jason's concealed hands.

"Who were you talking to?" Jason changed the subject.

"What?"

"Before you realized I was here. Who were you texting?"

"Ah...no one," Derek lied, unsure exactly how to bring up the conversation with Bethany and the fact that he'd given her a sample of the core liquid a couple of days ago. "I loaded the trip calculations into the phone as a back up this time...you know, just in case."

Jason just stared at his deceitful friend before revealing the iPad in his right hand as he placed the tablet on the counter between them.

"What are you doing with that?" Derek questioned.

"Push the button."

"What?"

"Go on," Jason insisted in the same, monotone voice.

Hesitantly, Derek complied, pressing the single button at the bottom of the device. The iPad's screen lit up to display a photo of a Midwestern lightning storm in the background of the security screen.

"Go ahead," Jason urged Derek to continue.

Staring at Jason, Derek slid his finger across the screen, unlocking the device to reveal he and Bethany's conversation.

You still haven't told me why you gave me his blood, was the last message received.

"Jason, I can explain—"

"—Explain what? You were curious, so you snuck a sample of the core liquid out and gave it to that whore to test."

"Whoa!" Derek responded, shocked at Jason's blunt and candid description. "I know your date didn't go well the other night but Bethany is still my friend."

"She climbed out of a bathroom window to get away from me," Jason revealed the date's true outcome.

Hesitantly, "I know."

"Really?" Jason's tone finally took on some emotion as sarcasm managed to sneak its way in. "Now, how could you possibly know that? Oh, that's right..." Sliding his finger down on the screen the conversation scrolled back to the previous night.

Derek: Where is he now?
Bethany: At the table. I climbed out the bathroom window.
Derek: What?
Bethany: He's weird.
Derek: I don't know about that.
Bethany: Half the time he just sat there staring at me silently.
Derek: I'm sure he was just nervous.
Bethany: Yeah, nervous and weird. I'd much rather see you tonight.
Derek: Can't tonight. I'm in the middle of something. Did you get a chance to run that sample I gave you?
Bethany: The blood.
Derek: It's not blood.
Bethany: It looks like blood. No not yet.

Derek: I really need that done soon.

Bethany: Ok. I'll be at the lab tomorrow. I'll run it then. Maybe we can get together and I can tell you the results in person. B===D~~(())

Derek: Dirty girl. You text your mother with those fingers?

Bethany: lol. Anyway, gotta go. Ride's here.

Derek: Night.

Bethany: Night.

The two just stared at one another until Derek, purely in the interest of breaking the awkward silence, blurted, "What are you doing going through my texts anyway?"

"Really?" Jason disregarded the question. "I think we're way past broken trust here. Don't you?"

"Listen, I'm sorry about Bethany," Derek stood up to meet Jason eye to eye across the counter.

Jason didn't respond.

"We have something far more important to discuss though, like why your blood is in the machine's core," Derek continued, his tone becoming more stern.

Again, Jason didn't respond. He just continued to stare at his friend before slowly reaching for the iPad and with a few taps, called up the image of himself tied to the bed.

Derek was speechless.

"It would appear that we have a lot to discuss," Jason spoke for him.

Derek just stared at the familiar image.

"How did you get that?"

Derek didn't have a response.

"Did you take it? Were you there that night?"

"No I didn't take it, Jason."

"But you were there?"

Derek hesitated.

"After all these years, how could you keep that from me?" Jason's voice quivered as his eyes started to well up.

"Jason, it's not what you think," Derek attempted to defend himself.

"You were the only one I ever talked to about that and now I find out you were there?"

"I didn't mean to be."

"Oh, you accidentally hid in the closet while that cunt set me up."

"Jason, calm down and let me explain," Derek began to circle the counter, attempting to calm his obviously distraught friend.

"Don't tell me to calm down," Jason wiped away a tear as he struggle to regain his composure.

"I didn't know what was happening until it was too late. Tyler told me to follow him. He said he had something to show me. Honestly, when he brought me up to the bedroom I thought he was going to tell me he was gay and hit on me," Derek joked with a smile to lighten the mood.

Jason didn't laugh.

"Anyway, when we got up there, everyone was hiding in the closet. I didn't know what was going on and the next thing I knew, someone whispered 'they're coming' and they pulled me into the closet. I didn't know what they were planning. Honestly."

Jason just stared, processing the information.

"Jesus Christ, Jason, why do you think none of those pictures ever made it out. After you ran out of there I made everyone delete the pictures."

"What about that one then?" Jason motioned to the iPad as the screen went to sleep.

"Tyler managed to get that one out without me knowing. He emailed it to me a week later, threatening to send it to the entire school while spreading the rumor that I had set the whole thing up."

Jason looked at him inquisitively.

"I didn't. I swear," Derek defended himself again. "Anyway, I went over to his house and convinced him to delete the photo."

"Was that the—"

"—The broken nose," Derek smirked. "Yeah."

"Then why do you still have it?" Jason asked.

"I don't know why I didn't delete that copy. Over time I guess I'd just forgotten about it. There's no excuse but I'm so sorry that I never told you," Derek reached out, lightly grabbing hold of Jason's shoulder.

Jason sat down on the stool next to him.

"I would do anything to be able to go back and stop that night from happening," Derek continued.

Jason looked up.

"But you know we can't do that," Derek anticipated what his friend was thinking. "You said it yourself. Altering the past could have devastating consequences."

Jason lowered his head again.

"You need to put it behind you and move on. You can't let that one event haunt you for the rest of your life. No one in your life knows about it other than me and I'm certainly not going to tell anyone," he assured Jason as he grabbed the iPad, unlocked the screen and deleted the image. "See. Now it never happened."

Jason continued to sit silent, his eyes focused on the floor beneath the stool.

"Now, honestly. Why is the core filled with your blood?"

"Grandma Ushi always said I was special," Jason mumbled, his eyes still diverted downward.

"Huh?"

"You're going to do wonderful, amazing things is what she always told me. You're special. You have a gift, she said. For the longest time I didn't know what she was talking about. You know that it wasn't until she was on her death bed that she told me the truth?"

"The truth about what?" Derek asked, trying to get Jason to look up at him.

"The truth about who I am and where I came from. Hell, the truth about *what* I am."

"What you are?" Derek asked confused.

"Apparently it skips a generation."

"What does?"

"My great uncle had it, Grandpa Fook I used to call him, though I guess he wasn't actually my grandfather. He died when I was eleven, seven years before my grandmother told me the truth."

"Jason, I have no idea what you're talking about but you're scaring me."

"I was scared when she told me. At first I couldn't believe it. How could anyone believe something that crazy?

"What?" Derek asked impatiently.

"I tried to kill myself you know," Jason looked up briefly before returning his gaze to his tapping foot.

Derek eyes widened at the previously unknown information.

"Yeah, tied a rope to the basement rafters."

"Jason, I—"

"It wouldn't let me die though. It prevents you from dying."

Derek had no idea what Jason was talking about or what to say.

"Two weeks. I woke up in a corn field in Nebraska with no recollection of the previous two weeks. That's when I decided that I was going to figure this thing out; to harness the power that was inside of me.

"Jason, I don't understand. You need to tell me what's going on."

"I'll never forget the last thing she told me though. Jason, she'd whispered, fighting the cancer for every word. People won't understand. You have to keep this a secret. You are the last of this family. For your own safety and to ensure that our family's gift endures, you must keep this a secret. Promise me, she'd said. So I did. She died moments later."

"Jason—"

"—So what are we going to do about this?" Jason questioned, looking up at Derek with a hollow stare.

"What do you mean?" Derek asked confused.

"I can't break my promise to my dead grandmother. She was right. No one could understand. Not even you."

Preoccupied by the text and the photo and the unusual story, Derek hadn't noticed that Jason's left hand was still concealed behind his back. It wasn't until the light overhead struck the thin needle that he noticed the hidden weapon.

Plunging the syringe into Derek's thigh, Jason stared coldly into his roommate's fading eyes as he slumped to the floor.

"Not even you."

TWENTY-ONE

"What took you so long?" Bethany greeted Derek at the door with a smile and an enthusiastic hug.

Unable to muster the energy to even lift his arms, he just leaned into the welcoming hug as the world continued to spin out of control. He didn't know how he'd gotten to the girl's sorority. He didn't even remember telling her that he was coming over.

"Are you alright?" Bethany's excitement shifted to concern as she realized that she was the only reason Derek was still on his feet.

He wanted to say "no". He wanted to tell her that there was something wrong with Jason and that he'd been drugged with God knows what, but just as the syringe's chemical concoction had rendered his motor skills practically useless, they'd done the same to his vocal cords. All he could do was moan as a thin line of drool fell from the corner of his mouth, onto Bethany's shoulder.

"Jesus," Bethany proclaimed as she wrapped her arm around Derek's back and helped him into the house.

Looking around the elaborately decorated sorority, everything seemed to have a fog like quality. The members' pictures, both past and present, seemed to float instead of hang on the surrounding walls, and the eyes of the female bust beside the grand staircase seemed to follow them as they made their way toward the stairs.

"What happened to you?" Bethany questioned, her concern growing as they reached the first step.

"Oh my god," another sister gasped as she appeared at the top of the stairs.

"I need some water," Bethany looked up at the girl as she began coaching Derek up the first step.

"Do you need help?" the shocked girl asked as she hurried down the stairs.

"Just get me some water."

Reaching the bottom of the stairs the girl bolted down the hall, disappearing into the kitchen.

"Jason," Derek mumbled, causing more drool to escape.

"What?" Bethany questioned the nearly inaudible word as she struggled to maintain their balance.

"Sick," Derek added.

"I know you're sick."

"No. Sick," Derek repeated, forgetting to add Jason to the statement.

"I'll take care of you. We just need to get you upstairs."

"No," Derek protested as he stopped climbing and, turning his gaze back toward the front door, spotted Jason standing on the bottom step, staring up at them with the same cold look he'd offered just before jabbing the needle into his leg. "No!" Derek yelled as he lost his footing, nearly sending both he and Bethany tumbling back to the first floor.

Grabbing hold of both the banister and her suddenly startled friend, Bethany managed to regain both of their balance as Derek went down to one knee and using his hand to prop himself up, spun his attention back down the stairs.

"What is it?" Bethany asked confused as she too turned in the direction of Derek's terrified gaze, just in time to see her sister returning with the glass of water. "It's just Rachel."

Making her way up the stairs, Rachel handed Bethany the glass.

"Here, take a drink," Bethany instructed as she coaxed a tiny sip past Derek's lips.

"Do you need me to call an ambulance?" Rachel asked.

"No, I think he'll be alright. I just need to get him upstairs to lay down."

"Let me help," Rachel offered as she grabbed hold of Derek's other arm and, helping him to his feet, they managed to get him up the remaining steps, down the hall and into Bethany's room.

"You're sure you don't want me to call?"

"No. He just needs to rest," Bethany assured her as they stared at Derek who, upon reaching the pillow covered bed, had fallen face first into the comforter and lay motionless. "You go. Have fun."

"You're sure," Rachel questioned, hesitant to leave but based on her retreating motion, eager to remove herself from the situation.

"Yeah, I'm sure. Go."

Rachel didn't need any more convincing as she turned and quickly left.

Like a rowboat on the open sea, Bethany's bed seemed to pitch and roll with each passing wave as Derek struggled to make out the conversation taking place behind him. Fragmented memories of the night seemed to form and then fade away as quickly as they'd appeared, leaving his thoughts incomplete and his mind struggling to piece together the reality of the situation.

He heard the door close behind him as another wave hoisted the bed into the air before sending it plummeting downward again, the constant motion, combined with the flowery smell of the bed, stirring up the contents of his stomach as another blackout overtook him.

*****

"Derek. Are you alright?" Bethany's concerned voice whispered in his ear.

He wanted to answer but even though the seas had calmed and the wave of nausea had passed, he was still hesitant to open his mouth.

"Derek."

Chancing it, "Yeah," he moaned.

"Derek."

"I'm fine," he assured her.

"Derek."

"I'm okay. Just need to lay here."

Suddenly a shrill scream filled the room as Derek opened his eyes to the sight of Jason's face only inches from his, laying beside him on the floor.

"Fuck!," he exclaimed at the sight of his unexpected roommate as he slid himself back and closed his eyes, expecting the vision to disappear when reopened.

"Derek," the voice repeated again. This time it was clear that the voice had not been Bethany's but Jason's the whole time.

Reluctantly reopening his eyes, the vision remained as Jason repositioned himself to sit Indian style beside him.

"Where—?"

"—Where are you?" Jason completed the anticipated question. "I don't know how to tell you this," he spoke in a comforting tone. "You're dead Derek. There was an accident and I'm sorry to say it but…you didn't make it."

Derek just stared back at the familiar, yet oddly different man sitting beside him.

"I'm just messing with you," Jason laughed. "I had you though, didn't I."

"No," Derek thought, still confused over just about everything as he glanced back and forth at Jason's hands.

"Oh, you don't have to worry about that again," Jason chuckled. "No more needles. I just needed that to get you here."

"Where—?"

"—Where's here?" Jason once again completed the question. "You my friend are in a sorority house. Familiar territory I bet," he added with a grin.

"Bethany," Derek recalled being helped up the stairs and onto the bed on the other side of the room.

"You know, you sure did make a mess of things," Jason disregarded Derek's recollection. "You couldn't leave well enough alone. You just had to know what the mysterious fluid was. The magic, chemical concoction that I'd whipped up to make time travel possible. As if two college students...albeit brilliant ones, but college students nonetheless, could solve a century's old fantasy like time travel with some computer scraps and a chemistry set," Jason laughed. "That's absurd. Frankly, I'm shocked you went for it."

"What's wrong with you?" Derek questioned his dramatically different friend as he unsuccessfully attempted to prop himself up.

"What's wrong with me?" Jason repeated confused. "Wasn't it you that said I should lighten up; that I should be more outgoing and a little less...well...me."

"I don't think I said all that."

"Well that's what you meant," Jason asserted angrily. "I'm sorry," he smiled, the sudden anger fading from his eyes. "You know, I really wanted to tell you the truth. You were the one person that I thought I could trust with something like this but I guess I was wrong now, wasn't I?" he mimed a camera taking a picture.

"Jason, I—"

"—I know. I know. You didn't take the picture. You actually destroyed all of the pictures and I should be praising your heroics and yadda, yadda, yadda."

"I—"

"—Can't say I believe it, but it was a good story anyhow," Jason continued. "You know what? It's water under the bridge. Don't worry about it."

"Jason it's true."

"No. You know what's true? This. This right now is true. The situation we currently find ourselves in. That's what's fucking true!"

Derek watched as the previously unfamiliar anger returned to Jason's face, then faded as quickly as it had appeared.

"As I was saying...I wanted to tell you about the blood. Even though my grandmother had warned me to never tell a soul, you were someone that I thought I could trust but then you had to go and get *her* involved," he motioned toward the bed.

"Bethany?" Derek called out, finally managing to prop himself up on one elbow, as he unsuccessfully attempted to see the top of the bed.

"Now, I *knew* I couldn't trust her. I mean, how can you trust someone who'd rather climb out a window than offer the simple courtesy of seeing a date to its end?"

"Bethany, are you alright?," Derek called out concerned.

"She's fine," Jason assured.

"What did you do?"

"Hey!" Jason snapped. "You're losing focus here!"

Derek returned his concerned gaze to his roommate.

"You were so gung ho to find out what was in the core and now all you can think about is that little bitch." Calm again, "As I was saying, there was nothing special about your machine. Don't get me wrong, it's a beautiful display of craftsmanship. You should be very proud. The blood, my blood, however is the true star here. As much as I've tried to understand it, sadly it still remains a mystery to me. I haven't been able to find any record of even one individual outside of our family, with the same condition. I guess you could call it a defense mechanism, sort of like fight or flight. In this case it acts as the flight by somehow creating a link between here and there upon imminent death. Unfortunately I need to practically die to use it, and even then I don't have any control, as I found out with my little hanging experiment. That's where our...sorry...your machine comes into play. By delivering a targeted blast of electricity directly through the blood filled core, we managed to trigger the flight defense and with a bit of programming wizardry, I was able to not only harness but aim that reaction toward a specific place and time.

"You're insane."

"I'm insane? No, I'm very sane. It's you who's insane my friend," Jason asserted as he got to his feet. "Or at least that's what I'm counting on everyone thinking."

"Everyone?" Derek questioned confused.

"You see, even though I believe you were part of that whole bedroom scheme and even though you went behind my back to test my blood and who knows what other deceitful things you've done during our friendship, I still can't bring myself to kill you. I don't know. Call it a weakness, but I guess I still kind of like you. But seeing that I can't have you exposing my little secret to the world, I do need to get you out of the way," Jason explained as he made his way to the open bedroom window.

Derek struggled to sit up.

"After they see what you've done here, they won't believe a thing you say, especially if you start talking about time travel and magic blood and how your shy, timid roommate set you up."

"What did you do, Jason?" Derek pushed against the floor, fighting the waning effects of the drug.

"I didn't do anything," Jason insisted as he stepped out of the bedroom window, onto the sloped roof just below. "You were the one that texted Bethany, saying you were coming over. You were the one that everyone saw stumbling up to her front door and into her bedroom and you'll be the one they find in this room when I'm gone. No one knows about our little incident in the lab tonight. No one knows that I climbed in through this window and hid in the closet while you were stumbling around downstairs and no one knows the pleasure I took from slitting that little whore ear to ear," he punctuated his rant with a devilish grin before disappearing into the night.

Shuffling toward the bed, Derek pulled himself to his feet as Bethany's battered body came into view, the once white sheets now stained by the life which had been drained from her nearly decapitated head.

"I'm sorry I left earlier, I..."

Derek turned to see, a vaguely familiar girl standing in the doorway. Glancing at the body and then back at the new girl, "I didn't—"

Too terrified for an explanation, Rachel's scream drowned out Derek's plea of innocence as she turned and ran from the room, screaming for someone to call the police.

Though innocent, he knew that he didn't stand a chance against the evidence surrounding him. As quickly as his weakened legs could carry him, Derek stumbled toward the open window. Bethany's bedroom was only on the second floor, however, given the ten foot tall ceilings, it was still at least a twelve or thirteen foot drop to the bushes below. Luckily, the first floor jutted out from that side of the house, giving him a small, sharply sloped roof to step out onto to make his escape a bit easier.

Propping himself against the window frame he attempted to lift his leg, only getting it six inches off the carpet before its weight proved too much for his weakened body and fell back to the floor.

"In Bethany's room! He's still in there!" Rachel's voice echoed through the house.

He knew he didn't have much time. It wasn't the cops that were going to show up first. In a matter of moments the room would be filled with horrified and angry sorority girls. He wouldn't even live to receive his life sentence if they got to him first. Panicked and determined to find safety, he lifted his leg again, this time grabbing hold of his knee as his muscles started to tremble and managed to get his calf and the side of his foot onto the edge of the window sill. The hard part done, he shoved his leg through the opening just as Rachel reappeared in the doorway with two of her sisters.

Rachel knew where *not* to look as she focused her attention on Derek. The other two either hadn't been warned or hadn't understood the severity of their sister's claims as their eyes immediately turned to the bloodied corpse sprawled across the bed, sending one girl back into the hall and the other into a series of bent over, stomach churning convulsions.

Taking advantage of the girls' momentarily distracted states, Derek returned his attention to the window as he ducked beneath the raised pane.

"Stop!" Rachel screamed.

He didn't get a chance to see if the girl was charging him or not as the slope of the small roof proved too much for his trembling legs, and instead of cautiously stepping out onto the shingled surface and gently lowering himself down as he'd planned, his foot slid down the roof and off the edge, sending him on a somersaulting plummet toward the bushes.

"He's getting away!" Rachel cried from the window.

Looking up at the girl in the window from his dense, leafy bed, Derek knew he didn't have time to lay around and recover. Managing to free himself from his tangled prison of broken branches, Derek slinked out onto the manicured lawn and managing to get to his feet, ducked through a row of tall hedges.

"Come on! Hurry!" Derek could hear another girl cry from the front porch as police sirens joined the hunt in the distance.

Looking behind him as he stumbled through a neighboring property and onto a side street it occurred to him that he had no place to go. He couldn't go back to the dorm. It would only be a matter of time before the police came looking for him there. Besides that, Jason would probably be there, pretending to be asleep to ensure his own alibi. His only hope was the lab. He had to get to the machine. He had to—

The crack of a wooden plank breaking in two across his face put an instant end to all thought as his feet came out from under him and the blow of the shattered board in conjunction with the impact of the ground jarred his mind.

"You just don't know when to give up, do you?"

With the brief thunderstorm dissipating, pockets of stars danced overhead as Derek struggled to regain the breath that had been stolen from him by the impact of the ground. Pulling himself together, the stars' movement began to slow to a more tolerable spin as Jason stepped into view.

"Now, where do you think you're going?" Jason asked, pausing as if he actually expected a response.

Doing all he could to maintain consciousness, all Derek could do was groan.

"Did that hurt?" Jason asked, kneeling beside his fallen roommate. "Ooh, I guess I did hit you kind of hard," he poked at Derek's already swelling face. "Seriously though, where are you going? The dorm's back that way," he motioned back toward the sorority house. "But you wouldn't be stupid enough to go there. So where could you possibly go to escape what you've done?" Jason rubbed at his chin as the answer drew a smile to his face. "No... You weren't... You didn't think that... Then again, I do like that better," he spoke to himself.

Only half aware of Jason's presence, Derek closed his eyes in an attempt to calm the rolling ocean on which he lay.

"Tell you what," Jason continued as he fumbled through his pocket. "Since we've been friends for so long, I'm gonna help you out. I'm going to get you out of here but first you have to promise to cooperate," he emphasized as he withdrew another syringe from his pocket and, plucking the cap from the needle, leaned over his friend. "You, my friend, are going on a little journey," he smiled as he slid the needle into Derek's jugular.

The ocean calmed and the dancing stars overhead faded as the world was replaced by darkness.

TWENTY-TWO

"Unbelievable! You really don't feel that?"

Feeling just as he had when he'd awoke on Bethany's floor, Derek struggled to open his eyes, hoping to find himself in his bed with the TV on and the worst hangover in history, but the excited voice circling around him wasn't that of any known TV personality, though it *was* terrifyingly familiar.

"It's all over. Just like before."

Derek opened his eyes to the sight of Jason staring at his outstretched palms and kicking up dust and gravel as he paced excitedly around. Overhead, large bundles of wire crisscrossed the night sky and the previously passing storm appeared to be regaining its hold on the night sky with an even more ominous looking ceiling. He didn't need to look around. He knew where he was. Though this time he couldn't claim to be the least bit excited about it.

"Hey," Jason kicked at his awakening friend. "Wake up."

Fighting the second dose of the incapacitating concoction flowing through his veins, Derek slowly rolled his head from side to side as the waves beneath him once again began their nausea inducing ballet.

"You know, I wasn't sure that I could do this without you," Jason spoke as he sat down on the ground beside Derek and began poking at the iPad within the briefcase. "Sure, I watched you set it all up but I'll be honest, I don't know the first thing about this electric shit and all I could picture was being fried to a crisp trying to hook up those wires," he motioned to the cables that connected the device to the large transformers behind them. "You know what though?" he slapped Derek on the chest, drawing a hollow thud as Derek remained motionless, only wishing to be able to move in response to the blunt pain. "I did it and ta-da. Here we are."

Derek just stared up at him with as much of an unenthusiastic glare as he could muster.

"What? Not excited? Where's your adventurous spirit now? Don't tell me you're not at least a little excited by this still. I know we were just here but it's still pretty fucking cool, though it is a bit later in the day this time," Jason acknowledged his miscalculation as he looked around at the darkness of the surrounding woods. "Oh well, at least we're not siamese twins, right?" he laughed as he issued another slap. "Anyway, I've gotta be going but you enjoy your new home." Standing up, "oh, I almost forgot. Here." Reaching into the backpack, he pulled out the white medical coat and tossed it at Derek, the white fabric landing on his face and blocking his view as Jason depressed the button on the orb in his hand.

The transformers cracked and whirred as power surged through the yard. Rocking his head back and forth, the coat slid aside just in time for Derek to see Jason and the machine disappear, leaving behind a soft, fading glow as the super charged equipment returned to normal.

"Where was he going to go?" Derek wondered as he struggled to move his fingertip against the coarse gravel. Turning his head to the side once again, the white coat came into view as did a tiny paper sticking out of one of the side pockets.

Sarah
1342 Belmont St.

He'd been looking up Sarah's college address when Jason had shown up in the lab. Apparently Jason had finished the search for him and jotted the desired information onto the tiny scrap, but why? It was obvious that he'd snapped. He was the last person Derek would've ever expected to suffer from…whatever it was he was suffering from. Or, maybe this was the real Jason and for all those years he'd managed to keep up the Oscar worthy performance.

If the situation hadn't been so serious, he might have laughed at such a thought or at least cracked a smile. Jason was a normal guy or at least he used to be. This wasn't him. This was the result of years of torment, capped off by the perceived betrayal of his best and only friend. He'd come back for him. Once he calmed down he'd realize what he'd done and be back. But what about the blood? What was he talking about in the lab? Was what he said really possible? It had to be. His current predicament proved it. But how? And what about…oh God…Bethany. The memory of the butchered girl grabbed hold of his stomach and with a violent twist, finished the job that the waves had struggled to accomplish.

Struggling for command of his left arm, Derek wiped at his mouth before sliding his hand toward the paper, knocking it from the pocket and onto the ground. Jason hadn't written down the address to be nice, Derek realized. Reading the now visible, last line, his heart sank.

See you there

*****

"Daddy, Daddy! I did it!" Abby announced as she appeared in the doorway.

"What did you do?" Dustin questioned as he compared the register's contents against the report printed out on the receipt paper.

"Well, first I turned off the T.V. and then I put away my chair and then I threw away my trash..."

She was going to give him an exact play by play account of the last five minutes, Dustin thought as he signed the bottom of the receipt and slipped it under the rubber band that held the recently counted money together.

"...and then I picked up my crayons because I dropped them on the floor and they rolled everywhere. That took a while because I had to put them all back in the box but I was missing one so I had to look for it..."

"Ah huh," Dustin acknowledged that he was still listening as he bent down to punch the code into the safe just below the register. The door released with a click.

"That's a lot of money," Abby paused in her story when she saw the three large stacks of cash sitting on the top shelf of the safe.

"That's why it's kept in the safe," Dustin acknowledged the unusually large amount of money currently residing within the large steel box. Typically the owner never let money stack up for more than a day or two before making a run to the bank. Judging from the pile, today's take brought the total number of days to four.

"Is it yours?" Abby questioned.

"No sweetie. I wish it was but it belongs to the store."

"What is the store going to do with it? It's just a building. It doesn't need money."

Laughing, "Not the store itself, the owner of the store," Dustin clarified.

"Oh. Who's that?"

"Mr. Levrett," Dustin locked the safe and turned to

face his daughter. "You remember Mr. Levrett from this morning."

"Oh. I like him. He's funny looking."

"Yes, I guess he sort of is, but let's just keep that to ourselves. Daddy needs to keep his job so he can continue to buy you food and clothes and those pesky crayons," Dustin poked at his daughter's stomach, attempting to draw a laugh but failing as the mention of the crayons returned her memory to her story.

"You know where I found the missing crayon?"

"Where?"

"Under the crayon box. I looked everywhere but it was under the box the whole time. Can you believe that?" the precocious girl questioned with her hands on her hips.

"No I can't," Dustin mimicked his daughter's seriousness, drawing the laugh he'd been seeking.

"Don't make fun of me, Daddy," Abby giggled.

"Then don't be so silly," Dustin laughed as he hoisted his daughter into the air, drawing even more laughter.

Suddenly a loud bang rattled the glass door to the store, putting an abrupt end to the jovial moment.

Putting his daughter back down behind the counter, Dustin quickly grabbed the gun from on top of the safe. "Stay right here," he instructed his daughter as he cautiously peered over the countertop in the direction of the front door. The bottom half of the door was covered by a large Budweiser advertisement while the top half remained almost completely clear except for the security sticker and store hours posted to one side. From his vantage point he couldn't see anyone at the door.

Cautiously, he made his way around the counter, once again gesturing for Abby to remain where she was.

Abby acknowledged her father's command with a worried nod as she began pulling nervously at Mr. Pickles, the tattered stuffed bunny she'd had since she was a baby.

Holding the gun out in front of him, Dustin could feel his heart pounding at his ribs, the impact seeming to rattle his entire body as he struggled to hold the gun steady. Approaching the door, he still couldn't see anyone on the other side. The parking lot directly beyond the door was empty as well. His car was parked out back. All he could think, as he took each step closer, was that someone was suddenly going to smash the glass with a hammer or a bat or even worse, a gun and let themselves in to do who knows what to him and his daughter in order to get to the abnormally large amount of cash currently stashed in the safe.

Determined to protect his daughter, he pulled back the gun's hammer, ready for whoever might appear as he took one last step to bring himself within arm's reach of the door. The glass remained intact and glancing side to side he couldn't see anyone in the area.

"What is it Daddy?," Abby nervously asked.

Turning to his daughter, he saw Abby now standing in the open, beyond the protection of the counter.

"Get back behind the counter," he lightly scolded as he waived her back.

Satisfied that his daughter was once again out of sight, his mind returned to the door, though this time his love of horror films joined in lending worry to his thoughts as he expected the previously clear door to now be filled with the large ominous figure of a man, or a creature or whatever the hell had made the loud noise. Tightening his grip on the gun, he reluctantly returned his gaze to the door, relieved to see the still empty pane of glass and deserted world beyond.

Still unsure what could have caused the noise, he began searching his mind for possible, logical explanations as the thought of a bird came to mind. It could have flown into the window, he thought as he stepped even closer to the door, intending to look down at the sidewalk outside. As he leaned toward the glass, the shadowy outline of a man lying on the sidewalk came into view.

"Daddy?" Abby called from behind the counter,

worried that she could no longer see her father.

"I'm okay sweetie," Dustin assured the scared girl as he continued to look out at the mysterious man. He didn't look big or all that intimidating, he thought. In fact, he looked hurt.

Only half of the lights outside were currently working, reminding him of the forgotten task he'd promised Mr. Levrett he'd take care of earlier in the day but as the man shifted on the ground, a nearby light illuminated his familiar face. "What the hell?" Dustin gasped as he unlocked and opened the door to reveal the obnoxious young man from earlier in the day. "Are you alright?"

Struggling to see through the severe swelling on the left side of his face, Derek stared up at the familiar clerk. "Help."

"I'll call an ambulance," Dustin started to stand.

"No," Derek stopped him, reaching up and grabbing his arm, either unaware of the gun in the clerk's hand or just not caring. "Here." With his other hand, he reached into his pocket and pulled out the scrap paper with Sarah's address and held it up for Dustin to see.

"What's this?" Dustin asked, plucking the paper from Derek's hand.

"Need a ride," Derek instructed.

"You need a doctor," Dustin suggested, trying to get to his feet again, though failing once more as the man's surprisingly strong grip held him fast. "I'll call you a cab then."

"No time."

Confused, Dustin looked at the paper again, noting the girl's name at the top and the '*See you there*' written at the bottom. "Listen, I'm sure she'll understand if you're late."

"No," Derek insisted with his voice while pleading with his un-swollen eye.

"Well, I'm not going to drive you. I've got my daughter and that's all the way in the city," he explained, immediately wishing that he'd left his daughter out of it.

"My wallet," Derek fumbled to reach his back pocket on which he was laying. Managing to wiggle it free he held it up to the confused store keeper. "Cash is yours."

Dustin just stared at the wallet for a moment, confused by the man's persistence before finally taking it from his hand and peering inside. Three fifty dollar bills followed by a hundred and a couple of twenties greeted him as he peeled open the leather pouch. Looking up from the wallet full of cash he was greeted by a subtle nod from the injured man. Contemplating the offer, he looked back at the wallet and then toward his daughter who'd stepped out from behind the counter once again and stood watching her father while continuing to pull at poor Mr. Pickles worn stitching. Abby's mother would be off her shift at the hospital soon and he knew he had to get her home but this was easy money. Looking back at the wallet and then at the man, Dustin decided. "1342 Belmont street is it?"

Derek nodded.

"Let me bring my car around," he spoke as Derek released his grip and Dustin got to his feet, making his way to the back of the store as he emptied the contents of the wallet, plastic and all, into his pocket.

*****

Ding dong.

Startled awake by the unexpected, late night bell, Sarah sat up in bed as the fog of sleep faded away and her alarm clock lit room slowly came into focus.

12:08, the clock read.

Ding dong, the bell repeated.

"Who the hell?" Sarah questioned, confused as she tossed back the covers and made her way to the bedroom door.

Apparently her roommate Reyna had had the same confused response to the late night bell as they both opened their bedroom doors simultaneously, issuing each other the same confused stares.

"Are you expecting anyone?" Sarah questioned.

"No. Are you?" Reyna issued her own inquiry.

"No," Sarah answered as she opened her door all the way and stepped out into the hall.

"You're not going to answer it, are you?" Reyna questioned. "You don't know who that is and I sure as hell don't know who it is. How do you know it ain't no rapist or creepy homeless guy wanting to saw off your feet and use them for bookends or something?"

"Yes, it's a well read, homeless scholar with a homicidal need to keep his books neatly arranged on his cardboard bookshelves," Sarah smiled.

"You just go ahead and laugh. We'll see who's laughing when you lose those pretty little feet of yours. I'm getting my pepper spray," she declared before disappearing back into her room.

Ding dong.

Reyna did have a point, Sarah thought as she made her way along the short hall, exiting into the main area of the modest, two bedroom apartment with the kitchen and small eating area on her right, living room on her left and the beckoning door straight ahead. The only reason the two of them could afford a decent place and still pay tuition was the somewhat questionable neighborhood in which they resided.

Approaching the door, Sarah leaned toward the peephole just as a noise startled her, causing her to turn and find Reyna standing at the end of the hall, pepper spray in one hand and butcher knife in the other.

"Where'd you get the knife?" she questioned.

"I keep it in my underwear drawer," Reyna responded as if that answer sounded completely normal.

Glancing over at the butcher block on the kitchen counter, Sarah noticed that the butcher knife was missing. "Is that?" she started to question as she looked at the knife and then back at the kitchen. "You keep that with your underwear? Gross."

"My drawers are clean. Answer the damn door."

Turning back to the door, Sarah leaned toward the peephole through which the guy from the restaurant earlier that day came into view, holding a white coat and swaying back and forth. "It's that guy I told you about," she whispered.

"The one with the coat?" Reyna spoke back, disregarding the need to keep her voice down.

"I think he's drunk."

"Well you tell his drunk ass that he's too late. You missed your class and aren't interested. Some of us have class in the morning and need our beauty sleep. I gotta get some rest too."

Acknowledging her roommate's typical, smart ass remark with a look of false offense, she returned her eye to the door as the man reached for the doorbell once again and in doing so, was illuminated by the light in the hall.

Ding dong.

"Jesus," Sarah exclaimed as she caught a glimpse of the man's cut and swollen face.

"What!?" Reyna jumped, lifting the pepper spray and knife into the air in front of her, ready to attack as Sarah began disengaging the locks. "I know you ain't letting him in."

Turning the last deadbolt, Sarah yanked open the door.

"Are you okay?" Derek addressed her excitedly, though seeming a bit disoriented as he appeared unable to maintain his balance.

"What?" Sarah responded, unsure of the reason behind the question. "What happened?" she shifted the focus to his condition.

"God damn!" Reyna exclaimed as she joined Sarah at the door, ready to blind and then stab the late night visitor but quickly lowered her weapons upon seeing that someone else had apparently beat her to the punch.

"Is he here?" Derek continued the odd questioning.

"Is who here?"

"So you're alone?"

"Yeah, it's just us," Sarah answered.

"Don't forget about my boyfriend Terrance," Reyna added her imaginary boyfriend.

"Good," Derek offered an impaired smile before succumbing to his injuries and passing out in Sarah's arms.

TWENTY-THREE

3:00 am

The alarm clock on the night stand beside him was the only source of distraction from the explosively violent sounds of regurgitation escaping from the master bathroom. For the third time in the last hour now, he'd been awakened by the violently discarded covers and the sounds of his wife frantically darting for the toilet. The first time he'd immediately followed her, confused and unsure of the problem before having the door slammed in his face and being told, between the sounds of the chunky liquid discharge, that she didn't want him to see her like that and that she was okay and he should go back to bed. He'd done as he was told and ten minutes later, with teeth freshly brushed, Tabitha had returned to bed.

The next round he'd known better than to follow, though he had still climbed out of bed just in case, like a typical woman, she'd changed her mind and now wanted him to witness the vile display. Again she'd slammed the door shut but not before issuing a don't move an inch glare through the dimly lit room. Again, he'd done what he was told and again, ten minutes later the room was filled with the scent of peppermint.

This time he didn't even bother to get up. He knew better. This time he'd simply pulled the covers back up and rolled over to face the bright red digits of the time keeper to his left. The sounds from the other room were equally as loud this time, however had taken on more of a dry, hacking quality. The shellfish, which had been rejected earlier, had obviously run out, leaving nothing but the thin bile at the pit of her stomach to make the sudden, northerly journey.

Typically possessing a strong stomach, he was surprised to find himself also starting to wretch with each dry heave, leading him to contemplate just what he'd do if he himself needed the services of the occupied, porcelain god. He very well couldn't just burst through the door and shove his sick wife to the side. One, he'd feel horrible afterwards and two, when she was done puking all over the floor, she'd probably kick his ass.

Scanning the room, he quickly eyed the large, potted ficus beside the dresser and decided that, if needed, he'd fertilize the tree. Lucky for the tree however, the wretch inducing sounds began to die down and he managed to regain control of his own regurgitative reflexes. The welcome lull, followed by the familiar sound of running water signaled the end of what would hopefully be his wife's final bout with dinner.

"Never again," Tabitha announced in a strained voice as she appeared in the bathroom doorway, turning off the light and making her way back to bed.

"Are you okay?" Richard questioned as he rolled over to face his returning wife.

"I don't know what's wrong with me. I get the Pescatore all the time," Tabitha moaned as she slid back under the covers, laying her head on her husband's shoulder while making it a point to keep her mouth and potentially offensive breath aimed safely away from him.

"Maybe Georgio's got a bad batch of mussels this

time."

"You didn't get sick."

"That's because this time I was cheap and only got the Fettuccine Alfredo," Richard pointed out as he rubbed his wife's back.

"You're always cheap," Tabitha rebutted, turning her head to flash a smile before regretting the movement and returning to the crook between his shoulder and chest.

"Eighteen dollars is too much for a mediocre, eight ounce steak and noodles," he offered up his usual complaint when the topic of Georgio's came up in conversation. It was Tabitha's favorite restaurant and for that fact alone he didn't mind going; however, it didn't mean that he was about to drop a pretty penny on something he could easily prepare at home. It killed him to pay even eleven dollars for a bowl of noodles and sauce but at least it was a cheaper option and the salad and breadsticks easily offset the inflated price. "I'd much rather have—," he continued.

"—a ribeye on the grill at home," Tabitha completed the more than familiar rant.

"Well I would," Richard pouted.

"Can we drop the food talk for a while?" Tabitha requested as her stomach let out an audible protests. "I have a particularly important meeting in the morning and it probably wouldn't go over well if I upchucked all over Mr. Branson during my pitch."

"What are you pitching? Because if it's an ad for Pepto, that might just work," Richard grinned, proud of himself.

"Stop grinning. It wasn't that funny," Tabitha guessed at the broad smile likely occupying her husband's face. "It's for some new cleaning product called Fabrix. If you ask me it's just some cheap Resolve or Woolite ripoff but it's a new client and we could definitely use some of those right now."

"Perfect. First you throw up on him, then you clean him up with his own product. Get it all on tape and you've pitched the idea and shot the commercial all at once," Richard's grin grew.

"Maybe it wasn't dinner but instead your horrible sense of humor that made me sick," Tabitha joked with her own broad smile.

"No, I'm pretty sure it was the rotten mussels."

And with that, the covers flew, the door slammed and he was once again left to stare at the trembling ficus.

TWENTY-FOUR

"Hey! Ya made it!," Tyler exclaimed as he answered the door to find Derek standing on the other side.

"Aw shit, they invited you?" Derek feigned disgust while turning to walk away.

"Ha ha. Very funny asshole. This *is* my house."

"Technically it's your parents' house and frankly, I'm surprised they still let a prick like you live here," Derek stopped his retreat.

"The old man keeps telling me next year, college or not, I'm out. Now get inside," Tyler backed out of the way as Derek stepped inside.

The house was filled with the same familiar faces that filled the halls of Cannon High every day, only now they seemed noticeably happier, having exchanged their burdensome books for Solo cups filled with liquid escape.

"I actually don't know what I'm going to do," Tyler continued as they made their way into the busy living room, the noise of the over occupied space causing him to add to the growing roar with each word he spoke. "I didn't apply yet so I'm probably screwed already but that's probably a good thing. I might just take a year off or take a few classes at the community college until I figure out what the fuck I'm gonna do with myself. Hey, you wanna drink?"

"Sure," Derek reluctantly accepted the offer, his plan of using the search for a drink to escape Tyler's typical rambling now ruined.

Scanning the room of bobbing heads, Tyler spotted an unattended red cup on a nearby table and quickly claiming it, handed it to Derek.

Derek just stared at the already half finished beer and the trace of red lipstick lingering on the cup's white rim.

"So, I guess you don't have that problem?"

"Huh," Derek asked, confused by the vague question.

"College I mean," Tyler clarified.

"Oh," Derek responded. He didn't like to talk about where he was going. Though he enjoyed a very social existence he didn't really like to talk much about himself, especially when it might be construed as bragging.

"So, M.I.T. huh?" Tyler pushed the subject.

"Yeah, it's not a big deal."

"Not a big deal?"

"Hey!" a girl's voice suddenly erupted from the crowd; likely the drink's rightful owner.

"I'm just going for electrical engineering. I'm not going to be a rocket scientist or astrophysicist or anything exciting like that. Besides, I barely got in," Derek continued his modesty.

"It doesn't matter how you got in, just that you got in," Tyler finished his sentence with a slight stammer in his voice.

"Clearly the drinking started early," Derek thought as he realized now that he was never going to escape.

"Isn't that Jason kid going to M.I.T. too?" Tyler asked, before downing the rest of his beer and tossing the empty cup into the crowd.

Derek watched as the red projectile sailed across the room, striking a red lipped girl in the forehead and drawing another familiar, "hey!".

"He's such a tool," Tyler laughed. "I don't know why you hang out with him."

"Jason's a good guy. Sure he's a bit uptight and nerdy but he's a good guy."

"A bit?! That guy's the king of the nerds. I mean the guy's going to M.I.T.."

Derek just stared at his obviously inebriated acquaintance.

"I need another drink," Tyler changed subjects, obviously unaware of his previous statement. "You want another?"

"No, I'm good," Derek raised his untouched drink with a grin, hoping that his friend's alcoholic quest might free him from his company long enough to disappear into the crowd.

"Saw you empty handed," Brendan Silva suddenly emerged from the crowd with two new drinks, one of which he handed to Tyler.

"Asshole," Derek thought as he greeted the new arrival with a smile.

"Hey, Derek," Brendan greeted his friend with a hard slap to the shoulder.

While Tyler was too chatty, Brendan was way too touchy feely. The guy couldn't have a conversation without some sort of physical contact at least every couple of minutes.

"Hey Brendan."

"You're just in time," Brendan attempted to whisper, though given the noise, was probably just talking in his normal tone.

"In time for what?" Derek asked.

"He's here?" Tyler asked, obviously excited by the undisclosed news.

"They're out back. Come on. We need to hurry," Brendan almost giggled as he turned and made his way through the crowd to the roped off stairs.

"You gotta come," Tyler, pulling a move from

Brendan's playbook, grabbed hold of Derek's arm and pulled him toward the stairs.

Confused but curious, Derek followed.

"This is going to be a amazing. Hurry up," Brendan urged them along as he ducked under the improvised rope made of duct tape and leapt up the stairs two at a time.

"What's going on?" Derek asked, still not sure what could be so exciting upstairs when the party was clearly a first floor only event.

Neither Tyler nor Brendan answered as they reached the top of the stairs, sprinted down the hall and disappeared into a nearby bedroom.

Making his way toward the very door which had swallowed his two friends, Derek hesitantly glanced into the room before slowly stepping inside. The room was empty, other than a well adorned queen bed accompanied by the standard bedroom furnishings. Another door at the far end of the room stood open, revealing a white, porcelain tile floor that was most likely an adjoining bathroom. Obviously the master bedroom, Derek thought to himself.

"Psst!"

Derek turned to see Tyler's head poking out from between the partially open bi-folding doors of the master closet.

"What are we doing?" Derek asked.

"Get in here," Tyler insisted.

"Hurry up," Brendan's voice joined from within the small space.

Pushing the doors apart, Derek stepped into the dark, walk-in closet to find at least six other people in there with Tyler and Brendan.

"What are we—?"

"—Shh!," an unknown kid to his right silenced him as voices could be heard making their way down the hall.

Turning to his left, in hopes of finding someone who might let him in on what was happening, Derek was greeted by the glaring gaze of the red lipped girl from downstairs as she alternated glances between him and the lipstick stained cup in his hand. He just grinned and shrugged as the voices grew louder and Jenna Bishop entered the room.

Undisputedly the beauty of Cannon High, Derek finally understood why the closet was now full of men and what he now assumed to be a lipstick lesbian.

"Come on. I won't bite," Jenna coaxed her suitor into the room with the seductive waive of her index finger.

Derek knew that waive. Though he'd never been so lucky as to be on the receiving end of one from Jenna Bishop, he'd had his fair share of pant tightening encounter. Though he knew hiding in the closet at that very moment was wrong, he couldn't help but continue to watch with excitement, curious as to who the lucky bastard on the other end of that finger might be.

Watching as Jenna strategically sat at the end of the bed, her legs ever so slightly parted as an invitation to the man who approached, Derek couldn't help but turn his attention toward the unseen doorway, eager to see who had been fortunate enough to land the breathtaking blonde.

Quickly glancing at the girl beside him, Derek rethought the lesbian stamp as he noticed her gaze was also fixed upon the doorway. "She must know who the lucky guy is," Derek thought but instantly began questioning his own curiosity. Did he really want to know. What if it was someone he was good friends with. Though secure in his sexuality, he knew himself well enough to know that he'd never be able to separate the guy's face from his manhood which would make for a very uncomfortable remainder of the school year.

"Come on," Jenna continued to encourage her apparently shy mate.

Derek found himself wanting to yell, "get your ass in here" and "what the hell's wrong with you?" but all of his encouraging thoughts fell silent as his best friend appeared between the slats.

"There you are," Jenna smiled a devilishly sexual grin as she reached out for Jason to come closer.

"No way," Derek whispered, drawing angry stares from his closet-mates. "How in the hell is this possible," he questioned, keeping his thoughts to himself this time. Jason was a decent looking guy and all, but Tyler was right, he was a bit of a nerd and definitely not part of the Jenna click.

Obviously nervous, Jason slowly shuffled his way closer, stopping just short of her outstretched fingertips.

Apparently not interested in waiting any longer, Jenna leaned forward, grabbed hold of Jason's sweater and pulled him between her now fully parted legs. As their bodies met, Jenna rolled back, pulling Jason with her onto the bed and placing their lips on a collision course.

Not wanting to take his eyes off of the unbelievable events taking place just beyond the door, Derek couldn't help but notice the mixed reactions of excited disbelief and complete disgust from his fellow voyeurs. He could sympathize with the disbelief. If a situation like this were to be bet on in Vegas it would likely receive million-to-one...no...billion-to-one odds. It wouldn't even be worth betting on because it just wouldn't happen.

Watching as Jenna continued her control of the encounter and rolled Jason onto his back so that she was now straddling the shocked but excited teen, it suddenly occurred to Derek, what if this is all just a prank? Obviously everyone else in the closet knew that this was going to happen. What if this was all some sort of setup? On the other hand, what if it wasn't? If this *was* all part of some elaborate joke, Jenna was definitely deserving of the oscar as she began shoving her tongue down Jason's throat. It was possible that someone caught wind of the possible encounter, Derek thought. And with how quickly word spreads it was definitely conceivable that a handful of moral-less individuals could sneak in ahead of the horny couple to get their jollies from within a closet while the young pair went at it on the bed.

Torn on what to do, either step in and prevent a devastatingly embarrassing moment for Jason or remain silent and not interfere with a potentially amazing experience for his closest friend, Derek continued to watch as Jenna worked her way up Jason's body until she was sitting on his chest looking down at him while she slowly unbuttoned her blouse.

He knew Jason lacked experience when it came to girls. If this *was* a real encounter it would likely end embarrassingly anyway, as the sight of Jenna's bra would surely be enough to trigger a premature reaction. Surprisingly though, Jason managed to hang on as Jenna slid the lacy pink blouse off of her shoulders to reveal the hot red bra underneath.

Tyler and Brendan silently high-fived each other and Derek began to feel more at ease that this, as unbelievable as it was, was a real thing.

"Do you mind if we try something?" Jenna asked her pinned companion.

In a position where "no" just wasn't an option, Jason simply nodded as Jenna leaned to the side, reaching for the top drawer of the nightstand beside the bed. Opening the drawer, she withdrew a pair of silky red scarves and Derek began to wonder just how kinky Tyler's parents might be and why Jenna knows where they keep their instruments of erotic play.

"I want to tie you up," Jenna told Jason as she dangled the scarves over his head.

Again, unwilling to say anything that might cause the best night of his life to end, Jason remained silent as Jenna began tying him to the headboard.

"Is that too tight?" she questioned as she cinched the first scarf around his wrist.

"No," Jason quietly mumbled as she began on his other

hand.

Once the second knot was secured, Jenna again slowly slid down Jason's body until she was again laying on top of him, her astounding cleavage mere inches from his face.

Jason's nerves were clearly visible as occasional tremors rattled down his legs.

"Don't be nervous," Jenna comforted him as she began kissing his neck, slowly working her way down his chest and over his stomach. Lifting his shirt out of the way, she lightly ran the tip of her tongue around his belly button before looking up at her bound companion's look of sheer ecstasy. The look of ecstasy was quickly replaced by shock however as his belt buckle came undone, followed by the button and then zipper. With the skill of a tenured porn star, within seconds, Jenna had Jason's pants down around his ankles, his sneakers preventing their complete removal. But she had no plans of stopping there and as she reached for his briefs, Jason flinched.

"It's okay," Jenna assured him in a creepily mothering tone. "I'm going to make you feel so good. You'll remember this forever."

With that exciting promise, Jason relaxed and his underwear joined his pants once again.

"Just one more thing," Jenna paused, again reaching for the top drawer of the nightstand.

From it she withdrew a large purple dildo.

Caught completely off guard, Derek just stared in shock at the large rubber member.

Jason shared the same shocked and terrified look. "What's that for?"

"Oh," Jenna laughed, realizing how the situation looked. "It's not for you."

"Good," Jason sighed as he laughed nervously.

"No. I want you to use it on me. I was just getting it out," she continued to laugh as she placed the rubber toy on Jason's chest. "I just have to go get ready for you," she added as she slid off the bed and started toward the bathroom. "I'll be right back. Don't go anywhere," she teased as she disappeared into the adjoining bathroom, closing the door behind her.

Still in shock over the large member now resting on his friend's chest, Derek quickly scanned the closet to get everyone else's reactions and for the first time noticed cameras in a few of their hands, including Tyler's. "Oh shit," he thought, but it was too late. Suddenly the closet doors burst open, its temporary residents pouring out into the room pointing and laughing at a horrified Jason as he struggled to free himself from the silk knots around his wrists.

Remaining in the closet, Derek watched as the bathroom door also swung open to reveal a, once again, fully dressed Jenna, also pointing and laughing at the now very public scene.

Jason thrashed back and forth, launching the purple penis from his chest.

"You dropped something!" Brendan laughed as Tyler snapped photos.

Continuing to fight his bonds, Jason finally managed to get his right hand loose and quickly untied his left as he struggled to return his pants and underwear to his waist before stumbling to his feet and running from the room in tears.

Feeling horrible for his friend, Derek pushed through the crowd of laughing idiots to pursue his embarrassed friend but stopped at the door to the sound of his name.

"Derek!" the voice shouted.

Derek turned to see that all of the closet dwellers were now gone. Even Jenna was no longer standing in the bathroom doorway, pointing and laughing.

"Deerreek," the voice playfully beckoned.

Confused, Derek slowly made his way back toward the closet to find that the bi-folding doors had once again been closed.

"Derek," his whispered name escaped from between

the slatted doors as he grabbed hold of the two knobs and flung the doors open to reveal an empty closet, its only inhabitants comprised of clothing and an abundance of women's shoes.

"Over here," the whisper now sounded as if it came from the bed.

Spinning in place, the bed was empty.

"Warmer," the voice taunted.

Staring at the bed, Derek's eyes wandered to the dark void beneath it. "Hello," he called but received no response. "Whoever you are, come out. This isn't funny."

A faint snicker came from under the bed as Derek began to go down to one knee but was quickly stopped as he caught a glimpse of Jason's face over his right shoulder.

"Derek, wake up!" Jason snapped as he plunged a needle into his neck.

Derek's eyes shot open as he sat up on the unfamiliar sofa and grabbed hold of his neck, searching for the again, unwelcomed syringe. He quickly forgot about the dreamt attack however as his eyes widened at the ghastly sight of Sarah, disemboweled and lying across the coffee table, gasping for her last breaths just as Jason slit her throat.

"Ahhh!" Derek screamed, startled awake by the vivid nightmare.

Moments later Sarah emerged from her room, stunned and frightened by Derek's sudden cry.

"What the hell's going on!" Reyna shouted as she emerged from *her* room brandishing the same knife and pepper spray.

"Are you alright?" Sarah questioned as she made her way to Derek, taking a seat beside him.

"I told you not to let him stay here," Reyna complained from the hall.

"He was hurt. Someone obviously drugged him," Sarah rebutted her roommate's protest as she placed one hand on Derek's forehead while using her other hand to check his pulse.

Derek remained upright, though the still lingering effects of the drugs appeared to lull him back into a groggy, slumbering state.

"He probably shot that shit up himself and got his ass kicked by some other junkies. I'm going back to bed. Let me know if he dies so we can get some sleep around here." With that Reyna returned to her room, locking the door behind her.

"It's okay," Sarah ran her hand from Derek's forehead to the opposite side of his neck and gently pulled him toward her lap as she placed a pillow on her leg.

Unknowingly accepting the guidance, Derek laid his head on the pillow and returned to sleep.

TWENTY-FIVE

"Get a ride to school *one* day and the bus driver forgets you exist," Katie laughed as her bus blew right by her, apparently spotting her at the last second as the squeal of brakes erupted a couple of houses down. In her defense though, Mrs. McGuly was at least eighty years old and judging from the handful of exciting rides over the last couple of years, she was likely partially deaf and blind as well. It was amazing that she was still allowed to drive the giant yellow torpedo.

Catching up to the bus, the door folded back to reveal tiny Mrs. McGuly perched on her oversized vinyl seat, the same pleasant smile that had greeted her since elementary school still beaming through the added wrinkles and false teeth.

"I'm sorry dear. I didn't see you there," the old lady laughed as Katie climbed the steps.

"That's okay. I could use the exercise anyway," Katie smiled.

"You are looking a bit doughy child."

"Did she just call me doughy?" Katie questioned, exchanging looks with a young girl in the front seat who also seemed shocked by the comment.

She hadn't shared the news of her pregnancy with the old woman and apparently no one else had either. Mrs. McGuly came from a different generation when you didn't even have sex until you were married, let alone have a child. The news might come as such a shock to the old woman as to cause a heart attack and land the bus full of teenagers in one of the deep ditches alongside the road.

"Yeah, I guess I should start running again," Katie played along with a smile before turning to find her seat.

"There you go," the old lady lightly punched her on the shoulder before stretching to reach the handle that closed the door.

"What was that all about?" Latisha asked as Katie took a seat beside her.

"She just called me fat."

"You want me to cap the bitch?" Latisha joked.

"How many times do I have to tell you? You live in Cannon. You aren't black," Katie laughed at her friend; one of the only African American members of the ninety-nine percent white, small town.

"Just 'cause I ain't gangsta you tellin' me I ain't black. That some bullshit," Latisha laid it on thick. "I can take out some eighty yea' ol' cracka."

Katie just laughed. Though she agreed with the stereotype that women don't often make good comedians, Latisha was definitely the exception. No one had a quicker wit and no one could make her laugh like she could.

"Alright, in all sincerity though. You aren't fat," Latisha did a complete one-eighty in both tone and mannerism.

Katie just laughed harder.

"What? I'm being serious."

Katie continued.

"Cracka, you be trippin' o' somethin'," she struggled to maintain her composure as she too began to laugh. "Seriously though, I thought your dad was going to drive you until your timer popped."

"He's all talk. You know his schedule. Besides, I insisted that I didn't want this..." motioning toward her stomach "...to change anything.

"Well girl, it's going to change things. It's going to change a whole lot of things. Your timing was right though. In another week we'll be out of school for the summer. You'll pop the kid out sometime in late July and have a whole month to get back in shape for round two."

"There will be no round two," Katie corrected the loose description of her future.

"You sure? I hear Jordan might be coming back next year."

"What?" all previous humor in her voice vanished at the news of the possible return of her baby's now sixteen year old father.

"That's what I hear. I guess having a child twenty-four-seven cramps the lifestyle of a single, divorced man. Not so useful in picking up chicks when they themselves are old enough to knock them up."

"What? He didn't—"

"No, no, no. That's not what I meant. I mean his dad apparently doesn't like having him around is all," Latisha clarified.

"Oh, well that kind of sucks for him. I feel bad."

"Don't feel bad. Don't feel anything. Look what happened the last time you felt anything for him."

"Well I kind of do anyway."

"What about Mark? What's the plan for him? He obviously has a thing for fat chicks. You gonna bang him?"

Shoving Latisha toward the window, "Mark is a really nice guy. I'm sure he hasn't even thought about that."

"Does he have a dick?"

Shocked by her friend's blunt humor.

"I'm just saying. He's thought about it."

"It's not like that. He asked me to prom and that's it. I'm not looking for any kind of relationship right now.

I've got enough to deal with without throwing that into the mix.

"I guess you're right. He is kind of cute though, you know, for a nerdy guy. He's probably already drawn you into one of those little comic thingies he does."

"I doubt he's drawing me in anything," she defended, starting to turn red.

"The boy bought you and your unborn child a dress to prom. You're right, he probably doesn't have time to draw 'cause he's too busy digging the well in his basement. Just say no if he tells you to put the lotion in the basket. I'm just saying."

"Mark's a nice guy. He's just shy. I know he comes across as a bit awkward and weird but he means well."

"You're gonna bang him."

"Whatever," Katie dismissed her friend's obviously obnoxious mood.

"You at least gotta jerk him off."

"Jesus," Katie gasped as she looked around at the surrounding eyes pretending not to stare.

"What?" Latisha shrugged. "The boy did buy you a dress after all."

Katie just smiled uncomfortably.

"Ah, ah. You won't fit here," Latisha stopped a new passenger from joining them. "Can't you see the bitch is big as a house."

Again, Katie shoved her friend against the window.

TWENTY-SIX

Slipping past the slatted guard, a beam of morning sun pounded at Derek's eyelids, demanding entry. Though he couldn't remember much at all of the previous night, he did recall a lot of spinning and the unpleasant desire to hurl. That combined with vague memories of a dream involving a psychotic Jason and something to do with Bethany and blood and the time machine, he preferred to keep his eyes shut but sensing that he wasn't currently lying in his bed, he slowly parted his lids.

Much like his room, the white, popcorn style ceiling overhead greeted him to the new day and he began to feel better.

"There you are."

"Jesus," Derek shot up as a headache made its presence known.

"Whoa, whoa. It's okay."

Staring at the girl for a moment, trying to regain his focus, "Sarah?"

"Yes."

"What? Where? I...," Derek struggled to figure out what was going on just as the details of the previous night began to return. It wasn't a dream. It was all real; the blood, Jason, the machine, Bethany...oh Jesus Bethany, he lowered his head into his hands.

"I think you took something. You were pretty messed up."

"I didn't take it," Derek mumbled through his palms.

"Did someone do this to you?"

Derek just nodded.

"Who?"

"What happened? How could he...? Why?" Derek mumbled his thoughts as more memories slowly returned. He remembered something about Jason's grandmother and his family. Something about Jason committing suicide or not. It was all still fuzzy. He did remember a dream about the party and the dildo and hiding in the closet and waking up to find Sarah dead on the coffee table. Needing to confirm that she truly was sitting beside him, he slowly parted his fingers and turned toward her.

"Hi," Sarah greeted him confused.

"I told you you should have left him outside," Reyna uttered an "I told you so" from the kitchen table before shoveling another spoonful of cheerios into her mouth.

"Who the hell is that?" Derek dropped his hands from his face to locate the second mystery voice.

"That's my roommate, Reyna."

Reyna issued a half hearted wave.

"She wanted to pepper spray and stab you last night," Sarah joked.

"Still do," Reyna replied.

"Don't mind her. How do you feel?"

"My head's killing me," Derek grabbed his head again.

"That's just the drugs wearing off. I'd give you some aspirin but I don't want to add to whatever concoction you already have flowing around in there."

"That's alright. I've had enough drugs for one night."

"Junkie," Reyna muttered before taking another bite.

"R," Sarah scolded.

"No, its alright. I know how it looks, but I didn't do

this."

"Who did? It wasn't that guy from the restaurant yesterday, was it?" Sarah almost laughed at the ridiculous thought.

Derek just nodded.

"Oh. Why?"

"You wouldn't believe me if I told you," Derek almost laughed himself at the insane details of the previous night as he slowly got to his feet.

"You should sit," Sarah protested.

"I'm okay. You should be safe now."

"Safe?"

Derek froze trying to come up with an explanation.

"I mean...I should be fine now."

"When you showed up last night you kept asking if I was safe and if he was here. Did you mean him? Why would he come here?" Sarah grew concerned as did Reyna, reaching for the knife which she'd laid on the table beside the bowl.

"No. You're fine. I was just messed up is all. That shit did a real number on me. I must have been nearby, and in my altered state, looking for a familiar face is all."

"But how did you know where I lived?"

"Google," Derek nonchalantly replied.

"What's...Google," Sarah asked confused.

"It's a...it's a...phone book. At the pay-phone the cover said Google or something. Anyway, everything should be fine by now so I should get going," Derek insisted as he unsteadily made his way toward the door.

"By now?" Sarah continued the questions.

"Will you let him leave already," Reyna snapped from the table.

"I really am sorry to disturb you like this," Derek apologized as he struggled with the door."

Reaching in, Sarah unlatched the door and pulled it open.

"Thanks," Derek smiled.

"Oh, wait," Sarah quickly turned, running to the kitchen to retrieve the lab coat and his wallet. "These are yours."

"That's yours," Derek insisted, pointed at the coat. "And that...?" he pointed at the wallet.

"You were holding the coat in one hand and your wallet in the other when you showed up last night. I hope you don't mind that I looked inside. I was looking for a phone number of someone that I could contact for you. I think you were robbed."

Taking the wallet from Sarah's hand, he flipped it open to reveal that everything had been removed. They'd taken all of his cash, his IDs, his credit cards. They'd even stolen his old library card to the town library back in Cannon.

"You might want to cancel your credit cards before they use them," Sarah suggested with a sympathetic grin.

"I'd like to see their face when they try," Derek smiled, knowing that, technically, the cards hadn't even been issued yet.

Sarah just appeared more confused.

Holding the wallet up, "Thank you. For everything. Really."

"You should really sit—"

"—Sarah," Reyna interjected.

"It's alright. I appreciate it. Really."

Sarah just smiled.

"And thank you for not stabbing me," Derek peeked around Sarah to see Reyna.

"Don't forget about the pepper spray," Sarah whispered.

"And for not blinding me," Derek added.

"Don't mention it," Reyna nodded.

"Thanks again."

And with that Derek left, closing the door behind him.

"Are you crazy?" Reyna whined as Sarah joined her at the table. "That boy had serial killer written all over him."

"No. He seemed nice," Sarah disagreed, looking down

at the white coat in her hand.

"Nice, huh," Reyna raised a brow.

"What?" Sarah smiled.

"Well if he comes back, I'm gonna go Freddy Kruger on his ass."

TWENTY-SEVEN

Descending the short brick stairs to the sidewalk in front of Sarah's apartment, Derek paused, looking up and down the street at the familiar, yet oddly different scenery. Obviously the drugs had done a real number on his system last night since he hadn't really put together where he was. While the street itself was unfamiliar, the area wasn't. His dorm was actually only a couple of blocks to the north or at least it would be in about eighteen years and while familiar, everything seemed just a little bit off. While the eighties were still struggling to make a comeback in 2014, the opposite seemed true in 1991. Now they appeared to be struggling just to hold on as a darker, more drab sense of style seemed to be working its way into the closets of the busy residents making their way up and down the sidewalks.

Testing a theory, "Nirvana rules!" Derek blurted to a passing twenty something dressed in a ratty old, Mr. Rogers style sweater.

"Hell yeah," the kid responded enthusiastically as he threw his hand into the air for a passing high five.

Maybe this wouldn't be so bad after all, Derek considered. Though he'd spent his teen years in the mish-mosh of styles and trends that was the early two-thousands, he'd always had a special fondness for the nineties. Probably the result of growing up in a house where his mother was always playing Pearl Jam, Stone Temple Pilots, and of course, Nirvana. His young mind couldn't help but absorb those depressingly, angst filled musical poems. Continuing to look around, it was amazing that *anyone* made it out of this decade without blowing their brains out.

Realizing that Sarah and her potentially homicidal roommate could be watching him from the windows above, Derek stepped away from the stairs and started down the street. He didn't know where he was going. Where could he go? Jason had stranded him and taken the machine back to the future with him. His only hope was that Jason might have a change of heart and come back for him but with the limited twelve hour window already come and gone, his continued presence in this time was evidence enough that Jason wasn't coming back.

Checking for traffic, Derek jogged across the street and into a small park.

He could rebuild the machine he thought, quickly realizing how futile that effort would be. It wasn't the machine that was special. All that work. All those hundreds of hours building and testing and problem solving and for what? He'd basically built a twenty pound spark plug in a briefcase. Without Jason's blood, there was no hope of ever returning home. He couldn't go home to his parents. Hell, he wasn't even due to be born for another six months. If he showed up on his parents' doorstep claiming to be their stranded son from the future, one of two things would happen; his pregnant mother would either laugh him off the front steps or miscarry, bringing a definitive end to his dismal situation.

Taking a seat on one of the wooden benches, which lined a long winding jogging path, Derek just leaned back in defeat and turned his gaze skyward. Not overly religious, though not without faith either, he figured the only hope he had left was with the man upstairs, but since his soul was being occupied by an unborn fetus in this time he wondered if God would even be able to hear his prayers.

"What are we looking at?"

Startled, Derek returned his gaze earthward to find Sarah standing in front of him, staring up at the same patch of cloudless morning sky.

"First you show up at my restaurant and then my apartment and now I find you sitting on my bench," she met his eyes with a smile.

"Are you following me?"

"I should ask the same thing. You mind," she motioned to the bench.

Hesitantly, he slid over as she took a seat beside him.

"What are you doing here?" Derek rephrased the question.

"I told you, this is my bench."

Derek just stared at her.

"Okay, yes I'm following you. I didn't even bother to get fully dressed for fear you'd get too far away," she glanced down at her fuzzy blue pajama pants covered in tiny bananas.

"Why?"

"Let's just say that curiosity is sort of a problem for me. I don't like leaving things unresolved. I like closure and right now you're a big open ended mystery to me. Yesterday you showed up at the restaurant, delaying me and claiming that you could get me a new lab coat in time for my next class, which I missed by the way."

"Sorry."

"Then you show up at my door, beat to hell and completely wasted, asking me if *I'm* alright and if your obnoxious friend is there before passing out and mumbling in your sleep not to call the cops," she continued. "Then, this morning you wake up and rush out of my apartment but not before implying that I was somehow in danger but for some reason am now completely safe. If you ask me, I would be completely insane *not* to be curious."

Derek didn't know how to respond to the admittedly odd string of events. The truth wouldn't bring her the closure she sought. It would only add more questions. Staring into her awaiting gaze he did the only thing he could think of...deflect. "Aren't you worried that I'm some sort of mass murderer or something?"

"Are you?"

"Well, no but—"

"—Then that's good enough for me," she happily accepted.

Puzzled, Derek just stared.

"Listen, if I thought you were going to kill me I wouldn't have let you into the apartment last night. I don't take you as the murdering type."

Derek just continued to stare.

"And if I'm wrong, I still think I'm safe because, in your unconscious stupor last night, you sought me out for help which means you probably look at me as more of a friend than a potential victim."

"We don't even know each other. How could we be friends already?"

"Something also tells me that you're the type who makes everyone your friend...especially the ladies."

"Jesus," he thought. Did he have player written across his forehead? "I don't think your roommate shares the same opinion."

"Reyna? Don't mind her. She's just a little paranoid is all. She doesn't mean anything by it."

"Could've fooled me," Derek smirked.

"If she truly thought you were any danger, she never would have let me bring you inside."

"Isn't she worried that you're out here with me now?"

"Don't get me wrong, she's probably hiding in one of

the bushes as we speak, ready to jump out and gut you at any moment," Sarah laughed.

Derek didn't share Sarah's dark humor, as the image of her disemboweled body, sprawled across the coffee table, returned to mind.

Realizing that her words had had an obviously negative effect on him, Sarah canned the smile. "So, how about that closure," she placed the conversation back on track.

"Huh?"

"Let's keep it simple by sticking to the truth," Sarah's playful tone faded as it became obvious that she truly did want and believed she deserved some sort of truthful explanation.

Contemplating what might come from revealing the truth about his presence in her time, Derek recalled one of Jason's rants about changing the past and jeopardizing the future, though this time it admittedly didn't hold much relevance as his permanent present in this time had already severely compromised the time that followed. "What harm could there really be in letting one other person know the truth at this point?" he thought.

Focusing his attention and meeting Sarah's serious gaze with one of his own, "The truth?"

"Nothing but," Sarah leaned slightly closer in anticipation of his explanation.

"Okay...well..."

Raising her eyebrows, as if telling him to quit stalling, she waited.

"I'm from the future," he blurted the simplest of explanations, awaiting the anticipated laughter. Instead, she continued to stare at him as if what he'd just said was completely normal and expected. "Okay," he responded, puzzled by the lack of response. "Jason and I invented a time machine powered by what I thought was some sort of red, chemical concoction worked up by Jason but it turned out to be nothing more than his blood, which somehow has the ability to transport whoever's in contact with it, through space and time. Well, when a friend and I discovered that it was blood, Jason flipped out, killed my friend, tried to frame me for her murder and then stranded me in the year 1991...this year...with no hope of ever returning to my time, which is the year 2014," Derek finished his explanation with a much needed breath as he awaited Sarah's response.

Wrinkling her forehead, it was clear that she was trying to process the insanity that she'd just heard.

"I know how it sounds," Derek defended his story, realizing himself, for the first time, just how insane the whole situation sounded.

Slowly, Sarah's forehead smoothed and new wrinkles began to form around her mouth as the previously expected laughter finally arrived.

"There it is," Derek thought.

"Time travel, huh?" She laughed.

Derek just nodded seriously.

"I knew you were an interesting guy," Sarah continued her jovial response. "You seemed so smooth yet so frantic yesterday outside the restaurant. I wasn't sure how to respond at the time but after you left I realized that you'd somehow managed to make all that stress that I'd been feeling at the time, just melt away."

Now Derek wore a look of confusion. What should have been a story that landed him in the looney bin was actually turning out to be his best pickup line ever.

"You know, I waited over an hour for you to return? I don't know why but I was actually disappointed when you didn't." Jumping to her feet, she stood in front of him. "Tell you what. You're going to make it up to me tonight by taking me out to dinner and telling me who you really are."

Caught completely off guard by the flood of unexpected information, the only word he could muster was, "Okaaay".

"Good. It's a date then," Sarah turned, heading back

toward her apartment building. "Oh," she turned, continuing to walk backwards. "Try to lay off the drugs this time," she shouted before turning and disappearing from sight.

Sensing another pair of eyes on him, Derek turned to spot an old lady walking her pug through the park. Both her and the googly eyed fur ball seemed to issue disapproving stares.

The only response Derek had, was a baffled shrug.

TWENTY-EIGHT

"You don't look so good," Melody commented on her partner's pale complexion as she walked into the conference room.

"Thanks," Tabitha replied, knowing what she meant but still not appreciating it being pointed out.

"No, I mean—"

"—It's alright," Tabitha cut her off. "I know what I look like. I spent half the night on the bathroom floor," she explained as she took her seat beside the perky, healthy girl.

"Why didn't you stay home?"

"We can't afford to lose this client," Tabitha whispered, wishing to maintain the illusion of success that her and Melody had recently been forced to invent. In actuality, their company was hemorrhaging money.

As college friends, they'd spent countless nights in the dorms, imagining and strategizing how they would one day open their own firm in Boston and take the marketing world by storm. They imagined having all of the biggest clients like Nike and Coke; clients with money to burn on needless marketing campaigns for products that sold themselves.

After college they'd gone their separate ways, each taking jobs at large marketing firms around the country. Melody had spent a few years in Chicago and then San Francisco before coming back to Boston to work for Hirsh & Walice. Tabitha had followed a similar path, first in LA and then New York before also ending up at H&W, that is until it was discovered that Wilbur Hirsh and Herbert Walice were apparently heavily involved in insider trading. Within a matter of months the company's client pool had dried up and a couple months later, H&W closed its doors, leaving three-thousand employees high and dry.

Tabitha had had an offer to return to her old firm in New York and she was sure that she'd be able to find a spot for Melody there as well, but they both loved Boston. It was home and with husbands, and Melody with a two year old son, the idea of bouncing around the country just didn't seem fun anymore. So, each with a bit of savings and a hefty bank loan, they decided to make their once college fantasy a reality and opened Harmony Marketing, Inc..

The first six months had been amazing. With the sea of stranded clients created by the implosion of H&W and their familiarity with those company's needs, they were bringing in contracts left and right. The sudden success had led them on a hiring boom, bringing in many of the unemployed office staff they'd worked with previously. The office was filled with familiar faces and they'd made it a point to make the work environment a fun and relaxed place, with frequent after hours parties and a relaxed dress code when client meetings weren't scheduled. Unfortunately, the sight of jeans started becoming more and more common as meetings became fewer and fewer and once thought to be loyal customers, started migrating toward larger firms with more resources and proven track records. The excitement of the new guys in town had quickly worn off and reality began to set in.

As far as the staff was concerned, business was

booming. Both women did everything they could to create phony work in order to maintain the illusion of success, hoping that the next big break was just around the corner. Neither of them wanted to deal with the reality that they just couldn't afford to maintain the company at its current size without a steady client base to support it. Though they'd learned how to run a business in college and seen it in practice in the real world, it was quickly becoming apparent that neither of them had the stomach to deal with the harsh reality that was corporate America. So, out of sheer desperation, Tabitha had dragged herself into the office for a meeting with their last hope...Mr. Samuel Branson.

Son of Charles Branson, owner of one of the country's largest cleaning supply companies, Samuel Branson was looking to make a name for himself, separate from his father's multi-billion dollar empire and his first attempt was with a fabric cleaner he called Fabrix. They'd met with Mr. Branson and his associates a couple of weeks earlier to discuss his needs and things had initially looked very promising; that is until three days ago when Mr. Branson's office had called to inform them that they'd chosen to utilize another firm's services. Hearing this, Melody had instantly gone into crisis mode, dumping the contents of her desk into whatever empty boxes she could find around the office.

After a good cry in the ladies room, Tabitha had taken another approach. Crying and giving up wasn't going to do any good, and in a surprising moment of sheer will, she'd picked up the phone, insisted on speaking to Mr. Branson himself and somehow had convinced him to at least come in and listen to the ideas they'd been working on for him. Now they just hoped that the slides in the projector and proposals in the packets placed in front of each chair around the table were good enough to change his mind.

"Mrs. Tillmore," Tabitha's assistant appeared in the

conference room doorway.

Lifting her head out of her hands, Tabitha responded with a sickly gaze.

"Mr. Branson is here. He's on his way up now."

"Thanks, Joan," Melody answered for her partner. "You stay here," she addressed Tabitha, rubbing her back as she stood. "I'll go meet them."

"No, *I* convinced him to come. He's expecting to see me," Tabitha insisted as she got to her feet, suddenly aware of the floor's unsteady nature beneath her.

"No. You need to sit," Melody urged, seeing her partner's shakiness.

Tabitha just swatted at Melody's hand as she focused and steadied the moving building. "See. Everything's fine," she insisted before making her way out into the hall where she spotted Mr. Branson and his three associates stepping out of the elevator. "Mr. Branson, Sir.," she mustered all the strength she had to quickly make her way to the arriving entourage, and put on the most upbeat, healthy face she could manage.

"Mrs. Tillmore," Mr. Branson nodded, extending his hand to offer a firm shake.

She took a firm handshake as a good sign. It meant that he viewed her as a peer in the business world and not just a silly little girl trying to play CEO, like many of the men she often dealt with thought of her.

"I was surprised to receive your call. I know I told you that we were going with another firm, but I want you to know that it took real balls to get me on the phone and say what you had to say."

"Okay, maybe he views me too much like one of the guys," she thought to herself, also trying to recall what exactly she'd said on the phone. In reality she'd been so terrified that the entire phone call had been one big blur. The only information she remembered was the hello in the beginning and the date and time they'd agreed on for the meeting.

"Well, my partner and I are very confident that you and your associates will be more than impressed by what we have to show you."

"Let's hope so."

Nerves doing battle with her stomach's already acrobatic flips, Tabitha fought back the returning urge to vomit and directed the men toward the conference room. Entering the room, Melody looked as sick as Tabitha felt, as she circled the table to greet each of the men as they entered the room.

"Good afternoon gentlemen," Melody greeted the men, realizing instantly that it was only nine o'clock in the morning. "Mr. Branson, It's a pleasure to see you again."

Mr. Branson just offered a half grin.

"Please, take a seat gentlemen," Tabitha took over, aware of Melody's increasing nerves.

As instructed, the men each took a seat around the table with Mr. Branson at the center.

"So, as each of you know," Melody nervously began her pitch before the room had even settled from the noises of shifting chairs and rustling papers. "Harmony Marketing is a different type of marketing firm. We believe that in order to—"

"—Listen sweetheart," Mr. Branson interjected, the sexist remark seeming more suited for a crotchety old business man in his sixties rather than the thirty something who'd actually used it. "Miss Tillmore got us here, so no offense, but I'd like to hear the pitch from her."

Stunned by the rude and forward request, Melody just stood starring at the primped and polished business man.

"Of course," Tabitha jumped in, assuring Melody that she had it and waving for her to take her seat, which she did. "Well, as my associate was saying, Harmony Market—"

"—Let's just cut through the bullshit and get to the point. I know who you are and you know who I am. What do you have for me?"

Tabitha could feel the sweat pooling on her forehead, thankfully concealed by her overgrown bangs. "Thank God I didn't get my haircut like I'd planned," her mind took a momentary detour as her nerves grew.

"Okay. The plan," she reset herself, abandoning the rehearsed speech for a more direct and informal approach. How many of you remember the fifties?" the question came out before she realized how stupid it was given that only one member of Mr. Branson's team was old enough to have been alive during the decade and even then he was likely only a few years old.

All remaining color drained from both women's faces.

"That's a dumb question," Tabitha attempted to recover. "Why would you? But we all have an image of that decade in our heads, don't we?"

Okay, that's better, Melody felt a little better about where this was going.

"It was a simpler time. A less stressful time. Let's be honest, it was a time when men could be men because the women in their lives could be women."

Mr. Branson seemed puzzled, yet interested.

"Households weren't in turmoil because of the need for two working parents just to make ends meet. Let's face it, life today is insane, between getting the kids off to school in the morning and then spending a minimum eight hour day at the office before rushing home to get each child to a different athletic practice all the while trying to figure out how you're going to get some form of nutritious dinner down everyone's throats before going to bed, just so you can get up and do it all over again in the morning. It's nuts and who's the one that really suffers in this insanity we now call life?"

The room was filled with blank stares.

"Our homes," Tabitha answered her own question. "We live in complete and utter chaos and the state of our homes reflects it. That's why it's our belief that you need to make your customers feel like that time of simple domestic harmony is possible again with your product." Holding up one of the packets, Tabitha flipped open to an image of a Donna Reed type house wife happily cleaning her house. "We've put together a plan to attack all three fronts, television, print and digital. While every other company out there is fighting for a piece of the chaos, we believe that we can market to the simpler, more traditional side of your customers and in turn, create a brand for your company that could easily incorporate any and all future product," Tabitha finished with a smile, for the moment glad to find that the persistent nausea had passed.

Mr. Branson just stared at the two women, silently taking in what he'd just heard before offering a response. "Do you know what I think when I see that picture?" he started. "Women's suffrage."

Tabitha's sickness returned.

"I see a poor, beaten down woman with no self worth beyond that which is obtained by maintaining a clean house for her oppressive and likely abusive husband."

"Who'd have guessed that Mr. Branson was so into women's lib," Tabitha thought as she eyed Melody, who was staring out through the conference room's glass walls in search of more empty boxes.

"I don't want to speak for my colleagues here, but this image doesn't remind me of a simpler, happier time. It reminds me of an insensitive, careless moment in our history when only a middle class, white, American male had a chance at success, and frankly, that's not our core demographic, so if this is all you have, I'm sorry, but I'm going to have to pass," Mr. Branson rejected the pitch as he got to his feet.

Panicked and unsure about what they were going to do, not just in that moment with Mr. Branson, but in the coming months when the reality of the company's situation would finally have to be addressed and the people out there in the office would finally have to be told that, once again, they would be without work, Tabitha's face turned an even paler shade of white.

"Tab?" Melody noticed the sudden shift in her partner's complexion and demeanor as Mr. Branson and his associates began to head for the door.

Again the building seemed to dance beneath her feet as Tabitha tried to think of something that could salvage the disastrous moment, but instead her words were replace by another wave of nausea. Remembering what her husband had said the night before about throwing up on the client, she fought back the urge, but not before a wave of unconsciousness washed over her, causing her to fall forward and strike her head on the edge of the conference table.

TWENTY-NINE

"Katie," Mark whispered from the desk behind and diagonally to Katie's left.

Busy taking notes, Katie didn't notice his call.

"Katie," Mark whispered again, continuing to eye Mr. Burns who was currently distracted with the sample problem he was scribbling across the chalkboard.

"Hey," the girl directly to Katie's left whispered as she poked at Katie's shoulder then pointed over her own shoulder in Mark's direction.

"Thanks," Mark whispered in appreciation as Katie finally turned.

The helpful girl just nodded as she returned her attention to the lesson.

"What's going on?" Katie whispered, at the same time also keeping an eye on Mr. Burns.

With the senior class already out, the junior prom just a couple of days away and the end of the remaining students' school year just a week off, most of the teachers had already given up on teaching anything new, but not Mr. Burns. At the age of sixty three, he was still of the old school philosophy that, every day should be a day filled with learning. The new social norm of teaching to the test was unlikely to sink in at this point.

"I'm sorry," Mark continued the hushed exchange.

"For what?"

"For the dress."

"I love the dress."

"For being creepy I mean," Mark tried to explain in as few words as possible.

Apparently the word 'creepy' drew the helpful girl's attention as Katie saw her lift her head and turn her eyes upward as if she were listening to a conversation being had on the ceiling.

"Are you digging a well?" Katie asked with a smile.

"What?"

"Eh, hem," Mr. Burns drew their attention to the front of the class.

Katie and Mark instantly fell silent, offering their teacher an 'I'm sorry' bow of the eyes. After a moment, Mr. Burns returned his attention to the board and to the lesson he'd been teaching.

"Katie," Mark continued in an even quieter whisper.

Afraid of getting in trouble, Katie reluctantly turned again, this time holding up a clean page from her notebook on which she'd written, *write it.*

"Oh," Mark smiled as he flipped to a new page in his notebook and began writing, then cleared his throat to let her know that he was done.

Turning Katie read his message.

Like I was saying. I didn't mean to come across as creepy yesterday. And what well?

She turned back to her notebook to write a response before holding it up over her shoulder for him to read.

It was a bit forward but it was also sweet. You're not creepy. The one in your basement that you're going to lock me in.

She turned to see his expression. He looked confused. She added to the message.

Never mind. I love the dress and I can't wait to go with you on Friday.

Looking over her shoulder again this message drew a smile as he returned to his notebook.

Well I'm glad. I can't wait either. And it's in the shed.

What?

The pit is under the shed. I'm soundproofing it tonight.

Looking over her shoulder again, her smile was matched by his.

"Mr. Fossy. Miss Bishop," Mr. Burns broke away from his lesson again to scold the silently chatty couple.

Mark and Katie instantly dropped their notebooks.

"Even though school is over in a week, the same rules still apply. There's no passing of notes in class."

"Technically they weren't passing them," Nick corrected from the back row.

"Thank you, Mr. Peterson," Mr. Burns growled at the helpful student.

"You're welcome," Nick replied, thinking he'd actually been of assistance.

The class chuckled.

"Sorry Mr. Burns," Katie was the first to apologize.

"Me too," Mark quickly followed suit as Mr. Burns reluctantly returned to his lesson.

Looking over her shoulder, Katie shot Mark a playfully angry glare.

Mark just grinned sheepishly before mouthing, "Sorry."

THIRTY

"How are we feeling, Mrs. Tillmore?"

Managing to partially open her eyes, a tall, thin figure slowly came into focus, then quickly faded out again as Tabitha elected to re-close them. "Where am I?" she mumbled, trying to lift her arm.

"Whoa, I wouldn't do that," the man instructed as he placed his hand on her arm, encouraging it back down. "We've got you wired up pretty good and I wouldn't want you pulling out your I.V.."

"What?"

"You're in the emergency room, Mrs. Tillmore. You took a pretty good blow to the head. You may have a concussion. Just lie still and relax."

"Richard."

"Is that your husband?" the doctor questioned.

Tabitha nodded.

"I'm sure he's on his way. He should be here soon."

"My head," she moaned, noticing the throbbing pain for the first time.

"Like I said you had a pretty good fall. Hit your head on a table I hear. You should see the table," he joked, getting no response.

"Mr. Branson," Tabitha opened her eyes again, trying to sit up before the doctor once again encouraged her to lay back down.

"You really need to stay still, Mrs. Tillmore. We're going to take good care of you. You just need to relax."

As instructed, she again laid down and closed her eyes.

"Is Mr. Branson someone from your office?" the doctor continued the conversation, testing her mind as he also checked her wrist for her pulse.

"No, a client," she responded. "Important."

"Well I'm sure Mr. Branson will understand what happened and we'll have you back to work in no time," he assured her. "Now you just stay here and relax. I'm going to see if your husband is here yet, okay?" he added as he slipped through the curtain and disappeared.

Tabitha just nodded, unaware that the doctor had left.

"There you are," Melody spoke in a panic as she peeked through the curtain to find her friend lying on the bed.

"Melody?"

"Yes, it's me," Melody answered as she dropped her purse on the chair beside the bed and grabbed hold of Tabitha's hand. "They wouldn't let me in the ambulance. I got here as quick as I could. What did the doctor say?"

Parting her eyes, she attempted to bring Melody into focus. "Melody," she spoke with a smile as if just now realizing who she was talking to.

"Yes, it's me. What did the doctors say?" she asked again, worried by her partner's incoherent state.

"I'm fine. Nothing to worry about," Tabitha grinned.

"You're a tough one," Melody nervously laughed. "You wouldn't believe the amount of blood in the conference room."

"Mr. Branson," Tabitha appeared to come through a bit more as her eyes widened and Melody's face became clear.

"You did it," Melody smiled.

"What?"

"You did it. We got the Fabrix account," Melody

almost let out an excited squeal.

"How?" Tabitha asked, more confused now than she had been when they'd wheeled her into the hospital.

"The blood."

All Tabitha could offer was a look of painful confusion.

"You busted your head open pretty good on the table and got blood all over the carpet. Mr. Branson and his associates quickly rushed to help you and I...well...I didn't know what to do. I guess I sort of panicked. You know I'm not good in a crisis and cleaning comforts me so..."

Tabitha continued her look of confusion.

"...so I grabbed the bottle of Fabrix from the table and started to clean up the blood. Sorry," she offered Tabitha an apologetic grin for making it seem like the carpet was more important than her friend.

Tabitha just smiled, indicating that no offense was taken.

"Anyway, Mr. Branson saw how well his product was cleaning up the mess...that stuff really works by the way. The carpet looks almost new."

"Melody," Tabitha put her wondering partner back on point.

"Yeah, sorry. Anyway, when he saw me cleaning up the mess, he suddenly blurted out 'crime scene!' I had no idea what he was talking about. There was no crime involved. Then he went on and on about an ad campaign centered around spoofing shows like 'Twin Peaks' and 'Murder, She Wrote' and how, if the criminals had just used Fabrix, they'd have never gotten caught."

It was an oddly morbid campaign for a guy who'd just scolded her on the oppression of women and domestic violence but who was she to argue?

"He wants us to start putting together ideas immediately. Isn't that great?!" Melody's excitement finally got the best of her as she vocalized her excitement for the whole E.R. to hear.

"Well there seems to be an awful lot of excitement

coming from in here," a voice spoke as a white haired doctor parted the curtain and joined them in the enclosed space.

"I'm sorry," Melody replied embarrassed.

"No, don't be. We could use more of that around here," he laughed as he looked over Tabitha's chart. "So it says here you hit your head."

"Yeah, the other doctor said I might have a concussion."

"What other doctor?" the doctor questioned confused.

"The one that was just in here a few minutes ago," Tabitha pointed to the curtain.

The elderly doctor looked at Melody.

"I just got here," Melody responded.

"Well aside from the paramedics and nurses, I'm the first one to look at you," the doctor chuckled as he looked at the chart again.

"No, there was another doctor. An Asian guy. Young," Tabitha insisted.

The doctor looked up from the chart again with a worried look. "Well as far as I know, we don't have any young, Asian doctors in this E.R.. I would know. I do the hiring," he smiled. "Now let me get a look at that cut," he changed the subject as he moved toward her.

"Honey," Richard appeared in the curtain. "Are you alright?"

"I'm fine," Tabitha smiled.

"Are you the husband?"

"Yes," Richard addressed the doctor before turning back to his wife. "Your office called and said there'd been some sort of accident; that you'd fainted and hit your head or something."

"I'm alright," Tabitha smiled as Melody moved over so Richard could take her spot beside his wife. "The doctor says I could have a concussion."

"I never said that," the doctor corrected.

"The other doctor," she corrected.

"There is no other doctor," the current doctor insisted.

"What's going on here?" Richard asked, joining the confusion.

"Your wife hit her head Mr...," looking at the chart, "...Tillmore. There seems to be some understandable confusion going around," the doctor chuckled.

"Anyway, I'm fine," Tabitha smiled.

"She could have a concussion," the doctor interjected.

All three of them shot the old man a look.

"The good news is that I think I know what caused you to faint," the doctor added.

"I already know that. Stress," Tabitha replied.

"Well, only if that's what you're going to name it," the doctor smiled.

"What is this crazy old man talking about?" Tabitha wondered.

"Name what?" Richard verbalize what Tabitha and Melody were thinking.

"Mrs. Tillmore, you're pregnant."

"What?" Tabitha responded more in shock than joy.

Richard on the other hand lit up as worry instantly turned to delight at the news.

"Oh my god! Tab! That's so great! Congratulations!" Melody again addressed the entire E.R..

Tabitha couldn't share in the excitement however as panic once again started to come over her. She didn't have time to be pregnant right now. The company was collapsing and they'd just landed the client that could bring them back from the brink. She was going to have to work extra hard to ensure that they didn't fail and she just didn't see how being pregnant and having a baby was going to fit into all of that.

"I take it this wasn't planned," the doctor uncomfortably responded to Tabitha's worried stare.

"Are you sure?" she looked up at the white haired man.

"I can have them run the test again to confirm, but it says it right here. In about eight months you're going to be paying us another visit."

"Honey, this is great. I love you so much," Richard leaned in to hug and kiss her.

"I'll be in the waiting room," Melody, sensing the awkwardness of the situation, announced her departure. "Congratulations," she added much more timidly this time.

Not sure what to say, Tabitha looked down at her outstretched feet. Resting on the blanket, at the end of the bed, was a small folded piece of paper. "What's that?"

Stopping in her tracks, Melody turned around, following her friend's gaze to the small paper. Picking it up she handed it to Tabitha.

"Did you put this there?" Tabitha asked as she took it from Melody.

"No," Melody replied.

Silently, she glanced at her husband and the doctor. Both shook their heads no as well.

Confused, she opened the folded paper to reveal a single, handwritten sentence.

Do you like roller coasters?

Showing the note to her husband, he looked equally as confused.

"Damn it," the doctor interrupted their confused pondering as he touched Tabitha's bare wrist.

"What?" Tabitha asked.

"Oh, nothing. They just forgot to put an I.D. bracelet on you when you got here. No big deal but we wouldn't want to misplace you," he laughed. "I'll be right back," the doctor excused himself, followed by Melody.

Pushing his wife's hand and the paper out of the way, Richard took a seat beside her on the bed. "I know what you're thinking but it's all going to be alright," he attempted to comfort her. "It's not like we haven't talked about having kids."

"I know, but now isn't a good time with work and all-"

"—Listen, there's always going to be a reason to delay it. I think this is a good thing. Now the decision's out of our hands and we can move forward with our new family. I love you so much and I need you to trust me when I say that everything's going to be just fine. I promise."

Tabitha smiled. Richard always did have a way of making her feel better. He was the love of her life, and if he said that everything would be fine, she had no reason to doubt him.

"I love you too," She smiled as she pulled him close and tears of joy finally began flowing.

THIRTY-ONE

"How did I know you'd still be here," Sarah smirked as she rounded the corner, bringing Derek and the same park bench she'd left him on that morning, into view.

"Probably because you somewhat believe my story. I mean, where else am I going to go?" Derek swiveled his head back and forth.

"Ooor," Sarah pondered as she stopped in front of him, "you're a homeless crack fiend like Reyna suspects."

"Crack is whack," Derek responded with a grin.

Though she offered a polite smile, she had no clue what he meant by the random statement.

"That's right, she hasn't said that yet," Derek spoke aloud, though more to himself.

"Who?"

"Whitney Houston," Derek answered noticing her continued confusion. "Whitney Houston is around in 1991 right?"

"Yeah. I love her music. She has the most amazing voice. She's going to be in a movie next year...with Kevin Costner I think.

"The Bodyguard," Derek added.

"You heard about it too?" Sarah asked, clearly excited

about the cinematic event.

"I've seen it," Derek replied.

"Oh, there you go with the future thing again," she laughed. "Well I bet she's still a big deal in your time. That's a timeless voice. I bet she's still pumping out hits; her and Michael Jackson."

"What I could tell you," Derek mumbled.

"What?"

"Nothing. So, what are you doing here?" Derek questioned.

"Our date. Don't you remember?" Sarah asked.

"I wasn't entirely sure you'd been serious. I'm a mess. I have no car nor do I have any money. I can't say with any confidence that I'm the dating type at the moment."

"Well, I'd sort of expected you to go home, wash up and maybe hit the bank before picking me up."

Derek just stared at her, his eyes hinting at the pending explanation.

"...but you couldn't do all of that because you don't have a home in this time, nor do you have a car and won't open your first bank account for at least fifteen to sixteen years?" Sarah guessed.

Derek just shot her a "you got it" grin.

"You're really committed to this whole future thing aren't you?" she asked, for the first time a bit uneasy about his persistence. "You're not an actor or something, are you? You know, one of those actors who immerses themselves so much in their role that they never break character, even in their real lives?"

"No, I'm not an actor," Derek smiled. "I'm not that focused."

"Writer? You're not researching a book and trying to get into your character's mind are you?"

"I'm not that creative."

"So you're going to stick with the stranded time traveler story, huh?"

"The truth shall set you free, or in my case, strand me

with no hope of return," he grinned uncomfortably.

"Okay, well, I guess you have a lot to talk about during the game then," she played along with what she couldn't decide was either a persistent game or mental illness.

"What game?"

"Red Sox. First base line. Row sixteen. Seats three and four," she playfully pulled a pair of tickets from her pocket, fanning them out for Derek to see.

"No, I couldn't. Those must have cost you a fortune," Derek tried to hide his excitement.

"Yes, you could and no, they cost my *dad* a fortune. He and a bunch of guys from work went in on season tickets this year. But given his work schedule, among other family issues…" she showed contempt toward whatever she was referring to, "…he can't make it to all of his games, so lucky me," she smiled.

"How do you even know that I like baseball, let alone the Red Sox?" Derek struggled to get out the words, as if his mouth were reluctant to utter such a ridiculous question. He loved baseball, and growing up his whole life in New England, how could he not love the Red Sox? Such blasphemy was against the law or at least it should be; punishable by exile to New York.

"Given that your eyes almost doubled in size at the sight of the tickets…call it an educated guess," Sarah smiled. "Now come on, the game starts in about thirty minutes and its a fifteen minute walk from here," she turned, waving for him to follow.

With nothing better to do and nowhere else to go, Derek didn't have to think twice. A beautiful girl holding tickets to a game, insisting that he join her, what was there to think about?

*****

"Sosa, you suck!" Sarah yelled, drawing applause from the surrounding fans.

Derek didn't know what to say. Though never one to participate, he was accustomed to fan heckling, just never before from a woman. He was admittedly in awe and a bit turned on as he watched Sarah complete her rant as Sammy rounded first base on his way to second from a hard hit line drive to the wall.

With the White Sox player safely on second and the clamor of the crowd dying back down to a steady roar, Sarah turned, the intensity in her face melting away as she noticed Derek's shocked stare. Bowing her head, "Sorry. I get a little worked up sometimes."

"No. Don't be sorry. I think it's kind of hot, actually."

"Before my dad had tickets he used to get them from his job, so we'd get to go at least a couple of times a year. You think *I'm* bad, you should hear him. He almost got us thrown out one time."

"Well, he'd be glad to hear that you're continuing such a fine family tradition. What about your mother? Is she a rabid fan too?"

"My mother died a few years back."

"Oh, I'm sorry," Derek issued the standard response as he contemplated whether to continue with the subject or gloss completely over it in search of a more upbeat topic.

"It's okay. It was a long time coming. I mean," she stumbled over herself realizing how that sounded. "She was sick for a real long time and I didn't handle it very well."

Derek could see the pain behind Sarah's eyes as she attempted to conceal the tears beginning to lend a glossy quality to the large hazel orbs.

"Well he seems to have done a good enough job with you. I mean, aside from the aggressive hostility and fondness for drugged up strangers at your doorstep. I'd give him an A-...well...maybe a B+," Derek smirked as a tear glistened fist landed on his left shoulder.

"Look who's talking. I'd like to meet the parents of the man who stumbled to my door coked up and rambling about time travel. Do you have to visit them in the looney bin between certain hours or can you just drop in any time?" Sarah responded with her own snide smirk, her attention from the depressing topic successfully diverted.

Raising his hands, "Hey, hey, hey. Just hold it right there. One, it wasn't coke...I don't think...and two, I make sure to visit them at least twice a week. I'm a good son."

Sarah smiled as the crack of the bat instantly pulled her attention back to the field and onto the more important matter at hand...the game. "Come on!"

The crowd boomed as Sosa rounded third on his way for home. Fielding the ball off the wall, Greenwell reared back and released a rocket toward home. Barrelling toward Peña at the plate, Sosa dove forward, arms outstretched for the safety of the plate just as the ball struck the catcher's mitt with a snap.

"No!" Sarah cried as she began leading the crowd in a series of boos while the safe Sosa jumped to his feet and celebrated his way back to the dugout. "Do they win?" Sarah asked between boos.

"What?"

"The Sox. Do they pull it out?"

"Which ones," Derek looked at the similarly named teams.

"What do you mean which one's?" Sarah seemed agitated, though Derek knew it was just the fan talking and that she wasn't actually upset with him.

"How should I know?"

Frustration still lingering in her eyes, she turned, "You claim to be from the future, so tell me, do they beat these Windy City bastards?"

"I don't know. I haven't bothered to commit every game in history to memory."

"Then what good are you?" she joked through her frustration.

Searching his brain for anything to offer, "wait, 1991, this is the year Clemens wins the Cy Young!"

The anger evaporating from her face, replaced by excitement, "Oh yeah? He's my father's favorite player. So the Sox must do good this year. Do they break the curse?"

He wasn't sure if her excitement was a sign that she was starting to believe his story or just a frustrated fan grasping for any hope of one day seeing a World Series title come back to Boston. "No," he reluctantly delivered the bad news. "They fall apart late in the season. I think the Twins take it this year."

"The Twins? Now I know you're making this up. Who do they face, the Braves?" she laughed.

"Actually..."

"No," she stared at him shocked, before letting the smile push its way back to her pretty face. "You know, I don't know if you actually believe this time thing or not. You seem so put together, mentally at least," she gave his disheveled appearance a once over.

"Thanks?" He didn't know how to take the comment.

"I mean, I know how crazy the whole thing sounds and how impossible it is, but you seem so convinced," she stared into his eyes as if searching his soul for the truth.

A bit uncomfortable by the penetrating stare and spotting a Coke vender making his way up the other side of the section, he quickly raised his hand to get the young kid's attention before remembering his lack of cash.

Looking at Derek's face and then turning to see the soda kid making his way toward their row, Sarah knew exactly what he was thinking.

"That's okay. I've got it," she insisted, pulling money from her pocket.

"No, really. I forgot that I—"

"—No, it's no big deal. I'm actually kind of thirsty too," she held two fingers in the air as she handed the money to the guy beside her, who handed it to the girl beside him and so on until it made its way into the vendor's hands who traded it for two bottles.

"I'll pay you back," Derek insisted.

"Tell you what, prove to me that you are from, wherever you claim to be from, and we'll call it even."

"It would just be easier to pay you back," Derek sighed as the two bottles arrived in their neighbor's hands, who passed them along with a odd stare.

At first Derek didn't know what the man was staring at until he looked at Sarah's bottle and saw the odd paper ring loosely draped around its neck. Reaching over, Derek plucked the paper from the bottle.

Mass General Hospital

"Is that a—?"

"—Hospital ID," Derek answered before she could even get the question out.

Looking back down the line of people in their row, "But from who," she asked confused.

Tabitha Tillmore

"Tillmore, Tillmore," Derek repeated the name, trying to figure out where he'd heard it before.

"Who?" Sarah, still in the dark, simply wanted to know what was happening.

"Tillmore," Derek dug deep into his memory just as the name resurfaced. "Becky," he mumbled.

"Who's Becky?"

"Holy shit!" Derek exclaimed, drowned out by the crowd as Wade Boggs brought the crowd to their feet with a monstrous hit over the Green Monster.

Also jumping to his feet, Derek began frantically scanning the crowd.

With no idea what was going on, Sarah remained in her seat, staring up at her date's ghostly complexion.

"It's impossible. There's no way. There only a twelve hour window," Derek muttered as he scanned each face around them, only stopping when he realized Sarah's grasp on his shirt, insisting that he rejoin her in their seats.

"What's going on?"

He didn't know what to say. It was one thing to tell her that he was from the future. She didn't believe it and it had proved to be an odd, but light hearted way of breaking the ice. How could he tell her that he now believed his friend, the same one that he'd claimed had killed a girl the night before and then stranded him twenty-three years in the past, had somehow figured out a way to expand the window in which he could travel and was very likely with them at this very moment in the stadium? Fun crazy was one thing. Actual crazy was a completely different story.

"We have to get out of here," Derek insisted, trying to get to his feet but failing as Sarah again grabbed hold of his shirt and returned him to his seat.

"What's going on?" she insisted.

Staring into her eyes he knew she wouldn't settle for anything less than the truth, but at the same time he feared that having too much knowledge about Jason and what he suspected was going on, would only put her in danger. He already felt sick at the thought that his continued interaction with her had already put her life at risk, so looking into her eyes with intense sincerity, all he could muster was, "we have to go to the hospital."

THIRTY-TWO

"Daddy! The video stopped again!" Abby cried from the back room.

"$2.65 is your change," Dustin addressed the man on the opposite side of the counter as he handed him his change and slid his bag closer.

With a nod the man smiled, took his purchase and headed for the door.

"Daddy!"

"I'm coming sweetheart!" he responded to the impatient child as he made his way to the back room. "Now, what's wrong?"

"Elmo. He's stuck," Abby pointed at the frozen image on the screen.

"Again," Dustin huffed playfully. "That Elmo. I don't know what we're going to do with him," he smiled, as he approached the T.V., and kneeling beside it, began talking to the choppy, still image. "Hey, Elmo. What are you doing? You're killing me here."

"No daddy. You have to push the buttons," Abby laughed, pointing at the VCR on the shelf above the T.V.."

"What button? This one?" he joked, hitting the power button on the television.

"No!" the little girl giggled. "That one."

"Oh." Dustin stood up, pushed the play button on the VCR, then looked down at the television again.

"Daddy," Abby mixed laughter with a hint of frustration.

"What?" he smiled coyly.

"You have to turn the T.V. back on."

"Oh yeah. Silly me," Dustin playfully smacked his forehead as he again knelt down to turn on the T.V., bringing back the still frozen image.

"It's still broke."

"You know. I think you've worn Elmo out," Dustin turned to his daughter. It wasn't a surprise. This video was her favorite. She watched it at home with her mother constantly, and whenever she came over to his apartment, she was always sure to bring it with her. So of course she'd insisted on bringing it to the store with her for the second night in a row. "How about something else?"

"No, I want to watch Elmo," Abby whined.

"But I don't think—"

Just as he was about to explain to her that the tape might not work anymore, Elmo decided that break time was over and began dancing and singing again to the five year old's delight.

"Yay!" Abby celebrated as she bounced up and down and clapped at the return of her old friend.

Smiling, Dustin knelt down beside his daughter, staring at her as she excitedly watched the same show she'd seen literally hundreds of times. "I'm sorry you have to be here again tonight," he interrupted, though couldn't be sure that he'd actually been heard since Abby didn't offer a response. Mommy should be here very soon."

Abby just continued to watch the show.

"Do you think Elmo has red boogers too?" Dustin tested to see if his daughter was listening.

Again no response.

"I bet you he does. And when he sneezes big red

furry boogers fly everywhere."

Sill no response.

"I love you," he uttered as he stood and turned to head back to the store.

"I love you too," Abby responded, still refusing to take her eyes off the screen. "And that's gross."

Little butt-head, Dustin thought as the bell to the store's front door greeted another customer.

"I've got to go back to work sweetie," Dustin informed his daughter, but again, got no response. Shaking his head, he exited the back room and returned to the store, looking for the customer who'd just entered.

At first glance the store appeared empty. There were many isles and a lot of large displays which could easily conceal someone's presence though, so thinking nothing of it, he returned to his spot behind the counter and returned to the newspaper he'd been reading prior to helping the last customer.

Approximately twelve minutes after takeoff, Austrian Airlines Boeing 767-300 vanished from radar. Shortly after, reports of an explosion started coming in.

"There was a fireball in the sky and then a big boom," a Thai police officer described what he'd witnessed.

There were 223 passengers and crew aboard the flight at the time of the accident, all of which are presumed dead. The pilot, Thomas Welch was an American living in Vienna at the time and...

Pausing in his reading, Dustin glanced up, curious as to the whereabouts of the mystery shopper. Even if concealed by a display, he could usually locate a lone shopper by the clinking of glass as they picked through the abundance of bottles on the busy shelves, but since the bell had declared their presence, he hadn't heard a single sound. Shrugging he returned to the paper.

Bored with the typical stories of crime and death that the media seemed to love to print, he flipped to the sports section.

In a display of dominant superiority, the Pittsburgh Penguins trounced the Minnesota North Stars 8 - 0 to claim the Stanley Cup title in a lopsided 4 - 2 series.

Crash!

The sound of breaking glass yanked Dustin's attention away from the paper. "Son of a...," he huffed under his breath as he folded the paper back up and returned it to the shelf below the counter. "Don't touch it! Let me get a mop!" he yelled out to the clumsy shopper as he rounded the counter and returned to the back room where his daughter was now out of her chair and dancing along to the little red Muppet on the screen. "Having fun sweetie?" he greeted his daughter, who again either didn't hear him or chose not to answer. Grabbing the handle of the mop, he pulled the rolling bucket from the corner and returned to the store.

"Are you okay?" Dustin addressed the customer as he wheeled the cleaning supplies to the back of the store where he was sure he'd find a little old lady or embarrassed young woman standing over the shattered spirits.

As he was growing accustom to that night, he got no response.

"What do we got here?" he asked as he rounded a large display of Grey Goose vodka, expecting the clumsy customer to be there waiting, but instead, all he was greeted by was a broken bottle, sitting in a puddle of vodka. "Hello!" he shouted as he looked around the store, but again got no response.

"They must still be here," he thought as he left the mop in the bucket, carefully leaning the handle against a nearby shelf. The bell on the door hadn't rang again, so there was no way that they could have left. Wandering down the back isle, looking down each isle as he passed, he wouldn't have been surprised to find a kid cowering against a shelf, caught in the act while trying to steal the bottle of alcohol. It wouldn't have been the first time, but as Dustin rounded the last display, the last, empty isle came into view. Confused, he stood there for a moment, wondering where the mysterious shopper could have gone before turning around and making his way back toward the bucket, checking each isle for a second time as he passed. Still no one.

"Where the hell...?" the words faded as Abby returned to mind. Quickly he turned and made his way toward the muffled, musical number emanating from the back room. The last thing he wanted to find was some strange man in there with his little girl and given that he couldn't find the shopper anywhere else his heart began to race.

Rounding the doorway, the dancing little girl came back into view. She was alone. "Abby."

No response.

"Abigail!" Dustin raised his voice, startling the little girl and bringing an end to her dance as she spun around to the sight of her nervous and obviously stressed father. "Have you seen anybody?"

Confused, Abby looked around the room.

"Was anyone just in here with you?" Dustin clarified.

"Just you Daddy," Abby smiled as she returned to her video.

Completely confused as to how the mischievous shopper had managed to not only slip by him, but also allude the noisy bell above the door, Dustin turned to make his way back to the mess and in doing so, ran right into Abigail's mother.

"Fuck!" he exclaimed, jumping back.

Startled as well, Britney White also took a step back. "Nice language," she greeted her ex husband with her usual disdain.

"Mommy! Mommy!" Abby turned at the commotion, running toward her mother with her arms wide.

"Abby monster," Britney knelt down, dismissing

Dustin in exchange for a hug from her daughter. "I missed you."

"I missed you too mommy. How was work?"

"Work was good. How about you? You look hard at work."

"You know," Abby shrugged in her typical precocious manner, drawing a smile from her mother.

"Did you break the bottle of vodka?" Dustin interrupted the mother daughter reunion.

"What?" Britney turned, the look of disgust instantly returning.

"The vodka...at the back of the store. Did you break it?"

"I don't know what you're talking about. I just got here," she stared at him like he was crazy.

"Well someone was just in here and they broke a bottle at the back of the store," he explained defensively.

"Then get a mop and clean it up."

"I did. I mean, I was, but I couldn't find who broke it."

"Well maybe they left," Britney offered up the most logical explanation, tacking on a 'duh' with her facial expression.

"They couldn't have left, I didn't hear the...wait a minute. How'd you get in here?" Dustin asked confused.

Offering the same expression, "The door."

"But the bell," he raised an eyebrow as he moved past her and through the door to find that the bell, hanging above the front door to the store, had been removed.

"Son of a bitch," Dustin huffed at the missing bell.

"You ready to go pumpkin," Britney ignored her delusional ex as she made her way over to the VCR, bringing an end to the alphabet song.

"Yup," Abby responded, grabbing the pink, stuffed dog that she'd sat down next to the T.V..

"You've still got Saturday, right?" Britney paused beside a still baffled Dustin.

"What?"

"Saturday. You can still take your daughter that night, right? Damn it Dustin. You know that Charlie and I have a dinner to go to and—"

"—Yeah, yeah. I've got her. Not a problem," he cut her off before she could go into one of her typical, berating rants. "I wouldn't want you and *Charlie* to miss your precious dinner."

"I'll drop her off around five if that's okay with you," she chose to ignore his disdain for her boyfriend of nearly two years as she made her way back to the front door. "Come-on Abby."

"Bye kiddo," Dustin knelt down to give his daughter a hug.

"Bye Daddy. Love you."

"I love you too. I'll see you on Saturday. We can get pizza."

"And watch Elmo," Abby added.

Reluctantly, "And watch Elmo," Dustin resisted the urge to moan in agony.

"It's a date then," the little girl assertively nodded before running after her mother and out of the store.

Even though he and his ex didn't get along, he couldn't help but be grateful for the amazing little girl she'd given him.

Making his way to the back of the store, he grabbed the mop from the bucket and began pushing the larger bits of glass to the side while soaking up as much of the vodka as possible.

"Why the hell would they steal the bell?" Dustin contemplated the disappearance of the simplistic alarm system. "And how didn't I notice them taking it?"

"Eh hem."

Startled by the sudden sound of someone clearing their throat to his back, Dustin turned just in time to catch a glimpse of a grey goose in flight.

THIRTY-THREE

"Are you going to tell me what we're doing here?" Sarah demanded the explanation she'd been seeking ever since Derek had forced her to leave the game and catch a cab over to Mass General Hospital. Approaching the doors to the E.R., she'd finally decided that she'd had enough of his question dodging. Stopping in her tracks, she grabbed hold of his arm and brought him to a halt as well.

"What are you doing? We don't have time for this," Derek protested.

"Time. Ever since you showed up it's been all about time. You know what I don't have time for? Bullshit."

Derek was a bit taken aback by the sudden departure of the playful, carefree girl he'd just gotten to know. Now he sort of knew how Jason must have felt when she'd used the same scolding tone on him back at the restaurant.

"I want some answers, Derek, if that really is your name. Who are you? What are you doing here, really?"

"My name really is Derek and I already told you—"

"—Yeah the future thing. That was cute at first but I'm not eight. Time travel isn't possible, so what are you really doing here?

Deciding to leave the time travel portion out of it, he figured that she might at least go for what he suspected Jason was up to. "Alright. You see this?" he withdrew the hospital I.D. tag from his pocket. "This belongs to a patient by the name of Tillmore, Tabitha Tillmore."

As if that name was supposed to mean something to her.

"I think Jason put this on the bottle back at the game."

"Jason? Your crazy, homicidal friend from the future, Jason?" Sarah tried to figure out where this explanation was going and just how long she should listen before walking away.

"I think he's figured out a way to bend time beyond what we'd originally thought possible."

"The time thing again," Sarah turned to begin waving down another taxi.

"Yes," Derek grabbed her shoulder, spinning her back around to face him.

Surprised, she wore an expression of shock with a hint of fear.

"I'm sorry," he apologized. "I know how it sounds but you have to believe me. It's true. When we used the machine the first time we had very specific points in time that we could travel to. You see, the earth has to be aligned in exactly the same location as the time from which you're traveling. We had the ability to bend the trajectory of the jump a bit, but no more than twelve hours."

"That's the twelve hours you were mumbling about last night. That's why you said I was safe and that's why you thought you were stuck here," Sarah finally seemed to be catching on to what he was saying.

"Yes, but I don't think that's true anymore. Jason must have figured out a way to expand the window."

"In one day," Sarah was trying to comprehend the insanity that was coming from Derek's mouth.

"One day for us but it could have been weeks, months, hell, years for him. All that matters is that I think he did it and now I think he's come back."

"For this Tillmore chick."

"Yes...no...I mean, for her daughter."

"Her daughter? How do you know she has a daughter?"

"Because, in about fifteen years Jason is going to go out with her and she's going to ditch him at the amusement park."

Now she *knew* he was making this whole thing up. "Really? He's so unstable that he's going to come all the way back in time for the mother of a girl who ditched him in high school?"

"I know it sounds crazy—"

"—No, we're way past crazy," Sarah turned again to flag down a ride.

"It is crazy. There's a very dark side to Jason that I didn't even know existed until last night. I think you saw a hint of it in the restaurant the other day. That wasn't the Jason I knew who said those things to you."

"I thought you pressured him to be more outgoing."

"Yes, but you have to admit, there's outgoing and then there's offering sex for food...to put it politely," Derek softened Jason's words.

"Why, now?" Sarah moved closer to the curb, still searching for a cab as Derek followed.

"Well, I suspect that he hasn't figured out how to bend the trip enough to go after the actual girl yet."

"Yeah, but why not just hunt her down in his...your time? Why come all the way back here?"

"Because I'm here," Derek realized just how sick this situation was. Jason wasn't just back here for the girl. He was back for him as well. He obviously wanted him to know what he was up to, but why? Was he going to try and frame him for another murder or was this some sort of sick cat and mouse game that he was trying to get going. All he did know was that he had to get to Mrs. Tillmore and warn her before Jason could go through with whatever he had planned.

"Taxi!" Sarah shouted at a passing cab, snapping Derek out of his introspective trance.

"We don't have time for this. We have to get inside. According to this..." he held up the bracelet again, "...Mrs. Tillmore was checked in earlier today. We at least have to go in and see if she's still here."

"No. I don't have to go anywhere. Listen, you seem like a real nice guy...you might be a bit unhinged...but a nice guy nonetheless. I just don't have time for stories of time travel and psychotic best friends and revenge on the mother of a scorned lover," Sarah clarified to herself just how crazy this whole thing was as a cab finally pulled to the curb beside them. "You go ahead and alert Mrs. Tillmore, but let me warn you...," she added as she opened the door and took a seat in the back of the cab, "...if you go in there and tell her even half of what you've told me, you're going to end up in the psych ward instead of that E.R.." And with that final warning, the cab pulled away with Sarah in it.

Standing on the curb, watching the cab as it turned the corner and disappeared from view, Derek contemplated Sarah's advice. She was right. No one was going to believe him and he probably was going to end up in some psychiatric hospital, but he had helped to create the device that had brought about these events and it was his responsibility to do everything in his power to stop Jason, no matter what.

His determination rejuvenated, he sprinted for the E.R. doors.

*****

"I can't be pregnant and you can stop doing that. I'm knocked up, not crippled," Tabitha complained, freeing herself of her husband's over coddling grasp. Ever since they'd left the hospital he'd been carefully guiding her around with one hand on her arm and the other on the small of her back as if he expected her to collapse again at any moment.

Richard released his grip and ceased his escort as his wife entered the master bath alone, closing the door behind her. He wasn't offended by her harsh tone or short temper. She'd been through a lot already and the news of an unexpected pregnancy was something she'd have to get used to. He, on the other hand, was doing everything he could to contain his excitement.

"Can I get you anything?" he called through the door, his question going unanswered as his words were cut off by the sound of water coming from the bathtub faucet.

"I mean, how are we going to make this work!?" Tabitha continued to vocalize her nerves, shouting over the running water.

"We'll make it work."

"I know we'll make it work. We always make things work. This just isn't how I planned it. I don't have time to take care of a baby *and* run a failing company."

"Melody can pick up the slack for you."

"Melody is a brilliant Creative Director but she's no salesman. You can have the greatest idea in the world but it doesn't do any good if there's no one to sell it."

Leaning against the doorjamb, "I'm sure she'd do fine. Besides, you just landed that big deal today," he reminded her.

"*One* deal."

"Well it's one more than you had yesterday. You're going to be fine. The company is going to be fine and we are going to be fine," Richard leaned closer to the door as the water stopped.

She didn't answer.

"If we have to we..." Realizing that he was still yelling, even though he no longer had to compete with the roar of the running faucet, he turned the knob and slowly cracked the door. His wife's head came into view in the large mirror over the sink, though the rest of her body remained concealed by the porcelain walls of the oval, garden tub nestled in the corner. "If we have to..." he continued in a softer tone to announce his presence, "...we'll hire a nanny."

Pulling the washcloth from her eyes, she slowly tilted her head to the side to face her husband, who was now standing in the middle of the room, looking down at her. "And how are we going to afford that? We can barely afford this house right now."

"Well...you're not the only one who got a bit of news today," he hinted at the news he'd been keeping since he'd received the call from Melody that Tabitha was in the hospital.

Tabitha just stared.

"You know how I told you about that big job in Texas that my company was bidding on?" He took her continued interest as a "yes". "Well...we got it and they asked me to be the lead engineer on the project."

The worried frown, which had plagued Tabitha's face since the doctor had uttered those two life changing words, finally began to melt as a smile fought it way through. "That's great! Why didn't you tell me earlier?"

"The whole hospital thing and then the baby news. The timing didn't seem right."

"That's amazing," the frown began to return.

"What's wrong?" Richard watched as his wife's brief happiness slowly faded away.

"I'm sorry."

"For what?" he asked, taking a seat on the edge of the tub and placing a hand on her head, careful to avoid the large, stapled gash just above her forehead and partially concealed beneath her hairline.

"For being such a bitch."

"What?"

"You've had that news all day. It's probably been killing you to hold it in and all I've been doing is going on and on about how screwed we are and woe is me."

"I was wondering if it would ever end," he smiled.

"Ass," Tabitha's smile returned as she playfully swatted a spray of water in his direction.

Laughing, "It does mean a bit more travel but it also means a fairly significant raise," he continued.

"How much travel?" Tabitha questioned, concerned that she was now going to be left to raise a baby on her own.

"One week a month, tops," he assured.

Okay with that number, "how much more money?"

"Ten percent and this puts me one step closer to making associate with the firm and only five to ten years from partner."

She could tell that he was excited by the news. Ambition was what she'd always found most attractive about Richard. He was a go getter, incapable of failure, which is why, deep down, even though she truly was worried about being a mother, she really did believe that everything was going to be alright. "Congratulations, Mr. Tillmore," she smiled, looking into his eyes.

"Why thank you Mrs. Tillmore," he smiled back as he leaned in for a kiss. "Is there possibly room in there for another?" he scanned he tub, eyeing his wife's naked body beneath the ripples of steaming water.

"I don't know. There's two of us in here already. It's getting kind of crowded."

"Maybe I can join you and we can try for twins." ·

"I'm pretty sure it doesn't work like that," Tabitha grinned.

"But it could be fun to try," he smiled as he slid over the edge and splashed down beside her.

*****

Staggering through the E.R. doors holding his left arm, his original plan had been to fake a heart attack in hopes that such a serious ailment would allow him to bypass the cuts and broken arms and miscellaneous ailments filling the busy waiting room. As soon as he'd set foot on the white tile floor however, he'd instantly changed his mind, and, fearing drawing too much attention to himself, he'd quickly ducked into the sea of patient filled, blue plastic chairs.

His original plan, while likely to bypass the line, was also likely to land him in a hospital bed, hooked up to every machine available and surrounded by doctors and nurses, eager to correct his fabricated ailment. He needed to find Mrs. Tillmore, if she was still there, and if she wasn't, he needed to find something with an address on it so he could find her before Jason did. Having half of the E.R. staff standing over him, shoveling aspirin down his throat and hooking him up to I.V. drips seemed counterproductive to his cause. Instead he'd taken a seat in the far corner of the room, next to a mother who was tending to a nine year old soccer player while her two year old daughter watched from a stroller beside them.

"Boo boo," the little girl pointed at the large gash on her brother's knee as her mother pulled the makeshift bandage away from his leg.

Normally the sight of such an injury would have made Derek cringe but given the past twenty-four hours, he figured it would take a lot more than a sports injury to make him squirm.

"It hurts, it hurts," the boy cried as his mother looked around the room in frustration.

It was obvious that they'd been there for a while. The sun had been down for about an hour already. The boy's soccer game had likely ended hours ago. His bedtime had probably come and gone and his mother was clearly at her wits end; made even more evident as she eyed the nurse's station and mumbled something on the lines of "un-fucking-believable."

"Story," the little girl suddenly held up a book from the

stroller.

"Not now, sweetie," mom took the book from her daughter's hand and laid it back down on the tiny, built in tray next to her sippy cup. "I'm going to find out how much longer this is going to take," she turned back to her son, who continued to wince in pain as he held the paper-towel bandage over his knee. "Keep an eye on your sister. I'll be right back." Almost tripping over the massive purse/baby bag next to the stroller, mom weaved her way through the crowd toward the busy nurse.

"There's no hope", Derek thought. He'd have to saw off his own arm if he had any hope of getting back there and even then he'd still probably be sitting around for hours.

Turning his attention from the departing woman, his eyes locked with the two year old beside him, who was staring at him with an inquisitive gaze as if to say, "so, what's wrong with you?"

Derek smiled, then looked over at the little girl's brother, who traded tension for a zen like approach to pain management as he leaned back in his chair, head tilted back and eyes closed. Turning back to the little girl he was met with a giggling smile as if he'd done something to amuse the toddler, though he didn't know what. Over the giggles she grabbed her cup, and tilting back in the stroller, began sipping at the drink as a trickle of the red juice slipped from the corner of her mouth, down her chin and onto her tiny dress.

The sight of the juice gave him an idea. Glancing over at the nine year old Buddha again, then up at the impatient mother who was still at least three people deep in line, he leaned over and began feeling around inside the large baby bag. The little girl's puzzled look returned as she looked down at his hand buried deep inside her mother's property. Feeling something soft, he pulled a white cloth from the bag.

"Perfect."

Seeing his pleased smile, the little girl reciprocated with one of her own.

Checking the boy and the mother again, Derek pointed to the cup in the little girl's hand.

Confused, the little girl just stared at his outstretched finger, then up at his face.

Raising his brow, he reemphasized his request with a shake of his finger at the cup.

Again the little girl looked at his hand, though this time seemed to put the silent request together as her eyes wandered toward her cup. Looking up again, then back at the cup she finally realized what he was asking, and held her cup up for him to take.

With a smile, Derek took the cup and began dripping the deep red juice onto the white cloth as the girl watched confused. Once he was satisfied with the stain, he held the cup back out for her to take and mouthed the words, "thank you," which drew a big smile and a few bounces from the excited little girl as he got to his feet and wandered toward the check-in station with the freshly soiled towel around his hand.

"Excuse me," Derek pushed through the people waiting in line to yell at the obviously stressed young woman behind the counter.

"Where are you go—?" the little girl's mother started to protest Derek's cutting until she noticed the red stained cloth wrapped around his hand.

"I'm sorry," he apologized to the group of frustrated patients and parents as he approached the counter.

"Sir, you're going to have to—," Noticing the red towel. "Oh, my."

"Yeah," Derek looked down at his hand as he placed the other one over it and pulled it to his chest for fear that, if anyone got a good whiff of it, they'd notice its fruity nature. "The other girl checked me in already," Derek lied, hoping that there really was another girl, which given the woman's lack of protest, he figured there probably was. "I was just wondering if I could go back and get a new bandage while I wait to be seen."

"Let me get a nurse. That looks pretty bad," the young woman insisted.

"No," Derek motioned for her to sit back down. "It's not that bad, really. You're very busy with these people." He glanced over his shoulder at the crowd who apparently shared in the woman's concern as he noticed a distinct separation between himself and the next person in line. "I just need a bandage and if you could point me in the direction of the bathroom that would be great," he smiled, wincing a bit to make it more believable.

Returning to her seat, she pointed to the double doors over her left shoulder, at the end of the short hall. "You can go right through those doors over there. Just let them know that Jessica sent you back for a bandage."

"Thank you Jessica," Derek smiled, drawing a smile in return.

"Even with a cherry flavored, blood soaked hand he still had it," he thought as he headed for the indicated doors.

"Oh! The bathrooms are just to the left of the doors!" Jessica stood again to shout the forgotten directions.

"Thanks again!" Derek turned as they exchanged another smile and he watched the momentarily distracted, angry mob swarm Jessica's counter again.

Carefully pushing through the doors, still clutching the red rag in the event that he had to offer someone on the other side an explanation, the explanation for the long wait came into view as he saw busy nurses darting from one room to the next and stressed and tired looking doctors wandering from patient to patient, doing all they could to get ahead of the insane, emergency rush.

Clearly unnoticed, he breathed a sigh of relief as he ditched the cloth in a nearby trash can before making his way to the nurse's station. The pace behind the counter wasn't any slower than in front of it as nurses came and went, picking up charts and dropping off charts, all while the overwhelmed redhead behind the counter struggled to keep the mountain of paperwork beside her from toppling over while typing information into the computer.

"Excuse me," Derek greeted the overweight nurse behind the counter.

"Yes," she responded without looking up as her fingers continued to fly across the keyboard

"Hi, yeah, the girl out front, Jessica, told me that my sister was back here and I was wondering if you could point me to the right room," he looked around, feigning confusion.

"What's your sister's name?"

"Tillmore, Tabitha Tillmore."

"Tillmore, Tillmore, Tillmore," the woman's fingers stopped as she closed her eyes and thought for a moment. "Yeah, Mrs. Tillmore was discharged hours ago."

"Are you sure?" Derek asked, frustrated.

"Yes I'm sure," the woman responded with an exasperated sigh. "I just did the paperwork ten minutes ago," she glanced over at the neatly stacked files on the other side of the keyboard. "Now is there anything else that I can help you with?" she asked in a dismissive tone, however before Derek could answer, a loud crash drew the heavy woman from her chair. "Debby! Really?!" she cried out at a young girl who'd just dropped an entire tray of urine samples all over the hall.

Without so much as another glance, the woman made her way around the counter and over to the seventeen year old girl who'd already begun to cry as she hesitantly attempted to pluck each of the scattered containers from the yellow puddle surrounding her feet.

Finally managing to pull his attention away from the chaos taking place all around him, Derek returned his gaze to the stack of completed paperwork beside the computer. Looking around, he cautiously made his way behind the nurse's station, and ducking below the counter, he removed the stack of files from the desk and began flipping through them. Between the stack in his hand and the pile of unaddressed charts on the other side of the computer he wondered what the hell was going on that day or was this just a typical day in a Boston city hospital?

Johnson, Gilbert, Murray, he riffled through the names at the tops of the forms.

Perez, Michaels, Tillmore.

"What are you doing!?"

Looking up, Derek spotted the redheaded nurse standing on the other side of the counter looking down at him. He didn't have an answer, so he did the only thing he could think of. Pulling Tabitha's file from the stack, he threw the other files at the angry nurse as he leapt over the counter and bolted for the doors.

"Security!" the woman yelled as she tried to grab Derek as he passed, but failed as he contorted his body to stay just out of reach.

Somehow forgetting about the lake of urine, and young Debby still trying to salvage what she could from it, his foot hit the puddle as he began sliding down the hall, doing everything in his power to maintain his balance as his feet kicked the scattered cups even further from the girl's desperate reach.

Clear of the yellow ocean, he managed to regain his balance and burst through the doors, back into the waiting room where Jessica was still pleading with the angry crowd in front of her.

Running past her, "Thanks again, Jessica!" he yelled as he spotted a security guard emerging from another hallway.

"You! Stop!"

"You're welcome," Jessica, along with the rest of the waiting room, stood in shock as Derek nearly crashed through the automated glass doors, out onto the street.

Though glad to be out of the building, he knew that it was only a matter of time before the police showed up and with nowhere to run, he didn't know where he should go.

"Get in the car!" a voice suddenly called out to his left.

Turning, Sarah came into view behind the wheel of a car as she pulled alongside the curb.

"What are you doing here?" Derek asked, both surprised to see her and by her impeccable timing.

"Hey!" the security guard emerged from the building as Derek opened the car door and dropped into the passenger seat.

"Go! Go! Go!"

With the tires squealing, the car lurched forward just as the guard's hand smacked against the window.

"What the hell was that?" Sarah questioned, her adrenaline pumping as she weaved the car along the street, around the corner and out of sight of the hospital.

"I told them about the future thing and they tried to lock me up," Derek joked.

"See. I told you."

"Why'd you come back?"

"Something told me you might get yourself into trouble. I came back to stop you but I guess I was too late and now the cops are going to be looking for me too."

"I doubt they got a good look at you or your plates and you guys don't have traffic cameras or iPhones yet so I think we're fine.

Sarah just looked at him with a puzzled look. "What's an iPhone?"

Holding Tabitha Tillmore's stolen file up, "It's not important. I've got the address but we need to get some proof first. Head south."

Doing as instructed, Sarah took the on-ramp for I-93 South as she sniffed at the air. "Did you pee yourself?"

THIRTY-FOUR

"Here you go, Daddy," Katie entered the living room with a beer by her side and a bottle opener in her other, outstretched hand. "Can you give me hand with this? I can never get these things open when I want one," she smiled, unable to hold a straight face.

"Funny," Phil grinned as she lowered the bottle opener and handed him the beer.

"Who's winning?" Katie asked as she curled up on the couch beside her father's Lazy Boy recliner.

"Not the Sox," Phil huffed.

"White Sox?"

"Red Sox sweetie," Phil glanced over at his daughter, confused by the fact that they'd lived in Massachusetts her entire life, yet when it came to sports she still didn't know who the local teams were. Even if she *could* name the Boston teams she'd probably tell you that the Patriots played basketball, the Bruins played football, the Celtics played baseball and the Red Sox played hockey, even though they were currently standing in the middle of Fenway as shown by the new, twenty-six inch television in the corner.

"The picture looks really good."

"It does," Phil smiled proudly. He'd been talking about getting this TV for weeks, ever since they'd seen it at their local Bradlees a month earlier.

Tired of hearing her father talking about the television and how much he hated the old fifteen inch he'd been watching games on for the past six or seven years, she'd finally had enough and snapped at him during one of his rants the previous week. She'd blamed it on hormones at the time, which seemed to pass as a reasonable excuse and would be making its way into regular rotation. Really though, she was just tired of hearing about the television. He used to do the same thing with her mother. He'd see something he wanted but out of a sense of responsibility, would decide that it wasn't needed. For the next few weeks, all he'd do is talk about the item relentlessly until, just as she had done, her mother would finally snap.

"Just buy the damn thing!" She'd usually shout, followed by an apology and the hormone excuse as well.

Feeling justified in his purchase at that point, he'd run to the store and once again, the household could live in peace.

"I don't know how much better they can get," Phil continued his admiration for his new toy. "When I was your age, the only TV we had was a thirteen inch black and white set with two big knobs and three channels."

"That's horrible," Katie gasped. "What did you watch?"

"The only thing I really remember was the news and Mr. Ed."

"Did he read the news before Tom Brokaw?"

Phil again stared at his daughter.

"What?" Katie questioned her father's confused look.

"You don't know who the Red Sox are but you know the lead anchor for NBC's Nightly News?"

"I know who the Red Sox are," Katie smiled. "We don't even live in Chicago and I know who they are."

Phil couldn't tell if she was joking or being completely

serious, managing to conceal her emotions behind a blank face as she continued to watch the game.

THIRTY-FIVE

"Pull in there," Derek pointed to the dimly lit entrance, manned by a glowing sign which read, *Cranston Liquors - Lowest Priced Spirits in Town.*

"Do you really think this is a time to be drinking?" Sarah questioned as she pulled into the tiny, abandoned parking lot.

"We're going to need some sort of proof if we hope to convince Mrs. Tillmore that she's in danger."

"I'm not even sure I'm convinced yet," Sarah smiled as she pulled the car up to the front door. "Besides, what sort of proof do you expect to find in a liquor store, except 100 proof," Sarah couldn't help but chuckle at her own joke.

Though he found her inappropriately silly humor cute, he had only one thing in mind, get his ID back from the dickhead clerk and get to Mrs. Tillmore before Jason could.

"Seriously though...," Sarah's humorous tone subsiding, "...what are we doing here?"

"This is the guy that emptied my wallet last night," Derek responded, peering through the windshield at the dark store windows in front of them.

"The guy that was nice enough to drive you all the way into the city and leave you on my doorstep was the same guy you think robbed you?" Sarah asked confused.

"I guess nothing's free, is it?"

"What makes you think he still has your ID anyway? He probably just took your money and ditched everything else."

"Probably, but I have to at least check. What other proof do we have?"

"There you go with *we* again."

"Stay here. I'll be right back," Derek instructed.

Making his way to the door, he attempted to see inside, to confirm whether or not the same asshole was working, but between the tinted windows and dozens of advertisements plastered all over the glass, it was nearly impossible. Grabbing hold of the door, he pulled toward him, only to be denied by the rattle of the lock as it pushed against the door's metal frame. "What the hell?" he looked behind him at the glowing sign and then at the hours posted on the door.

Mon. - Friday, 9:00 - 11:00

"Looks like they're closed."

Turning, Derek saw that Sarah had gotten out of the car and was now standing behind her open door.

"I told you to stay in the car," Derek barked.

"I'm not a dog," Sarah protested as she closed the car door and joined him at the entrance.

Realizing that an argument with the independent and stubborn girl was pointless, "They're not closed. It's Wednesday. We have at least another twenty minutes," he pointed at the sign before wandering away from the door.

"Maybe they were dead and closed up early."

Derek didn't respond as he made his way along the side of the building and around the corner, out of view.

"Hey! Where are you going?!" Sarah shouted as she

followed.

Turning the corner, she saw Derek, walking along the side of the brick building and eventually disappearing, once again, around back. Jogging to catch up, Sarah rounded the corner to find Derek standing in front of a solid metal door.

"What are you doing?" she questioned as Derek looked the door up and down.

"I'm trying to figure out if the door has an alarm on it."

In her typically impulsive manor, she reached past him, grabbed the handle and pulled. To both of their surprise, the door swung freely open and to Derek's relief, no alarm sounded.

"You said we were in a hurry," Sarah shrugged before proceeding into the building.

Impressed by her dominance over the situation and apparent lack of fear, he quickly followed.

The back door led into a back storage room with a small desk in the corner, on which sat a small TV monitor and VCR, likely connected to the store's security cameras. The desk's chair lay upside down on a pile of boxes beside the desk, two of its wheels resting on the box beside it as a cheap plastic, elementary school type chair stood in its place in front of the desk.

"Hello!" Sarah called out suddenly.

"Jesus," Derek shouted in a hushed tone, almost reaching for her mouth to keep her quiet.

"What?"

"Do you want to get us shot?"

"I'd rather let someone know we're here than get my head blown off poking it though that doorway," she motioned at the door leading into the store. "Besides, I don't think anyone's here."

"And what makes you think that?" Derek asked, curious. "All of the lights are still on and the back door was open."

"Woman's intuition."

"Really?"

Sarah smiled.

Derek just shot her a look before slowly approaching the doorway. "Hello!" Noticing the look on Sarah's face, "What?" he whispered. "Male intuition."

"Doesn't exist."

"Hello!" Derek continued. The front door was locked! We were wondering if you could help us!"

"I told you, I don't think anyone's here," Sarah insisted from close behind him.

Having received no response, he decided to test her theory and slowly peeked around the doorjamb, hoping that the bullet would travel wide and lodge itself in the wall instead of his head. As the store came into view though, no gunfire arose and Derek realized that Sarah too, eager for a look, was leaning around him to get her own view of the empty space.

"See, told you," she smiled as they both stepped through the doorway.

Scanning the store as he walked, Derek made his way toward the front counter.

"What kind of idiot leaves on all the lights and leaves a door unlocked? It's like he's asking to be robbed. Maybe he left my stuff back here," Derek motioned behind the counter as Sarah wandered further into the store.

Rounding the counter, the gun, which Derek had feared existed, was laying on top of the safe, directly below the open, register drawer.

Looking around again, he suddenly had a very bad feeling about their situation as he made his way toward the open register. Surprisingly, all of the cash was still inside the till, only the coins were missing. "What sort of thief would steal only the coins?" he thought, staring at the register as the answer came to mind…"the interrupted kind."

"Eeek!" a scream suddenly filled the store.

Startled by the sudden cry, Derek leapt over the

counter and ran toward the scream. At the end of an aisle, toward the back of the store, eyes wide and hand over her mouth, stood Sarah, staring at the ground ahead of her.

"What?!" Derek shouted as he came up alongside her. She didn't need to answer him as the source of her scream became instantly evident.

"Is that?" Sarah spoke through her hand.

"Uh huh," Derek nodded as he struggled unsuccessfully to look way.

Sprawled across the linoleum floor was the body of the man he'd come to confront, only it looked as though someone else had already beaten him to it. On the floor beside the man was a broken bottle of Grey Goose vodka, its former contents sprayed all over the surrounding floor and displays. Its guilt in the recent murder evident by the red stains on its jagged edges and the dislodged shards still buried deep within the man's throat.

"What's in his mouth?" Sarah continued in her horrified and muffled speech.

Not noticing at first what she was referring to, Derek finally pulled his eyes away from the man's wounds. Sticking out of the man's mouth was what appeared to be a thin piece of plastic. Taking a step closer...

"Don't," Sarah grabbed his arm.

Freeing her grasp, he continued closer, carefully avoiding the diluted red puddle around the body.

"What is it?" Sarah asked again.

As he knelt down beside the body he made the mistake of looking into the dead man's wide open eyes. It didn't take a genius to see the horrific nature of his death but if there were any doubts, the terrified expression on the man's pale face was enough to put them to rest.

Concentrating on the barely protruding object, Derek tilted his head to get a better angle but still couldn't make out what he was looking at. Trying not to touch the dead man's skin, he grabbed the corner of the object.

"Don't touch it," Sarah gasped and turned away as

Derek pulled the thin plastic from the man's mouth. "What is it?"

Derek didn't answer.

"What is it?" she repeated turning and peeking through her fingers.

"My license," Derek held up the familiar card.

Confused, Sarah just stared at the odd looking license. It looked nothing like the laminated card in *her* wallet. Leaning closer, it did say Massachusetts Driver's License across the top with Derek's picture below but even more unsettling was the date of birth beside the picture.

11/18/91

"You...the date..."

"Hasn't happened yet?" Derek helped her find the words. Finally he could see that she was starting to believe his story.

"Wait a minute?" her belief began to fade, replaced by growing fear as she took a step back and placed her hands over her mouth again.

"What?" Derek looked up confused before realizing what she was thinking. "No, I didn't do this."

Continuing to back up, Sarah bumped into a wine display, knocking it and its bottles to the floor in a explosion of red.

Jumping to his feet, Derek reached for Sarah's arm to prevent her from falling.

Screaming, she turned and ran.

"Wait!" Derek cried, running after her, slipping on the wine and crashing into the shelf, adding even more bottles to the mix before catching his balance and chasing after her. "I didn't do this! You have to believe me!" he chased her back into the storage room/office. Grabbing hold of her arm he spun her around, causing their feet to tangle and sending them both stumbling into the television on the desk.

"Let me go!" Sarah cried, flailing at Derek as their current position had him pinning her against the desk, trying to regain his balance. "Let me go! Let me go! Please!"

Grabbing her wrists to stop her attack. "Listen. I didn't do this. I'm telling you the truth. Everything I've told you is the truth," he pleaded.

Unable to get free, she began to cry, causing him to release his grip as he noticed the image on the television screen.

"There!" he cried, pointing at the screen.

Sarah didn't know what to do. Everything inside told her to run. "Hit him as hard as you can and run," she told herself, but looking up through her blurred vision she realized that he wasn't even paying attention to her anymore, and had in fact taken a step back.

"See, I told you!" he cried at the screen. "That's him! That's Jason!"

Turning toward the TV, she saw what could have been Derek's friend from the restaurant the other day, though the image quality was poor and difficult to decipher. The screen was split into quadrants with Jason in the top right corner and the clerk standing beside a display in the top left, mopping the floor.

Forgetting all previous urges to run, Sarah leaned closer as Jason slowly crept from the upper right image, into the image with the clerk.

"Run," Sarah talked to the screen as if the events they were watching hadn't yet happened.

Slowly Jason moved closer to the clerk, coming to a stop only a few feet to his back. Removing a bottle from a display, he raised it into the air and with a momentary pause, swung the glass weapon.

Looking away, Sarah buried her face in Derek's chest as Derek continued to watch the attack. Sitting on top of the dazed man, Jason began savagely beating him until only faint movements told him that he was still alive. Then, apparently satisfied, Jason stopped, stood and began circling the man, seemingly talking to him, before once again kneeling down with his back to the camera as the man's legs began to thrash.

"Is it over?" Sarah spoke into his chest.

Derek continued to watch as the man's legs slowed and picking the broken bottle up off the floor, Jason sunk the jagged glass into the clerk's throat.

"Is it over?" Sarah repeated.

"It's over."

"We need to get to Mrs. Tillmore," Sarah looked up from his shirt.

Realizing she no longer needed convincing, he nodded. "I dropped my license. I have to get it. There's a gun behind the counter. Grab it. We may need it."

Sarah nodded, wiping her eyes as they both reentered the store.

Approaching the end of the isle, he knew what to expect but it didn't help as the body came into view once again. Having witnessed the brutal act now, the bruising and lacerations on the man's face were even more obvious and upsetting. Focusing his attention away from the body, Derek spotted his license on the floor beside the man's head. Carefully he reached down to pick up the alcohol and blood coated card but as he did, his foot slipped, kicking the side of the dead man's face and causing the silver and copper contents of the clerk's mouth to pour out across the floor.

THIRTY-SIX

The whirling fan overhead was an absolute necessity when it came to Tabitha's ability to get a good night's sleep. It had been that way ever since she was a little girl. Even during the winter months, when the temperature was in the single digits outside and the house was freezing because her father was too cheap to pay for oil, she'd insisted that it stay on all night. Some people like fans for the noise, others for the chill that it lends to the air. She liked it for both, but even though the fan was on its highest setting and a cascade of cool air was pouring down onto the bed, she still wasn't able to sleep.

Richard, on the other hand, was out like a light and had been since his head hit the pillow. He hated the cold and having the fan on all the time had been a big compromise, but it didn't seem to bother him as he sawed logs beside her, the blanket pulled almost entirely over his head so that only his hair was visible.

His hatred for the cold was the reason she kept having to fight for her own share of the covers, as yet another gentle tug stole her share of the heavy comforter.

"Stop," she whined, pulling the covers back up over her exposed shoulders.

She didn't know how he was doing it in such a deep sleep and without any noticeable movement, but that was the third time in the last minute that she'd had to fight to remain covered.

Restless and frustrated with the sandman's reluctant showing, she rolled over, nestling her head deeper within the down pillow and firmly tucking the covers under her shoulder.

It had been an eventful day, from literally using her head to land the deal with Mr. Branson, to finding out about her pregnancy. There were undoubtedly plenty of reasons for her brain's refusal to shut down. All she could do was run through the day's events over and over again, always ending with the same question, "What are we going to do?" She didn't feel ready to be a mother, but like it or not it was going to happen. Hell, it already had. Not only did she need to worry about herself, now she had to think about the tiny life already growing inside of her. It needed the proper nourishment; no more two pound burritos from the food truck that always parked outside the office building, no more cheese cake splurges just before going to bed, and no more eating entire pizzas from the Italian Pug Pizzeria just down the street. Thinking about it, it was a miracle that she'd managed to maintain her petite figure when she seemed to always be eating like a linebacker, trying to carb up for the big game. Now even that was a thing of the past, she sighed as Richard pulled at the covers again, this time unsuccessful in his attempt as she pressed her shoulder even harder into the mattress.

"Richard, stop," she nudged him.

As if he were the one being bothered, Richard let out a soft groan as he pulled at the covers again.

"Stop," her frustration grew as this time she had to grab the retreating covers with her hand to fight the increasingly aggressive nature of his attempts.

Suddenly the comforter yanked out of her hand, retreating toward the foot of the bed.

Startled, she turned her head in the direction of the stolen fabric only to spot a shadowy figure standing at the foot of the bed, the comforter held firmly in its grasp.

She screamed.

Startled awake, "What?! What is it?!" Richard shot up, looking at his wife and then following her terrified stare to the foot of the bed where he caught a glimpse of the figure. Having just been yanked from R.E.M. sleep however, he couldn't be sure that anything he saw or heard yet was real. Reaching for the lamp on the nightstand, he filled the room with the soft glow of the incandescent bulb and turned back to the shadowy figure, that was no longer there. Meanwhile Tabitha was still sitting up beside him, pressed against the headboard with her eyes closed and screaming at the top of her lungs.

"Honey! Honey!" he attempted to break through the shrill cries. Grabbing her arm, "Sweetie, Stop!"

Finally hearing her husband's voice she opened her eyes, her scream subsiding as she realized that the mysterious figure was gone.

"What's going on?" Richard asked.

"A man. There was a man standing at the end of the bed. He yanked the covers off," she frantically explained.

Looking back toward the foot of the bed he still didn't see anything except the comforter in a heap at the end of the bed. "I don't see anything."

"He was there. Right there," she pointed.

Even though he thought he'd seen something too, he figured that it was simply the result of one too many horror movies and being awoken in the most terrifying manner possible.

"There's nothing there," he assured her.

"But he was."

"Who?"

"I don't know. It was dark, but I know what I saw. Why are the covers piled up at the foot of the bed?" she attempted to convince him.

"Maybe you had a nightmare and kicked them off," he offered what he thought was a very reasonable and the most likely explanation.

"I wasn't dreaming, Richard."

"Well, maybe you don't think you were, but—"

"—I wasn't dreaming!" Tabitha snapped.

Richard remained quiet.

"I haven't been able to fall asleep since we came to bed. I've just been lying here thinking and fighting you for the..." Oh my God she thought as she realized that it hadn't been her husband at all. Her stomach sank.

"What?" Richard continued to look at her confused.

A loud bang suddenly came from downstairs, followed by what sounded like every pot and pan falling from the rack hanging over the kitchen island.

"See," Tabitha whined as she scrambled to pull the covers back over her.

"Get your gun from your nightstand and stay right here," Richard instructed as he opened the draw to his nightstand and removed his own 9mm.

Doing as instructed, from the perceived protection of the comforter, Tabitha retrieved her own gun. Nowhere near as intimidating as her husband's, she'd only agreed to getting the tiny pink .380 because she'd never believed that she would need it. Now, holding the gun firmly in her hands, she had to admit that she did feel a little better, but not much.

"Remember what I taught you?" Richard whispered, looking down at her gun.

As taught, she disengaged the magazine, confirming its full capacity before reinserting it into the gun and yanking back on the tiny slide to load the chamber.

"Good. Now stay here. I'll let you know before I come back in the room so you don't shoot me."

"You can't go out there," Tabitha protested the plan.

"Just stay here."

"Shouldn't we call the police?"

"The rack could have just given way. I don't want the police showing up for faulty craftsmanship," Richard smiled.

Frustrated, "There was a man in our room, Richard," Tabitha insisted. "Why do you need the gun then?"

"I'm just going to check it out. If I see anything, I'll come right back. Okay?"

"No, it wasn't okay," she thought, but she knew she wasn't going to win.

"Just stay here," he instructed for a third time as he checked the mag. and chambered a bullet.

Tabitha didn't respond as she watched her husband slowly open the bedroom door and disappear into the dark hall.

*****

Wondering what in the hell he was doing, but proceeding onward anyway, Richard slowly advanced down the hall toward the dimly lit staircase. As much as he wanted to believe that the contractor, who'd already proven to be worthless, had somehow failed in attaching the hanging rack properly, he couldn't shake the brief image of the shadowy figure at the end of the bed. Though nowhere near large in stature, it had clearly been that of a man, if it had even existed at all. Tabitha had a history of awakening in the night and seeing things that weren't there, though usually it entailed reasonably harmless things like spiders and snakes, never cover stealing, shadowy men.

Approaching the top of the stairs, he lifted up onto his tip toes and leaned forward in an attempt to get a view of the foyer without fully exposing himself to whatever potential danger awaited below. Seeing no signs of movement in the dimly lit space he proceeded forward.

Thankfully, if there was one thing the contractor did do right, it was the stairs. They were probably the most solid thing in the entire house with not one loose or squeaky board. He was convinced that the house could be bulldozed, blown up or burned down and still the stairs would remain standing.

Breathing a sigh at the end of his descent, Richard took a step toward the arched entry into the living-room, only to be greeted by a loud squeak from the wood floor beneath his bare feet. Frozen by the sound, he wanted to curse but maintained his cool as he shifted his weight to his other foot and slowly stepped around the vocal, oak boards as he glanced around the doorframe, into the equally dark living room. The kitchen was just on the other side through another arched opening. He could have turned in the opposite direction and taken the short hall through the foyer, but that way was all wood flooring with many known noisy spots. The living room was carpeted and squeak free, so he continued on, gun drawn, hoping for nothing, but ready for anything.

As he approached the other doorway, he paused and listened.

Nothing.

His heart pounding, he caught himself breathing heavy, potentially giving away his location to the man who could be waiting on the other side of the very wall behind which he currently stood. Taking a deep breath to quiet his lungs, he silently counted to three before leaping through the doorway, gun up and ready to fire at anything that moved.

The room was empty. The pots and pans, which he'd seen only an hour ago, hanging over the island, were now strewn about the kitchen floor. The rack that had been holding them lay half on the counter top while the other half remained attached to the ceiling overhead.

"Fucking idiot," Richard huffed as he flipped the light switch, thinking about all the other, even more insulting names he was going to call the man responsible for this mess.

Moving toward the island, looking up at the two small holes overhead where the steel cables had fastened the pot rack to the ceiling, he let out a sigh, placing the gun on the counter as he knelt down to start picking up the scattered cookware.

"It's alright!" he shouted. "It was just the god damned rack!"

"Are you sure?" Tabitha's voice responded faintly from upstairs.

"Yeah! I can't believe this," he continued, though more in a tone beneficial to only his ears. "You pay over a quarter of a million dollars to custom build a house and this is what you get. We would have been better off—"

His rant interrupted by the sound of a pan being kicked across the kitchen floor, Richard pivoted on his knee just as the blade of a knife pierced his neck, splitting his tongue and dislodging his eye as the tip came to rest within his right socket.

*****

Standing in the bedroom doorway Tabitha listened as the sound of a sliding pan, followed by a thud traveled up the stairs and down the hall. "You okay?!" she yelled, this time receiving no response as the clanking of more pans reached her ears. "Likely Richard cleaning up the mess," she thought as she slid her gun into her pajama pant's pocket and started toward the stairs. "I'll add it to the list of things to call the Coletti Brothers about," she spoke loudly as she began her decent to the first floor. "I don't think it's going to do any good though. They've already cashed the checks and even if they do come back out, I doubt their second attempt is going to furnish any better results," she almost laughed in frustration as she flicked at the light switch at the bottom of the stairs with no result. Looking up at the lighting fixture hanging overhead she couldn't help but chuckle. "I think I can fix that one," she eyed the dead bulbs just as the remainder of the house went dark.

Looking around confused, Tabitha reached for the switch again, flipping it up and down as if that single switch was going to bring back power to the entire house. "I didn't do that!" she announced as she ran her hand around the end of the railing and along the wall leading to the kitchen at the back of the house. "There's a flashlight in the drawer next to the cupboard."

Richard didn't answer, but the sound of the drawer, followed by a bright beam of light shining right in her eyes told her that he'd been listening.

"Honey," Tabitha complained, throwing her hands up in front of her face just as she slammed her knee into the decorative table along the wall. "Damn it."

She didn't need to see to know that her favorite plant, an orchid that Richard had bought her the day they'd moved into the house, was likely ruined as the sound of shattering ceramic and dancing rocks filled the hall. "Shit! No!" she whined, fighting the urge to drop to the floor to pick up the beloved plant, but still unable to see with the beam of light still aimed directly at her face. "Honey, please."

The light turned off.

"You didn't have to turn it off," she complained, the darkness seeming even more imposing as the effects of the light still swirled in her vision. Slowly the dim, moonlit hall came back into view but the shadow that had been her husband no longer stood in the doorway ahead. "Richard? Richard, turn on the light again. Where'd you go?" she remained hesitant to move, afraid of cutting her feet on the shards of scattered pottery. "Richard, I don't have my slippers on. There's ceramic everywhere. Turn on the light."

With that request, the flashlight sprang back to life, this time from the doorway to the den on her right.

Startled, "Jesus! How'd you get in there?" she

questioned, throwing her hands up to block the powerful beam of light from her eyes once again.

There was only one doorway to the den and she'd been standing beside it the entire time. Even in her temporary blindness she would have at least heard him passing directly in front of her. There would have been no way to avoid the mess in the hall. At least a few rocks and pieces of pottery would have been kicked. But she hadn't heard a thing, and now Richard was once again attempting to blind her with the emergency flashlight.

"What are you doing? Get the light out of my eyes," she grew frustrated.

The light went off again, but as the swirling lights faded, this time she could still make out her husband's shadowy figure, still standing in the doorway just three feet away.

"I hope you're having fun," she playfully snapped. "I knocked over the orchid. Shine the light down here so I can pick it up," she instructed as she knelt down in anticipation, but the light never came. Looking up at the unwavering figure, "Richard, it's not funny anymore. I'm tired. I don't care if the power's out. I just want to pick up my flower and get back in bed. It's been a long day."

Still no light.

"Richard?"

No response.

Deep down, instinct was screaming for her to run...telling her that something was wrong. For all she knew it had been screaming at her this entire time, but it was only now that she was hearing it as a faint click, followed by a beam of light showed her that the man standing in the doorway was not Richard.

Frozen by fear, Tabitha just stared up at the young man. "Richard," she whined before realizing that the man standing before her was the same young doctor who'd first treated her in the E.R. earlier that day.

He smiled, the shadows cast by the light under his chin,

twisting the normally friendly expression into a thing of sheer terror.

Somehow realizing, that for whatever reason, her husband wasn't able to help her, Tabitha broke free of her paralyzed state and bolted for the stairs. Though close, the front door wasn't an option. By the time she reached the door, undid the deadbolt and lock on the handle, the stranger would have her.

Rounding the end of the railing, leaping up the stairs three at a time she didn't bother to look back. It wasn't going to do any good to see the intruder close on her heels. She only hoped that she could reach the bedroom and lock herself inside where she could call for help before the stranger got a chance to carry out whatever he had planned.

At the top of the stairs the open bedroom door came into view. Without hesitation she dashed down the carpeted hall, darted into the bedroom and slammed the door shut, locking it and pressing her palms to the thin barrier, trying to catch her breath and calm her nerves.

"Hello, Mrs. Tillmore."

Tabitha spun to see that the shadowy figure was already in the room with her.

Back pressed to the door, "I'm pregnant," she whimpered.

Advancing toward her, the only response the man offered was, "I know."

*****

"This is a nice house," Sarah commented as she navigated the semicircular driveway, bringing the car to rest directly in front of the steps leading to the front porch.

"Very dark though," Derek noted, glancing back at the unlit light posts at each end of the driveway as well as the dark windows and extinguished lights on the front porch.

"Maybe they don't like to waste money," Sarah knowingly offered up an unlikely explanation. "Besides, they're probably in bed," her voice broke as she continued the attempt at self comfort.

Sharing in her obvious concerns, Derek took a deep breath and reached for the door handle.

"Wait," Sarah stopped him with a hand on his shoulder. "We don't have to do this."

"You don't have to do this...I do," Derek smiled.

"Why?"

"Jason's my friend. I'm partly responsible for this situation."

"How? You didn't make him kill that guy back at the liquor store. You didn't tell him to go off the deep end and hunt this woman down. Let's just leave. We can call the Tillmores from a pay phone and warn them about Jason. That's all you need to do."

Taking his hand off of the door handle, he placed it over hers. "Tabitha Tillmore isn't the only one in danger. There were others, one in particular and if I don't stop him now, Jason's probably going to go after her next. I have to do this."

Realizing that she wasn't going to convince him otherwise, all she could do was stare into his eyes. They possessed a comforting quality that seemed out of place given the situation, but nonetheless, was appreciated as she leaned forward and gently pressed her lips to his.

Caught off guard, Derek closed his eyes as a tear and then another rolled down Sarah's face, lending a salty quality to the sensual exchange. Countless kisses had been placed on his lips over the years, but none like hers. There was almost no movement, no sound, just the warm, moist touch of those velvety lips, lightly pressed against his. He'd been attracted to Sarah from that first meeting outside the restaurant and now it was clear that she'd felt the same.

Opening their eyes, they broke their embrace. He

wanted to tell her to stay in the car and that everything would be alright, but he didn't have to say anything. With a nod and a smile, she seemed to acknowledge the unspoken words of comfort as he broke eye contact and exited the vehicle.

The house was completely dark. Given its brand new appearance, he wouldn't have been surprised to learn that the Tillmores hadn't even moved in yet, but as he climbed the unexpectedly creaky front steps, he noticed the welcome mat in front of the door and a narrow placard hanging on the front door which read, *Welcome Home.*

Though apparently moved in, it was clear that they hadn't yet addressed the window coverings as most of the windows along the porch remained completely open to the outside world, the faint glow of the waning moon offering what limited resources it had to illuminate the house's interior. Pressing his face against the narrow window to the left of the door, he attempted to see inside but other than the faint, shadowy outline of a staircase, he couldn't see anything.

"Maybe this will help."

Startled, Derek turned to see Sarah behind him, holding her keys in the air. On the key ring, pinched between her fingers, was a tiny flashlight which she had turned on and was shining in his eyes.

"I thought I told you to stay in the car."

"No you didn't."

"Well I thought it," he added, taking the flashlight from her and shining it in the window.

The tiny light didn't do much, other than to expose a toppled plant and a floor covered in shattered pottery and rocks.

Sarah pushed in to see what he was looking at. "We have to get in there," she gasped.

Surprised by her willingness to go charging into a potentially dangerous situation, he took a step back and prepared to kick in the door, unsure if he'd even be able to without breaking his foot.

Anticipating his plan, Sarah reached for the handle and turning it, pushed the door open.

"It's open," she whispered.

"I see that."

Nervously, he stepped inside with Sarah close behind. He didn't want to just go charging up the stairs and into the master bedroom. There was still the chance that the power was just out and that the Tillmores had simply forgotten to lock the front door. The toppled plant and shattered vase could have been the result of no lights and a new environment. Maybe they'd bumped into the table, knocking the plant over and didn't have any candles or a flashlight to aid them in cleaning it up, so they left it for morning.

Derek continued to run logical explanations through his head as he slowly entered the living room. Sensing Sarah's growing fear through the tightening grasp of his arm, he paused in his advance. "Are you okay?"

Receiving a simple nod, he continued toward what appeared to be the kitchen. Shining the tiny light ahead of him, a bar height counter came into view, followed by a marble island covered in the debris of what appeared to be a fallen rack of pots and pans. Stopping at the bar, Derek shined the light around the room. Other than the mess on and around the island, everything seemed completely normal.

Sarah grasp tightened once again.

Looking over his shoulder to see what was wrong, he was met with a look of horror as she raised her index finger toward the island. At first he didn't see what was so horrific, just some pots and pans; but, scanning lower with the flashlight, the source of her panic and the future bruise on his arm became clear as the soft beam of light fell upon the bloody head of who he could only assume was Mr. Tillmore. Most of his body was hidden behind the island with only his head from the mouth up exposed to view, however, given the pool of blood around his head and a missing eye, there was no mistaking the man's condition.

Thump.

Startled by the sudden noise, Derek and Sarah both directed their gaze toward the ceiling, then toward each other.

"Upstairs," he whispered, though immediately questioned why. She'd obviously heard it as well.

Sarah looked terrified.

"Go back to the car," he instructed, turning back toward the living room.

Nodding, Sarah again took hold of his arm as they made their way back toward the front door. With a better sense of the house's layout and an eagerness to get outside, the brief journey back to the front door seemed much quicker than the initial trip in; however, upon reaching the foyer, they found that the door which they had left open behind them, was now shut. Pulling at the handle, it became evident that not only had someone closed the door behind them, but they had also locked the double keyed deadbolt, snapping the key off in the lock.

Spinning, Derek quickly scanned the foyer and surrounding doorways. All seemed quiet. "We're going to have to find another way out," he whispered, motioning back to the living room in hopes of finding a back door somewhere in the kitchen.

"Help me!" a muffled scream came from upstairs.

Stopping in the doorway to the living room, Derek turned to Sarah.

"Let's just go," she insisted. "We can call the police."

"Go. Find the phone and call the police, then get out of the house," he instructed.

"No, come on," she begged, pulling him toward the living room.

Derek stood his ground.

"I have to go up there," he insisted. "Go."

Reluctantly, she did as instructed as he turned for the

stairs.

Slowly making his way up the staircase, he noticed small red spots of blood every few steps as well as random pieces of what looked like tiny shards of ceramic from the broken flower pot. He didn't know what he was walking into but, against all rational thought, he continued on, pausing at the top of the stairs to assess which door he might be looking for.

Based on the noise from the kitchen, he knew the room was toward the back of the house. At the far end of the hall stood a wide open door to what appeared to be an empty bathroom. Three doors lined the remainder of the hallway; two to the right and one on the left.

Cautiously, he proceeded forward, approaching the first open door on the right. Peeking around the doorframe he scanned what appeared to be an empty bedroom, filled with boxes and a disassembled bed. Continuing on, he came to a stop in front of the open bathroom door with a closed door to either side of him. Choosing to go left, he pressed himself against the wall just to the side of the door as he reached for the handle, slowly turning it and pushing the door inward.

"Help!" a suddenly excited female voice called out from within the room.

Peeking into the room, the terrified woman came into view. Mrs. Tillmore was standing in the center of what appeared to be the master bedroom. She was dressed in baggy pajama pants and a silky night top, a flow of steady tears adding to a growing, dark stain in the center of her chest. Behind her stood Jason, peering over her shoulder as he held a blood stained hunting knife to her throat.

Though only a day had passed, Jason's appearance, much like his personality, was dramatically different. The glasses, that Derek had grown accustomed to seeing him in, were gone, likely replaced by contacts, and his usually neatly groomed hair had been buzzed, leaving only a dark shadow on top of his head.

"Please, don't be shy," Jason greeted his friend. "Come on in. Mrs. Tillmore's been waiting for you," he pulled the knife closer to her throat as she tensed with fear.

Cautiously, Derek stepped into the room, holding his hands out in front of him to let Jason know that he wasn't armed.

"Why don't you just go ahead and close that door behind you," Jason nodded at the door.

As instructed, Derek turned and closed the door.

"Ah, don't forget to lock it. We wouldn't want your little girlfriend out there to interrupt our reunion now would we?"

Derek did as he was told. "Jason, put down the knife."

"No hello for an old friend?" Jason seemed hurt by the lack of a greeting. "Two years go by and all I get is, 'Jason, put down the knife'," he mocked.

"Two years?"

"Oh, that's right. What's been two years for me has only been a day for you," he chuckled. "This whole time travel thing is kooky isn't it? Don't move," Jason pressed the knife tighter against the woman's throat as Derek attempted to take a step toward them.

Derek remained motionless.

"Jason, what are you doing?"

"I'm taking control."

"Control of what?"

"Life."

"What are you talking about?"

"Oh don't play naive with me. You know exactly what I'm talking about. You yourself said that I should lighten up and let loose a bit. Well, I'm here to tell you that I took your advice and, whoo! I've never been better."

"Jason, I didn't tell you to do this."

"Maybe not this exactly, but I have to say, once I realized my full potential, I knew exactly what had to be done."

"Full potential?"

"Oh, yeah. I guess I should explain how it is that I'm standing here right now. It took nearly two years for me to perfect it but..."

Suddenly Jason vanished.

More stunned than relieved by her assailant's mysterious disappearance, Mrs. Tillmore remained ridged and motionless as Derek rushed to her side.

"Ah ah ah."

Startled, Derek turned to see Jason standing in the very spot from which he'd just run. Beside him, her arm held firmly in his grasp, the hunting knife pressed against her side, was an equally stunned and frightened Sarah.

"What the—"

"—Neat trick, huh," Jason grinned.

"It's going to be alright," Derek attempted to comfort Jason's new captive.

"Is it Derek?," Jason pressed the tip of the blade against Sarah's side as she fought the urge to break down. "How do you expect her to believe anything you say when it's clear by the confusion on your face that you have no idea what's going to happen next?"

"How did you—?"

"—Jump? I know, it's not a very unique term but it really is the best way to put it."

"Where's the brie—"

"—The briefcase," Jason interrupted again. "Oh...I don't need that anymore."

"But that's impossible. The power source. You need a power source."

"No, I never said I needed a power source. I simply needed a way to trick my body, or I should say my blood, into thinking my life was in danger. A high voltage shock seemed like the most efficient and controllable method at the time; at least when the blood was inside the machine that is. When it's in me however...well...mind over matter my friend. Mind over matter."

"But—"

"—Now don't get me wrong it did take me quite some time and a bit of testing to finally figure that out," Jason added, holding up his wrist to reveal a series of cuts. "The razor would never get quite deep enough to do any real damage before my body would take over and remove me from the situation. However, I found that such brutal and real threats made controlling the jump nearly impossible. Just like the time I tried to hang myself. I was gone even before the rope pulled tight. Eventually I realized that it wasn't strictly the blood that was triggering the reaction. It was the adrenaline. Fear. My body's natural fight or flight reaction could be used to initiate a jump and that's when I learned how to control it. Once I managed to harness my fear, all that was left was fine tuning the control, so now..."

Again, Jason vanished but only momentarily as he almost instantly reappeared behind Mrs. Tillmore, the hunting knife once again across her throat.

Stumbling backward in disbelief, Derek stood beside Sarah.

"No neat little gadgets. No complicated programs. Just good old fashion brain power," he pointed at his head.

"That still doesn't explain what you're doing," Derek defiantly refused to act impressed.

"Let's face it Derek. I've spent my entire life being bullied by...well...just about everyone...including you."

"I—"

"—You're honestly going to tell me that you never thought yourself better than me. That we didn't always do what Derek wanted to do. That the whole fucking world didn't revolve around dear old Derek and his conquests."

"What are you talking about?"

"Her," Jason nodded in Sarah's direction.

"Me?" Sarah asked shocked.

"Not just you. Every one of you."

Sarah seemed confused.

Turning his attention back to Derek, "No matter the situation, you somehow always manage to come out on top. Everyone loves the outgoing and unpredictable Derek. No one ever wants the quiet and boring Jason. Well, all of that's going to change, starting here, tonight."

"Jason, what are you going to do?"

"I'm going to right all of the wrongs, all of the things in my life, all of those people who made me the pathetic little twerp that I was. I'm going to eliminate them all."

"But why now? Why here?" Motioning to the woman at the end of Jason's knife, "She has nothing to do with this."

"You said it yourself Derek. We're friends. I wouldn't want you to miss out on this monumental occasion. Besides, I want you to know what's coming. Because, when I'm done here, I'm going to take care of your little girlfriend's baby sister."

"What?" Sarah snapped.

"What does this have to do with her sister?"

"You really should learn their last names Derek."

Derek turned to Sarah with a look of confusion before turning back to Jason.

"Bishop," Jason added.

"Bishop?" Derek repeated in shock as he turned back to Sarah. "Your last name is Bishop?"

"Yeah, why?"

"Is your sister's name Katherine Bishop?"

"Katie, yeah why?"

"And she's pregnant," Jason added with a grin.

"How do you know that?" Sarah turned to Jason, more confused than ever.

"Your sister's in danger," Derek returned Sarah's attention to him.

"Danger? Why? What does she have to do with any of this?"

"Not her," Jason playfully interjected.

"Her daughter," Derek added.

"Her daughter? What are you talking about?"

"Just like the little slut currently growing inside of Mrs.

Tillmore here, your sister is going to give birth to the biggest cunt of them all."

"Fuck you!" Sarah snapped back at Jason. "What is he talking about Derek?"

"I'll explain later but now we need to deal with this situation," Derek whispered.

"If you two are done," Jason interrupted.

"Jason, put the knife down. You don't have to do this. There's a better way. You're better than this."

"That's right. I am better than this. I'm a fucking god."

"You're a fucking psychopath," Sarah mumbled.

"You know, I wasn't planning on it, but given your sister's ability to spawn the seed of Satan, I should probably do your future husband a favor and take care of you as well."

"Jason," Derek pleaded.

"What? You never know. Maybe it's you. I could be doing you a favor," Jason grinned. "But first..."

Removing the knife from Tabitha's throat, Jason buried the blade in her back as she let out a gasp and stood frozen in shock.

"No!" Derek lunged forward.

"Oh god," Sarah turned away in horror.

"See you at the dance." And with that, Jason vanished as the wounded woman fell into Derek's arms.

Lowering her to the floor, "You're going to be okay. The police are on their way," Derek turned to confirm Sarah's call.

Reluctant to let the woman see her response, Sarah offered only a slight shake of her head from side to side as Derek shot her a 'why not' look.

"The line was dead and then...," Sarah whispered.

Turning back to the woman in his arms, Derek pulled his hand out from beneath her to find that it was covered in blood.

Mrs. Tillmore just stared up at the ceiling overhead, her

only sound a slight gurgling as her lungs filled with blood.

"It's going to be alright. You're going to be alright," Derek continued to lie.

Slowly the woman's eyes wondered from the ceiling overhead, pausing briefly on Derek's tear filled eyes before coming to rest on her stomach. Unable to speak, she slid her hand onto her stomach, comforting her unborn daughter as they both passed.

THIRTY-SEVEN

"Katie, can you get the door?!" Phil yelled down the stairs, receiving no answer from his daughter who he'd last seen sitting at the kitchen table, shoveling down her second bowl of frosted flakes.

The girl's cereal addiction had gotten worse since being pregnant. At age six she'd gone through a phase where she had refused to eat anything but cereal for nearly two months before they'd finally convinced her to try something that didn't come from a box. She'd nibbled on two strips of bacon before extending her Kelloggs run another month.

The doorbell rang again.

"Katie!"

Again, no answer.

Struggling to get his belt through the final loop, he fastened the buckle and almost forgetting, zipped his fly before poking his head out of the upstairs master bedroom to issue one last, "Katie, door!"

Silence, then another bell.

Sighing, Phil shuffled down the stairs, unlatching the deadbolt as he reached the last step and pulled open the door to reveal his oldest daughter and some boy he'd never met.

"Sarah!" he exclaimed, struggling with the stubborn latch on the screen door before finally striking it with an open palm.

"Whoa!," Sarah laughed as she caught the violently opened door.

"Sorry about that. That damn thing's been sticking even worse lately. What are you doing here?" he leaned down to hug his daughter. "I thought you weren't coming home until next week."

"All of my finals were this week. I just took the last one yesterday so I figured I'd come home a week early," Sarah lied. She had three more finals; one tomorrow and two more the following Monday morning, none of which she'd come up with a good excuse for missing yet.

"Well, I'm glad you did," Phil continued his excited greeting as he looked up at his daughter's unknown guest, making eye contact for the first time. He seemed like a fairly intelligent guy. Something in his eyes gave him an educated and well balance look, however with his disheveled clothes, dirty hands and bruised face, Phil couldn't help but think trouble. "Who's your friend?"

"Daddy, this is Derek."

"Nice to meet you, Sir," Derek attempted to win over the large police officer Sarah affectionately called, Daddy. He'd intended to add points with a firm handshake but apparently looking to intimidate his daughter's new "friend", Mr. Bishop clamped down on Derek's hand like a set of vice grips.

"Likewise," Phil stared at Derek suspiciously as he continued crushing his fingers.

"Daddy," Sarah, whispered loudly for her father to stop.

Reluctantly, Phil did as she asked.

"Boyfriend?"

"No," Sarah responded after a short pause to consider what her father would prefer to hear.

"Shame," Phil smirked.

"Daddy," Sarah scolded, taking his attention off of Derek for the moment.

"Well, come on in," Phil waved the two into the living room. Why didn't you just use your key?"

"My keys are on my other key ring. I grabbed the wrong set when we left Boston," she lied, not wanting to share with her father the events of the previous night or the fact that her and Derek had spent the rest of the night asleep at a rest stop along I-90, though not much sleep had been had. They'd spent most of the night arguing over what they were going to do about Jason, and the liquor store and Mrs. Tillmore and now her very own sister. She'd argued for telling her father everything; about Jason and what had happened and what they feared was next, leaving out the time travel bit of course. Her father was an intelligent man, trained to tell when someone was lying, which is why she'd finally given in to Derek's wishes to hold off telling anyone anything until they had had more time to consider their options. Able to tell that she really believed what she was saying, he'd likely take her to Cannon Memorial for a psych evaluation before he believed the farfetched and horrific tale. Then, once he learned that at least the part about the murders was true, he'd surely arrest Derek and charge him with the unspeakable crimes. No, for now silence was their best friend.

"Sarah?" Katie called out surprised as she exited from the hall bathroom.

"Katie," Sarah unenthusiastically responded, drawing a look of confusion from Derek in return.

"What are you doing here?" Katie continued the uncomfortable welcome.

"School's out. Thought I'd come home a bit earlier."

"Oh. That's nice."

Derek's eyes bounced back and forth as the sisters exchanged uncomfortably hostile pleasantries before their father interrupted.

"You two," Phil scowled. "Quit this bickering and give each other a hug."

Reluctantly, the two girls embraced.

"See now, isn't that better?" Phil mediated the more pleasant greeting.

Katie eyed Derek with the same uncomfortable glare he'd received from her father only moments earlier.

"Are you alright?" Phil questioned his youngest daughter as he noticed her hand holding the lower portion of her stomach.

"Yeah, I'm fine," Katie replied, rubbing at her belly. "I think I just ate too fast or something."

"See. That's why I tell you to slow down. You need to give your body a chance to catch up with your eyes. Plus I'm sure all of that sugary cereal doesn't help."

Temporarily putting their differences aside to acknowledge the common, over protective element in both their lives, the two girls exchanged a look.

Confused and at a loss in this new and unexpected family element, Derek remained silent.

"Listen, I have to get to work...," Phil changed the subject, "...and as you can see, I'm not quite ready yet." While he had on the entire uniform, his shirt remained unbuttoned and his belt, while fastened, obviously required tightening by a couple notches to eliminate the awkward sag to one side. "Why don't you two catch up...," he took both of his daughter's shoulders as he directed them toward the kitchen, "...while I get to know our friend Derek here a bit better."

Looking over her shoulder on her way into the kitchen, Sarah offered an, "I'm sorry," look to Derek. She'd warned him of her father's overprotective nature, especially when it came to his daughters, but she couldn't help but feel bad when she saw the nervous fear on Derek's face.

*****

"So, getting big," Sarah broke the uncomfortable silence, immediately realizing the negative connotations of her statement. "I didn't mean…"

Katie just glanced down at her growing stomach. She was doing everything she could to conceal just how much she was showing. All of her pants had built in elastic at this point and all of her once favorite, form fitting shirts had been banished to the back of the closet in exchange for a whole new wardrobe of stylish, yet loose fitting tops. At six months she was starting to look like someone seven or eight.

"Katie, I really didn't mean—"

"—It's okay," Katie sighed. "According to Daddy, I inherited mom's baby carrying genes."

"That's true, she did get pretty big with you…not because you were fat."

"I know I'm big, but it's alright. My doctor says everything is progressing perfectly and in a few months I'm going to be holding my little girl.

Watching her sister as she held her stomach and talked about the life growing inside of her, Sarah couldn't help but realize that this was a completely different version of her sister than the one she remembered only four months earlier. The last time she'd been home had been during Christmas break which had also been the time that Katie had chosen to drop the baby bombshell on the family. Their father had at first been irate, demanding to know the father's name so he could race over there and "crush his nut sack with his nightstick," was how he'd so eloquently put it. By the end of the week he'd cooled down and accepted the reality of the situation, promising not to harm the boy and assuring his youngest daughter that he'd be there for her every step of the way. Things hadn't ended as well between her and her sister however.

They were once inseparable, but since she'd gone off to

college the dynamic between them had changed. Sarah was off making that unavoidable transition into adulthood while Katie had been left at home, an only child for the first time in her life. Add to it their mother's death and things hadn't been the same since.

The death of their mother had had very different effects on them. While Sarah had taken the tragedy as proof that life is short, and had pushed herself through the remainder of high school, placing second in her class, Katie had chosen a more destructive path. Instantly, her grades had plummeted. She'd grown more and more defiant toward both her father and sister, who'd struggled to keep her out of trouble. A new set of friends had led to early experimentation with alcohol and weed and then, a quick romp with Jordan McCandlis had given them the tiny life now poised to join their family.

At that point Sarah had had enough. She understood the pain her sister felt. Katie was four years younger and just entering her teenage years at the time of their mother's death but her downward spiral had taken its toll and the pregnancy had been the last straw. At that point she'd essentially written her sister off, leading to nearly no contact between them, the only words ever exchanged being, "I don't want to talk to her," whenever Sarah called home to talk to her father and asked if her sister was around.

"So have you come up with a name yet?"

Taking a seat on one of the barstools at the island, "I don't know, Daddy really likes Ruth and I keep having to remind him that it isn't the fifties anymore."

"She'd probably come out with a walker in toe," Sarah joked, pleased to see a smile on her sister's face. "What do you want?"

"I *was* thinking Isabella, but now I sort of like Jenna," Katie smiled at the name.

Though she no longer needed convincing when it came to Derek's story, hearing her sister utter the now familiar name of her future niece, Sarah couldn't help but get lost in thought.

"You don't like it," Katie snapped her sister back to reality.

"No. I do. It's pretty."

"Not Jennifer though, just Jenna," Katie added. "Everyone is named Jennifer it seems. I like the name, but I want her to be more unique than that…without giving her some crazy name like Celebration or Moonbeam.

"How about Destiny," Sarah suggested.

"Eew no," Katie instantly scowled. "That sounds like a name Daddy would say belongs to a stripper. Up next on the main stage, Destiny," Katie joked in an announcer's voice.

"Yeah, I guess you're right but what do you know about strip clubs?"

Glancing down at her stomach, "I think I know a lot more than I should at this point."

The two laughed.

"This is good," Sarah thought. After the way she'd reacted during Christmas and four months of no contact, she'd been afraid that their relationship had been irreparably damaged and that the close, sisterly bond they'd once shared could never be restored. After just a few minutes of light conversation though, things seemed just like they used to be when they were younger. Well, not entirely the same, Sarah thought as she glanced at her sister's stomach.

"So who is he?"

"Huh?" Sarah shifted her eyes upward.

"Your friend currently being grilled by Daddy."

"Oh shit. You think he's okay?"

"I don't know. You remember what he threatened to do to Jordan. You aren't pregnant are you?"

*****

"She's not pregnant, is she?" Mr. Bishop continued his interrogation.

"What?" Derek responded, shocked by the question. "No…I mean…I don't think so. I guess she could be, but it isn't—"

"—A simple no was the answer I was looking for," Mr. Bishop interjected.

Derek had just watched the man strap one gun to his ankle, another under his shirt and a third to his belt. Normally quick witted and perfectly capable of standing his ground under a barrage of questions, he suddenly found himself feeling like a high school dropout interviewing for the position of Chief Physician at John Hopkins.

"So where are you from Mr. Miller?"

"Cannon, Sir," Derek realized his mistake as soon as he made it.

"Really? I must know your folks then."

"Cannon, Michigan," Derek added with a grin of much needed confidence.

"Oh really. I'm from Michigan."

His grin faded.

"Never been to Cannon though. Is that near Detroit?"

Derek didn't know what to say. If he answered yes, and Sarah's father was from Detroit, he ran the risk of being caught in the lie. He knew the man was testing him. He was a police officer for Christ's sake. He was used to getting a read on people and he'd already made it clear that he didn't much care for him.

"It's a small little town. Most people don't even know it's there," he provided as vague an answer as he could come up with.

"Ah. I grew up in Detroit," Mr. Bishop added.

"Sorry."

"Excuse me."

"I mean…yeah, it's out in the western part of the state, nowhere near Detroit," Derek fumbled for a response, confident that the peculiar look meant Mr. Bishop didn't believe a word he was saying.

Staring at Derek with an analyzing gaze, Mr. Bishop slid his radio into his belt. "You know I don't trust you, right?"

"I'm aware," Derek kept his response short and simple this time.

"Good," Mr. Bishop took a step closer. "Because the only thing that matters to me in this entire world, are those two girls down there and my future granddaughter. And as much as I look forward to meeting Sarah's future husband and father of her children, it's not going to be you and it's not going to be now. Am I clear?"

"Crystal, sir. Just friends," Derek managed to stand his ground in the face of the looming officer.

"Good. Then let's go see what the girls are up to," he grabbed hold of Derek's shoulder with the same set of vice grips.

THIRTY-EIGHT

"Your dad hates me," Derek spoke up from the passenger seat of the car.

"He doesn't hate you," Sarah assured him.

"No. I'm pretty sure he does. And I might have told him that you're pregnant."

"What!? I'm not pregnant!"

"I know. Well, I don't know. How could I know that? See, that's exactly how it happened," Derek began to babble again, wondering what the hell was wrong with him today.

"Whatever. He knows that I wouldn't be stupid enough to let that happen." Thinking about what she just said and her sister. "I didn't mean it that way."

"I know what you meant. So what's up with you and your sister anyway?"

"What do you mean?"

"Really?" Derek grinned.

Not aware that the awkwardness between her and Katie had been that obvious, "We've had our disagreements over the years."

Derek just stared at her, not satisfied with her attempted dodging of the question.

"What? Alright, yes. I'm not thrilled that my sixteen year old sister is pregnant. I don't think that's all that shocking. Ever since our mother died she's been a bit of a mess."

Just as before when the sensitive subject had come up, Derek didn't know how to respond. "Sorry," was again all he could think to say.

"You said that already," Sarah looked over with a grin, sensing his level of discomfort with the topic. "Cancer," she added.

Derek nodded, not sure where to go with the conversation, especially given their current situation.

"Please don't get all squeamish around me now," Sarah instantly acknowledged the growing level of awkwardness in the car, eager to stop it from spreading any further. "Whenever you tell someone that your mother died of cancer they get all quiet and uncomfortable around you. It's life. It happens. She'd want me to move on and make the most of my life," she asserted.

He wasn't sure if she really believed what she was saying or if the rehearsed speech was simply a defense mechanism left unchallenged for all these years. With larger problems at the moment however, he chose not to push the issue.

"Where are we going anyway?" Sarah questioned, apparently also interested in a change of subject.

"Jason's house, or the house he grew up in at least," Derek answered.

"Why?"

"Maybe we can talk to someone about Jason."

"Didn't you say he was just born last week?" Sarah asked, aware of how strange that statement sounded, given that she'd just witnessed the apparent newborn kill a woman in cold blood the night before.

"What are his parents going to tell us?"

"Not his parents. Jason was born in Tampa. His parents were killed in a car accident when he was about three months old."

"That's horrible."

"His grandmother raised him after that. Jason said something about his grandmother and what she told him before she died. Something about the men in their family. I'm assuming it has to do with the time travel thing."

"You really think she's going to just come out and admit to a total stranger that the men in her family have the ability to bend time?"

"I grew up my whole life around Jason and his grandmother. She likes me."

"Not yet. You haven't even been born yet," Sarah pointed out.

"Shit," Derek thought. Now even he was getting confused. "Anyway, we need to do something. We need to figure out a way to stop Jason."

"Yeah, we need to tell my dad and sister the truth, so when he shows up we can be ready."

"Not yet. We have time."

"No, he has time. He has all the time in the world to plot out how he's going to kill my little sister and niece. We don't have time because we don't know when it's going to happen."

"Not true. Remember what he said last night?"

Sarah looked over at him with no idea what he was talking about.

"See you at the dance, he said," Derek repeated Jason's departing words. "It's the end of the school year. I can only assume he meant the prom. Since your sister is currently in school and not at a dance I can only assume that she's perfectly safe. Did she mention anything to you about going to the prom?"

"Yeah, some boy she knows asked her out the other day for something like the third or fourth time. She finally said yes and actually seems pretty excited about it."

"When is it?"

"Tomorrow."

"Tomorrow?" That was a bit sooner than he'd expected. He thought they'd have at least a week to work out a plan. Now they only had a little more than twenty-four hours.

"I say we tell my father and we all get the hell out of here," Sarah reasserted her opposition to Derek's current plan.

"And go where? Where can we go that Jason can't find us? Sure we could drop off the grid. We could abandon all credit cards, change our names, spend our entire lives ensuring that no photos are ever taken and that nothing exists that could give Jason, who has access to over two decades of information on the internet, even the slightest clue to where we are."

"What's the internet?"

"It doesn't matter right now. What does matter is that we understand that there is no running. Jason holds all the cards right now. We just need to figure out a way to stack the deck in our favor."

Sarah didn't respond.

He could tell she was upset and didn't fully understand what he was talking about. Though only a little over twenty years separated their lives, her world was a far different place than his. How could he explain social media and the vast database of information that modern technology had made accessible to anyone with interest and time. Instead he chose to just comfort her.

"Look. I know that you're worried about your sister and I promise you, if we can't figure out some way to stop him before tomorrow night, we'll tell your father and get your sister as far away from here as possible."

He could see a tear welling up in the corner of her eye as she continued to silently stare at the road ahead.

"Sarah."

Glancing over at him.

"I'm not going to let anything happen. I promise."

A tear rolled down her cheek as she offered a hesitant

smile before turning her attention back to the road.

He knew there was nothing he could say to make her feel any better, so he offered up a direction instead. "Turn right up here."

THIRTY-NINE

"I thought she wasn't coming home until next week," Latisha leaned against the locker beside Katie's.

"Excuse me," a voice arose to her back.

"She was, but for some reason she came home early and she brought home some boy with her," Katie continued sharing the morning's events as she proceeded to swap the books from her backpack for those in her locker.

"A boy?"

"Excuse me," the whisper of a voice spoke up again.

"Yeah. I mean I know we haven't really talked since…" looking down at her own stomach, "…but she and my dad talk at least a couple of times a week and I don't recall him mentioning anything about a boyfriend."

"The only time I remember seeing her with a boy was that one time three or four years ago…at that party…you know…the one that your family and neighbors used to throw every year where your father cooked a whole pig and then tossed its head around the backyard like it was a shot put."

Katie nodded.

"Must be a white people thing," Latisha added under

her breath.

Ignoring the judgmental remark, though she fully agreed with her friend's disgusted opinion, "That was the last block party before my mother became too ill, and that was our cousin that she was with," Katie added quickly, trying to avoid letting the whole sick mother thing intrude into yet another light hearted conversation.

"Pig head tossing, cousin dating…remind me again why we're friends."

"Excuse me."

"Excuse me!" Latisha turned around, obviously having heard the quietly intruding voice, and to that point having chosen to ignore it. "May I help you?"

The shocked girl stared up at the intimidating volleyball player and unable to form the words, simply pointed at the locker against which Latisha was currently leaning.

Realizing what the freshman girl wanted, Latisha quickly dialed back the attitude and hopped away from the locker. "Sorry."

"She wasn't dating our cousin," Katie explained.

"Huh," Latisha took up her previous stance on the other side of Katie's locker.

"Our cousin, she wasn't dating him. He was simply at the party."

"If you say so, but I definitely got the cousin banging vibe from those two."

Contemplating Latisha's implications, Katie quickly shook off the idea. "She was always too into her school work to have a social life. You don't graduate salutatorian and earn a free ride to college by sleeping around."

"Depends who you're sleeping with," Latisha grinned.

"Nice. I'm not even going to go there, though that would explain why you have a higher GPA than me."

"Hey," Latisha lightly punched Katie's shoulder.

"Striking a pregnant girl. It's a sad day indeed," Mark stepped from the flow of students, squeezing in next to Latisha.

Latisha just looked him up and down, shocked by his suddenly social demeanor. Since Katie had agreed to go out with him, even his posture and walk had appeared more confident. "What social cocoon did you just hatch from?"

"What?" Mark turned to Latisha.

"Never mind," she replied looking back at Katie who had one hand on her stomach as she grimaced in pain.

"I didn't hit you that hard."

"Are you okay?" Mark instantly moved closer, placing his hand on Katie's arm.

"Yeah, I think so," Katie groaned as the pain subsided, allowing her to return to an upright posture.

"What was that?" Latisha tried to get closer, not sure how she felt about Mark's suddenly protective intrusion into their friendship.

"I don' know. Just a strange pain I guess. Probably nothing to—"

Before she could complete another sentence, the pain returned, this time dropping her to her knees.

"Katie!" both Mark and Latisha cried as they each took an arm.

Realizing that something was obviously wrong, "I'm gonna get the nurse," Mark assured her as he pushed passed the few shocked onlookers and took off down the hall.

FORTY

"What are you going to say?" Sarah stopped Derek as he reached for the doorbell.

"I don't know. I'll think of something," Derek assured her as he pushed the button.

He really didn't know what he was going to say. He wasn't even sure who might answer the door. He and Jason hadn't met until kindergarten so he couldn't even be sure that Jason's relatives lived in the familiar house yet. All he knew was that the house seemed a lot smaller and less intimidating than it had back then. An old, two story Victorian near the edge of town, he remembered being terrified of it the first time he'd gone over to play. Though the house bore a welcoming white exterior, it was clear that it hadn't been maintained for decades and in numerous areas, its cedar shingle exterior appeared to be trying to free itself of its dried and brittle skin.

All of the windows bore heavy, dark drapes and the glass insert in the door was handmade with bubbles and imperfections that blocked and distorted any light that attempted to pass through it, though a change in light and a dark mass told them that someone was standing on the other side.

A soft click and a moment later, the door slowly began its inward swing.

Derek could sense Sarah's uneasiness as she seemed to lean away from the opening door, probably feeling the same thing he'd felt so many years earlier.

"Can I help you?" an elderly Chinese man finally greeted them as he slowly shuffled around the open door and into view.

"Hi, my name is Derek and this Sarah. We were wondering if anyone with the last name Fook lives here."

"Yes!" the man seemed instantly excited, though Derek couldn't figure out why.

"Is, Ushi Fook here," Derek continued hopeful."

"Yes! Come on in," the man responded with the same sudden excitement.

"See," Derek turned to Sarah as they accepted the invite and entered the house, avoiding the old man as he shuffled out of the way and started the process of re-closing the door.

With a thud, the large wood door retook its position within the ornate frame as the man latched the deadbolt and turned. "Oh, hi there," he seemed shocked by his visitor's presence.

"Hi," Derek nodded with a look of confusion.

"Can I help you?" the old man restarted the brief exchange.

"Ushi Fook? You said she was here?" Derek questioned.

"Ah yes! My baby sister. I think she's out with mother. She should be back any minute. Please come in," he waved them toward an adjacent room as he grabbed the walker he'd left beside the door and began the slow journey toward the den.

"I don't think he's going to be much help," Sarah whispered into Derek's ear as they followed the old man.

"I never met him, or at least I don't remember him. I guess I can see why," he remarked at the old man's advanced age and apparent senility.

"Oh heavens! Mr. Fook, what are you doing?" a female voice suddenly called out from across the hall.

Derek and Sarah turned to see a woman in her thirties carrying a dishtowel in one hand and a fork in the other.

"What have I told you about the front door?" the woman added, bypassing their guests as she took hold of the elderly man's arm and attempted to lead him to a nearby chair.

"I've got it," the jolly man instantly became hostile, obviously not fond of being helped to perform such trivial tasks.

Once the woman had Mr. Fook in the chair, she finally turned to acknowledge Derek and Sarah who remained frozen just inside the living room, unsure of where to go or what to say.

"May I help you?"

"…Yes," Derek hesitated.

"You'll have to forgive Mr. Fook," the woman, sensing Derek's hesitance, smiled. "He's a stubborn old coot," she added, issuing the old man the same pleasant grin.

Mr. Fook seemed happy as he sat in the chair, oblivious to the guests in his house.

"So what can I do for you?"

"We were hoping to speak with Ushi Fook," Derek told the housekeeper, or nurse or…whatever she was.

"Ushi Fook doesn't live here," the woman answered, this time it being her turn to be confused. "Oh, did he? Mr. Fook."

"Mr. Fook grinned."

"I'm sorry about that. He's not supposed to answer the door. Last time he did I found him out in the street trying to play kick the can in the middle of a kids street hockey game. Did he tell you that his sister was home?"

"He said she would be home momentarily," Sarah chimed.

"I'm sorry about that. Ushi Fook lives in Tampa,

Florida. Is there something that I can help you with?"

"We were just hoping to ask a few questions about this house for a report we're doing in school about New England architecture," Derek lied. "This being one of the oldest houses in town, we thought it would be perfect."

"That sounds interesting. You can try to talk with Mr. Fook. He's lived in this house his entire life. I'm sure he's got lots of interesting things he could tell you if you can keep him on track long enough.

"What's wrong with him?" Derek asked, realizing instantly that it wasn't any of his business and that he probably shouldn't have prodded.

"Alzheimer's," Sarah answered before the nurse could.

"That's right. How'd you know that?" the woman seemed impressed and a bit skeptical now.

"My grandmother has it. She doesn't even know who I am most of the time."

Derek looked at Sarah, unable to help but to feel bad for her. A mother with cancer and now a sick grandmother. What was next, an ill family dog?

"I'm sorry to hear that dear," the nurse responded with sympathy. "Well, Mr. Fook isn't quite that bad. He still knows who everyone is. He just has a hard time with the 'when' sometimes but that might be okay seeing as you've got questions about his past. He's good with stuff like that. Can I get you two anything to drink?"

"No thank you, I'm good," Sarah replied.

"No thank you," Derek added.

"Okay then." Turning to Mr. Fook. "These fine young students would like to ask you a few question about your beautiful house," the woman spoke very deliberately.

"My house?" Mr. Fook responded with a smile.

"Yes. Your house. I'm going to go finish the dishes. I'll be back with your pills in a few minutes, okay?"

"It's a sturdy house," he spoke, ignoring the woman.

"There you go," she turned to Derek. Looks like he's raring to go. Just better make it quick. There's no telling when he might get sidetracked."

With that, the nurse left the room.

Exchanging looks, Derek and Sarah took a seat on the couch opposite Mr. Fook.

Uncomfortable, Derek waved. "Hello Mr. Fook."

Mr. Fook just smiled.

Looking toward the doorway, through which the nurse had exited, and speaking in a hushed tone, "Mr. Fook, we have a few things to ask you about your family."

Mr. Fook continued to smile, which Derek took as a sign to proceed.

"Do you know the name Jason Fook? I believe he'd be your great nephew. He was just born about a week ago in Florida."

"Florida," Mr. Fook repeated. "My sister and I went to Florida once with our parents. Beautiful beaches. Ushi always did love beaches."

"Where is your sister now?" Sarah jumped in.

"Florida."

"Your sister lives in Florida?" Derek attempted to get clarification that they'd moved past the previous question.

Mr. Fook nodded in the affirmative. "She writes. Her and Ty."

"Have they written anything to you about Jason?" Derek probed.

"He'll be home soon."

Confused, they exchanged looks, assuming that the old man's mind was straying from the conversation.

"Who will be home soon?" Derek asked.

"Jason."

"Are Jason's parents planning a trip to come visit? That would be nice," Sarah guessed at the meaning behind the statement.

"No. Nesbits have him," Mr. Fook huffed.

"What's a Nesbit?"

"Nesbits took him home. Called him Oliver. Ty's going to get him back," he assured them as he pointed toward a desk against the wall.

"What's he talking about?" Sarah whispered in Derek's ear. Who's Oliver?"

"I don't know," Derek spoke as he stood, looking back at the doorway as he made his way to the desk.

"Who's Oliver?" Sarah continued the questioning.

"Do you like pie?" Mr. Fook abruptly changed the subject.

"I do like pie," Sarah played along, glancing over at Derek who was rooting around through the papers on the desk.

"My mother makes the best apple pie. Maybe she will make some for us when she gets home."

"That sounds great," Sarah agreed, unsure where else to go with such a scattered conversation.

"I think I have something," Derek mumbled from the desk.

"What?" Sarah asked.

Derek turned to see both of them staring at him, Sarah with a look of anticipation and Mr. Fook with a happy grin.

"A letter from his Sister," Derek added, continuing to read to himself.

"Oliver," Mr. Fook spoke.

"Who's Oliver?" Sarah asked again.

"Jason."

"What?" Sarah turned back to Derek.

"According to this, Oliver is Jason or at least he will be."

"I don't know who's more confusing to talk to, you or him," Sarah sighed.

Returning to his seat beside her, "It's all here. It appears that Jason was adopted by the Nesbits last week. Look, there's even a picture." Derek held up a Polaroid taken through the window of a hospital nursery. "That must be Oliver—"

"—Jason."

"Thank you," Derek looked up at the old man.

Mr. Fook continued to smile.

"I don't think Jason's parents were killed in a car accident," Derek turned back to Sarah. "I think he was kidnapped by his grandmother."

"This guy was your best friend for nearly twenty years, but you don't seem to know anything about him."

"Not the truth at least."

"Derek, if that's true," she pointed to the letter, "then this family is completely nuts.

Derek's eyes widened as he looked at Mr. Fook, expecting him at any moment to become aware of what they were talking about, but instead the old man was staring at the blank television screen.

"So what are we going to do?" Sarah returned Derek's attention to her.

"I need to at least ask him about the time thing."

"I don't think he's going to be much help. Besides we don't even know if he knows about it."

"Jason said it skips a generation. If that's true then Mr. Fook here is very familiar with the concept of time travel. We just have to find a way to get it out of him."

Turning back to Mr. Fook, both Derek and Sarah jumped back, nearly alerting the nurse with abbreviated screams as Mr. Fook came into view only inches from their faces. His smile was gone and in its place was a look of clarity and seriousness they had not seen since the moment the front door had opened.

"Mr. Fook," Derek nervously grinned. "I didn't see—"

"—No time travel. I warned her. Just as I had been warned, but I didn't listen and now look at me," he pointed to his head. "I'll keep telling her until she listens. You should do the same. Ty doesn't have to worry. He doesn't have the gift, so he doesn't even know. But Jason..."

"Mr. Fook?"

Derek and Sarah turned to see the nurse standing in the

doorway, a look of surprise on her face. Turning back to Mr. Fook they were met with the same carefree grin they'd seen moments ago, still only inches from their faces.

"Is everything alright?" the nurse questioned as she rushed to Mr. Fook's side and helped him back down into the chair.

"Yeah, fine," Derek attempted to compose himself. "Mr. Fook was just telling us about the secret door in the upstairs bedroom."

"Oh, I didn't know about that one," the nurse smiled. "You'll have to show it to me sometime, Mr. Fook."

"Is the pie done?"

"Do you want pie? I can check the freezer and see if we have one if you'd like."

Mr. Fook sneered at the thought.

"I think Mr. Fook's getting tired kids. Did you get what you needed?"

"I think so," Derek exchanged a look with Mr. Fook as he and Sarah stood from the couch.

"Good. Maybe you two can come back again and spend some more time with him. Aside from me and the letters he gets from his sister each week, he doesn't have much contact with the outside world."

Realizing that he was still holding the letter and photo in his hand, Derek slowly lowered them, hiding them behind his leg.

"But now I think he needs to lay down for a while," the nurse spoke as she helped Mr. Fook to his feet, sliding the walker in front of him.

"Thank you Mr. Fook for all of your help," Derek addressed the old man.

"Yes. You have a beautiful old house and I can't wait to write about it in our report," Sarah added.

"Do you kids mind letting yourselves out?" the nurse asked.

"Not a problem. Thanks again," Derek replied.

"Time travel," Mr. Fook mumbled as he slowly

shuffled toward a doorway on the opposite side of the room with the nurse by his side.

Derek and Sarah paused to look at each other nervously before heading for the door.

"Time travel?" the nurse laughed. "That would be pretty neat. Maybe you could go back and see this old house being built, or maybe change something in the past."

Derek hesitated for a second, listening to the woman's words as her voice faded as she and Mr. Fook exited the room, and Derek and Sarah stepped back out onto the porch.

"I know what to do," Derek declared as Sarah shut the door.

"What? Other than the truth about Jason's origins and his crazy father and grandmother, I don't think Mr. Fook told us anything to help us stop Jason from doing whatever he has planned.

"Not Mr. Fook. The nurse."

"The nurse?" Sarah asked confused.

"I have to go but I'll be back as soon as I can."

"Go? Go where? What about Jason? What about my sister?" Sarah was now completely confused.

"If this works, you, your sister, everyone will be fine. But there isn't a lot of time. I need a credit card and your car."

Sarah didn't know what to think anymore. In the last twenty four hours she'd learned that time travel wasn't just a concept for the movies, she'd found a dead body in a liquor store, she'd witnessed a poor woman get murdered right in front of her and she'd learned that a psychotic time traveling lunatic was hell bent on slaughtering her pregnant sister. Derek standing before her now claiming to have a solution, but only if he can borrow her credit card and car, was probably the most rational thing she'd heard yet.

Pulling her keys and credit card from her pocket, she placed them in his hand.

Jogging toward the car, "I'll drive you back to the house first. Don't tell your father until you hear from me."

"You'd better come back," Sarah asserted, staring over the roof of the car at him.

"I promise. I'll come back."

With that, they both got in the car and with a squeal, sped away.

FORTY-ONE

"Oh my god! Is everything alright?" Sarah slipped through the gap in the curtain to see her sister lying on the hospital bed.

"I'm fine," Katie replied.

"But dad's message on the answering machine. He said that you were in the hospital with some sort of pains. Is the baby alright?"

Not used to seeing a panicked and emotional side of her sister, Katie couldn't help but let a little smile slip out.

"What?" Sarah noticed the growing grin on her sister's face.

"You," Katie replied.

"Me, what about me? I was asking about you."

"I'm fine," Katie reassured her. "Just some minor pains. That's all."

"Minor pains don't usually land you in the E.R.."

"Okay, a little more than minor, but they're gone and I feel fine."

"What did the doctors say?"

"They mentioned something about Braxton Chicks or something."

"Braxton Hicks," Sarah corrected.

"That's it. They think it's just false labor pains. They said it was completely normal. Mine were apparently just a little more severe than usual. They're running tests now. Sit down. Relax. You look stressed. You've looked stressed since you got home this morning."

"You have no idea," Sarah thought as she took a seat beside the bed. She told Derek that she wouldn't say a thing about Jason until he contacted her, but how could she wait? Seeing her baby sister in the hospital, even though she seemed fine, was far more upsetting than she could have ever guessed it could be, and this was only a false alarm. What if the next time is for something far more serious, and she didn't do anything to prevent it? She had to tell her what she knew, no matter how crazy it sounded. She had to convince her father and sister that the threat was real and that they needed to pack up their things and leave town for a little while. Even though Derek swore that such a reaction wouldn't do any good, she at least had to try.

"Katie, I—"

"—So, Miss Bishop, we have your results back and everything looks fine."

"Do you know what it was?" Sarah stood from her chair, forgetting all about the Jason situation for the moment.

"This is my sister, Sarah."

"Nice to meet you," the doctor extended her hand.

More interested in knowing the cause of her sister's pain than meeting the doctor, Sarah shook the woman's hand while repeating her question. "Do you know what it was?"

"Is your father back yet?" the doctor turned to Katie.

Having not even noticed his absence, "Where *is* dad?"

There was a little incident out in the waiting room about ten minutes ago," the doctor explained. "He went out to deal with it until help could arrive. Do you want me to wait until he gets back?"

"No," Sarah answered before her sister even had a chance to.

"No, it's alright," Katie agreed.

"Like I said, everything looks fine. Your blood pressure was normal and the ketone test came back negative so like I'd suspected, we have nothing here but a perfectly normal case of Braxton Hicks."

"Is it normally so painful?" Katie asked, obviously relieved, but worried that it might happen again.

"False labor pains are very normal in the third trimester. It's simply your body's way of preparing for the real thing and while it is possible to have some pain, it's typically no worse than menstrual cramps. I think what you felt was a rare anomaly and I wouldn't expect it to happen again, but if it does, please don't hesitate to contact your OB-GYN. I'd rather you be seen than just assume everything's all hunky-dory, okay?"

Relieved, Katie nodded with a smile.

"What'd I miss?" Phil slipped through the curtain. "Oh good, you got my message," he greeted his oldest before turning his focus back to Katie. "So what is it? Is everything alright? How's the baby?"

Watching her father, Sarah now understood Katie's smile when she had first arrived and started the game of twenty questions.

"I was just telling your daughters that everything seems perfectly normal. All tests came back fine. I think it was just pre-labor pains."

"So what do we do? Does she need to be on bed rest?" Phil continued his worried questioning.

"I don't know that strict bed rest is in order, but given the severity of the pains that you described," the doctor turned back to Katie, "I don't think it would hurt to take it easy and stay off your feet for the next few days."

Instantly Katie's look of relief returned to that of concern. "What about the dance tomorrow night?

"I don't think—," The doctor began what she intended

to be a statement of reassurance, telling her young patient that it would be perfectly fine for her to attend the dance if she just took it easy, but was instantly cut off by Mr. Bishop.

"—I don't think that would be a good idea, sweetheart."

The doctor turned to Mr. Bishop as if she wanted to disagree.

"I mean. We don't want anything to happen to the baby," he defended his stance. Is a dance really worth it?"

"But Dad, I can't not go. What about Mark?"

"I'm sure Mark will understand. If he cares at all, he wouldn't want you putting yourself or the baby at risk."

Sarah and the doctor exchanged looks. She knew what the doctor wanted to say, but it was obvious that she didn't want to interfere with their father's parenting. She herself, under normal circumstances, would have gotten all over her father for such an overprotective stance, but this was perfect. With Katie forced to stay home, Jason's dance plans would be ruined. Aware that it wasn't an absolute solution to the situation, it might at least buy her and Derek more time to figure things out. Besides, if Katie's pregnancy *was* in any kind of danger, she didn't need the stress of hearing that someone out there wanted her dead. That sort of news alone could throw her into labor and potentially cause her to lose the pregnancy. No, for now she would remain quiet like Derek wanted.

"Sarah, will you talk some sense into him," Katie turned to her sister for help.

"I think Dad's right."

"What!"

"It's not worth the risk," Sarah and the doctor this time shared disagreeing glances.

"I have other patients to tend to," the doctor excused herself from the escalating family squabble. "I'll have the nurse bring your discharge papers," she added before disappearing through the curtain.

"I can't believe you're taking his side," Katie stared at her sister in disbelief.

"There aren't any sides here," Phil interjected.

"You know, I shouldn't be surprised. I know you think you're better than me."

"I'm not better than you," Sarah respond in shock.

"Yes you do. Ever since mom died you've had a problem with me."

"I haven't had a problem with you. I've had a problem with some of the decisions you've made."

"Girls," Phil attempted to gain control of the escalating tone of the situation.

"Like getting pregnant?" Katie asked.

"Yes, I guess so, but that doesn't matter now because here we are and all I'm trying to do is keep you and the baby out of danger."

"Danger? What danger?"

"Shit," Sarah thought. "Safe from getting hurt," she poorly recovered.

"No one's going to get hurt here. The doctor said I was fine."

"She also said that you should take it easy for a few days," Phil added.

"This is ridiculous," Katie huffed as she slid off of the bed. I'll be in the car. You can wait for the papers," she announced as she slipped past her father and disappeared through the curtains.

Turning back to his oldest, Phil offered a, "Thank you."

She wanted to tell him that they were wrong, but given the benefits of the situation, she simply responded with, "You're welcome."

His look of appreciation suddenly turned to confused as he did a quick look around before asking, "Where's Derek?"

FORTY-TWO

For a second time in the last couple of days he'd found himself in a hospital trying to obtain information he had no right knowing.

After a three hour flight from Springfield, Massachusetts to Tampa, Florida, Derek, using the limited information he'd gleaned from Mr. Fook's letter, had made his way to St. Joseph Hospital's maternity ward, where he'd told the nurses that his sister had just given birth to his first nephew. Thankfully, the flawed security had him passing right in front of the nursery before reaching the nurse's station where he had to sign in, so he'd had plenty of time to pick a name from one of the plastic bassinets before greeting the nurse behind the counter. Luckily, this time around, she'd been closer to his age and reasonably attractive to boot, so starting a friendly conversation had been easy. It was clear that she was relatively new to the job and obviously drawn to the work by her love of babies, so striking up a flirtatious conversation had been relatively easy. Hell, he had all the ammo he needed crying in the next room.

Within five minutes he'd earned the nurse's number and more importantly, her trust as she was temporarily pulled away from her station to assist one of the other nurses in moving one of their…larger mothers who, based on the second nurse's loudly whispered explanation, refused to get up and move herself because, she quoted, "I just had my hoo-ha split in two and it's swollen like a mother-fucker."

"Obviously one of the hospital's more classy patients," Derek had thought as he'd added, "lucky kid," to the conversation, also a bit too loudly as both girls had turned and grinned before disappearing into the eloquent woman's room.

The yelling and complaining from the room down the hall had assured him that he had some time, so instead of hunting through piles of papers, he'd gone right for the computer. Within minutes he'd found everything he needed: Jason's birth name, to which he'd mumbled, "poor kid," forgetting who he was talking about; his birth mother's information; which room she'd been in; which bassinet had been his and most importantly, the names of the adopting parents and their address.

With the woman down the hall screaming that her vagina was stuck, whatever that meant, he'd confidently taken the time to print out a copy of the stolen records as well as written a quick thank you note with the cartoon image of a baby with a curly-Q strand of hair on top of its otherwise bald head. She'd deserved some sort of thank you he'd thought, given that *this* unlawful act hadn't ended in a brief chase through the hospital, nor had he found himself hydroplaning across a sea of urine this time.

Now, standing outside of the Nesbit's house and more importantly, Oliver…Jason's nursery window, he was left to wonder if he'd actually be able to follow through with what he'd just traveled fifteen hundred miles to do.

*****

"Oh my god. Come on already," Derek mouthed as he

continued to peer through a gap in the nursery's curtained window, at the man sitting across the room in a rocking chair with baby Jason cradled in his arms.

Crash!

The lightening had been increasing ever since he'd slipped through the neighbor's yard and clumsily climbed and fallen over the Nesbit's back fence. Thankfully, it was only that though…lightening, and the normally accompanying rain hadn't yet arrived. Removing his gaze from the window, Derek slid back into the shadows of the narrow walkway between the house and property dividing fence.

"How do people live like this, he thought?" looking over the fence at the neighboring house no more than fifteen feet away. He'd grown up on the south shore of Massachusetts where most houses were relatively spread out from one another. Sure he'd had neighbors, but if you wanted to spy on them effectively, you had to invest in a telescope or at least a pair of binoculars, not simply pull a chair up to the window with a bowl of popcorn and wait for the show to begin. Sure he'd spent the last four years living in Boston but that was different. That was a city, and he'd been living in a dorm where privacy was a luxury typically not afforded. It wasn't a permanent residence. These people practically lived right on top of one another and they'd paid a hefty sum to do so. Florida was officially off his list of future homes…if he ever saw home again, he thought, standing back up to check the nursery once again.

Inside, Mr. Nesbit was finally placing Jason into his crib, obviously nervous that his newly asleep son might awaken at any moment.

Crash!

Mr. Nesbit froze, closing his eyes at the thought of what the sudden boom might bring. Slowly opening them again, it became apparent on Mr. Nesbit's face that the lightening had gone unheard by the baby as he let out a little smile before turning and exiting the room.

"Finally," Derek thought as he took a step back to contemplate exactly how he was going to get inside the house. He hadn't tested the window before because of the father's presence, so taking a step forward he lightly pushed up on the closed window.

Locked.

"Shit!" he exclaimed, quickly covering his own mouth as he stared at the window horrified by his own carelessness. He couldn't afford to get caught. How could he explain to the police why he was standing outside the window of a newborn he had no relation to? He couldn't. If he got arrested, it meant Sarah and her sister were on their own, which meant Jason would get what he was coming for. He couldn't let himself get caught, he had to get inside and put an end to this madness.

Crash!

With the latest explosion's sound waves rippling through his ears, he suddenly knew what to do. Looking around his feet on the dark, shadowy ground, Derek began searching for something, anything that could be used to break the window; a task which proved to be relatively easy with Mr. Nesbit's apparent plans to replace the grass gap along the side of the house with stone pavers. Hoisting one of the surprisingly heavy stones from the pile, Derek positioned the smooth rock inches from the window as he glanced toward the sky, waiting for God's next strike.

The storm was rolling in fast, so it didn't take long and with a perfectly timed jerk of the hands, the small square of glass forfeited its defense, allowing him to reach inside and disengage the latch as the first raindrop struck the top of his head. Carefully returning the stone to the pile, Derek again pushed up on the window, this time slowly inching it upward in its casing, just enough so that he could pull himself up and through the opening, landing on the floor with a soft thud.

Freezing in his carelessness, he listened; one for the

sound of the sleeping infant beside him and two for the returning footsteps of Mr. Nesbit who was surely on some leveling listening to his son's room through the baby monitor on the changing table. Everything remained quiet, except for the soft patter of rain against the window and roof overhead as the storm finally decided to arrive.

"Alright dumbass," Derek thought as he got to his feet slowly, careful not to make any more careless noises as he crept up to the edge of the wooden crib. On his back, Jason slept peacefully, his pacifier tightly clenched between his tiny lips and moving up and down with each deliberate suck.

"How could something so innocent, so harmless turn into such evil?" he thought as his gaze traveled from the sleeping child to the cheerful decor of the surrounding room. It didn't really matter how it had happened, he answered his own question as his wandering gaze returned to Jason. All that mattered was what Jason was going to become…had become. Something had to be done to stop him and back at Mr. Fook's house, he'd concluded that this was the only way.

Quickly looking around again, he spotted a large, pink, stuffed bunny beside the crib; probably a gift from someone who hadn't been briefed on the sex of the adopted child. The color less important than its function, Derek plucked the bunny from the nearby tabletop, his hands shaking as he held it out in front of him.

There was no going back from this point. It had to be done. Nonetheless, he knew that this horrible act would haunt him for the rest of his life. With his hands shaking, he lowered the pink animal down into the crib, positioning its white stomach over the sleeping baby's face and, fighting back tears, began to press.

It took a moment for the child to respond, the gap between reality and slumber not quite bridged until the tiny mind acknowledged the odd sensation of the heavy object impeding its ability to get air. Once aware of his situation, at least on an instinctual level, Jason's arms and legs began kicking and flailing, though lacked any real coordination to mount any sort of effective defense.

With his head turned and eyes closed, Derek leaned further into the crib, pressing the pink fur harder against the child's face.

"Hey!"

His eyes bursting open, Derek didn't have time to see who had shouted the exclamatory term, but he didn't need eyes to figure it out. Within seconds, Mr. Nesbit had his arms wrapped around him, tugging and pulling at his body and arms, trying to remove him and the bunny from his son's crib.

A blunt pain to his ribs, followed by another and then a blow to the head almost made Derek release his grip of the homicidal rabbit, but focusing on the task at hand, he stood his ground as more painful blows connected with his increasingly battered body. No matter what, he couldn't succumb to the all out assault launched by the irate father. As horrible an act as he was committing, it was the only way. He could end it right then and there, no one else would have to die. Bethany wouldn't end up sliced to pieces on her bed. The liquor store clerk could continue to be the same asshole behind the counter. Mr. and Mrs. Tillmore would get to watch their daughter grow up to become prom queen and Sarah's sister wouldn't have to die. As painful as each blow was, he had to hang on until it was done, even if it meant he himself being killed in the process.

With another blow to his temple, the room began to spin. That, combined with a high pitched shriek, momentarily broke Derek's focus as Mr. Nesbit finally managed to pull him away from the crib and with one more devastating blow to the face, dropped him to the floor.

Bordering on unconscious, everything seemed to move in slow motion as Derek looked up at the hatred and confusion in Mr. Nesbit's eyes and then watched as the man returned his attention to the crib, his look of confusion suddenly even more profound.

Realizing his opportunity, Derek stumbled to his feet and, not as shocked by the empty crib as Mr. Nesbit was, he darted toward the door, knocking Mrs. Nesbit out of the way as he stumbled into the hall, colliding with the opposite wall before stabilizing himself and heading for the front of the house. Reaching the end of the hall, the front door came into view as did the sight of the naked infant lying on the floor in the center of the living room. Too shaken up to even consider that this may be his last opportunity to strike, he was out the front door and running down the rain soaked street, adrenaline the only thing keeping him conscious.

FORTY-THREE

"Where are you going?" Phil questioned over his coffee mug as his daughter entered the kitchen, backpack over her shoulder.

"School," she answered surprised by the question.

"Didn't you hear what the doctor said yesterday?"

"That I'm perfectly fine."

"No, that you should take it easy for the next few days. That means no school today. I want you to stay home and rest. I'll give you a note on Monday."

"Dad," Katie whined.

"Katie, I'm serious. You should take it easy. It's better to be safe than sorry."

"But I'm fine. I haven't had any more pains and I feel fully rested. Actually, I think last night was the best sleep I've ever had," she added, realizing that she may be laying it on a little too thick.

"I'm glad you're feeling better, but you're still not going to that dance tonight," Phil countered, knowing full and well the true reason behind her persistence.

"That dance is the prom. Are you really going to insist that your daughter miss her prom?"

"Junior prom. Your real prom isn't until next year.

345

Besides, when I was your age, there was no such thing as a junior prom."

"When you were my age dinosaurs still roamed the earth," she smiled, attempting to use humor as a way of possibly swaying her stubbornly overprotective father.

However, his stoic expression told her that, not even her usually well received jokes were going to persuade him this time.

"Katie. I love you. I know that you're upset about missing out on the dance, but I need you to understand the importance of your health. We're not only talking about you right now," he motioned toward her stomach. "You have someone else who's depending on you to keep her safe."

"Now she definitely wasn't going to win," she thought. He'd used the, "you're going to be a mother," guilt trip on her. How could she argue with that one? So instead, she just dropped her bag on the floor beside the barstool and took a seat.

"Good morning," Sarah greeted her father and sister as she entered the room.

"Morning," Phil offered in an exasperated tone.

Katie said nothing as she sat in front of a glass of orange juice that her father had poured during their squabble.

Sensing the tension in the room, "What's going on?"

"Child abuse," Katie mumbled, keeping her eyes on the glass before her.

Phil grinned at his younger daughter's childish humor. "Nothing. Your sister is devastated about missing school."

"Really?" Sarah asked. "When did you...oh," she finally realized the true reason behind the tension. Just as she'd felt yesterday, she wanted to tell her father to relax; that Katie would be perfectly fine to go not only to school but the dance as well and that she could use the whole rest of the weekend to relax but again, considering the benefits of the current situation, she continued to side with her father. "At least it's only your junior prom."

"That's what I said," Phil added, feeling validated.

"Oh, God, now I sound just like Dad," Sarah thought, but couldn't go back now. "I didn't even go to my junior prom," she continued. "And Daddy, I don't even think they had junior proms back then."

Even more validated, Phil smiled as he sipped at his coffee.

"Hell, I don't even think the wheel had been invented yet," Sarah added with a smile.

"No, it had just come out," Phil quickly retorted. "And it's a good thing because I don't know how I would have been able to pick your mother up without that horse drawn buggy."

Katie didn't respond as her father and sister exchanged grins.

Ding dong.

"Mike's early today," Phil acknowledged as he glanced at the clock on the microwave.

"How is officer Lucern?" Sarah asked with a smile.

He knew what she meant. While nearly eighteen years her senior, his partner's immaturity and boyish good looks often gave people the impression that he wasn't much past his mid to late twenties, and once a few years back, Sarah had chosen to inform him of how hot she thought his partner was. He wasn't sure if she still felt that way or just liked seeing him squirm, as she often found a way to work the topic into almost any conversation. "How's the weather? Hot like your partner? So, what are you doing this weekend? I don't know, maybe your partner." The timing and means were random and often uncomfortable, but he was glad to have such an open and comfortable relationship with his oldest. They'd always been close, likely because they had much the same personality. Katie had taken after his wife, which was likely the reason for her rebellion once her mother was gone.

"Engaged," Phil answered his daughter's intentionally uncomfortable question with a pleased smile.

Sarah let out a little frown, causing him to again question her seriousness as he made his way to the door.

"You're early," Phil greeted Michael as he pulled open the door, surprised to find a delivery driver standing on the other side, holding a large FedEx envelope and clipboard. "Oh. I'm sorry. I thought you were someone else."

The man smiled, not sure how to respond, other than to hold out his clipboard and say, "I need you to sign here."

Taking the clipboard, Phil signed on the line, handed it back to the driver and took the envelope as the young man quickly turned and started back down the path without another word.

"Not exactly Mr. Personality," he thought as he started to close the door, then, realizing that he didn't recall seeing the FedEx truck parked along the curb, turned back in the direction of the departing man who was now gone. Looking up and down the street confused by the man's sudden disappearance, he simply shrugged his shoulders and closed the door.

"Who was that?" Sarah asked, entering the living room.

"I'll be in my room...*relaxing*," Katie huffed as she passed her prison guards and quickly made her way upstairs to her bedroom.

Shaking his head with a smile, Phil stared at the envelope. "You expecting anything?"

"No," Sarah replied. "Open it."

Again shrugging his shoulders, he tore at the perforated strip and tipped the envelope on its side as a VHS tape slid out into his hand.

The top of the tape simply read, *RCA*, but a handwritten label along the side said, *play me*.

Confused, Phil looked inside the envelope, expecting to find a letter or something that might explain what the tape was or where it had come from.

Sarah didn't need a note. She didn't know exactly what might be on the tape, but she had a good idea that, whatever it was, it wasn't good.

"Dad, aren't you going to be late for work. You should probably finish getting ready."

"I have time. Mike's not even here yet. Do you have any idea what this is?" he looked up from the mysterious cassette.

Poorly attempting to conceal her worry, she shook her head no, as her father returned his attention to the tape and started toward the television.

"What are you doing?"

"It says play me."

"Do you do everything a tape tells you to do?" she uncomfortably joked.

"Don't know. This is a first," he smiled as he fed the tape to the VCR and turned on the television.

"Why don't you go finish getting ready and I'll watch the tape. I can tell you what's on it."

"Why don't you want me to watch this tape?"

"I don't care if you watch it," she lied. "I just don't want you to be late."

"I've got time," he assured her as the static on the screen cleared and the security footage a what appeared to be a liquor store came into focus.

"What the hell?" Sarah thought, recognizing the liquor store from the night before. The mystery of who the tape was from was now clear, but why would Jason send it to her father? It would show Jason killing the poor man currently seen mopping the floor. It would make it that much easier for her to tell her father the truth about what was really going on. He'd definitely believe her now. She wouldn't have to wait for Derek to figure something out. Her father would believe her and do everything in his power to protect her sister. What benefit did Jason get by giving them this evidence? And then she saw it.

With his back turned, a second man entered the image,

but it wasn't who she'd expected. Instead, it was Derek, slowly approaching the distracted man. It was Derek carefully plucking a bottle from a nearby display and it was Derek, smashing the man upside the head.

"How...?" she thought, even more confused than she had been in the last couple of days.

"What is this?" her father turned to her. "Is that?—"

She didn't know how to respond other than to continue staring at the familiar footage as Derek sat on top of the stunned man's chest and began forcing every coin from the cash register down his throat before using the jagged bottle to put an end to the clerk's struggle.

"Oh my God," Phil gasped at the horrible image on his television. "Sarah, what is this?" he asked again, even more concerned.

"Dad, I can explain. That's not Derek."

He just stared at her in disbelief. It sure as hell looked like the boy she'd brought home yesterday and who'd mysteriously disappeared less than eight hours later. "Not Derek?"

"It was Jason."

"Jason? Who's Jason?"

How was she going to explain this? It was hard enough trying to explain the truth without sounding completely insane. Now she had to tell her father that the image on the screen wasn't real and expect him to believe that her unbelievable story was?

"He's a friend of Derek's. Was a friend...," she corrected, "...until—"

"—Until what? Until Derek did this?" he turned back to the screen.

"I told you, that's not Derek."

Standing, the man in the video turned and then approached the camera overhead, pausing to look straight into the lens. It couldn't have been any clearer that the man in the video *was* Derek.

"He was with me all night. Someone must have

messed with the video. That's not what happened."

"You knew about this?" Phil seemed even more shocked.

"He stole Derek's wallet. We were trying to get it back."

"That guy stole Derek's wallet so he killed him?"

"No. Jason killed him and then somehow changed the video to make it look like Derek did it. He's from the future."

Phil didn't know what to say to that as a knock came from the front door, shortly followed by the doorknob turning and the door opening inward to reveal Derek, standing alongside Phil's partner.

"He says he knows you," Michael entered first, referring to Derek who followed close behind.

"Son of a—!"

"—Daddy, no!" Sarah jumped in her father's way as he made a b-line for a very surprised and battered looking Derek.

Michael didn't know what was going on as he watched his partner push past his daughter and grabbing hold of the stranger's arm, shove him up against the wall as he reached for the handcuffs on his nonexistent belt.

"What's going on!" Derek shouted surprised, his face being pressed into the wall by the angry officer's forearm.

Realizing that he hadn't finished getting ready yet, Phil turned to his partner. "Cuffs!"

With still no idea what was going on but realizing that he should help his partner, Michael handed his cuffs to Phil and helped to restrain Derek as they were applied.

"Daddy stop!" Sarah cried.

"What's going on?" Katie called from the top of the stairs, shocked to see her father and his partner restraining her sister's boyfriend.

"Go back to your room!" Phil shouted as he secured the cuffs.

"What did I do?!" Derek protested, his words slurred

by the wall.

"You're under arrest for murder," Phil began reading him his rights.

"Murder?" Michael responded shocked.

"Anything you say can and will be used against you."

"Daddy, let him go! The tape's not real!"

Completely confused, but eager to find out what had happened prior to his arrival, Michael looked over at the image on the T.V.. Frozen on the screen was a black and white close up of the man in custody, but more telling was the image of what appeared to be a dead body lying on the floor behind him.

"Do you understand these rights?" Phil finished.

Derek didn't know how to respond. He'd just arrived back from Tampa, ready to tell Sarah that his plan had failed and that they were going to have to somehow convince her father about the whole situation with Jason. He wasn't prepared to be brutally attacked again, this time for reasons unknown.

"Do you understand these rights?!" Phil repeated.

"Yes," Derek mumbled.

Pulling him away from the wall, Phil shoved Derek toward his partner. "Put him in the car. I'll get the tape."

Glancing over at the television, Derek finally understood what was going on as Mr. Bishop's partner guided him back out the front door.

"Daddy, he didn't do anything," Sarah pleaded.

"Is anyone going to tell me what's going on? What did he do?" Katie asked, now from halfway down the stairs.

"Didn't I tell you to go back to your room?!" Phil barked as he ejected the tape and quickly made his way into the kitchen.

Following her father, "Jason altered the tape," she continued to plead Derek's innocence as her father grabbed his gun and belt from the counter and quickly made his way toward the front door.

"Listen," he turned and paused to address his pursuing

daughter. "I don't know what's going on, but you and I are going to have a long talk when I get back. Now look after your sister," he ordered as he disappeared onto the front porch, closing the door behind him.

"And I thought Daddy was hard on my boyfriends," Katie joked.

"Shut up," Sarah snapped as she ran for her keys.

FORTY-FOUR

"Now, we're going to go over this one more time," Phil leaned across the table, stopping within mere inches of Derek's face, "Why'd you do it?"

"I told you. It wasn't me," Derek repeated the same explanation he'd been giving for the last two hours since being arrested, booked and chained to the interrogation room table, behind which he now sat.

The frustrated officer withdrew, dropping back in his chair on the other side of the table. "Really?" he uttered in frustration, eyeing his partner who stood behind Derek on the other side of the room. "We have a tape of what is unmistakably you killing that clerk, and you want to continue to claim that it was some other guy? What was his name?"

"Jason," Derek mumbled.

"Yes, Jason Fook, the grandson of nice old Mr. Fook's sister you said."

"Yes," Derek insisted. "He must have doctored the tape."

"What, does he work for George Lucas or something? Tapes can be altered, I'll give you that, but this thing is clear as day. Do you wanna watch it again?"

"I really don't," Derek thought. He'd already been forced to watch the horrific footage three times since being placed in the room. The television and VCR on the rollable cart still stood at one end of the table and Sarah's father seemed more than eager for another showing to get his point across. He could understand the officer's disbelief. The footage was very well done, but that wasn't hard to believe given the amazing editing software available to Jason in his time. While the early nineties weren't exactly the stone age, a lot had changed in the last twenty three years but he'd so far opted to leave the whole, I'm from the future explanation out of his defense. It was hard enough for them to believe that a video could be so well altered. How exactly could he convince them that his presence in their time was the result of magical blood and a machine that he'd built into a briefcase? It even sounded ridiculous to him.

"Do ya?" Phil asked again, holding the remote, his finger ready to push play.

"No."

"Then why don't you tell me what's really going on."

"I already told you who did it."

"Yeah, this Fook guy. Your roommate."

"Yes, but there's something I didn't tell you," Derek glanced up at the clock, concerned by the time. More than half the day had been wasted already and Sarah's sister was running out of time. At this point the chances of figuring out a solution in time were slim so he decided to level with the guy, even if it meant sounding like a lunatic and probably spending the rest of his life in prison. "There are more victims."

"You killed someone else?" Phil seemed shocked by the unexpected confession.

"No, Jason."

"Of course," Phil sighed.

"Are you going to take this serious or not?" Derek raised his voice.

Taken aback, Phil leaned forward. "Alright, I'm listening."

"Tabitha Tillmore. Her and her husband were killed last night at their house in Scituate.

Phil just stared into Derek's eyes. He appeared to be telling the truth, or at least he believed he was. Looking up at Mike, "Go check it out."

Nodding, Officer Lucern left the room.

"And you didn't kill these people?" Phil continued to probe.

"No."

"So how do you know about it?"

"I was there. I saw Jason do it."

"So you were an accomplice?"

"No. We tried to stop him but couldn't."

"We?"

"Shit," Derek thought. So far he'd left Sarah completely out of this. Other than telling her father that they'd recently met, he hadn't said another word about her and had avoided the subject whenever it came up.

"I meant I," he lied.

"Is my daughter somehow involved in this?"

"No."

"Don't fuck with me. My daughter brings you home from college unexpectedly. Nobody knows who you are or what your story is. Hell, I didn't even know she was seeing anybody.

"We're not—"

"—Shut up."

Derek complied.

"Where was my daughter when you saw this Fook character killing them?"

"I don't know. I didn't see Sarah until early yesterday morning when she picked me up."

"For a murderer, you don't lie very well. Let's hope you can find a lawyer better at it than you are."

Derek didn't know how to respond as he leaned back in

his chair, wanting to tell the man that his other daughter was next, but unable to find the words.

Seeing the defeated look in Derek's eyes, Phil also leaned back in his chair, the soft click and the squeak of the interrogation room door, finally breaking the deafening silence between them.

"It's true," Michael whispered in Phil's ear as he looked at Derek. "Two bodies, Mr. and Mrs. Tillmore, killed sometime the other night."

"How?" Phil looked at Derek.

"Mrs. Tillmore was stabbed in the back and Mr. Tillmore...well."

He could tell that his partner was bothered by the details he'd just received from the Scituate police department. He'd spent his entire career in the town of Cannon. The worst things he'd had to deal with so far were juvenile delinquents and the occasional domestic violence calls. Never murder.

"Any witnesses?" Phil whispered back, continuing to keep an eye on Derek.

"Just one. The next door neighbor claims to have heard some sort of commotion. She said that she saw a man, matching his description, getting into a car with...someone else."

"Shit," Derek thought.

"Who?" Phil looked up at his partner.

"The description sounds like Sarah."

Phil turned back to Derek. What had been a look of frustration and anger toward Derek, instantly became a rage filled hatred as he stood from his chair and grabbed Derek by the front of his shirt.

"Phil!" Michael exclaimed, worried about what his partner might do.

"You listen here you little shit," Phil addressed Derek through clenched teeth.

Derek had nowhere to go. His hands and feet were cuffed together and chained to the table. He didn't know if the incensed father was going to push, punch or shoot him.

"I don't know what you have gotten my daughter into but you can rest assured that—"

"—Your daughter is in danger," Derek blurted out. Why not he thought. He was going to be convicted for the murders that Jason committed anyway. His only defense was that a man, with the ability to travel through time, had come back to enact revenge on the mother's of the girls who had wronged him in high school. Yeah, that should be an easy sell to a jury.

"What did you say? You're not going to mention Sarah ever again or I'm going to—"

"—Not Sarah, Catherine, Katie. She's next."

"You're not going to touch my daughters, either of them," he lifted Derek out of the chair, pulling him halfway across the table.

"Phil," Michael urged his partner to relax.

Very calmly, given his threatened position, "Not me. Jason. You don't have much time."

Phil just stared at the surprisingly relaxed man in his grasp before releasing his grip, sending Derek crashing back into his chair. "Lock him up," he turned.

"Where are you going?" Michael asked.

"To have a word with my daughter," he grumbled as he yanked the door open and stormed out of the room.

FORTY-FIVE

"Sarah! Sarah, are you here!? We need to talk!"

Emerging from her room, Katie made her way to the top of the stairs where she saw her father standing just inside the front door, staring up at her.

"Where's your sister?"

"I thought she was with you."

"Why would she be with me?" Phil asked confused.

"She grabbed her keys and left right after you took what's his name away this morning. I thought she'd followed you to the station."

"Well she didn't," Phil sighed. "Do you have any idea where she might have gone?"

"No," Katie shrugged.

"Great."

*****

"Sarah. What are you doing here," Officer Lucern addressed his partner's daughter with surprise.

"I need to see him Mike," Sarah skipped the pleasantries and got right to the point.

"Your father's not here. He went home to speak with

you."

"Not my father," she glanced at the doorway leading to the holding cells in the basement.

"I can't let you do that," he held his hand up as Sarah took a step toward the door."

"And why not?"

"I don't think your father wants you talking to the suspect right now."

"He's not a suspect, Mike."

"Well I beg to differ. Right now he's being held on the suspicion of murder, with video evidence to back it up. I think that more than qualifies him as a suspect."

"I don't care what evidence you think you have against him. Your evidence is wrong," Sarah continued to stare him down. "Now you're going to let me in there or I'm going to tell my father about our little…you know…thing from a few years back."

Michael's face instantly turned ghost white at the threat.

She would never risk his career with such news but he didn't need to know that. Besides, nothing illegal had been done, but she was pretty sure that her father would explode at the news that his then eighteen year old daughter had been part of a three month affair with his long time partner and closest friend shortly before she'd gone off to college. It had ended on mutual terms, both realizing the eventual outcome of such a forbidden relationship. She'd gone off to school and he'd continued by her father's side as if nothing had ever happened. Occasionally, they'd exchanged awkward glances whenever she'd come home for a long weekend or holidays, some of which her father had noticed, but she'd managed to play those off with uncomfortable jokes about how hot his partner was, and had managed to keep him in the dark.

"You wouldn't. I thought we agreed that—"

"—Mike, I just need five minutes. The dispatcher buzzed me in and the other guys are in the back office. No one needs to know that I'm down there. My father won't find out," she assured him.

Nervously, he stared into her eyes. He could keep her presence in the basement from the others and he believed that she wouldn't tell her father. Hell, for over three years she'd kept the much bigger secret, but she also seemed a bit nervous and uneasy, which told him that, if denied, she might just go ahead and break her long time silence. It was a risk not worth taking.

"You have five minutes."

"Thanks Mike," she smiled as she again went to take a step toward the door, stopped once again by the officer's halting hand.

"But if you get caught down there, I'm going to claim to have never seen you and that you snuck in on your own. Alright?"

"Got it," she smiled. "You're looking good. You been working out?"

"Go," Mike grinned as she hurried through the door.

*****

"What are you doing here?" Derek leapt from the holding cell bench to meet Sarah at the bars.

"I had to make sure you were alright," Sarah nervously looked back over her shoulder, down the hall from which she'd just come.

"Did you break in?" Derek followed her nervous gaze.

"No," she laughed.

"Well I'm assuming that your father doesn't know. So, how'd you get down here?"

"It's not important. Listen, I went back to speak with Mr. Fook after you were arrested."

"And?"

"You were right about Oliver...I mean, Jason and the adoption."

"Sarah."

"They *are* planning on kidnapping him; his

grandmother and father I mean. Mr. Fook never really came right out and said it, but I understood what he meant. I didn't get much else before he forgot what he was saying and offered me another pie. The man must really like pie..."

"Sarah."

"But anyway, it gave me an idea. What if we contact the Nesbits and let them know what's going on."

"Sarah."

"Maybe we can stop this—"

"—Listen to me!" Derek finally managed to interject.

She fell silent.

"I know all about it. I went to Tampa last night. I went to the Nesbits."

"You did?"

"Yes."

"Why didn't you tell me?"

Looking around the room at his current situation.

"Right, but why didn't you tell me where you were going?"

"Because I didn't want you to be involved anymore than you already are."

"Involved. How could I be any more involved? I'm probably going to end up right beside you in that cell if we get linked to the Tillmore's."

"I told your dad about the Tillmore's. He knows everything."

"Everything?"

"Well not everything. I told him about Jason but I didn't mention you or the part about the future. Anyway, it doesn't matter. You need to get home and get your sister out of here. Run as far away as possible."

"I thought you said running wouldn't do anything."

"It probably won't but it might buy you a little bit of time to figure something else out."

"What about the Nesbits?"

"What?"

"You said you went to the Nesbits. What happened?"

"They aren't going to be of any help."

"But you told them right? Did you tell them about Jason's grandmother and father? Did you tell them about Jason?"

"I...," Derek hesitated as he contemplated whether or not to share details about the previous night's events and his unspeakable part in it.

"What am I thinking?" Sarah interrupted. "Of course they didn't believe it. Hell, I would still think you were nuts if I hadn't seen it with my own eyes."

Satisfied with letting Sarah jump to her own conclusions...for now at least, he redirected the conversation back to her sister. "Your sister can't go to that dance, alright?"

Sarah smiled.

"What?"

"My sister was in the hospital yesterday."

Derek wasn't sure how that news constituted a smile.

"She's alright," Sarah realized the contradictory quality of her expression to the news. "She's not going to the dance. One thing you have to know about my father is that he's very protective.

"You think?" Derek again scanned his surroundings.

"He's not letting her go tonight. She has to stay home and rest."

"Great! That should buy you a little bit of time. Jason seems to want me involved. He wants me there to witness it. You need to get your sister as far away from me as possible."

"But, what are you going to do? You didn't commit those murders."

"The evidence seems to say otherwise," Derek sighed. "Listen, don't worry about me. I'll be fine. Something tells me that Jason's not going to want me in here permanently. He's just toying with me. Like I said, he's going to want me there when it's time, which is why you and your sister need to leave, now."

Sarah didn't know what to say. She knew the truth. She didn't want to see Derek charged with crimes that he didn't commit, but she also wanted her sister to be safe.

"Go," Derek insisted.

Reluctantly, Sarah took a step back, sensing that there was more on Derek's mind than just her sister's safety. "What else happened in Tampa?" she asked.

Derek just lowered his head, ashamed of what he'd done, but more ashamed that he'd failed and that Sarah's sister was still at risk. Without looking up, he simply said, "Go."

FORTY-SIX

The sound of the doorbell echoed throughout the house. Its first chime instantly grabbing the attention of the impatient father waiting in the armchair in front of the dark and silent television. There would be no need for a second.

Leaping from his seat, Phil all but flew to the front door, expecting to find his oldest daughter standing on the other side. Why she was ringing the doorbell and not using her new key would be a question, but it would have to wait in line behind some much more serious and worrisome ones first.

"Where have you been?" Phil yanked open the door, surprised to find a boy on the other side.

He was dressed in what appeared to be a tux, though it's loose fit and strange blue hues made him look more like a clown or someone who might belt out a singing telegram at any moment. At his side hung a large black duffle bag, in which were probably a bunch of helium filled balloons that he'd probably set free at the finale of his song.

"May I help you?"

"Mr. Bishop?" the entertainer asked.

"Yes," Phil answered apprehensively.

"My name is Mark."

Phil just stared at him confused.

"Mark Fossy," the kid clarified.

"Oh, Mark," Phil finally recognized the name. "Katie's Mark," he smiled, though instantly wanted to cringe after playing back what he'd just said.

Mark smiled and bowed his head.

"He's obviously much more timid than his obnoxious brothers" Phil thought, as he stared down at the awkward looking kid before him.

"Is Katie here?" Mark finally managed to harness his nerves and make eye contact again, though barely.

"She is but... Didn't she tell you that she can't go to the dance tonight? She was in the hospital yesterday." Wow, this was going to be awkward if he was the one breaking this news to the kid, Phil thought.

"Oh, I know. I was there. I know she can't go. She told me and I understand completely. Whatever's best for her and the baby."

"Maybe this kid's not so bad after all", Phil thought.

"I just wanted to stop by and bring her something," Mark held up the bag.

"And what's in the bag?" Phil questioned, his suspicious police nature picturing a bag full of cocaine or fire arms, even though he knew he was being absolutely ridiculous.

Knowing what Katie's father did for a living and noticing the look of suspicion on his face, Mark placed the bag on the threshold between them and pulled back the zipper, revealing the bag's contents.

Phil, seeing what was inside, instantly shot the nervous kid a puzzled look.

*****

Knock, knock, knock.

"Daddy, since when do you knock?" Katie questioned from her bed, her eyes fixed on 'Saved by The Bell's' Screech. "Don't turn out like him," she whispered to her stomach.

Realizing that he still hadn't entered, Katie sighed and meandered over to the door, her eyes still fixed on the T.V. nerd's wild antics.

"Finally believe in privacy?" she greeted her father as she opened the door but instead of the familiar, parental figure she'd expected to find on the other side, in his place stood Mark. Caught off guard by his presence and his colorful outfit, she did a quick double take of the television, and for the first time realized that she had a thing for Dustin Diamond.

"Hey Katie."

"Mark. What are you doing here?"

"I just wanted to make sure you were feeling alright."

"I'm okay. Listen, I'm sorry about the dance," she apologized again for the last minute cancellation but stopped in her tracks as she stared at his outfit. "I did tell you, right?"

"Yeah."

"Phew," she breathed an internal sigh of relief. She already felt bad enough for canceling their date. She would have felt horrible if she'd then forgotten to tell him about it.

"If I told you, why are you all dressed up then?"

"May I come in?" Mark avoided the question.

"I guess so, but leave the door open. My dad has an open door policy," she rolled her eyes as she returned to her bed, sitting down on the edge as Mark moved into the center of the room and placed the black duffle bag on the rug in front of him."

"What's in the bag?" Katie questioned curiously.

Anticipating the question, "I need you to close your eyes."

Confused and still staring at the bag, she wondered

what was inside, cocaine or maybe firearms, she thought, then laughed at herself for how obvious it was that she was her father's daughter. "You're not going to chloroform me or anything, are you?" she joked.

"Just close your eyes," Mark repeated.

"Okay," she complied. "Because my dad's on high alert tonight. Apparently my sister is dating a mass murderer or something, which could go one of two ways for you, depending on whether or not you're suspected of murder as well."

"Open them," Mark interrupted her rambling.

Opening her eyes she instantly saw the clear plastic container which Mark had placed on her lap and the gorgeous orchid corsage within it.

"It's beautiful," Katie looked up, the smile already beaming from her face doubling in size as she saw Mark kneeling before her, a mirror ball dangling from one hand and in the other, a flashlight, the reflections of its beam dancing around the room.

"I know you can't go to the dance but that doesn't mean that the dance can't come to you, right?" Mark smiled.

Katie's face glowed with excitement as her eyes welled. "Yes," was the only response she could muster through her overwhelming emotions as she leapt forward and threw her arms around the amazing man before her.

"I really hope you two didn't just get engaged," Phil spoke from the doorway with a smile.

"Daddy," Katie let go of Mark and took a step back.

"It's okay," he approved the show of affection. "I'd say he earned that one."

Katie just smiled as Mark put down the flashlight and took her hand.

Staring at the young couple, Phil dreaded what he was about to do but realizing that his little girl was growing up, he felt confident in his decision. "Shouldn't you be getting ready?" he asked his daughter.

"What do you mean?" Katie questioned, confused.

"The dance. It starts soon. Shouldn't you be getting ready?"

Her lips finding even more elasticity to expand the already ear to ear smile on her face, "Really?" she squealed.

Phil just smiled and nodded as his daughter traded Mark's hand for a running hug with him.

"Thank you Daddy. I love you so much. Thank you."

"And I love you, now hurry up. You don't want to keep him waiting," he whispered in her ear.

With one last squeeze, she released her grip and turned back to Mark. "Just give me ten minutes, fifteen tops."

"I'll keep him entertained downstairs while you get ready," Phil motioned for Mark to join him.

"Daddy, be nice."

"What? I'm always nice," Phil grinned as Mark slipped past him, into the hall and the door swung shut.

FORTY-SEVEN

Staring at the caged clock on the wall, all Derek could think about was Sarah and her sister throwing things into a suitcase and loading up the car for their impromptu trip. More likely though, Sarah was in the middle of an argument with her father, trying to convince him of the unbelievable truth that was the last couple of days. All he could hope was that she would have better luck getting through to him than he had.

"Almost time," a voice suddenly arose to his back.

Turning, Derek's heart dropped. Sitting on the bench on the other side of the cell, holding the same hunting knife on his lap that he'd used to carve up Mrs. Tillmore, sat Jason. Beside him, passed out on the bench, was the disheveled man the cops had brought in only twenty minutes earlier and who had since been filling what had been a peacefully silent cell with eardrum rattling bouts of snoring.

"Did I snore like that when we were roommates?" Jason asked.

Derek didn't answer.

"What, no hello?" Jason smiled.

"You son of a—," Derek took a step toward him.

"—Ah ah," Jason lifted his finger as his other hand moved the knife from his lap to a precarious position over the throat of the sleeping man; the tip of the blade resting ever so delicately against his Adam's apple as he playfully twirled it back and forth between his fingers.

Derek stopped. "What the hell do you want?"

"An apology for one."

"An apology!?" Derek snapped, realizing how well his voice carried in his concrete surroundings. There was no point in alerting the officers upstairs. If he called to them, yelling that the killer was in his cell, Jason would just disappear and he'd be made to look even more crazy than he already did.

"Yes, an apology," Jason insisted.

"I'm sorry you're an asshole."

"Not exactly what I was looking for," Jason shook his head.

"Well sorry to disappoint you. How about you settle for a simple fuck you then."

"Derek. Derek, Derek, Derek. So vulgar," Jason continued to spin the knife, the man's skin twisting beneath the blade ever so slightly. "Then again, what else should I expect from a baby killer?"

He didn't think his heart could fall any further from his chest, but now he wouldn't have been surprised to look down and find both his heart and stomach lying on the cold grey floor beside him.

"Surprised? How'd I know?" Jason guessed at what his former friend was thinking.

Derek didn't have a response.

"I was there. Remember? Sure you do. It was only about…," looking at where his watch would have been if he wore one. "That's right, we don't really use watches anymore do we?" he joked, knowing that Derek, like most of their generation, relied solely on his cell phone for just about every bit of daily information. "How are you getting by without it?" Jason smiled.

"I've managed."

"I'm sure you have. You always do."

"What does that mean?"

"It means that no matter what unfortunate situation good old Derek finds himself in, he always seems to come out on top."

Staring at Jason, Derek had no idea what he was talking about, but was sure that he'd elaborate.

"He sleeps halfway through a midterm after an all night rager and still manages to ace the test in the twenty minutes he has remaining. Even after getting his ass beat by a girl's much larger, linebacker boyfriend, he still manages to take the girl home and not only does he fuck her for the next three weeks, but he also receives a hefty, 'I'm sorry,' check from the athletic department to ensure that the incident never found its way to a court room or the media. And my favorite," Jason chuckled, "He gets stranded twenty three years in the past and what does he do?...No, he doesn't find himself in jail or living on the streets with no real identity, other than the one he shares with the child version of himself—"

"—Jason, what are you talking about? I am in jail."

"Only because I chose to put you here. Do you want to know what I'm really talking about? Her."

"Who?"

"Who do you fucking think? Her. Sarah. That bitch you've been running around with trying to figure out how to stop me."

He still had no clue what Jason was talking about, but he didn't like Sarah being brought up in the conversation.

"You think I just ditched you here and forgot all about you?" Jason continued. "No. While I spent the next two years trying to harness the full potential of my gift, I still had to use the machine and while it somewhat limited my ability to travel to any point I desired, it did get better. I continued to find minor tweaks in the programming that broadened my options when it came to jump points. I used those advancements to check in on you from time to time; a year after I left you here, two years, then five, ten, you get the point. And do you know what the common element was every time I watched you?"

Derek had a guess.

"Her. Every time, there she was, right by your side, devoted and as loving as a wife could be."

"Wife?" Derek asked surprised.

"And two rat kids," Jason added.

Derek didn't know what to think. He knew he had strong feelings for Sarah and he suspected that she felt something for him, but he never would have guessed that she'd be the one he'd finally settle down with, especially given the extremely odd manor in which they'd met.

"It was then that I realized that, no matter what I did to you, you would always find a way to turn it around and show how much better you were than me."

"Jason, I don't think I'm—"

"—And then you had to go and do it," Jason interrupted.

Derek was again confused.

"Sure, I might have pushed you to take such a drastic measure but I never had any intention of harming you. As much as I've always hated you for being smarter and more popular and better looking, I would've never done what *you* tried to do."

"Jason, you killed those people. You were going to kill Sarah's sister."

"Oh, I still am. I assure you of that. But I never would have killed you. And as much as I might want to right now, I still don't think I have it in me to kill my lifelong friend."

Though still worried about Katie and whomever else might be on Jason's list, Derek breathed a sigh of relief as something in Jason's eyes told him that he was telling the truth.

"Jason, you—"

"—do you love her yet?"

"Jason—"

"—Do you love her?" Jason insisted.

"I don't know, I—"

"—I sure hope so, because I can't wait to see the look in your eyes when I cut out her heart," Jason sneered, raising the knife into the air over the snoring man.

"No!" Derek leapt toward Jason just as he disappeared, the knife remaining behind, falling through the air and sticking into the bench, millimeters from the sleeping man's throat.

Plucking the knife from the bench, Derek turned to see Jason now standing on the other side of the iron bars.

"Sorry to chat and run but I've got a prom to attend," Jason smiled as he looked up at the ceiling overhead. "But since I can't have anybody interfering with my date," he returned his evil gaze to Derek and smiled just before vanishing once again.

*****

"Ruth, did you get that notice from town hall?" Michael asked as he entered the dispatch room where sixty two year old Ruth Mater had spent the last thirty two years acting as the police department's dispatcher, 911 operator and front desk receptionist.

The room wasn't anything impressive. Though there were two stations with matching equipment, Cannon being the small town that it was, there had never been much need for more than one dispatcher to be on duty at a time, so as usual, Ruth manned the space alone.

"Ruth. The notice from town hall. Did Gerald bring it by yet?" Michael repeated the question, this time looking up from the papers in his hand and noticing the woman's arm across the desk, her head nestled in the crook of her elbow. "Another headache?" he asked, knowing her history of migraines.

It wasn't often that she got one at work so debilitating that she couldn't perform her duties, but it did happen on occasion.

"Do you want me to give Abigail a call? I'm sure she wouldn't mind coming in a bit early," Michael approached the woman, placing his hand on her shoulder. The moment his hand made contact with the grey haired woman's spring colored sweater, he knew that it wasn't a headache that she was suffering from.

With the slight pressure of his touch and the imbalanced weight of the slumped woman, the rolling chair on which she sat began slowly moving away from the desk, revealing a steady stream of blood, flowing over the edge of the desk and onto the vinyl floor below.

"What the…?"

Stopping the rolling chair with his foot, he grabbed both of the woman's shoulders and pulled her upright in the chair. The river of blood, pouring from her neck onto the desk, now began turning the bright yellow sunflowers of her sweater a crimson hue.

"Shit!" he exclaimed as he turned to call for help from the other officers down the hall.

"Hello Officer…," Jason greeted the panicked cop as he buried the blade of the blood stained knife deep within Michael's belly. Reading the officer's name tag, "…Lucern," he finished his greeting with a smile.

The shock of the unexpected attack causing his body and vocal chords to seize, all Michael could do was stare into the sadistic face of his attacker as he twisted the blade and pushed it even further into his abdomen.

"I don't think you'll be needing this," Jason pulled the officer's hand away from his gun, which he'd failed to fully withdraw from its holster.

"Who the—?"

Without hesitation, Jason pulled the gun from Michael's belt, turned and dropped the new arrival to the scene, all while continuing to hold the hunting knife firmly in his other hand.

The lights began to flicker and then dim as unconsciousness approached and the unknown man, staring at the shot officer, yanked the knife from his stomach. Dropping to his knees, Michael finally managed to fight through the shock, and get a signal to his hand, but as he reached toward his attacker, the room went dark and he fell forward at the man's feet.

Kicking the fallen officer's hand off of his shoe, Jason stepped out into the hall and without hesitation raised the gun to his left firing three shots at the two officers charging toward him just as a third, much older man in uniform rounded the corner to his right.

Having heard the gunfire, the white haired chief of police already had his gun drawn and spotting his officers being fired upon, did not hesitate in raising his own weapon to fire off two shots of his own. However, as the bullets erupted from the gun, Jason vanished from the hall, allowing the two stray shots to find their new targets. The first bullet struck a window at the other end of the hall, sending glass erupting into the interrogation room while the other bullet finished the job that Jason had started by striking the second charging officer in the head, dropping him onto his already fallen friend.

"Nice shot old man," Jason whispered in the man's ear, startling the elderly chief who stood in shock at what he'd just done, before pulling the trigger and splattering the wall with blood, skull and strands of red stained, white hair.

*****

"Shit!" Derek exclaimed as gunshots erupted overhead.

Reaching between the bars he jammed the tip of Jason's knife into the lock on the cell door, wiggling and twisting it back and forth in hope of somehow getting free and stopping what was taking place upstairs. With each shot however, his panic increased as did his aggression with the lock until finally, the tip of the blade snapped off, causing him to drop the knife to the floor, his only hope for freedom sliding out of reach.

"Ahhmm," the sleeping man on the bench suddenly moaned and shifted, the sound of the gunfire apparently more startling to his inebriated brain than the tip of Jason's knife, delicately balanced upon his throat.

As the man turned onto his side, a tiny, metallic noise joined in the commotion as something fell from beneath the man, striking the concrete floor and bouncing under the bench. Moving toward him, Derek scanned for the source of the odd sound, but didn't see anything until he was kneeling beside the unconscious drunk. In the shadows, against the wall, was a single key.

"Son of a bitch," Derek huffed as he grabbed the key.

Somehow he knew that it didn't belong to the unconscious man sleeping off his day of indulgence. The key didn't go to the man's car. It didn't open his house, nor did it open a locker at a fitness club, by the looks of the overweight bench warmer. Jason had placed the key beneath the man during his little visit. As much as he'd enjoyed setting him up for the murder of those people, he apparently didn't want his best friend to miss out on the action that remained, especially now that he was furious about the attempt on the much younger version of himself. He wanted Derek there when he went after Sarah's sister and more importantly, when he went after Sarah herself.

Returning to the lock, Derek again reached through the bars and rubbing the key against the lock managed to extract the remainder of the broken blade before inserting the key, disengaging the lock and pushing the door open to freedom.

FORTY-EIGHT

She didn't know what she was going to say to her father. She knew he was home. A cruiser was parked in the driveway. Typically, he and Michael rode in together, since Michael lived only a few blocks over, but as she'd learned from her visit earlier to the station, he'd apparently left early in hopes of having a few words about the unusual and alarming situation in which she was currently involved.

Turning the doorknob, Sarah took a breath and entered the house.

"Where the hell have you been?"

The anticipated question struck her ears even before her other foot could cross the threshold.

"Daddy, we need to talk," Sarah ignored the question.

"You're goddamn right we need to talk," Phil respond in the same angry tone. "What the hell are you involved in? Do you know that your boyfriend is suspected of not one but three murders now."

"Daddy, I can explain everything, but right now we need to get Katie and get out of here."

"Get out of here? What are you talking about?"

"We don't have time. I can explain in the car but we have to go now. Get some things together. I'll grab

Katie."

"Wait!" Phil barked, stopping Sarah mid stride on the stairs.

"I know it sounds crazy and you have no idea what's going on, but you need to trust me," Sarah pleaded.

Something in her voice and panicked eyes told him that he should listen. As confused as he was, his daughter had never been one to exaggerate or stir up drama. If she was this worked up over whatever she was talking about, he should probably put aside his current anger and listen.

"I need to get Katie, Dad," Sarah repeated as she started to take another step.

"Your sister's not up there."

"Where is she then, the kitchen?" she reversed her direction and rejoined him in the living room.

"I sent her to the dance," Phil answered, confused by the sudden look of panic on his daughter's face.

"You what?"

"That Mark kid showed up and I realized that I shouldn't be so protective. After all, the doctor did say she was fine," he finally acknowledged his stubborn disregard for the doctor's actual opinion. "So she got ready and went to the dance. They left about fifteen minutes ago."

"Shit!" Sarah exclaimed.

"What the hell is going on?" Phil asked.

"We need to get to the dance," Sarah declared, turning toward the front door.

"Mr. Bishop. Officer Bishop," a staticky voice called from the kitchen.

"Who was…?" Phil turned and headed for the source of the voice.

"Mr. Bishop, this is Derek. Please answer."

"Derek?" Sarah rushed to join her father who grabbed his radio from the counter.

"What the hell are you doing on the radio?" Phil snapped. "Where's Officer Lucern?"

"He's right here. He's hurt badly though."

"What the hell did you do?"

"Phil," a faint, whisper came over the radio.

"Mike," Phil responded, hearing the weakness in his partner's voice. "Mike what happened?"

"The kid was right, Phil. He was right."

"Mike! Mike!" Phil panicked, yelled into the radio.

"He's dead sir," Derek returned to the radio.

"I'm going to hunt you down and I'm going to—"

"—Daddy. It wasn't him. Didn't you hear Mike," Sarah fought through her own tears. "It was Jason. Katie's next."

Phil turned to his daughter in shock. "What has that boy told you?"

"You have to get to the dance. I'm on my way there now," Derek squawked across the radio again.

"Derek didn't do anything Daddy, but right now we need to get to Katie before Jason does," she pleaded.

Having never been more confused than he was at that moment, Phil stared into his daughter's tear filled eyes and realized that what she was telling him was probably true. His youngest was in danger and he needed to be there to protect her.

FORTY-NINE

"Alright, slide in a bit closer. There. Hold that pose and say cheese."

The flash of the photographer's camera bounced off of the ornate, glass chandelier hanging over the function hall lobby behind the young, well dressed couple.

"Next," the man behind the camera summoned his next subjects as the current couple bounced away smiling and kissing their way into the ballroom.

Serving as Cannon Town Hall, as well as the local community center, function hall and even playhouse to the local theatre group, the oldest and largest building in town was usually the focal point of any and all activities. As soon as Katie had set foot on the polished marble floors of the lobby, she had fallen in love with the place.

Squeezing Mark's arm, the two exchanged a smile as they stepped in front of the camera and positioned themselves on the two white "X's" taped to the floor.

"Alright, slide in a bit closer," the photographer repeated the directions he'd likely say a few hundred times more before the night's end.

Pushing in closer, Mark placed his arm behind his date, placing his hand on the small of her back.

Feeling his hand ever so gently pressed against her, she became overwhelmed by a feeling that she hadn't felt since her mother had touched her in the very same way. It was a comforting touch; a touch that sent a warm tingle throughout her body and told her that the owner of that touch would do everything in their power to lookout for her and care for her no matter what the situation.

Looking up at Mark, the smile on her face changed ever so slightly from that of excitement to that of happiness as Mark, apparently feeling the same way, offered the same expression.

"The camera's over here guys," the photographer interrupted the moment, drawing their momentarily distracted glances just as the flash erupted. "Next!"

"Ready," Mark turned to Katie once again.

Nodding, she took his hand as they entered the ballroom.

*****

Siren blaring, Phil skidded the Crown Vic. to a stop behind a photography truck parked in front of the function hall.

"Stay here while I find your sister," Phil ordered as he reached for the door.

"No," Sarah barked defiantly, opening her door and stepping out onto the curb.

Leaping from the vehicle, "Get back in the car and let me handle this. I don't want you getting hurt."

Ignoring her father's demands, Sarah turned and ran toward the front door.

"Sarah!" Phil rounded the car, passing behind the photo truck and stopping in his tracks as something caught the corner of his eye.

Backing up a few steps, he glanced inside the back windows of the van, spotting the body of what he assumed was the photographer, sprawled across the floor, covered in blood.

*****

The ballroom was amazing. The Junior Prom Committee had voted on a 1930's swing theme. The entire room was decorated in black and white and a live swing band and professional dancers filled the stage. Hundreds of students filled the dance floor, some attempting to mimic the acrobatic moves of the dancers on stage while others just did their best not to embarrass themselves.

He'd never been one for dancing, but seeing the look of excitement on Katie's face, Mark knew he'd have to put aside his fears for at least one night. His only hope was his date's current medical state and her father's last words before granting them freedom.

"Take care of my daughter and no swing dancing," Mr. Bishop had said.

At the time he'd been too terrified of the uniformed father to give it much thought, but now he wondered if he'd known the dance's theme or if it had simply been his attempt at humor. Either way he'd probably get his wish. He doubted that he'd even have the strength to twirl his date around like the professionals on stage, even if she wasn't pregnant, and something told him that she wouldn't want that anyway. Either way, before any type of dancing could occur, he needed to use the little boy's room.

"I'll be right back!" Mark shouted over the loud music.

Katie turned.

"I need to use the bathroom! You going to be alright for a moment?!"

With a squeeze of his hand, Katie nodded in the affirmative and released her grip as Mark disappeared into the crowd.

*****

For such an elegant building, the architect had left much to be desired with the bathrooms. As he stood at the middle urinal, he couldn't help but let his eyes wander up the dully painted wall, to the simple plaster ceiling overhead. One would think that a bathroom in a building of such ornate decor would have at least had some type of decorative features. Even though it was just a bathroom, there should have at least been some sort of crown molding. The counters had not been cut from the finest marble but instead appeared to be some sort of marble colored laminate and the plain, countertop sinks were topped by dull, unpolished, stainless steel faucets.

"Maybe I'm being too critical," Mark thought as the bathroom door opened and his new bathroom companion took up a position in front of the urinal beside him. After all, he acknowledged, he could be a bit critical sometimes. Since the age of eight he'd been telling his parents that he wanted to be an architect. Eager to encourage his dreams, they must have bought every set of Legos, Constructs and Lincoln Logs in the state. His room had been filled with dozens of Rubbermaid containers, filled to the top with the blocks of creativity.

Smiling at the memory of building tiny plastic and wooden cities, he couldn't help but smile as the man beside him caught his attention.

"Hey," Mark addressed the stoic man on the other side of the narrow divider. "Taking a break from the old camera, huh?"

The photographer didn't acknowledge him in any way.

"Okay," Mark thought as he zipped his pants and reached for the handle just as a sharp pain drew his attention back to his neighbor.

The photographer, who had previously pretended to be oblivious to the man beside him, was now staring right at him, a cold blank look upon his face as his gaze slowly shifted downward.

Following the man's wandering stare, Mark too shifted

his vision down along the man's shoulder, then to his outstretched arm to his hand and eventually to the knife buried in his side. Looking back up in shock, he was met by a simple smile on the young man's face as he yanked the knife from his flesh.

Stumbling backwards, Mark struck the corner of the nearby row of stalls before bouncing off of them and crashing into the counter. As he held his side and stared in shock at his wound in the mirror the photographer stepped away from the urinals.

Without anymore hesitation, Mark turned and staggered toward the door, the now excruciating pain in his side begging him to stop as every little movement pulled and twisted the open wound and drew more and more blood as his pant leg joined his shirt in adopting their new color.

"This dance is wicked," the bathroom door flung open to reveal Peter Broward, a member of the varsity football team.

"Watch out geek," Peter instantly addressed Mark as the two almost collided in the doorway before spotting the pool of blood on the floor beside the sink and the trail leading to Mark. "Man, are you alright?"

Looking over his shoulder for the photographer, "Run," Mark addressed his new company only to find his attacker was gone.

"What do you mean, run? What happened?" Peter asked.

"This," a third voice answered.

Turning, Mark spotted the photographer now behind Peter just as the man plunged the same knife into the football star's right ear.

*****

Though she was thrilled that her father had let her go; with Mark in the bathroom, the realization that she was completely alone was starting to sink in. Other than

Latisha, who was apparently planning a fashionably late entrance, she'd managed to burn the bridges to more than a few friendships over the last few years and becoming pregnant hadn't helped much with her social standings either. She'd gone from moderately popular to sideshow freak with each passing month.

She'd gotten used to the looks, well, maybe not used to them, but it certainly wasn't as uncomfortable as it had been the first few weeks after her condition had started to be noticed, and word began to spread around the school. She'd cried herself to sleep many a night during that time. *Now* she was excited to meet the little girl growing inside of her and everyone else's opinions just didn't matter.

"Who brought the whale?" Katie overheard one of the girls ask a nearby friend as she pointed and smiled.

"Whatever," Katie thought as she turned to watch the band on stage. They were pretty decent. They also looked surprisingly young given the style of music being played. Big band swing wasn't exactly the hip or expected form of music for a bunch of guys in their early twenties.

Suddenly a blood curdling scream brought all music to a halt as each of the band members, as well as everyone on the dance floor, and even the obnoxious girls at the table, all turned to the back of the ballroom. Turning, Katie spotted some commotion near the bathrooms as numerous students fled from that direction while the remainder of the crowd remained fixed on the sight of Peter Broward, staggering from the bathroom and collapsing to the floor in his blood soaked tuxedo with a large knife, protruding from the side of his head.

"Oh my god," Katie gasped, placing her hands to her mouth before realizing where Peter had come from. "Mark."

As teachers rushed to Peter's side, Katie too started toward the bathroom, pushing her way through the sea of traumatized onlookers before coming to an abrupt halt at the edge of the crowd as another man exited the bathroom. Unlike Peter, this second man was not a student, however she did recognize him. He'd taken their photo just minutes ago. However now, instead of a camera in his hand, he was holding what appeared to be a gun.

Seeing the weapon, the teachers at Peter's side jumped to their feet and backed away as the photographer raised the gun in their direction and very calmly approached his victim.

Katie wanted to run. Every instinct told her to hightail it out of there, but frozen with the same fear that was apparently keeping everyone else in the inner circle from fleeing, she continued to watch.

Seemingly oblivious to the hundreds of eyes surrounding him, the photographer stopped beside Peter's body, the football player's open eyes and lack of movement confirming his condition. With a smile, the man began whistling a little tune as he placed the leather sole of his shoe on Peter's head and leaning over, yanked the blade from the jock's skull.

The crowd gasped as crying began to break out from numerous directions.

Wiping the blade off on his khakis, the photographer looked up at the crowd, and zeroing right in on Katie, simply said, "say cheese," before vanishing into thin air.

Baffled by what they'd just witnessed, the group of onlookers remained frozen for a moment, until the same girl who had called Katie a whale, issued another statement; this time in the form of a high pitched scream.

Like a gunshot starting a race, the scream sent everyone fleeing toward the exits. The bottleneck of bodies instantly created an impenetrable wall, on the other side of which Katie spotted her father and sister trying to fight their way through.

"Daddy!" Katie screamed as she started toward them.

"Out of the way!" Phil yelled at the sea of terrified kids pushing him away from his daughter.

"Katie, were coming!" Sarah yelled as a panicked student crashed into her, knocking her to the ground.

"Sarah!" Phil cried as he turned from Katie for moment to help his fallen daughter.

"Katherine Bishop," a voice behind Katie whispered as a hand grabbed her shoulder.

Spinning around, Katie saw the photographer standing behind her.

Anticipating the scream, the man slapped his bloodied hand over her mouth while issuing a "shhh," as his eyes traveled down to her stomach and then back up to her face. "We wouldn't want to upset the little one now, would we."

Katie didn't know what to do. Standing in the center of the abandoned dance floor, she could run in any direction but where was she going to go? There was no way she was going to get through the fleeing mob. Her eyes darting from side to side, she suddenly spotted a glowing exit sign on stage.

"That's him! That's him!" Katie heard her sister shout, followed by her father screaming "Katie!" as he fired a shot into the air in a desperate attempt to make a hole in the crowd.

Taking advantage of the photographer's momentary distraction, Katie knocked his hand away and bolted for the stage.

Rolling his eyes, Jason let out a sigh before locking eyes with the advancing officer who'd finally managed to break through the crowd, and was now charging across the dance floor. With a grin, Jason closed his eyes and disappeared.

Hesitating in his advance, Phil stared at the spot where his daughter's attacker had just stood. "What the…?" he commented as Sarah finally caught up to him.

"Katie," Sarah refocused her father's attention as they looked up to see Katie on the stage and running for the stage right exit.

"Katie! Stop!" Phil shouted, his command going unheard as his daughter almost crashed through the door, sliding to a halt as she grabbed the handle and yanked the door open.

"We're not done yet," Jason greeted her on the other side as the door swung open.

Screaming, she tried to slam the door shut again, but was out muscled by Jason as he shoved the door out of the way and grabbed a handful of the girl's hair as she turned to flee.

Charging her attacker, Phil ignored the three steps and leapt onto the stage, almost losing his footing as the rug beneath his feet slid, knocking over a couple of microphone stands.

"Whoa! Dad! Careful there," Jason taunted as he pulled Katie to his chest, pulling her head back by her hair and placing the knife to her throat.

Pointing his gun at the man, Phil continued to move forward.

"I don't think you get it. You move. She dies," Jason clarified the assumed understood rules. "Or maybe you'll understand this better." Lowering the blade from the terrified girl's throat, he pressed it against her stomach.

Phil stopped.

"Yeah. Now you understand."

"Shoot him!" Sarah shouted from the dance floor beside the stage.

Keeping himself concealed behind the crying girl, Jason shot Sarah a look before returning his attention to her father.

"I don't think so, Phil. I *can* call you Phil right?"

Phil didn't respond, keeping his gun trained on its target.

"While I don't doubt your abilities with that thing, you and I both know that you wouldn't take the chance of shooting your little girl…s."

"What do you want?" Phil growled.

"I have a little business with your granddaughter and then, I'll be on my way."

"My granddaughter?" Phil asked in shock, having no idea what the unborn child could possibly have to do with this.

"Though...I did make a promise to a friend a little while ago," he glanced back at Sarah again.

"Jason, put the knife down," Sarah calmly pleaded.

"I've got big plans for that one, Phil."

"You're not going to touch my family."

"Really," Jason tilted his head to the side as he turned the knife and began fake jabbing at Katie's stomach, stopping the tip of the blade just before making contact with the fabric of the pink dress while taunting, "I'm not touching her. I'm not touching her."

Terrified Katie squealed with each fake jab until finally closing her tear filled eyes just as Mark came charging across the dance floor and, diving onto the stage, toppled Jason like an angrily thrown bowling ball picking up the spare.

Opening her eyes at the commotion, Katie turned to see Mark and the photographer crash into a group of spare musical instruments. Though her father was only twenty feet in front of her, her last thought had been focused on the door to her back, so seeing her chance, she turned.

"Katie!" Phil shouted as his daughter disappeared through the open door. "Go! Find her!" he yelled to Sarah before charging the pile of instruments dancing on top of the struggling kids.

Following her father's instructions, Sarah leapt onto the stage and ran after her sister, leaving her father to deal with Jason.

"Let him go!" Phil ordered as he approached the scuffle, his gun drawn on the commotion before realizing that it was only Mark under the pile of guitars and brass instruments. "Mark! Where is he?!"

Caught up in his battle with the pile of metal and wood,

Mark too hadn't even realized that he'd been fighting with nothing but a pile of inanimate objects as he ceased his struggle and looked up at the gun pointed at him.

"Mark, you're hurt," Phil addressed the boy, spotting his blood soaked side.

"So are you, Dad."

"Look out!" Mark shouted, pointing over Phil's shoulder as Jason's knife pierced the right side of his neck and erupted from the left with a spray of blood.

With the shock of the unexpected attack, Phil's hand jerked and with it, a single shot erupted from his gun, striking Mark in the chest.

Twisting the knife, the blood spurting from the officer's jugular sprayed out, soaking the nearby stage curtains as the accompanying crimson river gushed out over his shoulder, down his arm and onto the floor where, after a brief struggle, Phil eventually fell.

Taking the gun from the dead officer, Jason turned to Mark who, though bleeding from the chest and side now, was still struggling to get away as he shoved aside a toppled trombone in his attempt to flee.

As the boy dragged himself across the stage, Jason slowly followed, giving Mark hope with every second that he delayed his attack, while at the same time confirming the inevitable with every exchanged glance as Mark occasionally looked over his shoulder.

With more important things to do, Jason stepped on the back of Mark's knee, halting his forward progress.

Realizing his fate, Mark gave up, placed his forehead on the stage floor and began to weep as Jason raised the gun.

*****

The sound of the second shot made her jump just as much as the first had. She could only hope that her father was alright and that this nightmare was over as she made her way down the dimly lit hall.

"Katie. Katie, where are you?" Sarah whispered, looking in each room that she passed.

This part of the building appeared to be used as a community center for the arts, each room having an almost school-like setup with desks, art tables, posters of music charts and color pallets on the walls.

"Katie. It's Sarah. Where are you?"

"In here," the musty air responded with a faint whisper.

Not sure where it had come from, Sarah stopped and listened. There were only two rooms left ahead of her, but she hadn't entered and thoroughly checked each room that she'd already passed, so Katie's response could have come from anywhere.

"Where?" Sarah asked, waiting for a response until finally another "Here," came floating through the air.

The sound had come from behind her. Turning, she rechecked the room she'd just passed. As before, it was dark. Stepping just inside, she searched for a light switch, finding three beside the door. The first switch snapped upward with a faint click but offered no visual aid. Trying the second, she again got no response so she wasn't surprised when the third also refused to help.

She'd seen enough horror films to know how this went. The lights were out, probably because the killer, in this case Jason, somehow disabled them. He was probably anticipating that her foolish curiosity and need to find her sister would lead her to adventure carelessly further into the room where he was likely waiting to jump out and make her pay for such stupidity. Well if this *was* a trap and she *was* playing the part of the silly girl, she'd just have to be ready to defend herself. Spotting a collapsed umbrella, standing in a brass pot beside the door, she stepped further inside. Though not an ideal weapon, she was pleased to see that the umbrella possessed a steel point on the end. Though not sharp, it did at least add some formidability to the impromptu weapon.

Holding the umbrella in both hands, she ventured into

the room.

"Katie. Are you in here?" she whispered.

There was no response. Continuing further into the art room, Sarah slowly bobbed between a sea of tall easels, each holding a large canvas with varying depictions of the same, human like figure. With no windows however, the further she got from the dim light of the hall, the harder it became to safely navigate without bumping into a few of the artistic renderings. Grabbing hold of one of the canvases as it teetered on its perch, Sarah stopped.

"What am I doing?" she whispered to herself. "Obviously Katie's not in here," she thought. She would have responded by now and if she wandered any further into the room she ran the risk of becoming trapped if Jason was by chance plotting an attack.

Deciding to return to the hall, she turned just as a large dark figure entered her vision. Screaming, she swung the umbrella, striking the figure and stumbling backwards as the towering object fell toward her.

Throwing her arms up over her head, she ran into an easel, sending it toppling into another nearby wooden tripod and then another. The sound of metal and wood filled the room as Sarah froze in fear, waiting for the pain of Jason's attack, however as the last object rolled to a stop beside her, she was relieved to have survived the commotion, injury free. Relaxing, she lowered her arms.

"Sarah."

Again she screamed, turning toward the door where a bright light was shining in at her.

"It's me," the figure turned the light on himself.

"Derek," Sarah sighed with relief. "What did I—?"

Pointing the light at the floor, the scattered components from a suit of armor lay all around her, the only portion remaining on the platform being that of two feet and a precariously balanced leg. Adding to the mess were the toppled easels and scattered canvases on which various, childlike interpretations of the intricate, metallic figure had been formed.

"What are you doing? Where's your sister?"

"I don't know. I think she's down her somewhere. She ran when——."

Knowing what was coming, Derek prepared for the question.

"My dad. Did you see my dad?"

He didn't know how to respond, but then again, he didn't have to. She could see it in his eyes, and instantly her's began to fill with tears.

"We need to find your sister," Derek attempted to refocus her attention on the task at hand.

There would be plenty of time for mourning but they'd be mourning the loss of one more if they didn't hurry.

"Where did you see her last?" Derek pressed.

Before she could answer however, the sounds of a poorly played trombone filled the basement.

Looking toward the door, Sarah simply said, "across the hall," as she recalled the room filled with musical instruments.

Attempting to avoid the scattered debris, they hurried toward the door and stepped into the hall. The music room was dark, just as the art room had been, the light from the hall only managing to penetrate about five feet before succumbing to blackness.

"Stay behind me," Derek whispered as he withdrew a gun from his waistband and advanced toward the room.

Before he could even set foot inside the threshold though, the lights snapped on, illuminating the dozens of instruments, all laid out in a large, neat circle around the room. At the center of the room was Katie, gagged, and bound to a chair with Jason standing beside her, the trombone to his lips and his cheeks puffed as he struggled to make even one crisp note from the large brass instrument.

"Let her go," Derek demanded as Sarah joined him in the doorway.

"Katie!"

Terrified, Katie struggled to speak through the rag tied around her mouth as Jason continued to blow one bad note after another, the tune he was attempting to play finally coming together as Derek recognized the theme music to Jeopardy.

Finishing the final jeopardy theme with those two familiar notes, Jason tilted the trombone to one side to get a better look at his new guests. "Not bad, huh?" he smiled, pleased with himself. "Can you believe that it took me two months to finally be able to play that?"

"You could have used two more," Derek critiqued.

"Ouch," Jason placed his hand over his chest. "I guess you're right though. Music was never really my strong suit," he acknowledged as he placed the trombone back on its stand beside the chair.

"Let her go, Jason," Derek threatened, holding the gun out in front of him.

"A gun? Really? Have you not learned anything yet?" Jason sighed. "Alright, how does this go?" he groaned as he moved behind Katie, who grew more historical as her captor's hands rested upon her shoulders. Ducking down behind his hostage, Jason taunted, "go ahead, shoot," as he bobbed back and forth, first looking over Katie's right shoulder and then her left before finally standing back up and taking his position beside her once again. "We both know who's in control here, so why don't you just put the gun down and—"

Two quick shots erupted from the gun. Sarah jumped and Katie screamed a muffled cry as Jason vanished, the two bullets striking the cymbals of a drum set to her back. Almost instantly, while the cymbals still chimed, Jason reappeared, now on Katie's right side as Derek pulled the trigger again, sending three more bullets into the far wall. Again, Jason disappeared.

"This is just getting silly now," Jason responded to the attack from the far end of the room, his chair tipped back and feet up on the desk behind which he sat. "Are you done yet? Eventually you'll run out of bullets and we'll be right back where we started."

Realizing the futility in any continued attack, Derek lowered the gun.

"Good," Jason vanished once again.

Scanning the room, trying to figure out where he'd rematerialize, Derek and Sarah exchanged a look as no sign of Jason could be found until...

"Now, back to business."

Turning, they spotted Jason once again standing beside Katie as he grabbed the trombone from the stand and, yanking off the slide, issued a menacing smile before plunging the two pronged, brass weapon into Katie's stomach.

"No!" Sarah screamed as her sister's eyes widened, the slide passing clean through and exiting her back as she slumped forward in the chair.

"You son of a—!" Derek charged Jason as Sarah ran to her sister's side.

Squaring for the impact, Jason vanished, sending Derek careening into the drum set.

"Katie! Oh god Katie!" Sarah cried, pulling the gag from her sister's mouth and lifting her head to look into her fading eyes. "I'm so sorry. I'm so sorry."

Unable to speak, tears ran down Katie's face as she stared at her sister in shock before lowering her gaze to the shiny brass object protruding from her stomach."

"Oh god, no," Sarah grabbed the trombone slide, ready to pull, then reconsidered for fear of opening the wound and potentially causing her sister to bleed out. It wasn't until their eyes locked again that she realized what was running through Katie's mind. Though unable to speak, her eyes said it all. "The Baby."

"It missed," Sarah attempted to comfort her sister as she took another look at the wound. "It's alright. She's okay," she continued, but quickly realized the futility of her words as she met her sister's eyes once again, but this time, couldn't find Katie within them. "No!"

"Awe."

Looking up, Sarah saw Jason standing right where he had been when Derek had charged. Jumping to her feet she swung, surprised as she landing a solid right.

Holding his jaw, Jason smiled just as Derek connected with his lower back, sending them both tumbling into a nearby cello and pair of violins. Ending up on top of the fallen psychopath, Derek began delivering blow after blow. Obviously too distracted by the wave of attacks to gather enough concentration to initiate a jump, Jason took hit after hit.

With each landed blow, Derek could feel things turning in his favor, right up to the moment that a violin exploded against his right temple, dropping him to the floor beside Jason who remained motionless for a moment, stunned by the beating he'd just received before finally getting to his feet and tossing the remains of the string instrument's handle to the floor.

"Fuck! You hit hard," Jason laughed, wiping at his bloodied nose with the back of his hand as he yanked the gun from Derek's waistband and standing over his friend, firing two shots into his chest.

"No!" Sarah screamed.

Sensing Sarah's closing distance, "Ah, ah, ah," he raised the gun in her direction as Derek struggled to get to his feet.

"Really, Jason turned to see his friend on one knee. Firing off another shot, Derek dropped.

Wanting to run to his aid, but blocked by the man between them, Sarah just watched as Derek gasped, then fell motionless.

Staring at his fallen friend, "You know, I'm recalling a certain promise I made," Jason turned back to Sarah, wrapping his gun holding arm around her as he drew his knife and placed it against her chest. "Do you know what it was?"

Closing her eyes, anticipating her end, she didn't know what else to do but weep.

"There, there," He mocked. "It's not that bad. It will be quick, well...maybe not. You'll probably survive the cutting...and maybe the rib cracking."

Sarah wept harder.

"It is a shame though, I really did want him to see me tear that precious little heart from your chest." Glancing over her shoulder, "then again," he added, looking down her shirt. "It would be a shame to let such perfection go to waste. After all, who's going to take care of you now? Daddy's gone. Sis is gone. Even your precious boyfriend didn't make it."

Opening her eyes again, she hoped to see some sort of movement from Derek, but he remained on the floor just as still as he had been.

"Hell, I guess I'm about all you have left," Jason continued. "Maybe you and I could have a future together. What-a-ya think?"

Sarah didn't answer as she continued to stare through her tears at Derek.

"Alright, I realize that it might not be easy at first but I think, with some time, you could begin to feel differently. I really can be a likable guy."

Still she said nothing.

"Argh," Derek started to moan.

"Derek!"

"Mother...," Jason raised the gun and fired the last two rounds.

Seeing Derek's body jump and then fall still again with the fourth and fifth shots, Sarah screamed, just as a tingling sensation began to spread across her skin and Jason, closing his eyes, uttered "Hang on."

FIFTY

As the brilliant flash of light faded, the room slowly came back into focus, only it wasn't the same room. The instruments were gone, replaced by a roaring fire in a large brick fireplace and a portrait of some elderly, asian woman hanging above it. Beside the fireplace was an armchair…a very familiar armchair actually.

"That's impossible," Sarah whispered, though she shouldn't have been surprised by anything given the unbelievable events of the last couple of days.

Confirming her suspicions, she turned her head to the left, spotting the expected desk in the far corner of the room. It was the same desk on which Derek had found the letter about newly born Jason. Instead of the pile of papers and books that had been on it earlier that day, there now stood a large electronic device that resembled a television, though she'd never seen a T.V. quite that large nor with such oddly flat dimensions.

"Some rush, huh?"

Sarah spun around to find Jason standing right behind her.

Anticipating her scream, Jason slapped a hand over her mouth.

"Not that anyone can hear you. I just hate that sound."

Sarah redirected the expression of fear to her eyes instead.

"You're a smart girl," Jason lowered his hand. "Do you know where you are?"

"Mr. Fook's house," Sarah answered.

"Technically the house belonged to my great grandmother, Ushi Fook" Jason motioned to the woman in the large portrait. "The man you're referring to was her brother, Jian, which is a bit ironic if you ask me because I can't remember a day of his life that he wasn't sick," Jason chuckled.

Sarah just stared at him.

"Healthy. His name meant healthy," Jason clarified, annoyed that he had to explain his humor. "He died when I was young so I never really got a chance to know him anyway. My great grandmother however, I knew her very—"

"—You don't know do you?" Sarah asked.

"Know what?" Jason paused, confused.

"What made him sick," she clarified.

Jason just stared at her, not sure what she was talking about.

With a smile, "Keep this up and you'll find out eventually," she wiped away her tears.

"Keep what up? What the hell are you talking about?"

"The jumping," a third voice chimed in from the other side of the room to Jason's back.

Grabbing hold of Sarah, Jason spun around as he brought the knife to her throat.

She'd spotted the man, standing in the corner, as soon as she'd turned around to face Jason. Though she hadn't been able to see his face, she knew who it was.

"Jian and I had the same conversation," the voice continued as Derek stepped out of the shadowy corner of the room, though it wasn't the same Derek that either of them remembered. Though the years had been kind to him, the lines in his face, coupled with the smattering of grey in his beard, told Sarah that some time had passed.

"What the fuck? Don't you die?" Jason asked in frustration.

"Bulletproof vest," Derek answered. "Maybe you should've shot me in the face."

"Good idea," Jason responded, raising the gun one more time and attempted to pull the trigger before noticing the slide locked in the empty position. "Shit," he tossed the gun to the floor, raising the knife to Sarah's throat instead.

"It's going to kill you," Derek continued as he slowly inched forward, causing Jason to slide toward the large, open doorway leading to the foyer.

"What is? You?" Jason laughed.

"The jumping," Sarah added.

Jason shot her a look of confusion.

"Jian had a brain tumor, not to mention he was senile as fuck," Jason continued his retreat.

"And what do you think gave him that tumor?" Derek continued toward them.

"Stay back," Jason grabbed hold of Sarah's hair, further exposing her neck as he pressed the blade to her flesh.

"Jason, put down the knife. It's over," Derek stopped his advance.

"Over," Jason laughed. "Are you fucking blind. Who's got the knife? You know, I was a bit disappointed when I thought I'd killed you. I really did want you to watch her die, and as luck would have it, I'll still get my wish."

"I'm not going to let you do that, Jason."

"Really? And how are you planning to stop me?"

"I'm not."

"That's what I thought," Jason laughed.

"He is," Derek motioned behind them.

Turning, Jason caught a glimpse of a younger Derek, just as the baseball bat struck his skull.

*****

"Jason. Wake up. How hard did you hit him?" Jason could hear a male voice ask, though he felt too weak to open his eyes.

"I don't know," a second male voice answered. "Hard enough."

"Guys, I think he's coming to," Sarah interrupted.

"Arghh," Jason moaned.

"Jason," Derek leaned in close, separating one of Jason's eyelids with his fingers.

"His pupils are dilating," Sarah added. "That's good."

"Jason, wake up," Derek slapped the semiconscious man.

The impact of the hand sent a wave of pain through his already throbbing head. "Ah!" he cried, finally managing to open his eyes, though it took a moment for the room and the three figures standing in front of him to stop spinning.

"Is it working?" the younger version of Derek asked as Sarah grabbed Jason's bound wrist, checking for a pulse.

"His pulse is slow but strong. It's wearing off. We need to do this quick before he regains the ability to jump," Sarah answered.

"Do what?" Jason asked, finally regaining his sight and realizing that they'd tied and duct taped him to a folding metal chair. "What did you do to me? Who the—", Jason looked back and forth at the young and old versions of his friend.

"Drake," the younger version of Derek introduced himself with a nod.

"Drake?" Jason asked confused.

"Yeah, my parents thought it would be odd to name their newborn son after the twenty two year old version of himself," old Derek attempted to clarify, though based on the look on Jason's face, a more elaborate explanation was needed. "Once I came to and realized that you'd taken

Sarah, I tried to figure out how I was going to get her back. It didn't take me long to realize my only option. I didn't have the ability to snap my fingers and follow you. I had to do it the old fashion way and wait. During that time I managed to convince my parents who I was."

Jason shot him a dismissive look.

"I was just as surprised as you. They really are an understanding couple. A few 'impossible to know family secrets' and I had them questioning, but it wasn't until that first look into their newborn's eyes…," Derek motioned to Drake "…that I finally had them sold."

"Fine. Now there are two of you to kill," Jason either accepted what he was being told or didn't really care as he closed his eyes, but after a few seconds, opened them again, confused by his continued captivity.

"That's not going to work right now," Derek added.

"What did you do?" Jason panicked, closing his eyes again.

"Oh...we just shot you up with a little something to thin your blood and slow you heart rate," Sarah smiled.

"We had a lot of time to think this through."

"Without proper blood flow, your brain lacks sufficient oxygen," Drake explained.

"You see, I developed this theory that your ability doesn't just stem from the genetic mutation in your blood. It also requires a strong mind to process the vast amount of data necessary for such a reaction," Derek continued. "My guess is that this is why not everyone in your family could do it."

"It's only the males and every other generation," Jason dismissed the insulting allusion. "My grandmother was a brilliant woman."

"Insanity doesn't denote brilliance," Drake mocked.

"Though in your case, I guess they just might go hand in hand," Derek added.

"Fuck you."

"Guys, we're running out of time," Sarah interjected,

holding Jason's wrist again.

"Don't touch me, bitch."

Kneeling down beside Jason, Derek picked up the open briefcase and placed it on Jason's lap.

"I destroyed that," Jason looked down at the device in disbelief.

"I'm sure you did," Derek replied as he punched away at a cell phone in his hand, the device responding with a beep, followed by a low hum. "I built another one."

"Fine, send me wherever you want. As soon as this shit wears off I'll be right back here slitting your fucking throats or maybe I'll just wait a while; keep you looking over your shoulders for the rest of your lives. There's nothing you can do to stop me. I'm invincible and you know it, so go ahead. Hit the button. Nothing's gonna change what I've already done nor will it stop what I'm going to do. You're all gonna die like that little slut's father and sister.

"You want the honors," Derek turned to Sarah, holding out the phone.

"Gladly," Sarah took the phone, turning back to Jason, "This is for my family, asshole."

As she touched the screen, the device began to hum louder as a static charge built in the air around them, and soft crackling gave way to much louder snaps. Then, with a burst of light, the briefcase, Jason, and the chair on which he sat, were gone.

With a sigh of relief, Sarah placed the phone on the table and turned to face Derek and the much younger version she'd grown accustom to. Though separated by a twenty-five year age difference, they were both familiar. Sure, Drake was the spot on, visual match to what...up until half an hour ago...were her only memories of Derek but it was in their eyes where the two diverged. Though very much the same, they'd both lived completely different lives, and in that moment it was perfectly clear how she felt as she ran into Derek's arms, and placing her hand to his older, hairier face, she looked into those familiar eyes as their lips joined.

"What if he does come back?" Sarah suddenly interrupted their embrace.

Looking at his younger counterpart, "I don't think that's going to be possible."

"Quivering jello," Drake smiled.

"What does—?" Sarah started to question before Derek cut her off with another, even more passionate kiss.

FIFTY-ONE

"Isn't he beautiful?" Jennifer's eyes glistened at the sight of little Oliver through the nursery window.

"Do all hospitals use the same blanket manufacturer?" Bill stared at this new born son, his mind obviously in a completely different place than his wife's.

"What?"

"The blankets they're all wrapped in," he motioned to the room full of infants. "They're all the same; a white blanket with a blue stripe."

Jennifer just stared at her husband. She knew he was apprehensive about being a father for the first time. Throughout the adoption process he'd shown signs of hesitation, but this was the worst yet. The day was finally here, and instead of staring lovingly at their new son, he was more concerned with the sales statistics of a blanket manufacturer.

"I'm only bringing it up because I'm pretty sure the same blanket is in my baby pictures and I'm willing to bet that every television show and movie I've ever seen used the same blankets as well."

"Bill."

"Don't you find that pretty amazing?"

"Bill."

"I mean, there have to be other companies that produce them. Or maybe there's some national design standard that every company has agreed on."

"Bill!"

Acknowledging his rambling, Bill stopped talking.

"I know you're nervous," Jennifer comforted her husband, wrapping her arms around him and looking up into his eyes. "I'm nervous too, but everything is going to be alright. In a couple of days you, me and Oliver are going to be home and we're going to be the happiest family ever. There's nothing that can come between us and there's absolutely nothing for you to worry about. You're going to be a great father. Now, shut up and enjoy the moment."

Smiling, he knew she was right, so taking her advice, he turned his scrutinizing attention away from the identical blankets and focused on his sleeping son.

"Isn't he precious?"

Turning, Bill and Jennifer spotted Mrs. Brown standing in the doorway of the hospital room across the hall.

"Breathtaking," Jennifer replied. "Again, I can't thank you enough for choosing us."

"I can't take the credit. Tiffany had the final decision," Mrs. Brown joined them at the window. "She may not have been thinking when she got herself into this situation, but she really is a smart kid. Besides, I would have chosen you guys anyway. We just want the best for the baby, and I…*we* think you two will be perfect parents."

"Remember, we want you guys involved as much as you feel comfortable," Bill reminded the would be grandmother. "We consider you both as much a part of our family as Oliver."

"I appreciate that. We both do."

"Mom."

"What are you doing out of bed?" Tiffany's mother turned to see her daughter standing in the hospital room doorway.

"I needed to use the bathroom," Tiffany leaned against the doorframe, obviously still uncomfortable and a bit groggy from delivering the night before.

"Okay, I'm coming. Excuse me," Mrs. Brown excused herself from the Nesbits.

"Of course," Jennifer motioned her toward her daughter.

"I want to see him," Tiffany stepped into the hall wincing in pain as she grabbed the doorframe, her mother rushing to her side.

"You need to lie down," her mother grabbed her other arm as a nurse also rushed to her side.

"You shouldn't be moving around yet," the nurse scolded the teenage girl.

"I want to see him," she insisted.

"Sweetheart, are you sure about that? Didn't we talk about giving it some time before—"

"—I know what we agreed. I changed my mind."

Jennifer's eyes widened in fear as she squeezed Bill's arm.

"Not about that," the girl addressed the Nesbits, realizing how her comment could have been taken. "You two are perfect. I'm still going to sign the papers. I just want to see him. They took him away so fast last night that I didn't even get to hold him. I just want to see him through the glass."

Exchanging looks, Mrs. Brown nodded her approval to the nurse who turned to retrieve a wheelchair from the nurse's station. With her mother's assistance, Tiffany carefully lowered herself onto the doughnut shaped pillow, placed on the chair by the nurse, before being wheeled alongside the Nesbits.

"Isn't he perfect?" Jennifer commented to the young girl, whose eyes began to well up at the sight of her son.

With a nod, Mrs. Brown signaled for the nurse to retrieve little Oliver so that they could get a better look at him through the glass. Agreeing, the nurse disappeared around the corner.

"He's the most beautiful thing I've ever seen," Tiffany smiled with a quiver in her voice as a tear broke free and ran down her cheek.

Appearing in the nursery doorway, the nurse smiled at her audience as little Oliver began to squirm in his clear, plastic basinet as if anticipating his first meeting with his new parents.

"Oh look," Jennifer pointed excitedly as she tightened her hold on Bill's arm.

The maternity ward had been busy the last couple of days and Oliver's basinet was at the center of a sea of newborns. Passing the first child, the nurse looked down with a big grin. It was clear that she loved her job; her favorite part being the times she had direct contact with the babies. Making her way to Oliver's Basinet, she plucked the clipboard from the tiny bed, confirming that she had the right child, before returning it to the tiny hook and reaching for the now fully awake child.

He didn't need to see his wife's face. The numbing sensation in his left arm told him everything he needed to know. The truth was, he was just as excited.

Sliding her hands under Oliver, the nurse prepared to lifted the blanket wrapped baby from his bed, but hesitated as the lights in the nursery suddenly dimmed, then brightened, before dimming again with a slight flicker.

"What was that?" Mrs. Brown commented on the strange power surge.

As the lights returned to normal, the nurse shrugged to the crowd at the window before returning her focus to the task at hand. Reaching for the baby, she slid her hands under him before pausing once again, but this time in reaction to an odd sensation traveling up her arms. Pulling her hands out from beneath the blanketed infant once again she noticed the faint blonde hairs on her arms standing straight up as the sensation continued its migration toward her shoulders and across her neck to her head.

"What the...?" Bill commented, eyes wide as the nurse's shoulder length, bob haircut stood on end, and a static, crackling sound slowly began to build as the lights, once again started to flicker.

Turning to the window, eyes wide with fear, the nurse started to take a step back toward the nursery door, just as a flash of bright light erupted over Oliver's crib, followed by a loud electrical snap and a shock wave that sent the terrified nurse flying toward the large glass window. Striking the glass with her face, a small trail of blood marked the cracked glass as the stunned woman slid down the large window and collapsed to the floor.

Shielding his eyes from the intense light, Bill looked up from the injured woman. The blast that had sent the nurse face first into the window had also pushed all of the other mobile basinets to the outer edges of the room, leaving Oliver's basinet by itself at the center.

"What's going on!?" Jennifer yelled, as she, Mrs. Brown and Tiffany continued to look away from the bright electrical light show continuing from within the nursery.

Wanting to answer, but silenced by his brain's inability to comprehend what he was witnessing, Bill continued to stare silently awestruck, as the bright light slowly faded while blue arcs of electricity continued their dance around the room.

"Bill, what is it?" Jennifer looked up at her husband's stunned expression while continuing to shield her face, before realizing that the light had dissipated.

Still unable to answer, Bill continued to stare, mouth agape.

Lowering her hand from her face, Jennifer turned in search of her own answers, though instantly wished she hadn't as the only reaction she could muster was a blood curdling scream that instantly drew the attention of the other two onlookers.

At the center of the room, still in the basinet, was the very child who only twelve hours earlier had entered the world, filling a long felt void in their lives, only now...he wasn't alone. With him was a man, sitting on a metal chair, head back and screaming, though his cries were muffled by the loud electrical noise and wall between them.

It wasn't the man's mysterious appearance from the bright light. It wasn't even his cries of apparent pain or anger that were most disturbing. What baffled the horrified onlookers the most, was the man's apparent cohesion with both the basinet and Oliver.

Finally breaking free from his immobilizing shock, Bill ran toward the nurse's station, and the entrance to the nursery.

The last bit of air erupting from his lungs in an gurgled scream, Jason lowered his head, momentarily pausing on the three, aghast onlookers before continuing down to the face of the screaming infant protruding from his chest. He didn't need an explanation. He knew where he was, and he knew what had happened.

The terrified newborn thrashed as much as his little body could, his head rolling back and forth while his arms bounced up and down on the mattress in front of Jason, while his tiny feet kicked against the other end of the firm surface to Jason's back.

With each violent shift, Jason could feel the infant pulling at his insides as their bodies were now one, their skin fused perfectly at the center of his chest and back. Not knowing if they were going to live or die, as the lightening storm continued around them, Jason slid his hands under the shoulders and head of the infant, the nurturing touch calming his younger self.

A pound at the glass pulled his attention away from the child as a woman he'd never seen before began beating her fist against the transparent wall, screaming as tears poured down her face.

"Hey!" Bill yelled as he appeared in the nursery doorway.

Ignoring the threatening cry to his rear, Jason returned his focus to the life cradled in his hands, making eye contact with the infant as a wave of calm washed over them both.

Closing their eyes, as if sharing the same thought, they vanished.

Stranger Than

FOOK

"Come on. You have to come up," Justin begged, leaning over from the passenger seat for another denied kiss.

"I told you, I'm not going up to your room because you're drunk and all you want is sex right now," Kristy laughed as she continued to dodge her boyfriend's aggressive advances.

"Nooo!" Justin protested, filling the car with the stench of Jack Daniel's and beer as he slipped a hand between her thighs.

"No! Bad boy," Kristy playfully scolded her inebriated date as she grabbed his wandering hand and playfully slapped him across the face, drawing a brief look of shock, followed by a devious smile and ultimately another advance.

"Ooh! You know I like it rough. We could do it right here. Come on."

"Justin," Kristy whined, but did not shove him away this time as he began kissing her neck.

"Right here in the car," he mumbled between kisses.

"Right here? In front of your dorm? What if someone sees us?"

"Let them watch. You're so fucking hot. You have nothing to be embarrassed about."

"I wasn't worried about me."

Pausing in his exploration of her neck, he was met by a broad grin. "Ha ha," he smiled before locking his lips to hers, stopping any further protests. She didn't fight the aggressive advance this time as she reclined the driver's seat, inviting him across the center console as their lips remained one. "This is actually going to happen," he thought to himself, shocked that his forward approach had actually worked.

It wasn't like they hadn't done it yet. By relationship standards, theirs was still fairly new, having met only two months earlier at the beginning of the school year, but things had started off hot and heavy and had continued to progress rapidly. They'd done it in a back room at a party; in a locked, nightclub bathroom; they'd even done it in a stranger's motor home in a quiet residential neighborhood one night. This girl was definitely adventurous and he really didn't have any reason to complain, but with each daring act, the line was moved, which only begged him to move it further.

Though she wasn't a prude by any means, she *was* hesitant about putting herself in any situation with a real likelihood of being caught or seen by another person. He didn't look at this hesitation as a turn off though. He looked at it as a challenge. Though no stranger to landing attractive girls, he was particularly proud of Kristy, and something inside of him wanted nothing more than to show her off...in every way possible.

"Wait," Kristy attempted to speak around Justin's lips as he continued his advance, having blindly unbuttoned her blouse like a pro but stumbling a bit with the intricate belt keeping him at bay. "Justin. Justin wait."

"What?" he pulled back, taking the pause in action to look down at the damned contraption around her waist. "What's wrong?"

"This isn't comfortable. Why don't we get in the backseat?" she flirted.

He wasn't going to argue. He had been expecting her to put an end to this daring tryst at any moment, which is why he'd been hurrying through her clothing and probably why he was having so much trouble with the belt. If she wanted to get in the back seat, he wasn't going to argue.

That meant that this thing was a done deal. The only problem he could foresee was figuring out where to move the line to next.

Sliding back over the console, he started to recline the passenger seat, to make it easier to slide up and over, into the backseat.

"No!" Kristy blurted as he placed his foot against the dash in preparation for the climb. "I don't want to damage the car. Let's just get out and go around."

"If she wants me to go around, I'll go around," Justin silently complied as he lowered his foot, popped open the passenger door and jumped out, closing the door behind him as he reached for the backdoor's handle.

Click.

"It's locked," Justin complained as he repeatedly pulled on the handle before leaning over to look back in at the girl who was buttoning her blouse. "What are you doing? Open the door."

Ignoring her boyfriend's pleas, Kristy continued buttoning her blouse, readjusting herself as she returned her seat to its upright position.

Figuring that she couldn't hear him, Justin reached for the front passenger door again. It too was locked. Peering in the window again, his date was once again completely clothed and checking herself in the rearview mirror before turning to offer a "sorry" through the glass.

"Sorry? Just open the door."

"Good night, Justin. I'll talk to you tomorrow."

"This isn't funny," Justin complained as the car's engine started. "Where are you going?"

Continuing to ignore the ongoing protests outside her car, Kristy put the car in gear and pulled away from the curb, glad to see that Justin had chosen not to chase after her. Though she felt bad about giving him what was sure to be an excruciating case of blue balls, she did have her limits and there was no way in hell she was going to do it in the backseat of her car while parked in front of a busy boy's dorm.

Bewildered by the sudden cold shoulder, Justin just stood at the curb, watching as his date's car rolled down the street. A brief flicker of the brake lights gave him hope that this was all just a cruel joke, intended to make him suffer for being so forward, but the hope was short lived as the red lights faded and Kristy's car disappeared around the building.

With a lowered head and a mumbled "great," he turned and headed for the door.

*****

At just over fifty-thousand a year, not including room and board, one would think that a school, such as Cornell, would hire only the best contractors for building renovations. When Justin had visited the school last summer, he'd instantly fallen in love with not only the university's law school, but the town of Ithaca itself. The quaint northeast charm of the surprisingly busy little town had far more to offer than the dull, endless cornfields he had grown up with back in Nebraska. On top of that, the school had promised its incoming freshman that it would be undergoing a multimillion dollar facelift over the next year, prior to their arrival, with most of the money being spent on onsite housing. The once drab and outdated buildings were going to be turned into, "modern technological suites," was how the senior giving them the tour had put it. So far the only thing he'd seen was a fresh coat of paint in the lobby and free Wi-Fi throughout the building. It was hardly impressive. To make matters worse, the construction that was supposed to have been completed by the beginning of the school year, looked as though it had hardly even been started. There were holes in walls where pipes were being fixed. Only about half of the lights worked and if you were lucky enough to still have a functioning bathroom in your room, the odds of getting even lukewarm water were about fifty percent. Thankfully he and his roommate still had one such room.

Arriving at his floor, Justin quickly hopped from the elevator. He'd considered foregoing the finicky contraption altogether after spending two hours trapped in it the week before, however given his current intoxicated state, getting stuck for a couple of hours sounded far better than taking a tumble down the dimly lit stairwell. Hardly anyone used the stairs. He could lay there for days before the elevator broke again, giving someone a reason to stumble upon his broken body.

Safely on his floor, his thoughts returned to the bathroom inside his "suite" as he turned and proceeded down the hall, running his hand along the wall to keep the wobbly building from knocking him to the floor. With Kristy gone, the unfriendly combination of Jack Daniel's and Keystone Light had quickly taken the opportunity to make their presence felt as the two unlikely companions pushed at the lining of his bladder, searching for any means of escape. Though he would have preferred the more erotic sensation of evacuating his loins, given the urgency with which his two alcoholic companions were pleading for freedom, something told him that this was going to be the best piss he'd ever taken.

Not even noticing the lacy black underwear hanging from the doorknob, Justin twisted the handle and was denied access by a soft click as the knob shifted only slightly in his hand before coming to a sudden stop.

"What the hell?" Justin glanced up at the chipped numbers on the door, confirming that he was at the right room.

309

Confident that he was at the right place and recalling his roommate telling him earlier that he'd be home studying all night, Justin tried the door again, not entirely sure why he expected a different outcome or why he was surprised when he was again denied entry.

"God damn it," he fumbled in his pocket for his keys, pulling them out and holding them only inches from his face as he attempted to pick the right one from the ring of blurry metal.

Somewhat confident that he'd picked the right one, he began lining the key up with the center of the knob, since the keyhole was all but invisible at that point. As the key searched every surface of the round brass handle, he finally noticed the feminine object hanging right in front of him.

Lowering the key, he grabbed the underwear, lifting them into the air to examine them before giving them a quick sniff and returning them to the doorknob. He knew what they represented. Even though he was a freshman, the random object hanging from the doorknob was a universally understood symbol in college. Most people used socks, or even a hair tie. He liked to slip an unused rubber around the knob, but not before spitting in it to get the full effect. He couldn't think of a better way to ensure privacy. "His roommate, obviously didn't care as much about privacy," he thought as he placed his ear to the door, while once again trying to silently slip the key into the lock.

Annoyed by their continued imprisonment, Jack and Keystone suddenly banded together to issue one final assault, sending a wave of pain across his lower abdomen and causing him to forego the excitement of busting in on his roommate nailing some random slut. Instead, fighting through the pain, he traded the keys for his fist and began banging on the door.

"Dude, I gotta piss! Open the door!"

"Fuck off! I'm busy!"

"I gotta go and I'm drunk as shit! I can't get my key in!"

"Well I've got mine in just fine, so go away!"

"Just open the door!" Justin continued to plea as another assault caused him to start dancing.

"Use the one down the hall!" his roommate shouted, obviously not willing to be interrupted during his conquest.

"Asshole," Justin mumbled as he turned and quickly began staggering toward the common bathroom at the other end of the hall. He would have continued to argue with the selfish prick, but given the urgency of the situation, the fight seemed futile and the eventual outcome devastatingly embarrassing.

Again running his hand along the wall as he quickly shuffled toward the disgusting room at the end of the hall, he imagined what he was about to walk into. As more and more private bathrooms went down on the floor, more and more people were using the tiny public lavatory, and not just any people, college guys. The place was disgusting. Unless you were a trained deep sea diver and capable of holding your breath for extended periods of time, you were almost guaranteed to ingest at least some of the fecal cloud always lingering in the poorly up-kept room. However, with comfort the priority, Justin didn't even bother to take a deep breath before bursting through the door and making a b-line for the first of three urinals to his left.

Fighting with his zipper as it momentarily caught on a stray thread, he contemplated just dropping his pants all together but thankfully didn't have to as the thread snapped and the satisfaction of freedom was quickly replaced by the ecstasy of relief. With every muscle in his body relaxed, Justin leaned forward, placing both hands against the cool tile wall as Jack and Keystone once again parted ways.

"Where is he?" a faint whisper attempted to compete with the sound of urine against porcelain.

Unaware of the voice, Justin instead opened his eyes to the realization of what he was touching. Quickly yanking his hands away from the wall, he was surprised to see that the white tile surface was amazingly clean. Even head high it wasn't uncommon to see the glossy wall mottled with tiny yellow blotches. Pushing the final few ounces of fluid from his bladder, he looked down at his urinal, as well as the two to his right. They too were remarkably clean.

"About fucking time," he mumbled as the stalls to his back came to mind. Urinals were one thing. The disgusting shit closets were a whole different story. Pivoting to his right, shaking the last few drops free as he peered over his shoulder at the open stalls, he was again amazed at the level of cleanliness around him. That coupled with the faint scent of vanilla from what appeared to be a newly installed automatic mister overhead actually made the heavily used room somewhat tolerable.

"I don't see him."

"What the fuck?" Justin finally noticed the voice as his attention snapped from the electronic machine overhead to the showers on the opposite side of the room. Quickly zipping his pants, he stepped away from the urinal, staring at the two showers. Both curtains were pulled tightly shut, even though no water was running, and given the fabric's opaque nature it would have been nearly impossible to figure out which one housed the mystery guest if it hadn't been for the fact that the bottom of the curtains hovered nearly two feet above the ground.

It was clear that the shower on the left was empty, but the other one... Where Justin expected to find a pair of bare feet topped by naked, hairy calves was instead a pair of dirty feet nearly hidden beneath what looked to be a dirty and disheveled antique white dress.

"Where is he? I don't see him," the female voice repeated.

"Hello?" Justin called out to the woman.

"Show me. Show me where he is."

"Hello. Miss," Justin inched forward, tilting his head to the side in an attempt to get a better view through the crack between the curtain and the tile wall.

"Where is he?" panic changed to grief as the confused

420

woman began to weep.

"Miss, you're in the men's room," Justin again tried to get the woman's attention as he stopped only a foot from the separating curtain.

"I know," the woman responded.

"Then what are you doing in here?"

"I will. I swear."

"What?" Justin asked confused, sensing now that he wasn't the intended recipient of her words.

"I promise. Just give me back my son."

Clearly the woman needed help and from what he could see she was dressed, so taking a deep breath, Justin grabbed hold of the curtain and pulled it aside. Standing in the far corner with her back turned to him, the woman continued to weep with her face in her hands.

"Holy shit are you alright?" Justin looked the woman up and down. The tattered qualities of the dirty dress that he'd seen beneath the curtain continued all the way up her body, culminating at her back where the fabric around one shoulder had been completely torn away revealing large bruises and bloody cuts that disappeared beneath the remainder of the intact, old looking fabric. Rushing into the shower, though reluctant to touch her, Justin stopped right behind her. "Do you need help? Who did this to you?"

"He has my son," the woman finally addressed her new company, the grief in her voice slowly fading as a monotone quality took over.

"Who? Who has your son?"

"The witch."

"Witch? What witch?" Justin asked. It was clear that someone had beaten the crap out of this woman, but now he was thinking that she was on something as well. Given what he knew so far, which wasn't much, he began fabricating a scenario that included the twenty-something year old woman as an actress in the school's theatre department. Given her odd attire, he assumed that she was part of some play set in the late 1700's. All he could guess was that she'd gone to some party after a show, had had a few too many, or was slipped something, before someone beat and or raped her, but that didn't explain the kid.

"Where is he?"

"I don't know where your son is. I think I should call the police and get you some help."

"I know you know where he is," the woman's voice grew angry.

"No, I really don't know where he is," Justin was surprised by the sudden accusation. He didn't even know who this woman was. How could he know her son, let alone where he was? "The police will find your son. Right now we need to get you to a hospital."

"Where is he?" the woman repeated, even more upset.

Feeling uncomfortable, Justin began to take a step back but not before the woman spun around, grabbing hold of his head with both hands and with remarkable strength, pulled his face to within an inch of hers.

"I know he's here. So where is he?" the woman spoke through her clenched teeth, rage burning in the back of her eyes.

Terrified, Justin attempted to pull away but couldn't fight the woman's incredible strength. This wasn't just a battered woman. There was something else behind those eyes; something far more sinister. Preparing to punch, kick, bite; anything to get away, he clenched his fist, but never got the chance as the diminutive woman's lips parted, filling the room with a blood curdling scream.

*****

"Holy shit. This girl's amazing," was the only thought repeatedly running through Corey's mind as he watched the white sheets bob up and down with each pleasurable sensation.

High school had been fun and he'd nailed his share of loose girls, but nothing compared to the quality of ass he'd landed since the beginning of the semester…and he was only a freshman. "How much better could it get?" he thought, his mind taking a break from the hidden vacuum at his waist to contemplate the remaining three and half years of his college career.

The suction ceasing, the sheets began to rise as young Miss Hoover silently indicated that she was through. Disagreeing, Corey gently placed his hand on the sheet outlined shape of her head as he encouraged his conquest back to work. Obediently, the sheets resumed their dance.

He hadn't gone out that night looking for a meaningless one night stand…at least not consciously. Truthfully, he never went out looking for it. He didn't have to. Genetically blessed with the best of his parents' genes, his mother's model looks and his father's superior intelligence, girls naturally flocked to him, and those that didn't, he easily convince them that they should. What's her name beneath the sheets hadn't required very much convincing. She'd been in front of him in line while he waited to pick up a pizza that would hopefully fuel him through the remainder of his cram session for tomorrow's Biology exam. He'd first noticed her ass, accentuated by the tight black yoga pants and branded by the word *Tasty* in bold yellow lettering. "It might as well say 'stick it here'," he'd thought at the time, not noticing that he'd been busted until the girl had cleared her throat, drawing his stare upward to a pleasantly unexpected, flirtatious smile. A five minute walk and a hot and heavy elevator ride later and they'd both been naked in his bed with the pizza remaining uneaten on the nightstand.

"Oh my god," Corey's mind was returned to the action beneath the covers as the urge to finish suddenly presented itself. Not sure how she'd feel about that, though he could guess, he fought back the sensation as he turned his mind to something less erotic. His roommate. Instantly Justin's face came to mind and his soldiers retreated. That was about the only thing Justin was good for. He hadn't chosen to be bunked with the immature and filthy asshole. In fact, he was supposed to have a private room, but with the ongoing building renovations leaving the private dorms uninhabitable, he was forced to pair up with the prick for what he'd been told would only be a semester, though he suspected that it would be much longer.

It wasn't just the fact that Justin's side of the room looked like a cluttered, food soiled mess, even by a hoarder's standards. The guy just wasn't likable. He always bragged about how he'd fucked every girl in his high school and how he'd even landed a couple of teachers, but he wasn't fooling anyone. Since the beginning of the school year he'd been nailing the same girl and for someone supposedly so experienced, he thought fucking your "girlfriend" in someone else's parked RV was wild and exciting. "Amateur," Corey thought.

Bang! Bang! Bang!

"I said use the fucking bathroom down the hall!" Corey shouted in response to the second round of banging at the door.

The sheets stopping once again, Corey pushed them back into action.

Bang! Bang! Bang!

"Holy shit. I'm going to beat your fucking ass!" Corey protested through clenched teeth as he tossed the covers aside, revealing the startled blonde between his legs as he prepared to ensure that Justin would never be able to knock on a door again. Before he could get to his feet however, the locked door exploded inward, the knob of the door lodging in the adjacent drywall as young Hoover screamed and Justin appeared in the doorway with the girl's black panties tightly clenched in his hand.

"What the fuck, dude!?" Corey swung his leg around the frightened girl as she frantically gathered enough fabric to at least partially conceal herself. He didn't care that he was naked or that he was currently sporting a massive boner. He and his erection were going to pound the living snot out of the unwelcomed company. Getting to his feet, he took a step forward but hesitated as Justin signaled "stop" with his empty hand.

"Sit down," Justin addressed his perplexed and angry roommate.

"Sit down? You have a lot of fucking nerve bursting in here? I told you to use the fucking bathroom down the-"

"—Down the hall?" Justin finished the naked kid's sentence. "He did that."

"He? Are we referring to ourselves in the third person now?" Corey mocked, something about Justin's calm and creepily confident demeanor keeping him from advancing any further.

"Where is he?" Justin ignored the question.

"Who? I don't have time to play hide and seek right now. I'm kind of in the middle of someone," Corey motioned to the girl who was trying to reach her pants on the floor while remaining covered.

"Where is he?" Justin repeated.

"I don't know. You tell me. Where is he?" Corey continued his mocking attitude. "Who the fuck are we talking about?"

"Drake," Justin answered.

"Drake? Drake who?"

"Drake Miller," Justin clarified.

"I don't know any Drakes, so why don't you take your perverted ass and—"

"—He was here," Justin interrupted. This was his room. What year is it?"

"What? Are you fucking on something man?"

"What year is it?" Justin insisted, the anger in his voice growing.

"Fuck you. You know what fucking year it is."

Staring at his defiant roommate, Justin paused to take a breath before screaming, "What fucking year is it?!"

The girl froze in place, her arm still outstretched for her pants.

"2018," Corey nervously replied taking a step back, shocked by the level of rage being exhibited by his usually even keeled roommate.

"Fuck. Were getting closer," Justin muttered to himself, while looking down at the ground.

"What are you talking about?" Corey asked, the anger in his voice slowly being overtaken by fear as Justin returned his insane, hateful gaze to the two naked coeds.

"I guess it will have to do though," Justin smiled.

"Dude. You need to get the fuck out of here," Corey addressed Justin as he knelt to retrieve the girl's pants from the floor beside him.

Dropping the wadded up panties, Justin turned his attention to a lacrosse stick leaning against the closet door.

Following his roommate's gaze, Corey tossed the pants at the girl and quickly began fumbling with his own.

Grabbing the piece of sports equipment, Justin turned back to his roommate, the two of them locking eyes, as he issued a menacing grin and closed the door behind him.

Want more?

Visit:

AuthorBrianDrinkwater.com

for extended previews and more

ABOUT THE AUTHOR

Brian Drinkwater is an American horror/suspense writer with a knack for mind bending stories of a darker nature. His first book, *Book of "The Grave"*, was released in 2013 with his follow up, *FOOK,* being release one year later.

Born in Southern California, but raised on Massachusetts' South Shore, Brian has been writing since he was a small child, often testing the boundaries of his school assignments by writing fictitious stories in place of daunting reports. He even invented an English poet his senior year of high-school in order to bypass the school's rule of 'no self written yearbook quotes'. Readers now know this poet as William Grave.

Though never a big reader, as odd as that may sound, Brian did grow up a fan of Dean Koontz, so it's no surprise that his writing style mimics that of the renowned author, with multiple storylines cohesively coming together by story's end. And with a knack for creating vivid characters with dynamic personalities, as a reader you'll find yourself rooting for, and sometimes against, the people who make up his imaginary world. But don't get too attached, because standard rules don't always apply, and not everyone makes it out alive.

Brian lives in Southwest Florida with his wife and son.